Praise for #1 *New York Times* bestselling author

DEBBIE WITHDRAWN
MACOMBER

"When God created Eve,
he must have asked Debbie Macomber for advice because
no one does female characters any better than this author."
—Harriet Klausner

"As always, Macomber draws rich, engaging characters."
—*Publishers Weekly*

"Macomber is a master storyteller."
—*RT Book Reviews*

"It is easy to see why Ms. Macomber is a perennial favorite:
she writes great books."
—*RomanceJunkies.com*

"Ms. Macomber certainly has a knack
for telling the story of small-town life."
—*Romance Communications*

"One of Macomber's great strengths
is her insight into human behavior—
both admirable and ignoble. Her ability to make her points
about it without preaching is another."
—*RT Book Reviews*

"Debbie Macomber writes characters
who are as warm and funny as your best friends."
—*New York Times* bestselling author Susan Wiggs

DEBBIE MACOMBER

Midnight Sons

VOLUME 1

MIRA®

Recycling programs
for this product may
not exist in your area.

ISBN-13: 978-0-7783-2912-1

MIDNIGHT SONS VOLUME I

Copyright © 2009 by MIRA Books.

The publisher acknowledges the copyright holder of the individual works
as follows:

BRIDES FOR BROTHERS
Copyright © 1995 by Debbie Macomber.

THE MARRIAGE RISK
Copyright © 1995 by Debbie Macomber.

For questions and comments about the quality of this book please contact us
at Customer_eCare@Harlequin.ca.

www.MIRABooks.com

Printed in U.S.A.

For Don and Mary Ann Adler
Don is my oldest cousin and Mary Ann one of my
dearest friends and a fellow cameo collector

Dear Friends,

Welcome to Hard Luck, Alaska, a small community near the Arctic Circle. The town has a rich and interesting history that I hope you'll enjoy. These books revolve around the three O'Halloran brothers—Sawyer, Charles and Christian—who own a flight service. The problem is, they keep losing their best pilots, until the brothers decide that the way to keep the men is to recruit women to their town. That's when the fun begins.

My husband worked on the Arctic pipeline back in the mid-1980s and came to love Alaska. Creating this series was the perfect opportunity for me to explore it for myself. Our research trip in the summer of 1994 proved to be one of the most rewarding and enjoyable experiences of my writing career. I fell hopelessly in love with Alaska, the sheer magnificence of the landscape, the vastness and beauty, the friendliness of the small towns. Even now, all these years later, I have warm memories of our time there. Wayne and I flew with bush pilots, trekked across the tundra and talked with anyone who was willing to tell us about their lives.

The Midnight Sons series holds a special place in my heart. It was the prelude to the Heart of Texas series, the Dakota books and eventually led to the Cedar Cove series. (Keep in mind that the Hard Luck stories were written in the mid-nineties, before cell phones, DVDs and the Internet became part of our everyday lives.)

Now I invite you to sit back and allow me to introduce you to some proud, stubborn, wonderful men—Alaska men—and show you what happens when they meet their matches. Women from the "lower forty-eight." Women a lot like you and me.

Debbie Macomber

P.S. By the way, I love hearing from readers. You can reach me at www.debbiemacomber.com or by mail at P.O. Box 1458, Port Orchard, Washington 98366.

CONTENTS

The History of Hard Luck, Alaska

Hard Luck, situated fifty miles north of the Arctic Circle, near the Brooks Range, was founded by Adam O'Halloran and his wife, Anna, in 1931. Adam came to Alaska to make his fortune, but never found the gold strike he sought. Nevertheless, the O'Hallorans and their two young sons, Charles and David, stayed on—in part because of a tragedy that befell the family a few years later.

Other prospectors and adventurers began to move to Hard Luck, some of them bringing wives and children. The town became a stopping-off place for mail, equipment and supplies. The Harmon family arrived in 1938 to open a dry goods store, and the Fletchers came soon after that.

When World War II began, Hard Luck's population was fifty or sixty people all told. Some of the young men, including the O'Halloran sons, joined the armed services; Charles left for Europe in 1942, David in 1944 at the age of eighteen. Charles died during the fighting. Only David came home—with a young English war bride, Ellen Sawyer, despite the fact that he'd become engaged to Catherine Harmon shortly before going overseas. (Catherine married Willie Fletcher after David's return.)

After the war, David qualified as a bush pilot. He then built some small cabins to attract the sport fishermen and hunters who were starting to come to Alaska; he also worked as a guide. Eventually he built a lodge to replace the cabins—a lodge that was later damaged by fire.

David and Ellen had three sons, born fairly late in their marriage—Charles (named after David's brother) was born in 1960, Sawyer in 1963 and Christian in 1965.

Hard Luck had been growing slowly all this time and by 1970 it was home to just over a hundred people. These were the years of the oil boom, when the school and community center were built by the state. After Vietnam, ex-serviceman Ben Hamilton joined the community and opened the Hard Luck Café, which became the social focus for the town.

In the late 1980s the three O'Halloran brothers formed a partnership, creating Midnight Sons, a bush-pilot operation. They were awarded the mail contract, and they also deliver fuel and other necessities to the interior. In addition, they serve as a small commuter airline, flying passengers to and from Fairbanks and within the northern Arctic.

In 1995, at the time these stories start, there were approximately 150 people living in Hard Luck—the majority of them male....

Now, almost fifteen years later, join the people here in looking back at their history—particularly the changes that occurred when Midnight Sons invited women to town. Women who transformed Hard Luck, Alaska, forever!

BRIDES FOR BROTHERS

Prologue

"What you really need are *women*."

Sawyer O'Halloran made a show of choking on his coffee. "Women! We've got enough problems!"

Ben Hamilton—the Hard Luck Café's owner, cook and just about everything else—set the coffeepot on the counter. "Didn't you just tell me Phil Duncan's decided to move back to Fairbanks?"

Phil was the best pilot Sawyer had. He wasn't the first one Midnight Sons had lost to the big city, either. Every time a pilot resigned, it was a setback for the Arctic flight service.

"Yes, but Phil's not leaving because of a woman," Sawyer said.

"Sure he is," Duke Porter piped up. Still clutching his mug, he slipped onto the stool next to Sawyer. "Phil quit because he couldn't see his girlfriend as much as he wanted. He might've given you some phony excuse when he handed in his notice, but you know as well as I do why he quit."

"Joe and Harlan left because of women, too. Because they couldn't meet any, not if they were living here!" It was Ben again. The ex-Navy "stew burner"—as the O'Halloran brothers called him—obviously had strong views on the subject. Sawyer often shared his opinions, but not this time. He had half a mind to suggest Ben keep his nose out of this, but that wouldn't be fair.

One of the problems with living in a small town, especially if you'd grown up there, was that you knew everyone, Sawyer reflected. And everyone knew you—*and* your business.

He might as well set up the Midnight Sons office right here in the middle of the café. His pilots routinely ate breakfast at Ben's, and the cook was as familiar with the air charter's troubles as the brothers were themselves.

Christian, the youngest O'Halloran, held his mug with both hands. "All right, if you won't say it, I will," he began, looking pointedly at Sawyer. "Ben's right. Bringing a few women to Hard Luck would keep the crew happy."

Sawyer didn't really disagree with him. "We've got a new schoolteacher coming. A woman." As a member of the school board, Sawyer had read over Bethany Ross's application and been impressed with her qualifications, but he wasn't sure the state should have hired her. She'd been born and raised in California. He still hadn't figured out why she'd applied for a teaching position north of the Arctic Circle.

"I just hope this teacher isn't like the last one," John Henderson grumbled. "I flew her in, remember? I was as polite as could be, circled the area a bit, showed her the sights from the air, talked up the town. The woman wouldn't even get off the plane."

"I'd still like to know what you said to her," Christian muttered.

"I didn't say anything," John insisted. "I mean, besides what I told you." He squinted at Sawyer. "The new teacher's not coming until August, is she?"

"August," Ben repeated. "*One* woman." He readjusted the stained white apron around his thick waist. "I can see it now."

"See what?" Fool that he was, Sawyer had to ask. It went without saying that Ben would be more than happy to tell him.

"One woman will cause more problems than she'll solve," Ben said in a portentous voice. "Think about it, Sawyer."

Sawyer didn't want to think about it. All this talk of bringing in women made him uncomfortable.

"One thing's for sure, we're not going to let John fly her in this time," Ralph said scornfully. "I got first dibs."

He was answered by a loud chorus of "Like hell!" and "No way!"

"Don't squabble!" Sawyer shouted.

Ben chuckled and slid a plate of sourdough hotcakes onto the counter toward Ralph.

"See what I mean?" the cook said under his breath. "Your men are already fighting over the new teacher, and she isn't even arriving for months."

Ralph lit into the hotcakes as if he hadn't eaten in a week. Mouth full, he mumbled something about lonely bachelors.

"All right, all right," Sawyer conceded. "Bringing a few women to Hard Luck might be a good idea, but how do you suggest we persuade them to move up here?"

"I guess we could advertise," Christian said thoughtfully, then brightened. "Sure, we'll advertise. It's a good idea. I don't know why we didn't think of it sooner."

"Advertise?" Sawyer glared at his brother. "What do you mean, *advertise?*"

"Well, we could put an ad in one of those glossy magazines women like to buy. You know, the kind with *lifestyle* articles." He said the word almost reverently. "What I heard, it's gotten to be the thing to place an ad about lonely men in Alaska seeking companionship."

"A friend of a friend sent his picture to one of 'em," Ralph said excitedly, "and before he knew it, he had a sackful of letters. All from women eager to meet him."

"I want you to know right now I'm not taking off my shirt and posing for any damn picture," Duke Porter said in an emphatic voice.

"Getting your photograph in one of those magazines isn't as easy as it sounds," Ralph warned after swallowing a huge bite. He shrugged. "Not that I've tried or anything."

"Things are rarely as good as they sound," Sawyer pointed out reasonably, pleased that at least one of his employees was thinking clearly.

"Those women aren't looking for pen pals, you know," John said. "They're after husbands, and they aren't the type who can be picky, either, if you catch my drift."

"So? You guys aren't exactly centerfold material yourselves," Ben was quick to remind them. He pushed up the sleeves of his shirt and planted both hands on the counter.

"As far as I can see," Sawyer said, "we don't have anything to offer women. It's not like our good looks would induce them to move here, now is it?"

John's face fell with disappointment. "You're probably right."

"What would work, then?" Christian asked. "We need to think positive, or we're going to end up spending our lives alone."

"I don't have any complaints about *my* life," Sawyer told his brother. Christian's enthusiasm for this crazy idea surprised him. Sawyer was willing to go along with it, but he didn't have much faith in its success. For one thing, he wasn't convinced there'd be any takers. And if there were, the presence of these women might create a whole new set of problems.

"You've got to remember women aren't that different from men," Christian was saying, sounding like a TV talk-show expert.

The others stared at him, and Christian laughed. "You know what I mean. You guys came up to Hard Luck, didn't you? Even though we're fifty miles north of the Arctic Circle."

"Sure," Duke answered. "But the wages are the best around, and the living conditions aren't bad."

"Wages," Christian said, removing a pen from the pocket of his plaid shirt. He made a note on his paper napkin.

"You aren't thinking about *paying* women to move to Hard Luck, are you?" Sawyer would fight that idea tooth and nail. He'd be darned if he'd see his hard-earned cash wasted on such foolishness.

"We could offer women jobs, couldn't we?" Christian asked. He glanced around to gather support from the other pilots.

"Doing what?" Sawyer demanded.

"Well…" Frowning, his brother gnawed on the end of his pen. "You've been saying for a long time that we need to get the office organized. How about hiring a secretary? You and I have enough to do dealing with everything else. It's a mess, and we can't seem to get ahead."

Sawyer resisted the urge to suggest a correspondence course in time management. "All right," he said grudgingly.

The other pilots looked up from their breakfasts. They were beginning to take notice.

"What about all those books your mother left behind after she married Frank?" Ben asked. "She donated them so Hard Luck could have a library."

Sawyer gritted his teeth. "A volunteer library."

"But someone's got to organize it," Christian said. "I've tried now and then, but whenever I start to get things straightened out, I'm overwhelmed. There must be a thousand books there."

Sawyer couldn't really object, since, unlike Christian, he'd never made any effort to put his mother's collection in order.

"That was very generous of your mother, giving the town her books," Ralph said. "But it's a shame we can't find what we want or check it out if we do."

"It seems to me," Christian said, smiling broadly, "that we could afford to pay someone to set up the library and run it for a year or so. Don't you agree?"

Sawyer shrugged. "If Charles does." But they both knew their oldest brother would endorse the idea. He'd been wanting to get the library going for quite a while.

"I heard Pearl say she was thinking of moving to Nenana to live with her daughter," Ben told the gathering. "In that case, the town's going to need someone with medical experience for the health clinic."

A number of heads nodded. Sawyer suspected now was not

the time to remind everyone that Pearl regularly mentioned moving in with her daughter. Generally the sixty-year-old woman came up with that idea in the darkest part of winter, when there were only a couple of hours of daylight and spirits were low.

"I know what you're thinking," Ben said, turning to Sawyer. "But did it ever occur to you that Pearl actually *would* leave if someone was here to take over for her?"

No, Sawyer hadn't. Pearl had lived in Hard Luck for as long as he could remember. She'd been a friend of his mother's when Ellen lived in Hard Luck, and a peacemaker in the small community. Over the years Sawyer had frequently had opportunity to be grateful to Pearl. If she did decide to move, he'd miss her.

"We can ask her if she's serious about wanting to retire," Sawyer agreed, despite his reluctance. "But I won't have Pearl thinking we don't want her."

"I'll talk to her myself," Christian promised.

"I could use a bit of help around here," Ben said. "I've been feeling my age of late."

"You mean feeling your oats, don't you?" John teased.

Ben grinned. "Go ahead and add a part-time cook and waitress to your list."

There were smiles all around. Sawyer hated to be the one to put a damper on all these plans, but someone had to open their eyes to a few truths. "Has anyone figured out where these women are going to live?"

It was almost comical to see the smiles fall in unison, as if they were marionettes and a puppetmaster was working their mouths. Still, Sawyer had to admit he was beginning to warm to the idea of recruiting women. Hard Luck could do with a few new faces and he wouldn't object if those faces happened to be young, female and pretty. Not that *he* was the marrying kind. No, sirree. Not Sawyer O'Halloran. Not after what he'd seen with his parents. Their unhappiness had taught him early and taught him well that marriage meant misery. Although, in his opinion, Catherine Fletcher bore a lot of the blame....

He shook his head. Marriage was definitely out, and he suspected his two brothers felt the same way. They must. Neither of them seemed inclined toward marriage, either.

He returned his attention to the dilemma at hand. No one appeared to have any answers to his question about where these women would live, and Sawyer felt obligated to point out the less-than-favorable aspects of their plan. The more he considered it, the more certain he became that this idea was impossible. Attractive, perhaps—especially in a moment of weakness—but impossible.

"It wouldn't have worked, anyway," he said.

"Why not?" his brother asked.

"Women are never satisfied with the status quo. They'd move to Hard Luck and immediately want to change things." Sawyer had seen it before. "Well, *I* don't want things changed. We have it good here."

"Yeah," Ralph agreed, but without much enthusiasm.

"Before we knew it," Sawyer continued, "the ladies would have rings on their fingers and rings through our noses, and they'd be leading us around like...like sheep. Worse, they'd convince us that's the way we want it."

"Nope. Not going to happen to me," John vowed. "Unless..."

Not giving him a chance to weaken, Sawyer went on. "We'd be making runs into Fairbanks for low-fat ice cream because one or other of them has a craving for chocolate without the calories." Sawyer could picture it now. "They'd want us to watch our language and turn the TV off during dinner and shave every day…and…"

"You're right," Duke said with conviction. "A woman would probably want me to shave off my beard."

The men grimaced as if they could already feel the razor.

Women in Hard Luck would have his pilots wrapped around their little fingers within a week, Sawyer thought. And after that, his men wouldn't be worth a damn.

Christian hadn't spoken for several minutes. Now he slowly rubbed his hand along his jaw. "What about the cabins?"

"The old hunting cabins your father built on the outskirts of town?" Ralph asked.

Sawyer and Christian exchanged a look. "Those are the ones," Christian said. "Dad built them back in the fifties before the lodge was completed—you know, the lodge that burned down? Folks would fly in for hunting and fishing and he'd put them up there. They're simple, one medium-size room without any conveniences."

"No one's lived in those cabins for years," Sawyer reminded his brother.

"But they're solid, and other than a little dirt there's nothing wrong with them. Someone could live there. Easily." Christian's voice rose as he grew excited about the idea. "With a little soap and water and a few minor repairs, they'd be livable in nothing flat."

Sawyer couldn't believe what he was hearing. A city gal would take one look at those cabins and leave on the next flight out. "But there isn't any running water or electricity."

"No," Christian agreed, "not yet."

Now Sawyer understood, and he didn't like it. "I'm not putting any money into fixing up those run-down shacks." Charles would have a fit if he let Christian talk him into doing anything so stupid.

"Those old cabins aren't worth much, are they?" Christian asked.

Sawyer hesitated. He recognized his brother's tone. Christian had something up his sleeve.

"No," Sawyer admitted cautiously.

"Then it wouldn't hurt to give the cabins away."

"Give them away?" Sawyer echoed. It stood to reason that no one would *pay* for them. Who'd want them anyway, even if they were free?

"We're going to need something to induce women to move to Hard Luck," Christian said. "We aren't offering them marriage."

"Damn right we're not." John gulped down a slug of coffee and wiped his mouth with the back of his hand.

"Companionship is all I'm interested in," another of the pilots added. "Female companionship."

"We don't want to mislead anyone into thinking this is about marriage."

"Exactly."

Sawyer looked around the room at his pilots. "Marriage is what practically all women are after," he said with more certainty than he actually felt.

"There's plenty of jobs in the lower forty-eight," Christian said in a perfectly reasonable tone. This was always where Sawyer ran into trouble with his younger brother. Christian could propose the most ridiculous idea in the most logical way. "True?"

"True," Sawyer agreed warily.

"So, like I said before, we've got to offer these women some incentive to live and work in Hard Luck."

"You want to give them the cabins?" Sawyer scratched his head. "As an *incentive?*"

"Sure. Then if they want to bring in electricity and running water they can do it with their own money."

Sawyer checked around to see what the others were thinking. He couldn't find a dissenting look among them. Not on Ben's face and certainly not on any of the others. He should've known Christian's idea would take root in the fertile minds of his women-starved men.

"We'd clean up the cabins a bit first," Christian said as though this was the least they could do.

"We found a bear in one of them last year," Sawyer reminded his brother.

"That bear didn't mean any harm," Ralph said confidently. "He was just having a look around, is all. I doubt he'll be back after the shot of pepper spray Mitch gave him."

Sawyer just shook his head, bemused.

"But it might not be smart to mention the bear to any of the women," Ben was quick to add. "Women are funny about wild critters."

"Yeah," John said in hushed tones, "take my word for it— don't say anything about the wildlife."

"Say anything?" Sawyer asked. The men made it sound like he was going to personally interview each applicant.

"To the women when you talk to them," Ralph explained with exaggerated patience.

"I'm going to be talking to these women?"

"Why, sure," Duke said, as if that had been understood from the beginning. "You'll have to interview them, you or Christian. Especially if you're going to offer them housing when they accept a job in Hard Luck."

"You'd better throw in some land while you're at it," Ben said, reaching for the coffeepot. He refilled the mugs and set the pot back on the burner. "You O'Hallorans got far more of it than you know what to do with. Offer the women a cabin and twenty acres of land if they'll live and work in Hard Luck for one year."

"Great idea!"

"Just like the old days when the settlers first got here."

"Those cabins aren't *on* any twenty acres." Sawyer raised his arms to stop the discussion. "It'd be misleading to let anyone think they were, or that—"

"No one said the cabins had to be on acreage, did they?" Duke broke in. "Besides, to my way of thinking, people shouldn't look a gift house in the mouth." He chuckled at his own feeble joke. "House, get it? Not horse."

"A year sounds fair," Christian said decisively, ignoring him. "If it doesn't work out, then they're free to leave, no hard feelings."

"No hard feelings." John nodded happily.

"Now, just a minute," Sawyer said. Was he the only one here who possessed any sense? He'd come into the Hard Luck Café for a simple cup of coffee, discouraged by the news that Phil was leaving. The morning had rapidly gone from bad to worse.

"How are we going to let women know about your offer?" Ralph asked.

"We'll run some ads like we said," Christian told him. "But maybe not in magazines. That'll take too long. I've got a business trip planned to Seattle, so we can put ads in the papers there and I'll interview the women who apply."

"Hold on," Sawyer said, frowning. "We can't go giving away those cabins, never mind the acreage, without talking to Charles first. Besides, there are antidiscrimination laws that make it illegal to advertise a job for women only."

Christian grinned. "There're ways around that."

Sawyer rolled his eyes. "But we really do need to discuss this with Charles." Their oldest brother was a silent partner in the O'Hallorans' air charter service. He should have a voice in this decision; after all, they'd be giving away family-owned cabins and land.

"There isn't time for that," Christian argued. "Charles'll go along with it. You know he will. He hasn't paid that much attention to the business since he started working for Alaska Oil."

"You'd better have an attorney draw up some kind of contract," Ben suggested.

"Right." Christian added that to his list. "I'll do it tomorrow. I'll write the ad this morning and see about getting it in the Seattle paper. It might be best if we placed it in another city, as well. It wouldn't be much trouble to go down to Oregon and interview women from Portland. I've got plenty of time."

"Hey, good idea," John murmured.

"I'll design the application," Sawyer said reluctantly. This was happening much too fast. "You know, guys..." He hated to throw another wrench in the works, but someone needed a clear head, and it was obvious he'd been elected. "If any woman's foolish enough to respond, those old cabins had better be in decent shape. It's going to take a lot of work."

"I'll help," John said enthusiastically.

"Me, too."

"I expect we all will." Duke drained the last of his coffee, then narrowed his gaze on Christian. "Just make sure you get a blonde for me."

"A blonde," Christian repeated.

Sawyer closed his eyes and groaned. He had a bad feeling about this. A very bad feeling.

Chapter
1

It had been one of those days. Abbey Sutherland made herself a cup of tea, then sat in the large overstuffed chair and propped her feet on the ottoman. She closed her eyes, soaking in the silence.

The morning had started badly when Scott overslept, which meant he and Susan had missed the school bus. Seven-year-old Susan had insisted on wearing her pink sweater, which was still in the dirty-clothes hamper, and she'd whined all the way to school. Abbey had driven them, catching every red light en route.

By the time she arrived at the library, she was ten minutes late. Mrs. Duffy gave her a look that could have curdled milk.

But those minor irritations faded after lunch. Abbey received notice that the library's budget for the next fiscal year had been reduced and two positions would be cut—the positions held by the most recently hired employees. In other words, Abbey was going to lose her job in less than three months.

She finally got home at six o'clock, tired, short-tempered and depressed. That was when Mr. Erickson, the manager of the apartment complex, hand-delivered a note informing her the rents were being raised.

It was the kind of day even hot fudge couldn't salvage.

Sensing her mood, the kids had acted up all evening. Abbey was exhausted, and she didn't think reruns of *Matlock* were going to help.

Sipping her tea, she wondered what had happened to throw her life off course. She had a savings account, but there wasn't enough in it to pay more than a month's worth of bills. She refused to go to her parents for money. Not again. It had been too humiliating the first time, although they'd been eager to help. Not once had her mother or father said "I told you so," when she filed for divorce, although they'd issued plenty of warnings when she'd announced her intention to marry Dick Sutherland. They'd been right. Five years and two children later, Abbey had returned to Seattle emotionally battered, broken-hearted and just plain broke.

Her parents had helped her back on her feet despite their limited income and lent her money to finish her education. Abbey had painstakingly repaid every penny, but it had taken her almost three years.

The newspaper, still rolled up, lay at her feet, and she picked it up. She might as well start reading through the want ads now, although she wasn't likely to find another job as an assistant librarian. With cuts in local government spending, positions in libraries were becoming rare these days. But if she was willing to relocate…

"Mom." Scott stood beside her chair.

"Yes?" She climbed out of her depression long enough to manage a smile for her nine-year-old son.

"Jason's dog had her puppies."

Abbey felt her chest tighten. Scott had been asking for a dog all year. "Honey, we've already been over this a hundred times. The apartment complex doesn't allow pets."

"I didn't say I wanted one," he said defensively. "All I said was that Jason's dog had puppies. I know I can't have a dog as long as we live here, but I was thinking that maybe with the rent increase we might move."

"And if we do move," Abbey said, "you want me to look for a place where we can have a dog."

Her son grinned broadly. "Jason's puppies are really, really cute, Mom. And they're valuable, too! But you know what kind are my favorite?"

She did, but she played along. "Tell me."

"Huskies."

"Because the University of Washington mascot is a husky."

"Yeah. They have cool eyes, don't they? And I really like the way their tails loop up. I know they're too big for me to have as a pet, but I still like them best."

Abbey held out her arm to her son. He didn't cuddle with her much anymore. That was kid stuff to a boy who was almost ten. But tonight he seemed willing to forget that.

He clambered into the chair next to her, rested his head

against her shoulder and sighed. "I'm sorry I overslept this morning," he whispered.

"I'm sorry I yelled at you."

"That's all right." There was a pause. "I promise to get out of bed when you call from now on, okay?"

"Okay." Abbey closed her eyes, breathing in the clean shampoo scent of his hair.

They sat together for a few more minutes, saying nothing.

"You'd better get back to bed," Abbey said, although she was reluctant to see him go.

Scott climbed out of the chair. "Are we going to move?" he asked, looking at her with wide eyes.

"I guess we are," she said and smiled.

"'Night, Mom." Scott smiled, too, then walked down the hall to his bedroom.

Abbey's heart felt a little lighter as she picked up the paper and peeled off the rubber band. She didn't bother to look at the front page, but turned directly to the classifieds.

The square box with the large block printing attracted her attention immediately. "LONELY MEN IN HARD LUCK, ALASKA, OFFER JOBS, HOMES AND LAND." Below in smaller print was a list of the positions open.

Abbey's heart stopped when she saw "librarian."

Hard Luck, Alaska. Jobs. A home with land. Twenty acres. Good grief, that was more than her grandfather had owned when he grew raspberries in Puyallup a generation earlier.

Dragging out an atlas, Abbey flipped through the pages until she found Alaska. Her finger ran down the list of town names until she came across Hard Luck. Population 150.

She swallowed. A small town generally meant a sense of community. That excited her. As a girl, she'd spent summers on her grandparents' farm and loved it. She wanted to give her children the same opportunity. She was sure the three of them could adjust to life in a small town. In Alaska.

Using the atlas's directions to locate the town, Abbey drew her finger across one side of the page and down the other.

Her excitement died. Hard Luck was above the Arctic Circle. Oh, dear. Maybe it *wasn't* such a great idea, after all.

The following morning, Abbey reviewed her options.

She set out a box of cold cereal, along with a carton of milk. A still-sleepy Scott and Susan pulled out chairs and sat at the table.

"Kids," she said, drawing a deep breath, "what would you say if I suggested we move to Alaska?"

"Alaska?" Scott perked up right away. "That's where they have huskies!"

"Yes, I know."

"It's cold there, isn't it?" Susan asked.

"Very cold. Colder than it's ever been in Seattle."

"Colder than Texas?"

"Lots colder," Scott said in a superior older-brother tone. "It's so cold you don't even need refrigerators, isn't that right, Mom?"

"Uh, I think they probably still use them."

"But they wouldn't need to if they didn't have electricity. Right?"

"Right."

"Could I have a dog there?"

Abbey weighed her answer carefully. "We'd have to find that out after we arrived."

"Would Grandma and Grandpa come and visit?" Susan asked.

"I'm sure they would, and if they didn't, we could visit them."

Scott poured cereal into his bowl until it threatened to spill over.

"I read an ad in the paper last night. Hard Luck, Alaska, needs a librarian, and it looks like I'm going to need a new job soon."

Scott and Susan didn't comment.

"I didn't think it would be fair to call and ask for an interview without discussing it with both of you first."

"You should go for it," Scott advised, but Abbey could see visions of huskies in her son's bright blue eyes.

"It'll mean a big change for all of us."

"Is there snow all the time?" Susan wanted to know.

"I don't think so, but I'll ask." Abbey hesitated, wondering exactly how much she should tell her children. "The ad said the job comes with a cabin and twenty acres of land."

The spoon was poised in front of Scotty's mouth. "To keep?"

Abbey nodded. "But we'd need to live there for a year. I imagine there won't be many applicants, but then I don't know. There doesn't seem to be an abundance of jobs for assistant librarians, either."

"I could live anywhere for a year. Go for it, Mom!"

"Susan?" Abbey suspected the decision would be more difficult for her daughter.

"Will there be girls my age?"

"Probably, but I can't guarantee that. The town only has 150 people, and it would be very different from the life we have here in Seattle."

"Come on, Susan," Scott urged. "We could have our very own house."

Susan's small shoulders heaved in a great sigh. "Do *you* want to move, Mommy?"

Abbey stroked her daughter's hair. Call her greedy. Call her materialistic. Call her a sucker, but she couldn't stop thinking about those twenty acres and that cabin. No mortgage. Land. Security. And a job she loved. All in Hard Luck, Alaska.

She inhaled deeply, then nodded.

"Then I guess it would be all right."

Scott let out a holler and leapt from his chair. He grabbed Abbey's hands and they danced around the room.

"I haven't got the job yet," Abbey cried, breathless.

"But you'll get it," Scott said confidently.

Abbey hoped her son was right.

Chapter
2

Abbey took several calming breaths before walking up to the hotel desk and giving her name.

"Mr. O'Halloran's taking interviews in the Snoqualmie Room on the second floor," the clerk told her.

Abbey's fingers tightened around her résumé as she headed for the escalator. Her heart pounded heavily, feeling like a lead weight in her chest.

Her decision to apply for this position had understandably received mixed reactions. Both Scott and Susan were excited about the prospect of a new life in Hard Luck, but Abbey's parents were hesitant.

Marie Murray would miss spoiling her grandchildren. Abbey's father, Wayne, was convinced she didn't know what she'd be getting into moving to the frozen north. But he seemed to forget that she made her living in a library. Soon after placing the initial call, Abbey had checked out a number of excellent books about life in Alaska. Her research had told her everything she wanted to know—and more.

Nevertheless, she'd already decided to accept the job if it was offered. No matter how cold the winters were, living in Hard Luck would be better than having to accept money from her parents.

Abbey found the Snoqualmie Room easily enough and glanced inside. A lean, rawboned man in his early thirties sat at a table reading intently. The hotel staff must have thought applicants would arrive thirsty, because they'd supplied a pitcher of ice water and at least two dozen glasses.

"Hello," she said with a polite smile. "I'm Abbey Sutherland."

"Abbey." The man stood abruptly as if she'd caught him unawares. "I'm Christian O'Halloran. We spoke on the phone." He motioned to the seat on the other side of the table. "Make yourself comfortable."

She sat and handed him her résumé.

He barely looked at it before setting it aside. "Thank you. I'll read this later."

Abbey nervously folded her hands in her lap and waited.

"You're applying for the position of librarian, right?"

"Yes. I'm working toward my degree in library science."

"In other words, you're not a full librarian."

"That's correct. In Washington state, a librarian is required to have a master's degree in library science. For the last two years I've worked as an assistant librarian for King County." She paused. Christian O'Halloran was difficult to read. "I answer reference questions, do quick information retrieval and cus-

tomer service, and of course I have computer skills." She hesitated, wondering if she should continue.

"That sounds perfect. Hard Luck doesn't exactly have a
library at the moment. We do have a building of sorts...."

"Books?"

"Oh, yes, hundreds of those. At least a thousand. They were
a gift to the town, and we need someone who's capable of
handling every aspect of organizing a library."

"I'd be fully capable of that." She listed a number of responsibilities she'd handled in her job with the King County library
system. Somehow, though, Abbey couldn't shake the feeling
that Christian O'Halloran wasn't really interested in hearing
about her qualifications.

He mentioned the pay, and although it wasn't as much as she
was earning with King County, she wouldn't need to worry
about rent.

A short silence followed, almost as if he wasn't sure what
else to ask.

"Could you tell me a little about the library building?" she
ventured.

He nodded. "Actually it was a home at one time—my grandfather's original homestead, in fact—but I don't think you'd
have much of a problem turning it into a library, would you?"

"Probably not."

Already, Abbey's mind was at work, dividing up the house.
One of the bedrooms could be used for fiction, another for nonfiction. The dining room would be perfect for a reading room,
or it could be set up as an area for children.

"You understand that life in Hard Luck isn't going to be

anything like Seattle," Christian commented, breaking into her thoughts.

Her father had said that very thing the day before. "I realize that." She paused for a moment. "Could I ask you about the house and the land you're offering?"

"Of course."

"Well, uh, could you tell me about the house?"

She waited.

"It's more of a cabin, and I'd describe it as...rustic." He seemed to stumble on the word. "It definitely has a...rural feel. Don't get me wrong, it's comfortable, but it's different from what you're used to."

"I'm sure it is. Tell me about Hard Luck."

The man across from her relaxed. "It's probably the most beautiful place on earth. You might think I'm prejudiced and I can't very well deny it. I guess you'll have to form your own opinion.

"In summer there's sunlight nearly twenty-four hours a day. That's when the wildflowers bloom. I swear every color under the sun bursts to life almost overnight. The forests and tundra turn scarlet and gold and burnt orange."

"It sounds lovely." And it did. "What about the winters?"

"Oh, yes. Well, again, it's beautiful, but the beauty is kind of...stark. Pristine's a good word. I don't think anyone's really lived until they've seen our light show."

"The aurora borealis."

Christian smiled approvingly. "I'm not going to lie to you," he continued. "It gets mighty cold. In winter it isn't uncommon for the temperature to drop to forty or fifty below."

"My goodness." Although Abbey knew this, hearing him say it reinforced the reality.

"On those days, almost everything closes down. We don't generally fly when it's that cold. It's too hard on the planes, and even harder on the pilots."

Abbey nodded; he'd told her about Midnight Sons, the O'Halloran brothers' air charter service, during their phone conversation.

"What about everything else?" she asked. "Like the school. Does it close down, too?" He'd also explained in their previous conversation that Hard Luck had a school that went from kindergarten to twelfth grade.

"Life in town comes to a standstill, and we all sort of snuggle together. There's nothing to do in weather that cold but wait it out. Most days, we manage to keep the school open, though." He shrugged. "We rely on one another in Hard Luck. We have to."

"What about food?"

"We've got a grocery store. It's not a supermarket, mind you, but it carries the essentials. Everyone in town stocks up on supplies once a year. But if you run out of anything, there's always the grocery. If Pete Livengood—he's the guy who owns it—if he doesn't have what you need, one of the pilots can pick it up for you. Midnight Sons makes daily flights into Fairbanks, so it isn't like you're stuck there."

"What about driving to Fairbanks? When I looked up Hard Luck, I couldn't make out any roads. There is one, isn't there?"

"Sure there is—in a manner of speaking," Christian said proudly. "We got ourselves a haul road a few years back."

Abbey was relieved. If she did get the job, she'd have to have her furniture and other household effects delivered; without a road, that would obviously have been a problem. Flying them was sure to be prohibitively expensive.

"Do you have any more questions for me?" she asked.

"None." Christian looked at his watch. "Would you mind filling out the application form while you're here? I'll be holding interviews for the next day or so. I'll call you tomorrow afternoon, if that's all right."

Abbey stood. "That'd be fine."

Christian gave her the one-page application, which she completed quickly and gave back to him.

He rose from behind the table and extended his hand. "It was a pleasure to meet you."

"You, too." Even before she'd come in for the interview, she'd known she'd accept the position if it was offered to her. She needed a job, needed to support her family. If that meant traveling to the ends of the earth, she'd do it. But as she turned to walk away, Abbey realized she not only needed this position, she *wanted* it. Badly.

She loved the idea of creating her own library. But it wasn't just the challenge of the job that excited her. She'd watched this man's eyes light up as he talked about his home. When he said Hard Luck was beautiful, he'd said it with sincerity, with passion. When he told her about the tundra and the forest, she could imagine their beauty. She'd seen plenty of photographs and even a *National Geographic* documentary, but it was his words that truly convinced her. More than that, *excited* her.

"Mr. O'Halloran?" she said, surprising herself.

He was already seated, leafing intently through a sheaf of papers. He glanced up. "Yes?"

"If you decide to hire me, I promise I'll do a good job for you and the people in Hard Luck."

He nodded. "And I promise I'll phone you soon."

"Well?" Scott looked at Abbey expectantly when she walked into the house. "How'd the interview go?"

Abbey slipped off her pumps and curled her toes into the carpet. "Fine—I think."

"Will you get the job?"

Abbey didn't want to build up her son's hopes. "I don't know, honey. Where's Missy?" Since she paid the teenage babysitter top dollar, she expected her to stay with Scott and Susan for the agreed-upon number of hours.

"Her mother wanted her to put a roast in the oven at four-thirty. Susan went with her. They'll be back soon."

Abbey collapsed into her favorite chair and dangled her arms over the sides. Her feet rested on the ottoman.

"Are you finished your homework?" she asked.

"I don't have any. There's only a couple more weeks left of school."

"I know."

Abbey dreaded the summer months. Every year, day camp and babysitting were more and more expensive. Scott was getting old enough to resent having a teenager stay with him. Not that Abbey blamed him. Before she knew it, her son would be thirteen himself.

"Would it be okay if I went over to Jason's house?" he asked eagerly. "I'll be home in time for dinner."

Abbey nodded, but she knew it wasn't the other boy he was interested in seeing. It was those puppies that'd captured his nine-year-old heart.

Sawyer walked into the long, narrow structure that sat next to the gravel-and-dirt runway. The mobile served as the office for Midnight Sons. Eventually they hoped to build a real office. That had been on the agenda for the past eight years—ever since they'd started the business. During those years, Charles and Sawyer had built their own homes. Sawyer's was across the street from Christian's place, which had been the O'Halloran family home. Charles's house was one street over—not that there were paved streets in Hard Luck.

But they'd been too busy running Midnight Sons—flying cargo and passengers, hiring pilots, negotiating contracts and all the other myriad responsibilities that came with a business like theirs. Constructing an office building was just another one of those things they hadn't gotten around to doing.

Exhausted, Sawyer threw himself down on the hard-backed swivel chair at Christian's desk. Cleaning those old cabins was proving to be hard work. Much more of this, he thought ruefully, and he was going to end up with dishpan hands.

He'd been astonished—and impressed—by the willingness of their pilots to pitch in and make those old cabins livable. One thing was for sure; the log structures were solid. A few minor repairs, lots of soapy water and a little attention had done wonders. Not that a forty-year-old log cabin was going to impress a city girl. More than likely, the women Christian hired would take one look at those shacks and book the next flight south.

The phone pealed and Sawyer reached for it. As he did, he noticed the message light blinking.

"Midnight Sons."

"Where have you been all day?" Christian grumbled. "I've left three messages. I've been sitting here waiting for you to call me back."

"Sorry," Sawyer muttered, biting back the temptation to offer to trade places. While Christian was gallivanting all over kingdom come securing airplane parts, talking to travel agents, *meeting women* and generally having a good time, Sawyer had been wielding a mop and pail. In Sawyer's opinion, his younger brother had gotten the better end of this deal. As for himself, he'd seen enough cobwebs in the past week to last him a lifetime.

"You can tell Duke I found him a blonde," Christian announced triumphantly. "Her name's Allison Reynolds, and she's going to be our secretary—well, maybe."

Sawyer's jaw tightened as he made an effort to hold back his irritation. "What're her qualifications?"

"You mean other than being blond?" Christian asked, then chuckled. "I'm telling you, Sawyer, I've never seen anything like this in my life. I placed the ad in the Seattle paper, and the answering service has been swamped. There are a lot of lonely women in this world."

"Does our new secretary know she'll be living in a log cabin *without* the comforts of home?"

"Naturally I told her about the cabin, but, uh, I didn't have a chance to go into all the details."

"Christian! That's hardly a detail. She'll be expecting to see modern plumbing, not a path to the outhouse. Women don't like that kind of surprise."

"I didn't want to scare her off," he argued.

"She deserves the truth."

"I know, I know. Actually I offered her the position and she's thinking it over. If she decides to accept the job, I'll give her more information."

"You mean to tell me that out of all the women who applied, you chose one who isn't even sure she wants the job?" Sawyer didn't often fly off the handle, but his brother was annoying him more than usual.

"Trust me, Allison wants the position," Christian insisted. "She just needs to think about it. I would, too, in the circumstances." He paused. "Our ad certainly attracted a lot of attention."

Sawyer had carefully gone over the ad they'd submitted to the Seattle and Portland papers. He'd been concerned that they not inadvertently put in anything that might be misleading or violate the antidiscrimination laws. So there was nothing in the ad to suggest a man couldn't apply. No one wanted to deal with a lawsuit a few weeks down the road.

"I must've talked to at least thirty women in the past couple of days," Christian said, his voice ringing with enthusiasm. "And there were that many more phone inquiries."

"What about a librarian? Has anyone applied for that?"

"A few, but not nearly as many as for the position of secretary. The minute I met Allison—"

"Does she type?"

"She must," Christian answered. "She works in an office."

"Didn't you give her a test?" Sawyer asked, not bothering to conceal his disgust.

"What for? It isn't like she'll need a hundred words a minute, is it?"

Sawyer rubbed his face. "I can't believe I'm hearing this."

"Wait until you meet her, Sawyer," Christian said happily. "She's a knockout."

"Oh, great." He could picture it already. His crew would be hanging around the office, tongues hanging out over a dizzy blonde, instead of flying. Midnight Sons didn't need this kind of trouble.

"Don't worry about it," his brother said. "I've made a lot of progress. You should be pleased."

"It doesn't sound like you've done much of anything." Sawyer was fuming. He'd hoped—obviously a futile hope—that Christian would use a bit of common sense.

"Listen, I haven't made up my mind which woman to hire for our librarian. There were a couple of excellent applicants."

"Any blondes?" Sawyer asked sarcastically.

"Yeah, one, but she looked too fragile to last. I liked her, though. There's another one who seemed to really want the job. It makes me wonder why she'd leave a cushy job here in Seattle for Hard Luck. It's not like we're offering great benefits."

"But a house and twenty acres *sounds* like a lot," Sawyer said from between clenched teeth.

"You think I should hire her?"

He sighed. "If she's qualified and she wants the job, then by all means, hire her."

"Okay. I'll give her a call as soon as we're finished and make the arrangements."

"Just a minute." Sawyer shoved one hand through his hair. "Is she pretty?" He was quickly losing faith in his brother's judgment. Christian had already decided on a secretary, and he didn't know if she could so much as file. Heaven help them all if he hired the rest of the applicants based on their looks rather than their qualifications.

Christian hesitated. "I suppose you could say the librarian's pretty, but she isn't going to bowl you over the way Allison will. She's just sort of regular pretty. Brown hair and eyes, average height. Cute upturned nose.

"Now with Allison, well, there's no comparison. We're talking sexy here. Wait until John gets a look at her...front," Christian said, and chuckled. "She's swimsuit-issue material."

"Hire her!" Sawyer snapped.

"Allison? I already have, but she wants twenty-four hours to think it over. I told you that."

"I meant the *librarian*."

"Oh, all right, if you think I should."

Sawyer propped his elbows on the desk and shook his head. "Anything else you called to tell me about?"

"Not much. I'm not doing any more interviews for now. Allison and the librarian, plus the new teacher, that's three— enough to start with. Let's see how things work out. I've collected a couple of dozen résumés, and I'll save them for future reference. Unless I find a cook for Ben or—"

"Don't hire any more," Sawyer insisted. He was well aware that he sounded short-tempered, but frankly he was and he didn't care if his brother knew it.

"Oh, yeah, I meant to tell you. If Allison does take the job, she won't be able to start right away. Apparently she's booked a vacation with a friend. I told her that's okay. We've waited this long. Another couple of weeks won't matter."

"Why don't you ask her if next year would be convenient?"

"Very funny. What's wrong with you? I get the feeling you're envious—not that I blame you. I wish we'd thought of this a long time ago. Meeting and talking to all these women is a lot of fun. See you."

The phone went dead in Sawyer's hand.

Abbey's spirits were low. Dragging-in-the-gutter low. She hadn't got the job. O'Halloran would've phoned by now if he'd decided to hire her.

Scott and Susan, ever sensitive to her moods, pushed their dinner around their plates. No one seemed to have much of an appetite.

"It doesn't look like I got the job in Alaska," she told them. There wasn't any reason to keep her children's hopes alive. "Mr. O'Halloran, the man who interviewed me, was supposed to call this afternoon if he'd chosen me."

"That's all right, Mom," Scott said with a brave smile. "You'll find something else."

"I wanted to go to Alaska," Susan said, her lower lip trembling. "I told everyone at school we were moving."

"We are." Abbey knew this was of little comfort, but she

threw it in, anyway. "It just so happens that we won't be moving to Alaska."

"Can we visit there someday?" Scott asked. "I liked what we read in those books you brought home. It seems like a great place."

"Someday." *Someday,* Abbey realized, could be a magical word, filled with the promise of a brighter tomorrow. At the moment, though, it just sounded bleak.

The phone rang, and both Susan and Scott twisted around, looking eagerly at the kitchen wall. Neither of them moved. Abbey didn't allow the dinner hour to be interrupted by phone calls.

"The machine will pick up the message," she told them unnecessarily.

After the fourth ring, the answering machine automatically clicked on. Everyone went still, straining to hear who'd phoned.

"This is Christian O'Halloran."

"Mom!" Scott cried excitedly.

Abbey flew across the kitchen, ripping the phone off the hook. "Mr. O'Halloran," she said breathlessly, "hello."

"Hello," Christian responded. "I'm glad I caught you."

"I'm glad you caught me, too. Have you made your decision?" She hated to sound so eager, but she couldn't stop herself.

"You've got the job, if you still want it."

"I do," Abbey said, giving Scott and Susan a thumbs-up. Her son and daughter stabbed triumphant fists in the air.

"When can you start?"

Abbey was certain the library would let her leave with minimal notice. "Whenever it's convenient for you."

"How about next week?" Christian asked. "I won't return from my business trip until the end of the month, but I'll arrange for my brother Sawyer to meet you in Fairbanks."

"*Next* week?"

"Is that too soon?"

"No, no," she said quickly, fearing he might change his mind. She could take the kids out of school a week early, and she wouldn't need much time to pack their belongings. Her mother would help, and whatever they didn't take with them on the plane—like their furniture—she could have shipped later.

"I'll see you in Hard Luck, then."

"Thank you. I can't tell you how pleased I am," she said. "Oh, before I hang up..." she began, thinking she should probably mention the fact that she'd be bringing Scott and Susan. Despite the provision of housing, there was nothing on the application asking about children or family.

"I'll be with you in a minute, Allison," Christian said.

"Excuse me?"

"My dinner date just arrived," he told her. "As I explained, my brother will meet you in Fairbanks. I'll have the travel agency call you to make the arrangements for your ticket."

"You're paying my airfare?"

"Of course. And don't worry about packing for the winter. You can buy what you need once you arrive."

"But—"

"I wish I had more time to answer your questions," he said distractedly. "Sawyer's really the one who can tell you what you need to know."

"Mr. O'Halloran—"

"Good luck, Abbey."

"Thank you." She gave up trying. He'd learn about Scott and Susan when he returned. As far as she was concerned, the town was getting a great librarian—plus a bonus!

"You sure you don't want me to fly in and meet the new librarian this afternoon?" John Henderson asked, straddling the chair across from Sawyer. His hair had been dampened and combed down, and it looked as if he was wearing a new shirt.

"Be my guest." You'd think the Queen of England was flying in judging by the way folks in Hard Luck were behaving. Duke had arrived at Ben's this morning clean-shaven and spiffed up, smelling pungently of aftershave. Sawyer hid a grin. The next woman would follow in a few days, and he wondered how long it would take for everyone to get tired of these welcoming parties.

"You'll let John pick up the new librarian over my dead body," Duke barked. "We all know what happened the last time he flew a woman into Hard Luck."

"I keep telling you that wasn't my fault."

"Forget it! I'll pick her up." Sawyer looked away from his squabbling pilots in disgust and happened to notice the blackboard where Ben wrote out the daily lunch and dinner specials.

"Beef Wellington?" he asked.

"You got a problem with Beef Wellington?" Ben muttered belligerently. "I'm just trying to show our new librarian that we're a civilized bunch."

In Sawyer's opinion, this whole project didn't show a lot of promise. He'd bet none of these women would last the winter. The bad feeling he'd experienced when they first discussed the idea had returned tenfold.

"You talk to that Seattle paper yet?" Ben asked, setting a plate of scrambled eggs and toast in front of him.

"No." Sawyer frowned. The press was becoming a problem. It wasn't surprising that the media had gotten hold of the situation and wanted to do stories on it. They'd been hounding Sawyer for interviews all week—thanks to Christian, who'd given out his name. He was damn near ready to throttle his younger brother. And he was sorely tempted to have the phone disconnected; if it wasn't vital for business, he swore he would've done it already.

Now that the first woman was actually arriving, Sawyer regretted not discussing The Plan with their oldest brother. Although Charles was a full partner in the flight service, he was employed as a surveyor for Alaska Oil and was often away from Hard Luck for weeks on end. Like right now.

When he did get home, Charles would probably think they'd all lost their minds. Sawyer wouldn't blame him, either.

"Well, the cabin's ready, anyway," Duke said with satisfaction.

After they'd scrubbed down the walls and floors, Sawyer and a few of the men had opened up the storeroom in the lodge and dug out some of the old furniture. Sawyer had expressed doubts about sleeping on mattresses that had been tucked away for so many years, but Pearl and various other women—including several who were wives of pipeline maintenance workers—had aired everything out. They'd assured him that aside from some lingering mustiness, there was nothing to worry about. Everything had been well wrapped in plastic.

As much as Sawyer hated to admit it, the cabin looked almost inviting. The black potbellied stove gleamed from repeated scrubbing. The women had sewn floral curtains for the one window and a matching tablecloth for the rough wooden table. The townspeople had stacked the shelves with groceries, and someone had even donated a cooler to keep perishables fresh for a few days. The single bed, made up with sun-dried linens and one thin blanket, did resemble something one might find in a prison, but Sawyer didn't say so. Pearl and her friends had worked hard to make the cabin as welcoming as possible.

When he'd stopped there on his way to Ben's for breakfast, he saw that someone had placed a Mason jar of freshly cut wildflowers on the table. Right beside the kerosene lantern and the can opener.

Well, this was as good as it got.

"How are you going to know it's her when she steps off the plane?" Ben asked, standing directly in front of him and watching him eat.

"I'm wearing my Midnight Sons jacket," Sawyer answered. "I'll let her figure it out."

"What's her name again?"

"Abbey Sutherland."

"I bet she's pretty," Duke muttered.

His pilots gazed sightlessly into the distance, longing written on their faces. Sawyer wouldn't have believed it if he hadn't seen it with his own eyes.

"I'm getting out of here before you three make me lose my breakfast."

"You sure you don't want me to ride along with you?" John asked hopefully.

"I'm sure." Sawyer would also be bringing back the mail and a large order of canned goods for the grocery. He was flying the Baron, and he sincerely hoped Abbey Sutherland had packed light. He didn't have room for more than two suitcases, and he intended to store those in the nose.

Grabbing his jacket from the back of the chair, Sawyer headed out the door and across Hard Luck's main street toward the runway.

He could've flown into Fairbanks with his eyes closed, he'd made the flight so often. He landed, took care of loading up the mail and other freight, then—with a sense of dread—made his way to the terminal.

After checking the monitor to make sure the flight was coming in on time, Sawyer bought a coffee and ventured out to the assigned gate.

He was surprised by how busy the terminal was. Tourists, he guessed. Not that he was complaining. They brought a lot of money into the state. Not as much as oil did, of course, but they certainly represented a healthy part of the economy.

Even the airport was geared toward impressing tourists, he noted. The first thing many saw when they walked in was a massive mounted polar bear, rearing up on its hind legs. Although he'd seen it a hundred times, Sawyer still felt awed by it.

The plane arrived on schedule. Sipping coffee, Sawyer waited for the passengers to enter the terminal.

He glanced at each one, not knowing what to expect. Christian's description of Abbey Sutherland sure left something to be desired. From what he remembered, Christian had said she was "regular" pretty.

Every woman he saw seemed to match that description, such as it was. With the exception of one.

She was probably in her early thirties. She had two kids at her side. The little girl, who couldn't have been more than six or seven, clutched a stuffed bear. The boy, perhaps two or three years older, looked as if he needed a leash to hold him back. The kid was raring to go.

The woman wasn't *pretty,* Sawyer decided, she was downright lovely. Her glossy brown hair was short and straight and fell to just below her ears. Her eyes skirted past him. He liked their warm brown color and he liked her calm manner.

He also liked the way she protectively drew her children close as she looked around. She too, it seemed, was seeking someone.

With a determined effort, Sawyer pulled his gaze away from her and scanned the crowd for Christian's librarian.

Brown hair and cute upturned nose.

He found himself looking back at the woman with the two children. Their eyes met, and her generous mouth formed a smile. It wasn't a shy smile or a coy one. It was open and friendly, as if she recognized him and expected him to recognize her.

Then she walked right over to him. "Hello," she said.

"Hello." Fearing he'd miss the woman he'd come to meet, his eyes slid past her to the people still disembarking from the plane.

"I'm Abbey Sutherland."

Sawyer's gaze shot back to her before dropping to the two kids.

"These are my children, Scott and Susan," she said. "Thank you for meeting us."

Chapter
3

"Your children?" Sawyer repeated.

"Yes," Abbey said. It was easy to see the family resemblance between Sawyer and Christian O'Halloran, she thought. Both were tall and lean and rawboned. If he'd lived a hundred years earlier, he could've been on horseback, riding across some now-forgotten range in the Old West. Instead, he was flying over a large expanse of wilderness, from one fringe of civilization to another.

Whereas Christian had been clean-shaven, Sawyer had a beard. The dark hair suited his face. His eyes were a pale shade of gray-blue, not unlike those of a husky, Scott's favorite dog. He wore a red-checked flannel shirt under a jacket marked with the Midnight Sons logo. She suspected he had no idea how attractive he was.

"Hi," Scott said eagerly, looking up at Sawyer.

The pilot held out his hand and she noticed that his eyes softened as he exchanged handshakes with her son. "Pleased to meet you, Scott."

"Alaska sure is big."

"That it is. Hello, Susan," Sawyer said next, holding out his hand to her daughter. The girl solemnly shook it, then glanced at Abbey and smiled, clearly delighted with this gesture of grown-up respect.

"Could we speak privately, Ms. Sutherland?" Sawyer asked. The warmth and welcome vanished from his eyes as he motioned toward the waiting area. He walked just far enough away so the children couldn't hear him. Abbey followed, keeping a close eye on Scott and Susan.

"Christian didn't mention that you have children," Sawyer said without preamble.

"He didn't ask. And there was no reference to family on the application or the agreement Christian sent me. I did think it was a bit odd not to inquire about my circumstances, considering that you're providing housing."

"You might've said something." An accusatory look tightened his mouth.

"I didn't get a chance," she explained in even tones. His attitude was beginning to irritate her. "I did try, but he was busy, and I really didn't think it would matter."

"There's nothing in the agreement about children."

"I'm aware of that," Abbey said, striving to keep the emotion out of her voice. "As I already told you, I filled out the application and answered every question, and there wasn't a single one about dependants. Frankly, I don't think they're anyone's concern but mine. I was hired as a librarian. And as long as I do my job, I—"

"That's right, but—"

"I really can't see that it matters whether or not I have a family to support."

"What about your husband?"

"I'm divorced. Listen, would you mind if we discussed this another time? The children and I are exhausted. We landed in Anchorage late last night and were up early this morning to catch the connecting flight to Fairbanks. Would it be too much to ask that we wait for a more opportune moment to sort this out?"

He hesitated, then said in crisp tones, "No problem."

The pulse in his temple throbbed visibly, and Abbey suspected that it was, in fact, very much of a problem.

"I brought the Baron," he said, directing the three of them toward the luggage carousel. "All I can say is I hope you packed light."

Abbey wasn't sure how she was supposed to interpret "packed light." Everything she and the children owned that would fit was crammed into their suitcases. Everything that hadn't gone into their luggage had been sold, given away or handed over to a shipping company and would arrive within the month. She hoped.

"Look, Mom," Scott said, pointing at the wall where a variety of stuffed animals were displayed. Abbey shuddered, but her son's eyes remained fixed on the head of a huge brown bear. Its teeth were bared threateningly.

"That silly bear stuck his head right through the wall," Sawyer joked.

Scott laughed, but Susan stared hard as if that just might be possible.

When they'd collected all the luggage, Sawyer stepped back, frowning. "You brought *six* suitcases."

"Yes, I know," Abbey said calmly. "We needed six suitcases."

"I don't have room for all those in the plane. I'm not even sure how I'm going to get you, two kids, the mail and the rest of the cargo inside, much less enough luggage to sink a battle-ship. If you'd let me know, I could've brought a larger plane."

Abbey bit back a sarcastic reply. She'd *tried* to tell Christian about her children, but he'd been too interested in his dinner date to listen to her. She hadn't purposely hidden anything from him or Sawyer. And, good grief, how was *she* supposed to know how much luggage some airplane would hold?

"Never mind," Sawyer grumbled impatiently, "I'll figure it out later. Let's get going."

Abbey would've liked something to eat, but it was clear Sawyer was anxious to be on his way. Fortunately Scott and Susan, unlike their mother, had gobbled down what the airline laughably called a meal.

They loaded everything into the bed of a pickup and drove around the airport to a back road, which took them to an area used by various flight service operators.

"All that stuff belongs to Mom and Susan," Scott whispered conspiratorially as Sawyer helped him out of the cab. "They're the ones who insisted on bringing *everything*."

"Sounds just like a couple of women," Sawyer muttered. He led them to the plane.

Abbey wasn't sure what she'd expected, but this compact

dual-engine aircraft wasn't it. She peeked inside and realized that what Sawyer had said was true. There was barely room for her, let alone the children and all their luggage.

"There's only three seats," she said, looking nervously at Sawyer. It didn't take a mathematical genius to figure out that three seats wasn't enough for four people.

"You'll have to sit on my desk—the seat beside mine," Sawyer instructed after climbing aboard the aircraft. "And I'll buckle the kids together on the other seat."

"Is that legal?"

"Probably not in the lower forty-eight," he told her, "but we do it here. Don't worry, they'll be fine." He moved toward the cockpit, retrieved a black binder and a stack of papers from the passenger seat and crammed them into the space between the two seats.

"Go on in and sit down," he said, "while I see to the kids."

Abbey climbed awkwardly inside and carefully edged her way forward. By the time she fastened the seat belt, she was breathless.

Sawyer settled Scott and Susan in the remaining seat behind her. One look at her children told Abbey neither was pleased with the arrangement. But it couldn't be avoided.

"What about our luggage?" she asked when Sawyer slipped into the seat next to her.

He placed earphones over his head, then reached for the binder and made a notation in it.

"Our luggage?" she repeated.

"The suitcases don't fit. We're going to have to leave them behind."

"What?" Abbey cried. "We can't do that!"

Sawyer ignored her and continued to ready the plane for takeoff.

"How long is the flight?" Scott asked.

"About an hour."

"Can I fly the plane?"

"Not this time," Sawyer responded absently.

"*Later* can I?"

"We'll see."

"Mr. O'Halloran," Abbey said with a heavy sigh, "could we please discuss the luggage situation?"

"No. My contract is to deliver the mail. That's far more important. I'm not going to unload cargo for a bunch of silly female things you aren't going to need, anyway."

Abbey gritted her teeth. "I didn't bring silly female things. Now if you'd kindly—"

Sawyer turned around and looked at Scott. "Do you like dogs?"

Scott's eyes grew huge. "You bet I do," he answered breathlessly.

Sawyer adjusted some switches. "When we get to Hard Luck, I'll take you over to meet Eagle Catcher."

"Is he a husky?"

"Yup."

"Really?" Scott sounded as if he'd died and gone to heaven. He was so excited it was a wonder he didn't bounce right out of the seat.

"Um, about our luggage?" Abbey hated to be a pest, but she didn't like being ignored, either. It might be unimportant to

Buck Rogers here, but she'd rather they arrived in Hard Luck with something more than the clothes on their backs.

He didn't bother to answer. Instead, he started the engines and chatted in friendly tones with a man in the control tower. Come to think of it, he chatted in friendly tones with everyone but her.

Before Abbey could protest further, they were taxiing toward the runway.

In no time they were in the air. Above the roar of the twin engines, Abbey could hear nothing except the pounding of her heart. She'd never flown in a plane this small, and she closed her eyes and held on tightly as it pitched and heaved its way into the clear blue sky.

"Wow!" Scott shouted. "This is fun."

Abbey didn't share his reaction. Her stomach did a flip-flop as the plane banked sharply to one side. She braced her hands against the seat, muttering, "Come on! Straighten up and fly right, can't you?"

Still talking to the tower, Sawyer glanced at her and grinned. "Relax," he said. "I haven't been forced to crash-land in two or three months now."

"In other words, I haven't got a thing to worry about." Abbey shouted to be heard above the engines. She peeked over her shoulder to be sure Scott and Susan weren't frightened. They weren't—quite the opposite. They smiled at her, thrilled with their first small-plane ride. She, on the other hand, preferred airplanes that came equipped with flight attendants.

Abbey wasn't able to make out much of the landscape below. She'd been disappointed earlier; during the flight from Anchor-

age to Fairbanks, Mount McKinley had been obscured by
clouds. The pilot had announced that the highest mountain in
North America was visible less than twenty percent of the
time. He'd joked that perhaps it wasn't really there at all.

She glanced away from the window and back at Sawyer. He'd
already demonstrated a fairly flexible attitude to safety rules,
in her view. Now he took out the black binder he'd wedged
between their seats and began to write. Abbey stared at him.
Not once did his eyes shift from his task, whatever it was.

A light blinked repeatedly on the dashboard. Abbey knew
nothing about small planes, but she figured if a light was
blinking, there had to be a reason. They must be losing oil or
gas or altitude or *something*.

When she couldn't stand it any longer, she gripped his arm
and pointed to the light.

"Yes?" He looked at her blankly.

She didn't want to shout for fear of alarming her children,
so she leaned her head as close to his as possible and said in a
reasonable voice, "There's a light flashing."

"Yes, I see." He continued writing.

"Aren't you going to do something about it?"

"In a couple of minutes."

"I'd rather you took care of it now."

"There's nothing to worry about, Ms. Sutherland—Abbey," he
said. Lines crinkled around his eyes, and he almost seemed to
enjoy her discomfort. "All it indicates is that I'm on automatic
pilot."

She felt like a fool. Crossing her arms, she wrapped what
remained of her dignity about her and gazed out the window.

Sawyer tapped her on the shoulder. "You don't need to worry about your luggage, either. I've arranged with another flight service to have it delivered this afternoon."

He might have told her sooner, instead of leaving her to worry. "Thank you."

He nodded.

"What's that?" Scott shouted from behind her.

Abbey looked down to discover a streak of silver that stretched as far as the eye could see.

"That's the Alaska pipeline," Sawyer told Scott.

From the research she'd done on Alaska, Abbey knew that the pipeline traversed eight hundred miles of rugged mountain ranges, rivers and harsh terrain. It ran from Prudhoe Bay to Valdez, the northernmost ice-free port in North America.

Soon Abbey noticed that the plane was descending. She studied the landscape, trying to spot Hard Luck, excited about seeing the community that would be her home. She saw a row of buildings along one unpaved street, with a large structure set off to the side. Several other buildings were scattered about. She tried to count the houses and got to twenty before the plane lined up with the runway for its final descent.

As they drew close, Abbey realized the field wasn't paved, either. They were landing on what resembled a wide gravel road. She held her breath and braced herself as the wheels touched down, sure they'd hit hard against the rough ground. To her surprise, the landing was as smooth as any she'd experienced.

Sawyer cut the engine speed and taxied toward a mobile structure near the far end of the field. Abbey strained to see what she could out of the narrow side window. She smiled when she recognized a telephone booth. In the middle of the Arctic, at the very top of the world, it was comforting to know she could call home.

A burly man who resembled a lumberjack barreled out of the mobile structure. Abbey lost sight of him, then heard the door on the side of the aircraft open.

"Howdy," he called, sticking his head and upper shoulders inside. "Welcome to Hard Luck. I'm John Henderson."

"Hello," Abbey called back.

John disappeared abruptly to be replaced by the head and shoulders of another outdoorsy-looking man. "I'm Ralph Ferris," he said. Three other faces crowded in around the opening.

"For crying out loud," Sawyer snapped, "would you guys let the passengers out of the plane first? This is ridiculous." He squeezed past her, unsnapped the seat belt secured around Scott and Susan and helped them out.

Abbey was the last person to disembark. As she moved down the three steps, she found all five men standing at attention, as if prepared for a military inspection. Their arms hung straight at their sides, their shoulders were squared, spines straight. If any of them were surprised to see two children, it didn't show.

Muttering to himself, Sawyer stalked past Abbey and into the mobile office, leaving her alone with her children. He slammed the door, apparently eager to be rid of them.

Abbey felt irritation swirl through her. How could he just abandon her? How could he be so *rude?* What had she done that was so terrible? Well, she could be rude, too!

"Welcome to Hard Luck." Her angry thoughts were swept aside as a tall, thin older woman with gray hair cut boyishly short stepped forward to greet her. "I'm Pearl Inman," she said, shaking Abbey's hand enthusiastically. "I can't tell you how pleased we are to have a librarian in Hard Luck."

"Thank you. These are my children, Scott and Susan. We're happy to be here." Abbey noted that Pearl seemed as unsurprised by the arrival of two children as the pilots were.

"You must be exhausted."

"We're fine," Abbey said politely, which was true; she felt a resurgence of energy.

"You got any other kids in this town?" Scott asked.

"Are there any girls my age?" Susan added.

"My heavens, yes. We had twenty-five students last year. I'll have one of the boys introduce you around later, Scott." She turned her attention to Susan. "How old are you?"

"Seven."

Pearl's smile deepened. "I believe Chrissie Harris is seven. Her father works for the Parks Department and serves as our PSO on the side. PSO stands for public safety officer—sort of our policeman. Chrissie will be mighty glad to have a new friend."

"What about me?" Scott asked. "I'm nine."

"Ronny Gold's about that age. You'll meet him later. He's got a bike and likes to ride all over town on it, so there's no missing him."

Scott seemed appeased. "Are there any Indians around here?" he asked next.

"A few live in the area—Athabascans. You'll meet them sometime," Pearl assured him.

Looking around, Abbey felt a large mosquito land on her arm. She swatted it away. Susan had already received one bite and was swatting at another mosquito.

"I see you've been introduced to the Alaska state bird, the mosquito," Pearl said, then chuckled. "They're pretty thick around here in June and July. A little bug spray works wonders."

"I'll get some later," Abbey said. She hadn't realized mosquitoes were such a problem in Alaska.

"Come on—let's go to the restaurant and I'll introduce you to Ben and the others," Pearl said, urging them across the road toward a building that resembled a house with a big porch. A huge pair of moose antlers adorned the front. "This is the Hard Luck Café. Ben Hamilton's the owner, and he's been cooking up a storm all day. I sure hope you're hungry."

Abbey grinned broadly. "I could eat a moose."

"Good," Pearl said, grinning back. "I do believe it's on the menu."

Children.

Sawyer had no one to blame but himself for not knowing that Abbey came as a package deal. He was the person who'd so carefully drawn up the application. Obviously he'd forgotten to include one small but vital question. He'd left one little loophole. If Abbey had arrived with kids, would other women bring them, too? It was a question he didn't even want to consider.

Children.

He poured himself a mug of coffee from the office pot and took a swallow. It burned his mouth and throat, but he was too preoccupied to care. He had to figure out what they were going to do about Abbey Sutherland and her kids.

It wasn't that he objected to Scott and Susan. Abbey was right; her children had nothing to do with her ability to hold down the job of librarian. But they were complications the town hadn't foreseen.

First, the three of them couldn't live in that cabin. The entire space was no bigger than a large bedroom. Those cabins had never been intended as permanent living quarters, anyway. Sawyer remembered that initially he'd tried to reason with Christian and the others, but no one would listen, and he'd ended up taking the path of least resistance. He'd even helped clean the cabins!

In fact, he had to admit he'd become caught up with the idea himself. It had seemed like a simple solution to a complex problem. You'd think a group of men, all of whom were over thirty, would have the brains to know better.

Sawyer could only imagine what his older brother would say when he found out what they'd done. Charles would be spitting nails.

Sawyer passed his hand over his eyes and sighed deeply. He didn't understand what would bring a woman like Abbey Sutherland to Hard Luck in the first place. She wouldn't last, and he'd known it the moment he laid eyes on her.

It occurred to him that she might be running away. From her ex-husband? Perhaps she'd gotten involved in an abusive relationship. His hands formed tight fists at the thought of her husband mistreating her—at the thought of any man mistreating any woman.

Sawyer had seen for himself the dull pain in her eyes when she said she was divorced. He just wasn't sure why it was there. Understanding women wasn't his forte, and he felt himself at a real disadvantage. He lacked the experience, but he liked to think he was generally a good judge of character.

Then again, maybe he wasn't. There'd been only one serious relationship in his life, and that hadn't lasted long. Just when he was feeling comfortable with the way things were going, Loreen had started hinting at marriage. Soon those hints had become ultimatums. He'd liked Loreen just fine, but he wasn't anywhere close to marriage. Once he'd told her that, she left him.

Sawyer assumed that was how a lot of women felt. They wanted a ring to make everything official and complete. Well, he'd seen what could happen when a couple fell out of love. His parents were the perfect example of the kind of relationship he didn't want. They'd been chained to faded dreams and unhappy memories. So Sawyer had let Loreen go, and try as he might he hadn't once regretted his decision.

Sawyer didn't know how he was going to handle the problem of Abbey and her family. What he *should* do was put her and those two kids of hers on the afternoon flight out of Hard Luck.

But he wouldn't. Because if he even suggested it, twenty men would happily lynch him from the nearest tree. Of course, they'd have to go more than two hundred miles to find a tree tall enough for the job....

After he finished his coffee, Sawyer headed over to the café. It seemed half the town was there, eager to meet Abbey. There was no place to sit, so he stood, arms folded and one foot braced against the wall, hoping to give the impression that he was relaxed and at ease.

Ben, he noted, was pleased as a pig in...mud to be doing such a brisk business. The cook wove his way between the mismatched tables, refilling coffee cups and making animated conversation.

He lifted the glass pot toward Sawyer with a questioning look.

Sawyer shook his head. He sure didn't need another coffee. In fact, he shouldn't have had the last one.

He saw that Abbey was surrounded by four of his pilots. They circled the table where she sat with Pearl and her children, like buzzards closing in on a fresh kill. You'd think they'd never seen a woman before.

His crew was a mangy-looking bunch, Sawyer mused, with the exception of Duke, who was broad-shouldered and firm-muscled. One thing he could say about all of them was that they were excellent pilots. Lazy SOBs when the mood struck them, though. He didn't know anyone who could love flying as much as a bush pilot and still come up with the world's most inventive excuses to avoid duty.

Everyone plied Abbey with questions. Sawyer half expected all this attention to fluster her, but she handled their inquisition with graceful ease. He was astonished by how quickly she'd picked up on names and matched them to faces.

Ben sauntered over to his side. His gaze followed Sawyer's.

"Pretty, isn't she?" Ben said. "I wouldn't mind marrying her myself."

"You're joking." Sawyer's eyes narrowed as he studied his longtime friend.

Ben's heavy shoulders shook with silent laughter. "So that's the way it is."

"Which way is that?" Sawyer challenged.

"She's already got you hooked. In no time, you'll be just like all the others, fighting for the pleasure of her company."

Sawyer snorted. "Don't be ridiculous! I just hope we don't have any more women arriving with families in tow."

Ben's mouth fell open. "You didn't know about the kids?"

"Nope. Christian didn't, either, from what she said. Ms. Sutherland claims she didn't get a chance to tell him."

"Well, no one'll have a problem with a couple more kids in Hard Luck," Ben commented.

"That's not the point."

Ben frowned. "Then what is?"

"The cabins. Abbey can't live in one of those cabins with her children."

Ben leaned against the wall with Sawyer. "Yeah, you're right. So, what are you going to do?"

"No idea." Sawyer shrugged, trying to seem nonchalant. "It isn't like there's a house available for us to rent."

"Catherine Fletcher's place is vacant."

Sawyer shook his head. He wouldn't even consider approaching Catherine's family, and he doubted his brothers would be willing to do so either, regardless of the circumstances.

The bad blood between the two families ran deep. It would

take a lot more than needing an empty house to wipe out forty years of ill will.

Catherine Harmon Fletcher was in poor health now, and in a nursing home in Anchorage, close to her daughter.

Ellen, Sawyer's mother, had suffered so much unhappiness because of Catherine. But she no longer lived in Hard Luck either. She'd remarried and had relocated to British Columbia, as happy as Sawyer had ever known her. He didn't begrudge his mother her new life. He figured she deserved it after all the miserable years she'd endured.

"What about Pearl's? She's going to be moving in with her daughter," Ben reminded him.

Sawyer hated to see the older woman go, but she'd told him it was time for her to move on, especially now that her friends had mostly left.

"Pearl's not leaving until we hire a replacement and she's had the opportunity to train her," Sawyer said.

Ben mulled over the problem for several minutes. "What about the lodge?" he asked. "I know it's been years since anyone's stayed there, but—"

"The lodge?" Sawyer repeated. "You're joking!"

"It'd take a little work...."

"A little work!" Sawyer knew he was beginning to sound like a parrot, repeating everything the other man said, but the idea was ludicrous. The lodge was in terrible shape. It would take months of hard work and thousands of dollars to make it livable. If it hadn't been so much trouble, they would have refurbished it, instead of dealing with the cabins. But those, at least, were in one piece.

A fire had burned part of the lodge the year their father died, and not one of the three brothers had ever had the heart to get it repaired.

Their mother had always hated the lodge, which had become a symbol of everything that was wrong with her marriage, and she'd used the fire as an excuse to close it completely. If it'd been up to him, Sawyer would've torn the place down years ago. As it was now, the largest building in town stood vacant, a constant reminder of the father he'd loved and lost.

Ben wiped his forehead. "Yeah. The lodge wouldn't work. It's a shame, really."

Sawyer wasn't sure if Ben was talking about the abandoned lodge or Abbey's situation.

There was no easy solution. "I don't know what we're going to do," he muttered.

Ben was silent for quite some time, which was unusual for him. He studied Abbey and the children, then turned to Sawyer. "I guess you could send her back." His voice was carefully casual.

"I know."

"Is that what you plan to do?"

Sawyer felt a twinge of regret. "I can't see that we have any choice, do you?"

"It's a simple misunderstanding," Ben said. "No one's to blame. She should've told Christian about the kids."

The twinge had become an ache, and it didn't want to go away. "Maybe Christian should've asked." But it didn't matter; she was here now, there was no place for her to live and *he* had to deal with it.

Better Abbey should return to Seattle immediately, Sawyer reasoned, before he found himself making excuses for her to stay.

Chapter
4

Sawyer knew he wouldn't be winning any popularity contests around Hard Luck if he announced that Abbey Sutherland and her children had to leave. The best way to handle the situation, he decided after giving it serious thought, was for Abbey to back out of the contract on her own—with a little help from him.

He waited until everyone had finished eating before he worked his way over to the table where she sat with Pearl. "I'll show you to your cabin now," he offered.

She looked up at him uncertainly, as if she wasn't quite sure of his motives. "I'd appreciate that."

"Sawyer," Pearl said, placing her hand on his forearm.

Sawyer already knew what the older woman was about to say. Like him, Pearl must have realized immediately that Abbey and her children couldn't live in a dilapidated old cabin outside town.

"When can I meet your dog?" Scott asked eagerly.

"Soon," Sawyer promised. Eagle Catcher didn't take easily to strangers; the husky wouldn't allow the boy to come near him until after two or three visits. Sawyer decided he'd bring Scott over to the house that evening and show him Eagle Catcher's pen. But the kid would be long gone before the husky accepted him as a friend.

"I'd like to see the library, too, if it wouldn't be too much trouble," Abbey said.

"Of course," Sawyer said in a friendly voice, but a shiver of guilt passed through him. When he'd last spoken to his mother, he'd told her they'd hired a librarian. Ellen had been excited to learn that her gift to the town was finally going to be put to use.

Sawyer squeezed the four of them into the cab of his pickup and drove down the main road. There were a couple of short side streets, but none that anyone had bothered to name.

"What's that?" Susan asked, pointing to a small wooden structure that stood outside the mercantile. She giggled. "It looks like a little house on stilts."

"It's called a cache. We use it to store food and keep it safe from bears and other marauding animals."

"Alaska's got lots of bears," Scott murmured as if he was well versed in the subject. "I read about them in the books Mom brought home from the library."

"How come the cache has legs that look like they're wearing silver stockings?" The question came from Susan again.

"That's tin," Sawyer explained, "and it's slippery. Discourages those who like to climb."

"I wouldn't try and climb it," Scott said.

"I don't think he's referring to boys," Abbey told her son. "He was talking about the animals."

"Oh."

"Is it still in use?" Abbey asked.

"Yes, it is. I don't know what Pete keeps in there during the summer months, but it's a crude kind of freezer in winter."

"I see."

"Oh, this is Main Street," Sawyer said as they continued down the dirt road. Dust scattered in every direction, creating a dense cloud in their wake.

"I wondered if there'd be any leftover snow," Abbey said. She seemed to be trying to make polite conversation.

"It hasn't been gone all that long." Sawyer knew he should use the opportunity to tell her how harsh the winters were and how bleak life was during December, January and February, but he was afraid Abbey would see straight through him. He preferred to be a *bit* more subtle in his attempt to convince her to go home.

"Is that the school?" Scott asked, pointing to the left.

"Yup."

"It sure is small."

"Yup. We've got two teachers. One for grades one through eight and another for high school. We had more than twenty students last year."

"Ben told me you've got a new elementary teacher coming soon," Abbey said.

"That's right." The state provided living quarters for the teacher. The house was one of the best in town, with all the modern conveniences. It was a palace compared to the cabin that would be Abbey's.

They drove past the lodge with its ugly black scars. Susan pressed her face to the window, and Sawyer waited for another barrage of questions, but none was forthcoming.

"Is the cabin close by?" Abbey asked. They'd already passed the outskirts of Hard Luck.

"Not much farther."

She glanced over her shoulder, as if gauging the distance between the town and her new home.

Sawyer parked in front of the cluster of small cabins and pointed to the one that had been readied for her. Seeing it now, battered by time and the elements, Sawyer experienced a definite feeling of guilt. The idea of luring women north with the promise of housing and land had been a bad idea from the first.

"*These* are the cabins your brother mentioned?" Abbey kept her voice low, but her shock was all too evident.

"Yes." This was the moment Sawyer had dreaded.

"We're supposed to *live* here?" Scott asked in the same incredulous tone.

"I'm afraid so."

Susan opened the truck door and climbed out. The seven-year-old planted her hands on her hips and exhaled loudly. "It's a dump."

Sawyer said nothing. Frankly, he agreed with the kid.

"It looks like one of those places where you freeze meat in the winter, only it isn't on stilts," Scott muttered.

Without a word Abbey walked into the cabin. Sawyer didn't

follow; he knew what she was going to see. A single bed, a crude table and solitary chair, along with a woodstove. A small store of food supplies, stacked in a primitive cupboard.

"Mom," Scott wailed, "we can't live here!"

"It is a bit smaller than we expected," Abbey said. Her shoulders seemed to droop with the weight of her disappointment.

Hands still on her hips, Susan stood there, feet wide apart, as she surveyed the cabin. She shook her head. "This place is a dump," she repeated.

"Where's the bathroom?" Scott asked, giving the one-room interior a second look.

"There's an outhouse in the back," Sawyer told him. "Just take the path."

"What's an outhouse?" Susan asked her mother.

Abbey closed her eyes briefly. "Follow Scott and you'll find out for yourself."

The two disappeared, and Abbey turned to Sawyer. He thought she'd yell at him, call him and his brother jerks for misleading her. Instead, she asked, "What about the twenty acres?"

"It's, uh, several miles to the east of here," he explained reluctantly. "I have the plot map in the office and I'll show you later if you want."

"You mean to say the cabin doesn't sit on the twenty acres?"

"No," he answered, swallowing hard. When they'd initially discussed the details of this arrangement, it had all seemed equitable. Sort of. After all, Midnight Sons was picking up the women's airfare and related expenses. But at the defeated, angry look in Abbey's eyes, Sawyer felt like a jerk. Worse than a jerk. He wished she'd just yell at him.

"I see," she said after a long silence. Her voice was so low Sawyer had to strain to hear.

He clenched his hands into tight fists to keep from taking her by the shoulders and shaking some sense into her. Was she actually thinking of staying? Christian and the others were so starved for female companionship, they'd have promised the moon to induce women to move to Hard Luck. He didn't excuse himself; he'd played a major role in this deception, too.

"I found the outhouse," Susan said, holding her nose as she returned to her mother's side. "It stinks."

"What are we gonna do?" Scott asked, sounding desperate.

"Well," Abbey said thoughtfully, "we'll have to move a pair of bunk beds in here and add a couple of chairs."

"But, Mom…"

Sawyer glanced inside the cabin and groaned inwardly.

"We'll make it a game," Abbey told her children with forced enthusiasm. "Like pioneers."

"I don't wanna play," Susan whined.

"Maybe there's someplace else we can rent," Scott said, looking hopefully at Sawyer.

"There isn't." He hated to disappoint the boy, but he couldn't make houses that didn't exist appear out of the blue. He turned to Abbey, who continued to stare impassively in the direction of the cabin. He suspected she was struggling to compose herself.

"Could you show me the library now?" she finally asked. Apparently she wanted to see the whole picture before she decided. Fair enough. Sawyer hoped that once she'd had time to analyze the situation, she'd make a reasonable decision. The *only* reasonable decision.

They all piled back into the truck. On the drive out to the cabin all three Sutherlands had been filled with anticipation. The drive back was silent, their unhappiness almost palpable.

The urge to suggest that Abbey give up and leave was almost more than Sawyer could suppress. But he'd be tipping his hand if he so much as hinted she fly home. He'd say something eventually if need be, but he'd rather she reached that conclusion herself.

The log building designated for the library had once belonged to Sawyer's grandfather. Adam O'Halloran had settled in the area in the early 1930s. He'd come seeking gold, but instead of finding his fortune, he'd founded a community.

Since the day they'd heard that Christian had hired a librarian, Sawyer and the other pilots had hauled over a hundred or more boxes of books from Ellen's house, which was now Christian's.

The original O'Halloran home consisted of three large rooms. Abbey walked inside, and once more her disappointment was evident. "I'll need bookshelves," she said stiffly. "You can't store books in boxes."

"There are several in Mother's house. I'll see that they're delivered first thing tomorrow morning."

Her gaze shot to his. "Is your mother's house vacant?"

Sawyer knew what she was thinking. He shook his head. "Mom's remarried and out of the state, but Christian lives there now. Although he's away at the moment, as you know."

"I see."

A young boy who introduced himself as Ronny Gold walked his bicycle up to the door and peeked inside. Scott and Ronny stared at each other.

"Can you play?" Ronny asked.

"Mom, can I go outside?"

Abbey nodded. "Don't be gone long." She glanced at her watch. "Meet me back here in half an hour, okay?"

"Okay." Both Scott and Susan disappeared with Ronny.

Hands buried deep in his pants pockets, Sawyer watched as Abbey lifted a book, studied the spine, then picked up another. She handled each one with gentle reverence.

Sawyer waited until he couldn't bear it any longer. He'd planned to give her more time to realize she couldn't possibly live under these conditions. But if she wasn't going to admit it herself...

"It isn't going to work, Abbey," he said quietly. "It was a rotten idea, bringing women to Hard Luck. I blame myself. I should never have agreed to this."

"You want me to leave, don't you?" she asked in an ominously even voice, ignoring his comment.

Sawyer didn't answer. He couldn't, because he refused to lie or mislead her any further. What surprised him most was his own realization—that he'd have liked the opportunity to know her better. Instead, he was forced to send her back to Seattle, where she and her children belonged.

He steeled himself. He and Christian weren't the only ones at fault.

"You misled my brother," he said gruffly and couldn't decide who he was angriest with. Christian? Abbey? Himself?

"*I* misled Christian?" Abbey cried, her voice bordering on hysteria. "I find that insulting."

The anger that had simmered just below the surface flared

to life. "You duped him into hiring you without once mentioning that you had children!" Sawyer snapped. "I know there was nothing on the application about a family." That was one problem he was going to correct at the first opportunity. "But you should've been more honest, since you were aware that we offered housing as part of the employment package."

"*I* should've been more honest? That's the height of hypocrisy! I was told I'd be given living quarters and twenty acres of land, but you neglected to tell me the cabin's the size of a doghouse." She dragged in a deep breath. "How dare you suggest I broke the agreement? I'm here, aren't I?"

"You broke the spirit of our agreement."

"Oh, please! As for your free land, that's a big joke, too. You forgot to mention that it's so far from town I'd need a dogsled to reach it. If you want to talk about someone breaking the agreement, then let's discuss what you and your brother have done to me and my children."

At the pain in her eyes, he felt worse than ever. He had no defense, and he knew it. "All right. We made a mistake, but I'm willing to pay your airfare home. It's the least we can do."

"I'm staying," she said flatly. "I signed a contract, and I intend to hold up my end of the bargain, despite...despite everything."

Sawyer couldn't believe his ears. "You can't!"

Her eyes flashed. "Why can't I?"

"You saw the cabin yourself. There's no way the three of you could possibly live there, bunk beds or not. You might be able to manage this summer, but it'd be out of the question once winter sets in."

"The children and I are staying." She said this with such determination Sawyer could readily see that nothing he said or did would change her mind.

"Fine," he said brusquely. "If that's your decision." At best, he figured she'd last the night. By morning she'd be at the airfield with her luggage, anxious to catch the first plane out of Hard Luck.

An hour later Abbey sat on the edge of the thin mattress and tried to think. She hadn't felt so close to tears since the day she'd filed for divorce. In some ways, the situation felt very similar to the end of her marriage. She was being forced to admit she'd made a mistake. Another in what seemed to be a very long list.

It hadn't felt like a mistake when she'd accepted the job. It had felt decidedly right.

The problem was that she didn't want to leave Hard Luck. She'd painted a fairy-tale picture of the town in her mind, and when it fell short of her expectations she'd floundered in disappointment. Well, she'd been disappointed before and learned from the experience. She would again.

No matter how eager Sawyer O'Halloran was to be rid of her, she was staying.

Really, she had no one to blame but herself. Her father had told her the free cabin and twenty acres sounded too good to be true. She was willing to concede that he was right. But it wasn't just the promise of a home and land that had drawn her north.

She'd come seeking a slower pace of life, hoping to settle in a community of which she'd be a vital part. A community where she'd know and trust her neighbors. And, of course, the opportunity to set up and manage a library was a dream come true. She'd moved to Hard Luck because she realized being here would make a difference. To herself, to the town, to her children most of all. She'd come so Scott and Susan would only read about drive-by shootings, gang violence and drug problems.

Although her children's reactions to the cabin had been very much like her own, Abbey was proud of how quickly the two had rebounded.

"It isn't so bad here," Scott had told her when he'd returned to the O'Halloran homestead with Ronny Gold. Susan had met Chrissie Harris and they'd quickly become fast friends.

The sound of an approaching truck propelled her off the bed in a near panic. She wasn't ready for another round with Sawyer O'Halloran!

Sawyer leapt out of the cab as if he wanted to spend as little time as possible in her company. "Your luggage arrived." Two suitcases were on the ground before she reached the truck bed. Pride demanded that she get the others down herself. He didn't give her a chance.

Despite the ridiculous accusations he'd made, despite his generally disagreeable nature, Abbey liked Sawyer. She'd seen the regretful look in his eyes when he'd shown her the cabin. It might be fanciful thinking on her part, but she believed he'd wanted her to stay. He might not think it was practical or smart, but she sensed that he wanted her here. In Hard Luck.

He might provoke her, irritate her, accuse her of absurd things; yet she found herself wishing she could get to know him better.

That wasn't likely. Sawyer O'Halloran had made his views plain enough. For whatever reasons, he wanted her gone.

All the suitcases were on the ground, but Sawyer lingered. He started to leave, then turned back.

"I shouldn't have said that, about you duping Christian. It wasn't true."

"Are you apologizing?"

He didn't hesitate. "Yes."

"Then I accept." She held out her hand.

His fingers closed firmly over hers. "You don't have to stay in Hard Luck, Abbey," he said. "No one's going to think less of you if you leave."

She held her breath until her chest began to ache. "You don't understand. I can't go back now."

Frowning, he released her hand. "Why can't you?"

"I sold my car to pay for the kids' airfare."

"I already told you I'd buy your tickets home."

"It's more than that."

He hopped onto the tailgate and she joined him. "I want to help you, if you'll let me," he said.

She debated admitting how deeply committed she was to this venture, then figured she might as well, because he'd learn the truth sooner or later.

"My furniture and everything I own is in the back of some truck on its way to Alaska. It should get here within a month."

He shook his head. "It won't, you know."

"But that's what I was told!"

"Your things will be delivered to Fairbanks. There's no road to Hard Luck."

She wasn't completely stupid, no matter what he thought. "I asked Christian and he told me there's a haul road."

"The haul road is only passable in winter. It's twenty-six miles to the Dalton Highway, which doesn't even resemble the highways you know. It's little more than a dirt and gravel road. A haul road's much worse. It crosses two rivers and they need to freeze before you can drive over them."

"Oh."

"I'm sorry, Abbey, but your furniture won't go any farther than Fairbanks."

She took this latest bit of information with a resigned grimace. "Then I'll wait until winter. It's not like I have any place to put a love seat, do I?" she asked, gesturing at the cabin.

"No, I guess you don't." He eased himself off the tailgate, then gave her a hand down. "I need to get back to the airfield."

"Thanks for bringing our luggage."

"No problem."

"Mom. Mom." Scott came racing toward her. Keeping pace with him was a large husky. "I found a dog! Look." He fell to his knees and enthusiastically wrapped his arms around the dog's neck. "I wonder who he belongs to."

"That's Eagle Catcher," Sawyer said as his eyes widened in shock. "My dog. What's he doing here? He should be locked in his pen!"

That evening, Sawyer sat in front of a gentle fire, a book propped in his hands. Eagle Catcher rested on the braided rug by the fireplace. The book didn't hold his attention. He doubted that anything could distract him from Abbey and her two children.

In all the years he'd lived in Hard Luck, Sawyer had only
known intense fear once, and that had been the day his father
died.

He never worried, but he did this June night. He worried
that Susan or Scott might encounter a bear on their way to the
outhouse. He worried that they'd face any number of unfore-
seen dangers.

He couldn't help recalling that Emily O'Halloran, an aunt
he'd never known, had been lost on the tundra at the age of five.
She'd been playing outside his grandparents' cabin one minute
and was gone the next. Without a sound. Without a trace.

For years his grandmother had been distraught and inconsolable over the loss of her youngest child and only daughter.
In fact, Anna O'Halloran had named the town. She'd called it
Hard Luck because of her husband's failure to find the rich vein
of gold he'd been looking for; with the tragedy of Emily's death,
the name took on new significance.

Worrying about Abbey and her children was enough to ruin
Sawyer's evening. Surely by morning she'd see reason and decide
to return to Seattle!

Eagle Catcher rose and walked over to Sawyer's chair. He
placed his head on his master's knee.

"You surprised me, boy," Sawyer said, scratching his dog's
ears. He wouldn't have believed it if he hadn't seen it with his
own eyes. Eagle Catcher and Scott had acted as if they'd been
raised together. The rapport between them had been strong and
immediate. The first shock had been that the dog had escaped
his pen and followed Sawyer's truck; the second, that he'd so
quickly accepted the boy.

"You like Scott, don't you?"

Eagle Catcher whined as if he understood and was responding to the question.

"You don't need to explain anything to me, boy. I feel the same way." About Abbey. About her children.

He tensed. The only solution was for Abbey to leave—for more reasons than he wanted to think about. He prayed she'd use common sense and hightail it out of Hard Luck come morning.

The cabin wasn't so bad, Abbey decided after her first two days. It was a lot like camping, only inside. She could almost pretend it was fun, but she longed for a real shower and a meal that wasn't limited to sandwiches.

Other than their complaints about having to use an outhouse, her children had adjusted surprisingly well.

The summer months would be tolerable, Abbey thought, but she couldn't ignore Sawyer's warning about the winter.

As for her work at the library, Abbey loved it. Sawyer had seen to the delivery of the bookcases from his mother's house, along with a solid wood desk and chair for her.

The day after her arrival, Abbey had set about categorizing the books and creating a filing system. Someday she planned to have everything on a computer, but first things first.

"How are things going?" Pearl Inman asked, letting herself into the library.

"Fine, thanks."

"I brought you a cup of coffee. I was hoping to talk you into taking a short break."

Abbey stood and stretched, placing her hands at the small of her back. "I could use one." She walked to the door and looked outside, wondering about Scott and Susan, who were out exploring. It was all so different from their life in a Seattle highrise. She knew Scott and Ronny spent a good part of each day down at the airfield pestering Sawyer.

If Scott wasn't with Ronny, then he was with Sawyer's dog. Abbey couldn't remember a time her son had been so content.

Susan and Chrissie Harris spent nearly every minute they could with each other. In two days' time they'd become virtually inseparable. Mitch Harris had stopped by to introduce himself. Mitch, Abbey recalled, worked for the Department of the Interior and was the local public safety officer. He seemed grateful that his daughter had a new friend.

"I can't believe the progress you've made," Pearl said, surveying the room. "This is grand, just grand. Ellen will be delighted."

Abbey knew that Ellen was Sawyer's mother and the woman who'd donated the books to the town.

"I don't suppose you've seen Sawyer lately?" Pearl asked, pouring them each a cup from her thermos.

"Not a word in almost two days," Abbey admitted, hoping none of her disappointment showed in her voice.

"He's been in a bad mood from the moment you got here. I don't know what's wrong with that boy. I haven't seen him behave like this since his father died. He blamed himself, you know."

Abbey settled on a corner of the desk and left the chair for the older woman.

"What happened to his father?"

Pearl raised the cup to her lips. "David was killed in an accident several years ago. They'd flown to one of the lakes for some fishing, which David loved. On the trip home, the plane developed engine trouble and they were forced down. David was badly injured in the crash. It was just the two of them deep in the bush." She paused and sipped at her coffee.

"You can imagine how Sawyer must have felt, fighting to keep his father alive until help arrived. They were alone for two hours before anyone could reach them, but it was too late by then. David was gone."

Abbey closed her eyes as she thought of the stark terror that must have gripped Sawyer, alone in the bush with his dying father.

"If I live another sixty years I'll never forget the sight of Sawyer carrying his father from the airfield. He was covered in David's blood and refused to let him go. It was far too late, of course. David was already dead. We had to pry him out of Sawyer's arms."

"It wasn't his fault," Abbey whispered. "It was an accident. There was nothing he could've done."

"There isn't a one of us who didn't tell him that. The accident changed him. It changed Hard Luck. Soon Ellen moved away and eventually remarried. Catherine Fletcher grieved something fierce. That was when her health started to fail."

"Have I met Catherine?" Abbey asked, wondering why Pearl would mention a woman other than David's wife.

"Catherine Fletcher. Used to be Catherine Harmon. No...no, she's in a nursing home in Anchorage now. Her daughter lives there."

Pearl must have read the question in Abbey's eyes. "Catherine and David were engaged before World War II. She loved him as a teenager and she never stopped. Not even when she married someone else. David broke her heart when he returned from the war with an English bride."

"Oh, dear."

"Ellen never quite fit in with the folks in Hard Luck. She seemed different from us, standoffish. I don't think she meant to be, and I don't think she realized how she looked to others. It took me a few years myself to see that it was just Ellen's way. She was really quite shy, felt out of place. It didn't help any that she didn't have children right away. She tried. God knows she wanted a family. They were married almost fifteen years before Charles was born."

"You said Catherine got married?" Abbey asked, her heart aching for the jilted woman.

"Oh, yes, on the rebound, right after David returned from the war. She gave birth to Kate nine months later and was divorced from Willie Fletcher within two years."

"She never remarried?"

"Never. I thought for a time that she and David would get back together, but it wasn't to be. Ellen left him, you see, and returned to England. Christian was about ten at the time. She was gone well over a year." She shook her head, then sighed. "You can understand how David's death affected everyone in town. Especially Sawyer."

"Of course."

"What I don't get is why he's upset now. He's walking around like a bear with a sore paw, snapping at everyone."

Abbey gaped at her. "You think it's got something to do with me?"

"That's my guess. But what do I know?" Pearl asked. She drank the rest of her coffee and stood up to leave. "I'd best get back to the clinic before someone misses me." The clinic was in the community building, close to the school and the church.

She tucked the thermos under her arm. "So, are you staying in Hard Luck or not?" she asked. Her question had an edge to it, as if she wasn't sure she was going to like the answer.

Abbey told her the truth. "I'd like to stay."

"That doesn't answer my question."

Abbey grinned. "I'm staying."

Pearl's lined face softened. "Good. I'm glad to hear it. We need you, and I have a feeling Sawyer wants you to stay, too."

Abbey laughed in disbelief. "I doubt that." And if it was true once, she felt certain it no longer was.

"No, really," Pearl countered. "Unfortunately that boy doesn't have the brains of a muskrat when it comes to dealing with an attractive woman." She made her way to the door. "Give him time and a little patience, and he'll come around." With a cheerful wave, Pearl left.

Abbey returned to work and got busy unloading another box of Ellen's books. Knowing what she did now, the collection took on new meaning for her. Many of the books dated from the early to mid-fifties. Those were the childless years, when Ellen had yearned for a baby. Abbey suspected that Ellen O'Halloran had gained solace from these books, that they'd substituted for the friends she hadn't been able to make in this town so far from England.

As she set a pile of Mary Roberts Rinehart mysteries on the desk, she heard the distinctive sound of Sawyer's truck pulling up outside.

Her heart started to race, but she continued working.

He stormed inside and stood in the doorway, hands on his hips. His presence filled the room until Abbey felt hedged in by the sheer strength of it. "Have you decided to stay?" he demanded.

"Yes," she answered smoothly. "I'm staying."

"You're sure?"

"Yes," she said with conviction. And she *was* sure. During her conversation with Pearl, she'd made up her mind.

"Fine. You're moving."

"Where?" Abbey had been told often enough that there wasn't any other place available.

"You can stay in Christian's house. He phoned this after-noon, and he's decided to make a vacation out of this trip. I'll let him decide what to do with you when he gets home."

Chapter
5

"What?" Abbey's eyes flashed with annoyance—and confusion. "I'm not moving into your brother's home."

The last thing Sawyer had expected was an argument. Okay, so maybe he hadn't made the offer as graciously as he should have, but he had an excuse.

The woman was driving him crazy.

Worrying about her and those two kids stuck out on the edge of town had left him nearly sleepless for two nights. It wouldn't have bothered him as much if there'd been neighbors close at hand. But so far, the other cabins remained empty.

"You won't be there long," he said. And he'd thought he was doing her a favor! He should've known that nothing with Abbey would be easy.

She picked up another of his mother's books, handling it with respect, then added the author and title to a list. "The kids and I are doing well where we are. Really."

"There are dangers you don't know about."

"We're fine, Sawyer."

He inhaled sharply. "Why won't you move?"

Abbey's shoulders lifted in a small, impatient sigh. "It isn't *entirely* your brother's fault that he didn't know about Scott and Susan."

"True, but you aren't entirely to blame either."

"It's very thoughtful of you to offer me the house, but no thanks." She glanced up and gave him a quick smile. For a second Sawyer swore his heart was out of control, and all because of one little smile.

"All right," he said, slowly releasing his breath, "you can move into my house, then, and I'll stay at Christian's."

"Sawyer, you're missing the point. I don't want to put anyone out of his home."

"Christian isn't there to put out."

"I know that, but when he does return I'll have to go back to the cabin. There's nowhere else for me and the children to move. I can't see that shuffling us from one temporary place to another is going to help."

"But—"

"We're better off making do with what we have," she said, cutting off his argument.

"Are you always this stubborn?"

Abbey's eyes widened as if his question surprised her. "I didn't realize I was being stubborn. It doesn't make sense to play musical houses when we have a perfectly good— When we have a home now."

"The cabins were never intended to be full-time residences," he said, clenching his fists at his sides. He shouldn't admit it, especially since his brother had begun interviewing job applicants again, promising them free housing and land. Sawyer hadn't wanted him to do it, but Christian had gotten carried away. You'd think that with the Seattle press picking up on the story, Christian would reconsider his approach. At least— thank God—the reporters had stopped calling *him*. And nothing Sawyer could say seemed to dampen his brother's enthusiasm for the project. Christian was having the time of his life.

Well, when the next women started to show up, Sawyer decided, he'd let Christian escort them to those shacks and gleefully announce that here were their new homes. No way was he going to do it.

"I don't want you to think I'm being unappreciative," Abbey said.

"You're being unappreciative," he muttered. "Christian's place has all the conveniences. Surely the kids miss television."

"They don't." She hesitated and bit her lip. "Though I'll confess I'd like a...hot shower."

Sawyer could tell that she was tempted by the offer.

"I'm not comfortable knowing you're out on the edge of town alone," he told her. "Because of the kids... People in town would be mighty upset if something happened. Pearl's been at me to find you some other place to live." He didn't want her to think there was anything *personal* in his concern. "Anyway, Christian'll be gone a month or more."

"A month," Abbey repeated.

"Perhaps we could compromise," he said, walking forward

and supporting his hands on her desk. "You could move into Christian's house or mine, whichever you decide, until one of the other women arrives. Then perhaps you could share the place until a more viable solution presents itself." Her hair smelled of wildflowers, and he found himself struggling to keep his mind on business.

"When's the next woman flying in?"

"I'm not sure. Soon."

She took a moment to consider, then thrust out her hand. "Thank you. I accept your offer."

Relieved, Sawyer shook her hand as briefly as possible without being rude. The softness of her skin, her scent, her combination of vulnerability and fierce determination—it was all too attractive. Too disruptive. His world, so orderly and serene before her arrival, felt as if it had been turned inside out.

One thing was sure—he didn't like it.

"I'll stop by later and pick up your luggage," he said.

Her eyes moved to meet his, and she gave him another of those heart-tripping smiles. There was something so genuine and unself-conscious about it. Their eyes held a moment longer, and every muscle in his body was telling him to lean forward and kiss her. As soon as the impulse entered his mind, he sent it flying. The last thing he wanted was to become involved with Abbey Sutherland.

"Mom——" Scott burst into the room like a warlord roaring into battle "——can I have lunch at Ronny's? His mom said it's okay."

Sawyer leapt back so fast he practically fell over Eagle Catcher, who'd ambled into the room with Scott.

"Hi, Mr. O'Halloran," the boy said in a near squeak, then stared down at the husky. His face flushed with guilt.

Sawyer looked from the dog to the boy. "How'd Eagle Catcher get out of his pen?"

Scott lowered his head.

"Scott, did you let him out of his pen?" Abbey asked.

His nod was barely perceptible. "I went to visit him and he whined and whined, and I was going to put him back, honest I was."

Sawyer crouched down so he could speak to Scott at eye level. "I know you and Eagle Catcher are good friends, and I think that's great."

"You do?" Scott's eyes rounded with surprise.

"But it's important that you ask my permission before you let him out of his yard. Otherwise, I could come home and not know where he is."

"I went to visit him, but he didn't want me to leave," Scott explained. "Every time I started to go, he'd cry. I only opened the gate so I could pet him and talk to him. I must not have latched it very good, because he followed me."

"Next time make sure the latch is secure," Abbey told him sternly.

Scott's gaze avoided Sawyer's. "I might not have closed the gate all the way on purpose."

Sawyer tried to hide his amusement. "Thank you for being honest about it. Next time you want to play with my dog, all you have to do is come and ask me first. That won't be difficult, will it?"

"No, sir, I can do that."

"Good."

"Eagle Catcher only likes *me,* you know," Scott announced proudly. "He wouldn't leave the pen for Susan or Ronny." He closed his mouth when he realized what he'd admitted.

So the three friends had been in his yard and attempted to lure Eagle Catcher out of the fenced-off area.

"So, can I have lunch at Ronny's?" Scott asked again, obviously eager to change the subject.

"All right, but I want you to take Eagle Catcher back to his pen. Later on you and I are going to have a long talk about Mr. O'Halloran's dog."

"Okay," he said sheepishly, and before she could say another word, he dashed out the door, the husky at his heels.

Sawyer chuckled. "I can't believe the way those two hit it off. It's not like Eagle Catcher to become this attached to someone."

"I hope this doesn't develop into a problem," Abbey said. "He's got to understand that it's your dog, and he has to obey your rules. But Scott's always loved dogs, especially huskies, and we've never been able to have one. He was crazy about Eagle Catcher from the first time he saw him."

"The feeling appears to be mutual. Eagle Catcher's never had anyone lavish attention on him the way Scott does. They seem destined for each other, don't they?"

Abruptly Abbey looked away.

Sawyer wondered what he'd said that had caused such a startled reaction. Did she think he was talking about the two of *them?* If so, Abbey Sutherland was in for a surprise.

Sawyer wasn't interested in marriage. Ever. Not even to the beautiful Abbey Sutherland. He'd learned all the lessons he needed from his own experience several years before. And from his parents, who'd tried to make their marriage work, but only made each other miserable. Sawyer wanted none of that.

Rarely had Abbey enjoyed a shower more. She stood under the warm spray as it pelted against her skin and savored each refreshing drop.

Exhausted from a day of playing, Scott and Susan fell asleep the minute they climbed into the two single beds in Christian O'Halloran's guest bedroom.

Abbey was sleeping in the double bed in a second spare bedroom. Although Sawyer had repeatedly told her she was welcome in his brother's home, Abbey couldn't shake the feeling that she was invading Christian's privacy.

It was fine for Sawyer to offer his brother's house. But Abbey couldn't help wondering if he'd bothered to mention it to Christian.

After she toweled off, she dressed in jeans and a thin sweater and walked barefoot to the kitchen, where she made herself a cup of tea. It was difficult not to compare her stark living quarters at the cabin and the simple luxuries of Christian's home.

The kitchen was large and cheery, the white walls stenciled with a blue tulip pattern. The room's warmth and straightforward charm reminded her that Ellen O'Halloran had once lived here. Her touch was evident throughout the house.

Taking her tea with her, Abbey wandered onto the front porch and sat in the old-fashioned swing. Mosquitoes buzzed about until she remembered to light the citronella candle. The evening was beautiful beyond anything she'd imagined. Birds chirped vigorously in the background. The tundra seemed vibrant with life.

Although it was nearly ten, the sky was as bright as it had been at noon. Cupping the mug in her hands, she looked past the small patch of lawn to Sawyer's house across the street.

His home clearly lacked a woman's influence. He, too, had a yard, but there were no flower boxes decorating the window ledges, no beds blooming with hardy perennials. The porch was smaller, almost as if it had been added as an afterthought.

Drawing her knees up under her chin, Abbey gazed unseeingly at the house while she reviewed her situation. She'd taken the biggest gamble of her life by moving to Hard Luck. No one had told her she was playing against a stacked deck. But the stakes were too high for her to back down now. She wouldn't. Couldn't. Somehow, she'd find the means to stay and make a good life for herself and her children.

The front door of Sawyer's house opened, and he stepped onto the front porch. He leaned against the support beam, holding a mug in his hands. For what seemed a long time, they did nothing but stare at each other.

As if he'd reached some sort of decision, Sawyer set the mug aside and crossed the street. "Do you mind if I join you?" he asked.

"Not at all." Abbey hoped she didn't sound as shy as she felt. She slid over so there was plenty of room on the swing.

"My mother used to sit out here in the summer," Sawyer reminisced. "There were many nights I'd get ready for bed and I'd look out and see her sitting exactly where you are, swinging as if she was eighteen again and waiting for a beau."

A sadness crept into his voice, and from the little she knew about his parents' marriage, she guessed his perception could be right. His mother might well have been waiting for the man she loved to join her—the husband she'd once, and perhaps still, loved.

He seemed to have read her thoughts. "My parents didn't have a good marriage. Don't get me wrong—they rarely raised their voices to each other. In some ways I wish they had. It might have cleared the air. Instead, they practiced indifference toward each other." He hesitated and shook his head. "I don't know why I'm telling you all that. What about your parents?"

"They're great. They've had their share of squabbles over the years and still argue now and then. But underneath it, well, all I know is that they're deeply committed to each other." She paused, thinking about the fact that they'd disagreed with her move to Hard Luck. "My family gave me a firm foundation, and for that I couldn't be more grateful." She wondered how the conversation had become so personal. "I particularly appreciated that foundation when my marriage fell apart.

"My parents were wonderful. They'd never liked Dick, but they'd raised me to make my own choices and gave me the freedom to learn from my mistakes without I-told-you-so lectures." Abbey stopped, a little flustered. She hadn't meant to discuss her marriage, especially with someone she barely knew.

"Does your ex have contact with Scott and Susan?"

"No. And he hasn't paid a penny of support since he left the army. I haven't seen him in years, and neither have the kids. In the beginning I had a lot of anger. Not so much because of the money—that isn't nearly as important as everything else. Then

I realized it's Dick's loss. He's the one who's missing out on knowing two fabulous kids, and now I just feel sorry for him."

Sawyer reached for her hand and she held his tightly as tears clouded her eyes. She looked away, hoping he wouldn't notice.

"Abbey, I'm sorry. I didn't mean to pry."

"You didn't. I don't know what's wrong with me. I don't usually tear up like this."

"Maybe it's because you're a long way from home."

"Are you going to start that again—telling me I should go back to Seattle?" The argument had grown tiresome.

He didn't answer for a moment. "No." His free hand touched her cheek and brushed a tendril of hair aside. Their eyes met in a rush of discovery. It seemed inevitable that he'd kiss her.

It had been a long time since she'd been kissed. An even longer time since she'd wanted a man to kiss her this much. Sawyer lowered his mouth to hers and she leaned forward shyly.

As soon as Sawyer's mouth touched hers, she experienced a reawakening. She felt…cherished. For years she'd been the protector, standing alone against the world, caring for her children. She hadn't had either time or energy to think of herself as feminine and desirable. Sawyer made her feel both.

She opened her lips to him, and an onslaught of need stole her breath. She felt as though she'd taken a free-fall from twenty thousand feet.

Sawyer eased his mouth from hers, then brought it back as if he needed a second kiss to confirm what had happened the first time. His tenderness produced an overwhelming ache deep inside her. One that was emotional, as well as physical. Those feelings had been so long repressed she had trouble identifying them.

Sawyer lifted his mouth from Abbey's. Slowly she opened her eyes and found him studying her. His eyes were intense with questions.

She smiled, and at the simple movement of her lips he groaned and leaned forward, kissing her with a passion that left her breathless and weak.

Whatever happened to her in Hard Luck, whatever became of the housing situation, whatever took place between her and Sawyer from this point onward, Abbey knew that in these moments, they'd shared something wonderful. Something special.

He ended the kiss with reluctance. Abbey hid her face in his shoulder and took one deep breath after another.

They didn't speak. She sensed that words would have destroyed the magic. He gently rubbed her back.

"I'd better go home," he whispered after a while.

She nodded. He loosened his hold, then released her. Abbey watched as he stood, buried his hands in his pockets... and hesitated.

He seemed about to speak, but if that was the case, he changed his mind. A moment later, he whispered a good-night and walked across the street to his own home.

Abbey had the distinct feeling that they wouldn't discuss this evening. The next time they met it would be as if nothing had happened between them.

But it had....

After an hour of restlessly pacing the floor, Sawyer sat down at his desk and leafed through his personal phone directory. He needed to talk to Christian, the sooner the better.

He called Directory Assistance to get the number of Christian's hotel in Seattle—or, at least, his last-known residence there. Christian might not even *be* in Seattle anymore—but Sawyer swore he'd find him if it took the rest of the night.

He waited for the hotel operator to answer. As luck would have it, Christian was still registered at the Emerald City Empress. The operator connected him with his room.

Christian answered on the fourth ring, sounding groggy.

"It's Sawyer."

"What time is it?"

"Eleven."

"No, it isn't." Sawyer could visualize his brother picking up his watch and staring at it. "It might be eleven in Hard Luck, but it's midnight here. What's so important that it can't wait until morning?"

"You haven't called me in days."

"You got my message, didn't you?"

Sawyer frowned. He had; that was what had prompted him to move Abbey into Christian's house. "Yeah, I got it. So you're taking some personal time."

"Yeah. Mix business with pleasure. I might as well, don't you think?"

"*You* might think of phoning more often."

Christian groaned. "You mean to say you woke me up because we haven't talked recently? You sound like a wife checking up on her husband!"

"We've got problems." Sawyer gritted his teeth.

"What kind of problems?"

"Abbey Sutherland's here."

"What's the matter? Don't you like her?"

Sawyer almost wished that was true. Instead, he liked her too much. He liked her so much he'd completely lost the ability to sleep through an entire night. Either he was pacing the floor, worried about her living in that cabin alone with her two children, or he was fighting the instinct to walk across the street and make love to her. Either way, he was fast becoming a lunatic.

"I like her fine. That's not the problem."

"Well, what is?"

"Abbey didn't arrive alone." A short silence followed his announcement. "She brought her two children."

"Now, just a minute," Christian said hurriedly. If he wasn't awake earlier, he was now. "She didn't say a word about having any children."

"Did you ask?"

"No...but that shouldn't have mattered. She might have said something herself, don't you agree?"

"All I know is we'd better revise the application. Immediately."

"I'll see to it first thing in the morning." His promise was followed by the sound of a breath slowly being released. "Where's she staying? You didn't stick her in one of the cabins, did you? There's barely room for one, let alone three."

"She insisted that was exactly where she'd stay—until I convinced her to move into your house."

"My house!" Christian exploded. "Thanks a lot."

"Can you think of anyplace else she could live?"

There was a moment's silence. "No."

"I tried to talk her into moving back to Seattle, but she's stubborn." And beautiful. And generous. And so much more...

"What are we going to do with her once I return?" Christian asked.

"Haven't got a clue."

"You're the one who told me to hire her," his brother argued.

"I did?"

"Sure, don't you remember? I was telling you about Allison Reynolds and I mentioned there were two women I was considering for the position of librarian. You said I should hire the one who wanted the job."

So apparently Sawyer was responsible for his own misery.

"Maybe she'll fall in love with John or Ralph," Christian said hopefully, as if this would solve everything. "If she gets married, she won't be our problem. Whoever's fool enough to take her on—*and* her children—will be responsible for her."

Anger slammed through Sawyer, and he had to struggle to keep from saying something he'd later regret.

"Any man who married Abbey Sutherland would be damn lucky to have her," he said fiercely.

"Aha!" Christian's laugh was triumphant. "So that's the way it is!"

"How much longer do you plan to be in Seattle?" Sawyer asked, ignoring his brother's comment. A comment that was doubly irritating because it echoed one made by Ben the very day of Abbey's arrival.

"I don't know," Christian muttered. "I've been busy interviewing women, and I'd like to hire a couple more. I haven't even gotten around to ordering the supplies and plane parts. While I'm here, I thought I'd take a side trip up to see Mom. She'd be disappointed if I didn't."

"Fine, go see Mom."

"By the way, Allison Reynolds decided she wanted the position, after all. Take my advice, big brother, and don't get all excited over this librarian until you meet our new secretary," Christian said. "One look at her'll knock your socks off."

"What about a health-care specialist?"

"I've talked to a few nurses, but nothing yet. Give me time."

"Time!" Sawyer snapped. "It isn't supposed to take this long."

"What's your hurry?" Christian asked, and then chuckled. An evil sound, Sawyer thought sourly. "The longer I'm gone, the closer your librarian friend will be." Laughter echoed on the line. "I love it. You were against the idea from the beginning— and now look at you."

"I'm still against it."

"But not nearly as much as you were *before* you met Abbey Sutherland. Isn't that right?"

Abbey stood in front of the lone store in town, popularly known as the mercantile. It was decorated in a style she was coming to think of as Alaskan Bush—a pair of moose antlers adorned the doorway. She walked inside with a list of things she needed. The supplies she'd been given when she got to Hard Luck were gone. She also craved some fresh produce, but was afraid to find out what that would cost.

A bell over the door jangled, announcing her arrival.

The mercantile was smaller than the food mart where she bought gas back in Seattle. The entire grocery consisted of three narrow aisles and a couple of upright freezers with price lists posted on the door. A glass counter in front of the antique cash register displayed candy and both Inupiat and Athabascan craft items.

A middle-aged man with a gray beard and long hair tied back in a ponytail stepped out from behind the curtain. He smiled happily when he saw her. "Abbey Sutherland, right?"

"Right. Have we met?"

"Only in passing." He held out his hand for her to shake. "I'm Pete Livengood. I own the store and I have a little tourist business on the side."

"Pleased to meet you," she said, smiling back, wondering how much tourist trade he got in Hard Luck. "I want to pick up a few things for dinner this evening."

"Great. Let me have a look at your list and I'll see what I can do."

Abbey watched as he scanned the sheet of paper. "We don't sell fresh vegetables here since most folks have their own summer gardens. Every now and then Sawyer brings me back something from Fairbanks, but it's rare. Wintertime's a different story, though."

"I see." Abbey had hoped to serve taco salad that evening. She knew the kids would be disappointed.

"Louise Gold's got plenty of lettuce in her garden. She was bragging about it just the other day. I suspect she'd be delighted if you'd take some of it off her hands."

"I couldn't ask her." Abbey had only met Ronny's mother briefly. The Gold family had been very kind, and she didn't want to impose on their generosity any more than she already had.

"Things are different in the Arctic," Pete explained. "Folks help one another. If Louise knew you wanted lettuce for your dinner and she had more than she needed, why, she'd be insulted if you didn't ask. Most folks order their food supplies a year at a time. I'll give you an order form. Louise can probably help you with it better than I can, since you're buying for a family of three."

"A *year* at a time?"

"It's more economical that way."

"Oh."

"Don't worry about this list. I know how hard you're working setting up the library. I'll take care of everything you have here myself, including talking to Louise about that lettuce."

"Oh, but…I couldn't ask you to do that."

"Of course you could. I'm just being neighborly. Tell you what. I'll get everything together and deliver it this afternoon. How's that?"

"Wonderful. Thank you."

"My pleasure," Pete said, grinning broadly as if she'd done him a favor by allowing him to bring her groceries.

As the day went on, Abbey found herself waiting for Sawyer, hoping he'd stop by, wondering if he'd mention their kisses. Knowing he wouldn't.

Scott and Susan were in and out of the library all morning. Abbey enjoyed being accessible to her children; the experience of having them close at hand during the summer was a new one.

When she'd asked Pearl about day care, the older woman had thought she was joking. There was no such thing in Hard Luck. Not technically. Abbey knew that Louise Gold watched Chrissie Harris for Mitch, but there wasn't any official summer program for school-age children.

Scott and Susan were thriving on the sense of adventure and freedom. Their happiness seemed to bubble over.

"Hi, Mom," Scott said, strolling into the library, Eagle Catcher beside him.

"Once the library opens, we can't have Sawyer's dog inside," she told him.

"We can't?" Scott was offended on the husky's behalf. "That's not fair. I let him come everyplace else I go."

"Dogs can't read," she said, raising her eyebrows.

"I bet I could teach him."

She shook her head. "Did you ask Sawyer about letting him out of his pen?"

"Yup. I went down to the airfield. He was real busy, and I thought he might get mad at me, but he didn't. He said I'd been patient and he was proud of me." Scott beamed as he reported the compliment. "He's short-handed 'cause his brother's gone, and he had to take a flight this morning himself. I don't think he wanted to go, but he did."

"Oh." She tried to conceal her disappointment. "Did he say when he'd be back?"

"Nope, but I invited him for dinner. That was okay, wasn't it?"

"Ah…"

"You said we were having taco salad, didn't you?"

"Yes… What did Sawyer say?"

"He said he'd like that, but he wanted to make sure you knew about him coming. I told him you always fix lots, and I promised to tell you. It's all right, isn't it?"

Abbey nodded. "I suppose."

"I'll go see if Sawyer's back yet. I'll tell him you said he could come." Scott raced out the door at breakneck speed, with Eagle Catcher in hot pursuit. Abbey couldn't help grinning—it took the energy of a sled dog to keep up with her son.

She was barely aware of the afternoon slipping past until Pete Livengood stopped by with her groceries and surprised her with a small bouquet of wildflowers. His thoughtfulness touched her.

Abbey was straightening everything for the day when a shadow fell across her desk. She looked up to find Sawyer standing in the doorway, blocking the light.

He seemed tired and disgruntled. "Isn't it about time you went home?"

"I was just getting ready to leave."

"Scott invited me to dinner."

"So I heard." She found herself staring at him, then felt embarrassed and looked away. Her thoughts were in a muddle as she scrambled for something to say to ease the sudden tension between them.

"Pete Livengood brought me wildflowers," she blurted, convinced she sounded closer to Susan's age than her own.

"Pete was here?"

"Yes, he delivered a few groceries. He's a very nice man."

Sawyer was oddly silent, and Abbey tried to fill the awkward gap.

"When he stopped by, we talked for a bit. He's led an interesting life, hasn't he?"

"I guess so." Sawyer frowned. "Do you have any idea how old Pete Livengood is?" he demanded.

"No." Nor did she care. In fact, she couldn't think of a reason it should matter. He was a rough-and-ready sort who'd lived in Alaska for close to twenty years. Abbey found his stories interesting and had asked him questions about his life. Perhaps Sawyer objected to her spending so much time away from her job.

"Pete's old enough to be your father!"

"Yes," she said curiously. "Is that significant?"

Sawyer didn't respond. "I gave specific instructions that you weren't to be bothered."

"Pete didn't bother me."

"Well, he bothers me," Sawyer said abruptly.

"Why?"

Sawyer expelled his breath and glanced up at the ceiling. "Because I'm a fool, that's why."

Chapter
6

The atmosphere in the Hard Luck Café was decidedly cool when Sawyer came by for breakfast.

"Morning," he greeted Ben, then claimed a seat at the counter. Three of his pilots were there, and he nodded in their direction. They ignored him.

Ben poured him a cup of coffee.

"I'll take a couple of eggs and a stack of hotcakes." Sawyer ordered without looking at the menu.

John Henderson grumbled something Sawyer couldn't hear, slapped some money down on the counter and walked out. Ralph, who sat two stools down from Sawyer, followed suit. Duke muttered a few words, then he was gone, too.

Sawyer looked up, surprised. Three of his best pilots acted like they couldn't get away from him fast enough. "What? Do I have bad breath?"

Ben chuckled. "Maybe, but that ain't it."

"Why are they mad at me?"

Ben braced his hands on the counter. "I'd say it has something to do with Abbey Sutherland."

Sawyer tensed. "What about Abbey?"

"From what I hear, you had a word with Pete Livengood about him dropping off Abbey's groceries at the library."

"Yeah? So what?" To Sawyer's way of thinking, the old coot had no business interrupting her when she was at work. The library wasn't open yet. Besides, Pete hadn't brought that bouquet of wildflowers because he was interested in finding a good book to read. No, he was after Abbey. That infuriated Sawyer every time he thought about it.

Pete wasn't right for Abbey, and Sawyer wasn't planning to let him pester her while she was on his property. Okay, so maybe his family *had* donated his grandfather's cabin to the town. It didn't matter; Sawyer felt responsible for her. If it wasn't for Midnight Sons, she wouldn't even be in town.

"Just remember I'm a disinterested observer," Ben said. "But I've got eyes and ears, and I hear what the men are saying."

"So what's the problem?"

Ben brought the eggs and cakes hot off the griddle, and topped up Sawyer's coffee. "Ralph and John and a couple of the others object to you keeping Abbey to yourself."

Sawyer didn't see it that way. "What gives them the idea I'm doing that?"

"Wasn't it you who warned everyone to stay away from the library?"

"That isn't because I'm keeping Abbey to myself," he argued.

"The woman's got work to do, and I don't want her constantly interrupted."

"I sure don't remember you taking such a keen interest in your mother's collection before."

Sawyer wasn't going to argue further, although the whole discussion irked him. No one seemed to appreciate what he was trying to do. "The library will be open soon, and then the men can visit as often as they like."

That seemed to appease Ben, and Sawyer suspected it would appease the other men, as well.

"Next on the list of complaints," Ben continued, "the guys think you're inventing flights to keep the crew busy so you can court Abbey without interference."

"I'm not *courting* her," he said heatedly. "And what kind of old-fashioned word is that anyway?"

"You had dinner at her house, didn't you?"

"That's true, but Scott was the one who invited me." He hated having to defend his actions. That aside, it was the best dinner he'd had all summer. And he didn't just mean the food.

"Are you saying you don't have any personal interest in her?"

"That's right." Although he didn't hesitate, Sawyer wondered how honest he was being. It was a good thing no one knew he'd been kissing Abbey.

Ben narrowed his eyes. "You're not interested in her," he repeated. "Is that why you nearly bit Pete's head off?"

Sawyer sighed, his appetite gone. "Who told you that? I didn't so much as raise my voice."

"But you made it clear you didn't want him seeing her."

"Not before the library's open," Sawyer insisted. "This is the very reason I was against the idea of recruiting women in the first place. Look at us!"

"What?" Ben asked.

"A few weeks ago we were all friends. Don't you see what's happening? We're at each other's throats."

"Well, we got one thing settled, though, didn't we? You're not interested in her yourself."

"Of course not," Sawyer said stiffly.

"Then you won't mind if a few of the other guys develop intellectual interests that require research trips to the library?"

Sawyer shrugged. "Why should I care?"

"That's what I'd like to know," Ben said, and Sawyer had a feeling the old stew-burner was seeing straight through him.

"All I ask is that the guys give Abbey a little breathing room. Can't they wait until the library's open?"

"And when will that be?"

"Soon," he promised. "I understand she'll be ready to open it up to the public in a few days."

"Good. I'll pass the word along," Ben said, then returned to the kitchen.

Sawyer ate his breakfast, and although Ben was an excellent cook, the food rested in his stomach like a lead weight.

It didn't take him long to acknowledge that he was guilty of everything Ben had suggested. He'd gone out of his way to keep the men as far from Abbey as he could arrange. It hadn't been a conscious decision, at least not in the beginning. But it was now.

Abbey was putting away the last of the dinner dishes the following night when she heard Scott and Susan on the front porch talking with a third person. The weather had been warm, and she'd changed into shorts when she got home from work. Who'd have believed it would reach the mid-eighties in the Arctic? Despite everything she'd read, it hadn't seemed real until she'd experienced it for herself.

Drying her hands on a kitchen towel, she walked out to the porch to discover Sawyer chatting with her children. Eagle Catcher stood at his side.

"Hello," he said cheerfully when she joined them.

"Good evening." She'd been hoping she'd see Sawyer again soon. His eyes said he was eager for her company, too.

Being with him felt right. She loved the easy way he spoke to her children, his patience with Scott over the dog, his gentleness with Susan. Her daughter had adored him from the moment he'd held out his hand to her when they'd met at the airport.

"When are we going to see the northern lights?" Scott asked Sawyer. He'd talked of little else over dinner that night. "Ronny told me it's better than the Fourth of July fireworks, but no matter how late I try to stay up, it won't get dark."

"That's because it's early summer, Scott, and the solstice isn't even due for another two weeks. Wait until the end of August—you'll probably begin to see them then."

"Does it *ever* get dark in Alaska?" Susan asked.

"Yes, but just for a short time in the summer. Winter, however, is another story."

"Ronny told me it's dark practically all day," Scott put in, "but I knew that from the books Mom read when she applied for the job."

"What do the northern lights look like?" Susan asked.

Sawyer sat on the swing and Susan sat beside him; Scott hunkered down next to Eagle Catcher. "Sometimes the light fills the sky from horizon to horizon. It's usually milky green in color and the colors dance and flicker. Some folks claim they can hear them."

"Can you?"

Sawyer nodded. "Yup."

"What's it sound like?"

Sawyer's eyes caught Abbey's. "Like tinkling bells. I suspect you'll hear them yourself."

"Are they always green?"

"No, there's a red aurora that's the most magnificent of all."

"Wow, I bet that's pretty!"

"You know, the Inuit have a legend about the aurora borealis. They believe the lights are flaming torches carried by departed souls who guide travelers to the afterlife."

Abbey sat on the edge of the swing. Soon Susan was in her lap, and she was next to Sawyer. He looked over at her and smiled.

Her children seemed to have a hundred questions for him. He told them the story of how his grandfather had come to Hard Luck, chasing a dream, searching for gold.

"Did he find gold?" Scott asked.

"In a manner of speaking, but not the gold he'd been looking for. It was here, but he never really struck it rich. He died believing he'd failed his wife and family, but he hadn't."

"Why did he stay?" Abbey asked.

"My grandmother refused to go. They had a little girl named

Emily who disappeared on the tundra, and afterward my grandmother wouldn't leave Hard Luck."

"Did she think there was some chance Emily would come back?"

"She never stopped looking."

"What do you think happened to her?" Scott asked.

"We can only guess, but none of the prospects are pleasant. That's why it's so important for you never to wander off on your own. Understand?"

The two children nodded solemnly.

Abbey glanced at her watch, surprised by how late it was. When she'd read that Alaska was the land of the midnight sun, she'd assumed the light would be more like dusk. She was wrong. The sun was so bright she had to prop a board against the curtains in the children's bedroom to make it dark enough for them to fall asleep. As it was, their routines had started to shift. They stayed awake later and slept in longer.

"Bedtime," she told them now.

Her announcement was followed by the usual chorus of moans and complaints.

"Come on, Susan," Sawyer said, standing. "I'll give you a piggyback ride." He hoisted her onto his back and Susan giggled, placing her arms around his neck.

"You're next, partner," he told Scott.

"I'm too old for that stuff," Scott protested, but Abbey knew it was for show. He was as eager as his sister for a ride.

"Too old? You've got to be kidding," Sawyer said, his voice rising in exaggerated disbelief. "You're never too old for fun." Then, before Scott could escape, Sawyer clasped him around the waist and held him against his side.

Scott was giggling and kicking wildly. With a smile, Abbey held open the screen door, and Sawyer carried the children down the hallway to the bedroom they grudgingly shared.

"How about a cup of coffee?" she asked while the kids changed into their pajamas. "Or I could make tea."

His eyes brightened momentarily, then he shrugged and shook his head. "I can't. Thanks, anyway. I came over to tell you I talked to my brother about the housing situation."

Susan burst out of the bedroom wearing her Minnie Mouse pajamas and ran into the kitchen. Scott was close behind, his pajama top half over his head. When her kids were this excited, it was always a while before they settled down enough to sleep.

"Will you tuck me in?" Susan asked, gazing up at Sawyer.

He glanced at Abbey. "If it's okay with your mother."

They hopped up and down as if it were Christmas morning and they'd awakened to find the tree surrounded by gifts.

Taking him by the hand, Susan led Sawyer into the bedroom. Abbey followed, her arm around Scott's shoulders. Sawyer tucked each child into bed, but it was soon apparent that neither one intended to go to sleep.

"Tell us a story," Susan pleaded, wriggling out from under the covers. She hugged her favorite doll.

Scott, too, seemed to think this was a brilliant idea. "Yeah!" he shouted. "One with a dog in it." It went without saying that he would've welcomed Eagle Catcher in his bedroom had Abbey and Sawyer allowed it.

"All right," Sawyer agreed. "But then you have to promise to close your eyes and go to sleep."

Sawyer entertained them with a story for the next fifteen

minutes. He was obviously inventing as he went along, and Abbey was both charmed by his spontaneity and moved by his willingness to do this for her children. Afterward, emotion tugged at her heart as Sawyer bowed his head while each child recited a prayer.

A few minutes later, he slipped out of the bedroom. Abbey was waiting for him in the kitchen. She was boiling water for a cup of tea.

"Thank you," she whispered, not looking at him.

There was an uncomfortable silence, then Sawyer cleared his throat. "As I said, I spoke with Christian about the housing situation. It's clear to both of us that you and the children can't go back to the cabin."

"But I don't really have any choice, do I?"

"There's one vacant house in town." His lips thinned. "It belongs to Catherine Fletcher."

The name was vaguely familiar, and Abbey tried to recall where she'd heard it. Then she remembered the day Pearl Inman had stopped by the library and told her about Sawyer and his family, and some of Hard Luck's history. If she recalled correctly, the two families had been at odds since the 1940s right after World War II.

"Christian thought we should contact Catherine's family. She's in a nursing home now, and it's unlikely she'll ever return to Hard Luck."

"I'd be happy to pay whatever rent she feels is fair."

"Midnight Sons will pick up the rent," Sawyer said. "We promised you free housing when you agreed to move here, and that's what you're going to get."

"Do you think she'll let me have the house?" Abbey asked hopefully.

Sawyer frowned. "She's a cantankerous old woman, and it'd be just like her to refuse out of spite. I'm hoping I don't have to speak to her at all. Her daughter's far more reasonable."

"You don't like Catherine?"

"No," Sawyer said without emotion. "She went out of her way to hurt my mother, and I don't find that easy to forgive. It's a long story better left untold."

Despite his negative feelings toward the old woman, Sawyer was willing to approach her on Abbey's and the children's behalf. Every day Abbey found a new reason to be grateful for Sawyer's presence in her life.

"I appreciate what you're doing," she murmured. "Are you sure you don't have time for a cup of coffee or tea?"

His eyes held hers, and a warm sensation skittered through her. Hastily he shook his head. "I've got to get back." He looked past her down the hallway that led to the bedrooms. "You were right when you said your husband was the one to be pitied. Scott and Susan are great kids. They'd make any man proud."

He moved past her, then paused on his way out the door and kissed her. Only their lips touched. The kiss was brief and casual, as if they exchanged such an intimacy every day.

It didn't strike Abbey as unusual until he'd left the house. One hand covering her mouth, she watched him from the screen door.

His steps seemed to have an uncharacteristic bounce. He was

halfway across the narrow dirt road when he appeared to realize what he'd done. He stopped abruptly and whirled around.

"Good night, Sawyer," she called.

He raised his hand in farewell, then continued across the street to his own home.

"Midnight Sons," Sawyer barked into the receiver, stretching the phone cord as far as it would go so he could reach a pad of paper.

"Sawyer, it's Christian. Listen up. Allison Reynolds is on her way."

Sawyer blinked. "Who?"

There was a loud, exasperated sigh. "Our new secretary. I talked to her this morning, and she's back from vacation and ready to start work first thing Monday morning."

"Great. This is the woman who doesn't type, right?"

"She won't need to. Besides, there's more to being a secretary than typing. Don't worry, what she lacks in one area she makes up for in others."

That didn't warrant a comment. "Have you booked her flight?" he asked.

"Yeah. She's coming in on Friday morning. Same flight Abbey Sutherland did."

Sawyer wrote down the information. "I'll send Duke in to meet her," he said. That should quell some of the dissension among the men.

"Not Duke," Christian protested. "Send Ralph."

"Why not Duke?"

"He'll talk her head off, and you know what a chauvinist he can be. I don't want Allison's first impression to be negative."

"Fine. I'll send Ralph."

"Ralph," Christian repeated the pilot's name slowly. "No, maybe John would be better," he suggested.

John? It was his big mouth that scared off the last teacher! "Why not Ralph?"

"He's too eager, you know? He might say something that would offend Allison."

"Why don't you get your butt home so you can pick her up yourself?" It seemed to Sawyer that his brother was being *much* too particular.

"I would if I could get there in time. I've interviewed a nurse I think would be excellent. I know you asked me to wait on hiring anyone else, but this gal is perfect."

"Then do it." If she met the qualifications, Sawyer couldn't understand the problem.

"She's older. Way older. Pete Livengood's age."

"So?" All the better as far as Sawyer was concerned. Then maybe Pete would stop showing interest in Abbey.

"I was hoping to find someone younger. Attracting women to Alaska isn't as easy as it sounds. I get plenty of calls, but once they hear exactly how *far* north we are, they start asking a lot of questions." He paused. "I had to do some fast talking to convince Allison to give us a try."

"Every position can't be filled with Allison clones," Sawyer said testily.

"I know. I know. Listen, I'll talk to you again soon. I'll want to know how Allison's adjusting."

"Fine."

"Any word from Charles lately?"

"None, but I expect he'll show up any day, hungrier than a bear and meaner than a wolverine." Their eldest brother kept his own hours. He was often gone for weeks at a time, then would blow into town with his geological equipment and stay for a month or two. There was a restlessness in Charles that never seemed to ease. Sawyer didn't question it, but he didn't understand it, either.

He spoke to his younger brother for a few more minutes. Sawyer hung up the phone to find John Henderson standing on the other side of the desk.

"You got a minute?" the pilot asked nervously.

Sawyer nodded. "Sure. What's the problem?"

"Not a problem as such. It's more of a...concern."

"Sit down." Sawyer motioned toward the vacant chair.

"If you don't mind, I prefer to stand," the other man said stiffly.

Sawyer arched his eyebrows and leaned back in his chair. "Suit yourself."

John folded his hands. He seemed to need a couple of minutes to gather his thoughts. Finally he blurted, "Me and a few of the other guys aren't happy with the way things are going around here."

"What things?"

Once more it appeared that John was having difficulty speaking his mind. "You've got an unfair advantage, and it's causing hard feelings."

Now Sawyer understood. After his talk with Ben, he should've realized sooner that this discussion wasn't about Midnight Sons at all. John had come to talk to him about Abbey.

"You're upset because I asked you not to disturb the new librarian while she organizes the library."

"Yes," he said angrily. "You ordered us to stay away until the library's open, but I notice the same doesn't apply to you."

"I'm her contact person," Sawyer explained, keeping his voice calm and even. "She needs someone who can help her, answer questions and so on."

"Let *me* be her contact person," John argued. "Or Duke. None of us would pester her. We just want to drop by the library and make her feel welcome. Everyone knows what happened when Pete went to see her. It wasn't right that you chewed him out for doing his job."

"Pete delivers groceries now? That's news to me."

"Come on, Sawyer, get real. If Abbey stopped by here and needed something, wouldn't you be willing to take it to her?"

Before Sawyer could respond, John continued.

"Of course you would. She's pretty and she's nice, and heck, I thought when we came up with the idea of bringing women to Hard Luck, we'd at least get to talk to them now and then."

Sawyer released a lengthy sigh. "Perhaps I have been a bit...overprotective."

Henderson's jaw tightened. "The guys are saying you want her for yourself."

Sawyer opened his mouth to disagree, then realized they had more than enough evidence to hang him. "You could have a point there."

"That's what we think. All we're asking is that you drop the restrictions on the rest of us. It's only fair. You have my word of honor that I won't bother her, and the others won't, either."

Sawyer couldn't see any choice. If he didn't do it, he'd have a mutiny on his hands. "Fine," he said reluctantly.

John relaxed. "No hard feelings?"

"None," Sawyer assured him. He picked his notepad and peeled off the flight information Christian had given him. "In fact, we've got another woman due to land on Friday. Would you be willing to pick her up?"

"Would I?" John's face broke into a wide grin not unlike the expression on Scott's face when Sawyer had given him permission to play with Eagle Catcher.

The pilot quickly composed himself. "I'll have to check my schedule."

"Do that and get back to me."

Abbey had no idea what was happening. She'd had four visitors in the past hour. Each had produced a valid reason for coming to the library. She hadn't realized how eagerly awaited the opening of the library was. In light of such overwhelming interest, she decided to do just that the next morning.

Abbey finished for the day and collected her things. She'd been visited by everyone but the one person she was aching to see.

As she walked toward Christian's house, she recognized the familiar sound of Sawyer's pickup behind her. She turned and waved.

He slowed to a crawl. "Heading home?"

"Yeah."

"How about a ride?"

She laughed. "It's less than two blocks."

Sawyer leaned over and opened the passenger door. "I thought I'd take the scenic route. Where are Scott and Susan?"

"In the yard. They wanted to run through the sprinkler." The temperature was in the low eighties for the second day in a row, and the kids loved it.

"Grab your swimsuit and a towel, and I'll take you and the kids to my favorite swimming hole," Sawyer suggested.

Abbey brightened. "You're on."

Scott and Susan came racing toward the truck when Sawyer pulled up.

"Hey, kids, want to go swimming?"

"Can Eagle Catcher come, too?"

"Sure. Hop in the back," Sawyer told them. "I'll just run and get my swimming trunks."

As he did that, Abbey hurried into the house and slipped out of her clothes and into her bathing suit. She almost hadn't packed it with the move. She threw on some shorts and a T-shirt, then grabbed towels and clothes for the children.

Sawyer drove out to the airfield and loaded them into a plane. He explained that this type had pontoons so it could land on the water. It was a tight squeeze with kids and dog, but they managed. The kids thought it was great fun.

"How far is this swimming hole of yours?" Abbey asked once they'd taxied off the runway and were in the air.

"Far enough for the kids to appreciate it when we get there."

From the air, there seemed to be a huge number of lakes. She did remember reading that there were—how many lakes? A lot—in Alaska, but knowing a geographical fact sure hadn't prepared her for actually seeing it. Above the noise of the engine, Sawyer told them he was taking them to an all-around favorite spot of his. Not only was the swimming great, the fishing was good, too.

It must have been an hour, perhaps longer, before Abbey noticed they were descending. She cast an anxious look at Sawyer before the plane glided gracefully onto the smooth water.

Once the engines had slowed, Sawyer steered the aircraft toward shore.

"Does anyone know we're here?" she asked.

"I left a note for Duke."

"But—"

"Trust me," he said. "I wouldn't take Scott and Susan anywhere they wouldn't be perfectly safe." He patted her hand. "You, too."

"The kids have only had a few swimming lessons, but they're not afraid of the water." The lake was so clear Abbey could see the bottom. Near the shore, where Sawyer stopped, it appeared to be just three or four feet deep.

Various shrubs grew along the shoreline. Abbey recognized wild rose bushes and knew that in a month or so they'd be crowded with small, vibrantly pink flowers. It was easy to imagine the beauty they'd add to this already beautiful scene.

The minute they could step out of the plane, Scott and Susan were splashing about in the shallows. "It's cold, Mom!" Scott grinned at her, his teeth chattering. "Wow, and does it ever feel good!"

"It's lovely," she agreed, dipping in one foot. "What's the name of the lake, Sawyer?" She was thinking she'd look for it on a map when they returned to town.

Sawyer shrugged. "There are three million lakes in Alaska. They don't all have names. Let's call it...Abbey Lake."

"Abbey Lake!" Susan laughed.

"I like it," Abbey said, playing along. "It has a nice ring."

"Can we go in deeper now?" Scott asked. "I wanna swim."

"Hold your horses," Sawyer told him, tugging his shirt out of his waistband. He was undressed and down to his swimming trunks in almost no time; it took Abbey a little longer. Soon Sawyer and the two children were in waist-deep water and Scott and Susan were taking turns swimming short distances.

Abbey sat on the edge of the pontoon and dangled her feet in the water. It felt cold, but wonderfully invigorating.

"Come on, Mom! The water's great once you get used to it," Scott assured her.

"I think she might need some help getting wet," Sawyer teased.

"No...no! I'm fine." She saw the first splash coming in enough time to cover her face. But her defenses were hopeless against the concerted efforts of the other three. Within seconds she was drenched. "All right, you guys, this is war. The men against the women."

For a short while, pandemonium reigned. Abbey and Susan might have done more damage if they hadn't been laughing so hard. Abbey stumbled out of the water and onto the shore.

A few minutes later, Sawyer joined her. He wiped his wet face with his forearm, then sat next to her on the sun-warmed sand. He kept his gaze trained on the children, who continued to wage war and fun.

"This was a fantastic idea," she said, wringing out her hair. "Thank you for thinking of us."

"I've been doing a lot of that recently," he said in a low voice. "Thinking of you," he clarified. "I feel my brother and I misled you about Hard Luck."

"I was the one who made the decision to come. I knew what I was getting into. It's true the housing situation is a problem, but at the time you didn't know about the children."

"I wanted you to leave when you first came."

"I know," she said unevenly. His determination to be rid of her still rankled.

He glanced at her, his eyes intense. "I don't feel that way anymore."

"I'm glad," she whispered, finding it hard to keep the emotion out of her voice. She sighed, thinking how fortunate she was to have met Sawyer. He was wonderful with her children— wonderful with her. *To* her.

He looked away abruptly, as if the conversation had grown more personal than he'd intended. "When will the library open?"

"Funny you should ask. I had several inquiries this afternoon. I thought I'd place an Open sign on the door first thing in the morning."

"Terrific," he said, but it seemed to her that his response lacked enthusiasm.

Scott trotted out of the water and stood before them.

With some relief, Abbey turned her attention to her son.

"I was just watching you," he said, directing the comment to Sawyer, "and it looked like you wanted to kiss my mother." He grinned, scrubbing water from his eyes with both hands. "You can if you want to," he announced, then raced back into the lake.

Chapter
7

At nine o'clock the following morning Abbey printed a huge Open sign and posted it outside the library. It wasn't long before her first customer arrived.

At five past nine, John Henderson ambled in, hands in his pockets. He was tall and husky, his boyish good looks set off by a thatch of honey-colored hair.

"Good morning," she said in a friendly tone.

"Mornin'," he returned almost shyly. "Nice day, isn't it?"

"Sure is," Abbey agreed. The weather was unseasonably warm this year, she'd been told.

John wandered around the library scanning the rows of books. Everything was cataloged and carefully arranged—fiction in alphabetical order, nonfiction according to subject and children's books. She hoped to order some new titles soon.

"Is there anything I can help you find?" Abbey asked, eager to be of assistance.

"Yup."

"What do you like to read?"

"Romances," John said.

His choice surprised her, but she didn't let it show. Romances were generally considered women's fiction, but that didn't mean a man couldn't enjoy them.

"I need something that'll teach me how to tell a woman she looks even prettier than a shiny new Cessna."

"I see." She suspected it would take more than a romance novel to help him in that area.

"I want to be able to tell her how pretty I think she is, and how nice, but I need to know the right way to say it without riling her. Whenever I try to talk to a woman, all I seem to do is make her mad. Last time I tried, I didn't do so well."

Abbey walked over to the bookshelves and pretended to survey several titles while she thought over the situation.

"It's important that I learn how to talk to a certain woman right," John continued, "'cause another man's got a head start on the rest of us." His voice tightened. "But that's not important now, all things being equal, if you know what I mean."

Abbey didn't, but feared an explanation would only confuse her further. "You might look down this row," she finally advised, directing him to books on etiquette and social behavior.

"Thanks," John said, grinning widely.

Abbey returned to her desk. No sooner had she sat down when Ralph Ferris, another of Sawyer's pilots, strolled in. He paused when he saw John. The two men glared at each other.

"What are you doing here?" Ralph demanded.

"What does it look like?"

"I've never seen you read a book before!"

"Well, I can start, can't I?" John glanced nervously at Abbey. "I have as much right to be here as you."

"Is there something I can help you find?" Abbey asked the new man.

"I see you shaved," Ralph taunted under his breath. He held his nose. "What kind of aftershave did you use? It smells worse than skunk cabbage."

"I borrowed yours," John muttered.

The two men engaged in a staring match, then each attempted to force the other away from the shelves. Bemused, Abbey watched Ralph ram his shoulder against John's. She saw John retaliate, jabbing the point of his elbow into Ralph's side. "Excuse me. If you two are going to fight, I'd prefer you didn't do it in the library," she admonished in her sternest librarian's voice.

The men scowled at each other, then rushed to stand in front of her desk. John spoke first. "Abbey, would it be all right if I stopped by at your house this evening?"

"How about dinner?" Ralph said quickly before she could answer. "Ben's cooking up one of his specials—caribou Stroganoff."

"Dinner?" Abbey repeated, not knowing what to say.

Before she could respond, Pete Livengood marched in. His hair was dampened down as if he'd just stepped out of the shower. He carried a heart-shaped box.

"Chocolates," the two pilots said together. They sounded furious—and chagrined—as if they'd been outmaneuvered.

"Women like that sort of thing," Abbey heard one whisper to the other.

"Where are we going to get chocolates?" John murmured.

"I've got an extra can of bug spray," Ralph said. "Do you think she might like that?"

It was turning into one of the most unproductive days Sawyer had ever spent.

His men had invented one excuse after another to delay their routine flights. He didn't need anyone to tell him they'd gone to the library, and they weren't interested in checking out books, either.

Sawyer found himself increasingly impatient and ill-tempered. He refused to ask any of the men, but his curiosity made him incapable of concentrating. What was happening at that library? And how was Abbey reacting to all this attention? The prospect of her being with someone else drove him crazy.

Restlessly he stood in front of the office's only mirror, wondering if he should shave off his beard. He'd never asked Abbey how she felt about it. Although he'd worn a beard for more than ten years, he'd be willing to remove it if she asked.

He ran a hand along his face, then returned to his desk, slouching in the seat.

John had come back from the library first, clutching an old edition of Emily Post and a couple of paperback romances. Sawyer found him intently reading one of the love stories during his coffee break. He watched as John scanned a page or two, then set the book aside and stared into space, apparently mulling over some important matter.

Ralph had gone to the library that morning, too. He'd

returned sporting a book on the history of aircraft, which he proudly showed to Sawyer.

"I understand another woman's coming in this week," Ralph said, lingering inside the office. He glared at John accusingly.

"That's right," Sawyer answered absently, reading over a flight schedule before handing it to Ralph.

"I'd like to ride along."

"You already have a flight on Friday."

Ralph lifted one shoulder in a shrug. "Duke'll take it for me. He owes me one."

Sawyer didn't hesitate long. If two of the most woman-hungry of his men were vying for Allison Reynolds, maybe they'd leave Abbey alone. So he agreed—with one stipulation. Duke had to willingly consent to the change in plans. Sawyer refused to arbitrate in a conflict over this, he told Ralph, and he didn't want to hear another word about it. The other man's face fell as he walked out of the office and toward the airfield.

The day dragged by, with every pilot somehow managing to visit the library. The minute Sawyer was free, he hurried there himself. He knew something was wrong the minute he stepped inside.

Abbey sat at her desk reading, and when the door opened, she raised her head. Eyes narrowed, she slapped the book shut. After observing the loving way she'd handled the books earlier, that action surprised him.

"Good afternoon," he said warmly.

No smile. No greeting.

He missed the way her eyes lit up whenever they met. He missed her smile.

He tried again. "How's your day going?"

Silence.

"Is, uh, something wrong?"

"Tell me," she said in tones as cold as a glacier, "exactly why was I hired?"

"Why were you hired?" he repeated slowly, not understanding her anger, let alone her question. "Hard Luck needed a librarian to organize a lending library."

"And that was the *only* reason?"

"Yes."

"Oh, really?" she spat out, her eyes blazing.

"Abbey, what's wrong?"

She stormed to her feet and folded her arms. The fire in her eyes was hot enough to scorch him from ten feet away. "All your talk about me breaking the spirit of the agreement! I can't believe I fell for that. You had me thinking you were upset because I hadn't told you about Scott and Susan. Well, everything's clear to me now."

"That's settled and done with. No one blamed you—it was as much our fault for not asking."

Abbey shook her head, but Sawyer wasn't sure what she meant. It did seem to him, though, that she was close to tears. He stepped toward her, but stopped short of taking her in his arms.

"Stay away from me."

"Abbey, please—"

"It wasn't a librarian you wanted," she said. "You and your men were looking for—" she paused as if she didn't know how to continue "—entertainment."

"Entertainment?"

"I don't know how I could've been so *stupid*. The ad practically came right out and said it. Lonely men! You weren't interested in my library skills, were you? No wonder everyone was so upset when I showed up with children."

"That's not true," he flared. He did value her professional skills—and he didn't want her dating *or* "entertaining" any other man. Today, with every unattached male in Hard Luck visiting the library, had made that very obvious.

"If the men in town are so lonely, why didn't you just advertise for wives?"

"Wives? We wanted women, but we didn't want to have to marry them."

Abbey's mouth fell open. "Oh. That makes it all right, then."

"We offered you a house and land, remember."

"In exchange for what?"

His temper was rising. "Not what you seem to think. We offered jobs, too, you'll notice."

"*Invented* jobs, you mean."

"Okay, we *could* have organized the library with volunteers. But there was a reason for coming up with jobs."

"I'd be glad to hear it."

"Well, for one thing, no one wanted to be responsible for supporting a bunch of women."

"Is that what you think marriage is?"

"Damn right."

Abbey swallowed tightly. "You've told me everything I need to know." Her voice broke on the last word, and Sawyer felt shaken.

He tensed, knowing he'd botched this entire conversation. He wondered how he could explain the situation to her— without making things worse.

"It's lonely up here, Abbey. If you want to fault us for feeling like that, then go ahead. I was losing pilots left and right. Christian and I had to do *something* to keep them happy, and the only solution we could come up with was, uh, importing a few women." He knew that hadn't been the best way to put it, but he plunged on. "We wanted female companionship without the problems of marriage. We—"

"In other words, you wanted these 'imported' women to relieve the boredom." She closed her eyes as if he'd confirmed her worst fears.

"Did something happen today?" he asked, clenching his fists. "If anyone offended you, I'll personally see to it that he apologizes."

"*You've* offended me!" she cried.

"Why? Because I didn't offer to marry you? One woman's already tried to lure me into that trap."

"Trap?"

"I'm not going to marry you, Abbey, so if that's what you want, you'd better get this straight, right here and now. I brought you here so you'd be friends with a few of my men." Too late he realized how that must sound. "You know what I mean."

"I know *exactly* what you mean."

Sawyer could see that Abbey was in no mood to be reasonable. She'd already made up her mind, and nothing he said would change it. "We'll settle this later," he said gruffly.

She didn't respond.

Sawyer had to force himself to leave the library. He started down the walk, paused and started back, then stopped again. What a mess. He hated unfinished business.

Scott rode down the street on Ronny Gold's bicycle and pulled to a stop beside him. "Hi, Sawyer!" he said enthusiastically.

Sawyer's gaze was still locked on the library door. "Hiya, Scott."

"How's it going?"

"Good," Sawyer lied.

"Ronny let me ride his bike. I'll sure be glad when mine gets here. How much longer do you think it'll take the shippers to haul our stuff to Hard Luck?"

Sawyer's eyes reluctantly drifted from the library to the boy. It seemed heartless to tell him the truck wouldn't make it to town anytime this summer.

"You miss your bike, do you?"

"It'd be neat if I had it, 'cause then Ronny and I could ride together."

"I've got an old bike from when I was a kid. I think it's in the storage shed. Would you like me to see if I can find it for you?"

Scott's eyes lit up. "Gee, that'd be great!"

"I'll go look for it right away," Sawyer promised, eager for an opportunity to prove himself a family friend, instead of the fiend Abbey thought he was. He really didn't understand what had upset her so much. "I mean, what did she think when she answered the ad?" he muttered to himself.

It took some doing to locate the old bicycle, which was

hidden in the back of the shed behind twenty years' worth of accumulated junk. Old though it was, the bike wasn't in bad shape.

Sawyer hosed it off in the front yard. When he finished the task, he happened to look up—and saw Abbey walking home.

He straightened, standing in the middle of his yard, the hose in his hand dripping water. He stared at her. With every bone, every muscle, every cell in his body, he ached to know what he'd done that was so wrong. More important, he needed to know how he could fix it.

Without even glancing in his direction, Abbey disappeared into the house. Not long afterward Scott approached him, frowning.

"The old bike doesn't look like much, does it?" Sawyer said, drying off the padded seat and chrome fender with an old T-shirt. "But I think once I get her cleaned up a bit and give the chain a shot of oil, it'll be fine."

"No, the bike looks great," Scott said, his sudden smile brimming with pleasure. But some of his enthusiasm faded when he looked over his shoulder. "I have to get home."

"If you wait a few minutes I'll have the bike ready for you."

"I better get home."

Sawyer nodded in the direction of his brother's house. "Your mother seems upset about something."

"I'll say," Scott said. "She's *real* upset."

Sawyer stared at the front door, and the ache inside him intensified. He wouldn't rest until he'd sorted out this business with Abbey. "Maybe I should try to talk to her."

"Not now, I wouldn't," the boy advised.

Sawyer realized—with some embarrassment—how inept he was at dealing with women. Inept enough to accept advice from a nine-year-old boy. Still, if Scott thought it best to wait, he would.

"You'd think she'd be happy," Scott said with a long sigh. "Grandma and Grandpa kept telling her she should go out on dates, but Mom never wanted to. She went out sometimes, but not very often. Now she's all upset because some guy asked her to dinner."

"Who?" Sawyer demanded before he could censor the question. "Never mind, Scott, that's none of my business."

"Well, Grandma wants her to get married again. I heard them talking once, and Grandma was telling my mom that it's wrong to let one bad experience sour her on marriage. She said there were lots of good men in this world and Mom would find one of 'em if she tried. Do *you* think my mom should get married again?"

Marriage wasn't a subject Sawyer felt comfortable discussing. "I...I wouldn't know."

"Mom's never said anything to us, but I'm pretty sure she gets lonely sometimes. Did you know Mr. Livengood asked her to marry him today?"

"What?" A fierce, possessive anger consumed Sawyer. He threw down the hose and was halfway out of his yard before he realized he couldn't very well wring Pete's neck. No matter what his feelings toward Abbey, Sawyer had no right to be angry. If Pete wanted to propose to her, that was his prerogative. He himself had no say in the matter.

"Scott!" Abbey had come out onto the porch to call her son. Sawyer might as well have been invisible for all the attention she paid him. "Dinnertime."

"In a minute, Mom."

"Now," she insisted.

"You'd better go," Sawyer said. "I'll bring the bike over after dinner."

"Okay." He dashed across the street, stopping when he reached the other side. "Sawyer," he called, "don't worry. Mom still likes you best."

Unfortunately the boy's opinion was no comfort at all.

Abbey couldn't eat; the food stuck in her throat. It felt as if she was swallowing gravel. The baked salmon certainly felt that way in the pit of her stomach.

Scott and Susan had never seemed more talkative, but she found it difficult to respond to their comments and questions.

"Sawyer said I could use his bike until mine gets here," Scott said, glancing expectantly at Abbey.

She'd been such an idiot. It had taken her virtually the whole day to figure out what was happening. Every unmarried man in town—most of them, anyway—had made a point of visiting the library, and it wasn't to check out books. No, it had more to do with checking out the librarian.

The newspaper ad had claimed there were lonely men in Hard Luck, but that wasn't the reason she'd applied. Not at all!

"Isn't it neat of him to lend me his bike?" he asked.

Abbey had to think about the question before she could answer it. "Very nice."

"Did Mr. Livengood really ask you to marry him?" Susan piped up, her dark eyes wide with curiosity.

"Would you like some more rice?" Abbey asked, intent on

changing the subject. The last thing she wanted to do was discuss the miserable details of her day.

"He said he was serious," Scott said. "I overheard him telling Mrs. Inman that he wanted to get his bid in before anyone else."

Abbey groaned. How many more proposals would she have to endure? Apparently Sawyer was the only man in Hard Luck who *wasn't* interested in marriage. His ridiculous comment about her trying to lure him into marriage still rankled. As if she'd even *consider* such a thing.

"Are you going to marry him?" Susan asked.

"Of course not. I barely know Mr. Livengood."

"I think you should marry Sawyer," Susan said thoughtfully. "Do Scott and I get to choose a new husband for you? 'Cause if we do, I bet Scott'd want Sawyer, too."

"I am not marrying Sawyer O'Halloran," Abbey said, obviously with more vehemence than she'd intended, because both children gave her odd, confused looks.

"Why not?" Scott asked. "I like him."

"He told us a bedtime story and took us swimming and named a lake after you, Mom. Don't you think he'd be a good husband?"

Abbey's shoulders sagged. "Let's not talk about Sawyer right now, okay?"

Scott and Susan accepted her request without comment, for which Abbey was grateful. They both began to chatter about their new friends and their plans and Eagle Catcher and what they'd done that day.

She was grateful her children had adjusted so well to life in such a small community. A town that lacked the amenities and resources they were used to. She'd been certain they'd find plenty of reasons to miss Seattle. They hadn't, even though they'd left behind their friends, their grandparents, their whole lives.

So had she.

After dinner Abbey was sitting alone at the kitchen table, drinking coffee and reviewing the woeful events of her day, when there was a knock at the door. She answered it to find Sawyer standing on the stoop. Her heart thumped wildly.

His eyes held hers for so long it took her a minute to realize he had the bike her son had mentioned.

"Wait here and I'll get Scott," she told him.

A muscle worked in his jaw. "I brought the bike over for Scott, but it's you I want to talk to." Nothing showed in his eyes, but she felt the power of the emotions he held in check.

The same emotions churned inside her.

"Abbey, please. Tell me what happened today."

"You mean other than two invitations to dinner and a marriage proposal? Oh, I nearly forgot—I was invited to inspect one pilot's fishing flies."

Sawyer closed his eyes. "That'd be John."

"Right. John. There were gifts, too."

The muscle in his jaw jerked again. "Gifts?"

"A bit of inducement, I suspect."

"I apologize for the behavior of my men. If you want, I'll drag every one of 'em down here to apologize."

"That's not what I want," she said coldly.

He heard the phone ring, and with unconcealed relief, Abbey went to answer it.

* * *

Sawyer took the mail run into Fairbanks himself. He found he could think more clearly when he was in the air. The roar of the plane's engines drowned out everything but the thoughts whirling inside his head.

He'd heard there were only two laws a pilot needed to concern himself with. The laws of gravity and of averages. Whoever had said that hadn't taken into account the laws of nature—of physical attraction between a man and a woman.

Abbey confused him. Never had he been this attracted to a woman. The few kisses they'd shared had been a shock to his senses. He imagined the excitement, the satisfaction, of making love to her....

Yes, he wanted Abbey. But even a saint couldn't find fault with the way he'd behaved toward her.

Frustration gnawed at him, eating away at his confidence. Granted, he hadn't been completely in favor of Christian's plan, but he didn't think it was unethical or unfair. It wasn't a question of false pretenses. Well, except for the cabins, which they had—slightly—misrepresented. He didn't want to force anyone, man *or* woman, into a relationship. Not everyone wanted to become romantically involved; it was a personal decision. This way there was no pressure, but for the life of him, he couldn't make Abbey understand that. Offering women jobs instead of marriage meant everyone had a choice when it came to romance. Surely that was as much to the women's benefit as the men's!

The mere thought of her accusations infuriated him. He'd noticed it hadn't taken her long to bring up the subject of marriage.

Did he want to marry her? Did he love her?

Somehow Sawyer found it easier not just to think at thirteen thousand feet but to confront his emotions. What did he know about love? Not much, he decided. From his earliest memories, his parents had been at odds. He felt sure that his parents had genuinely cared for each other, but in every other way theirs had been a bad match. Bringing his mother from the sophistication of London, England, to a primitive little community like Hard Luck couldn't have helped, either. Ellen had gone back to England, taking Christian with her, when Sawyer was thirteen. He'd never forgotten the desolate look on his father's face when the plane took off with his mother and youngest brother aboard.

It was the one and only time Sawyer could ever remember his father getting drunk. And he realized now, as an adult, that it was regret he'd seen in David's eyes.

Sawyer was well aware, as was Charles, when their father began seeing Catherine Fletcher. He often wondered if David would have filed for divorce had Ellen not returned.

At first everything was better. His parents had decided to make a new start, and for a while, life in the O'Halloran household was smoother and more pleasant than it had ever been. Sawyer had missed his youngest brother and his mother. At fourteen he hadn't understood the nature of his parents' relationship; all he knew was that he and his brothers were happy. Ellen had come back. They were a family again.

Unfortunately it didn't last. Everything suddenly changed, and his mother moved out of their bedroom. To the best of Sawyer's knowledge, Ellen and David never slept in the same room again. Later, after the lodge was built, they didn't even sleep in the same house.

No one needed to tell Sawyer why this had happened. His mother had learned about David's affair with Catherine. No one needed to tell him how she'd found out, either. Catherine had taken pleasure in breaking his mother's heart, destroying the tentative beginnings of happiness.

Sawyer had never understood why his parents didn't divorce. In the end, it was almost as if they'd *looked* for ways to make each other miserable.

No, his parents hadn't taught him about love. Nor had he learned much about it in the years since.

Until Abbey…

His mind filled with thoughts of her and Scott and Susan. If she was so distraught about her agreement to work in Hard Luck, he'd release her from any obligation, real or imagined. She was free to go. He'd personally escort her and the children to Fairbanks and see them off.

His heart beat high in his throat at the possibility of losing Abbey.

But if Sawyer admitted he loved her, he'd have to make a decision, and he wasn't ready for that either. They'd met less than two weeks ago. One thing was certain, though—he could no longer picture Hard Luck without her.

When Sawyer returned later that afternoon, he found Scott riding the old bicycle at the airfield. He spotted Eagle Catcher first and smiled to himself as he taxied the Cessna over to the hangar.

"You sure do fly good," Scott told him with admiration when he climbed down from the cockpit.

"Thank you, Scott."

"Are you going to take me up with you like you said?"

"Yeah, someday."

The boy's face fell. "That's what you said last time."

Sawyer remembered how much he'd disliked being put off when he was a kid. "You're right, Scott. I did say you could fly with me. Let's check the schedule."

"You mean it?"

"Yes, but we'll have to ask your mother's permission first."

Scott kicked the dirt with the toe of his sneaker. "I don't think you're her favorite person right now."

"She's still mad, is she?"

"Yup. She told Mr. Livengood she wasn't interested in marrying him. He looked like he was real disappointed, but you know what? I think he would've been surprised if she said yes."

"Maybe I should talk to her." Or try, although heaven knew he'd done that often enough.

"I wouldn't," the boy said.

"Well, have you got any other ideas, then?" Sawyer resigned himself to asking a nine-year-old boy for advice.

"The other guys brought her dumb gifts. Mom doesn't care about bug spray. She doesn't like mosquitoes, but we've gotten real good at keeping them away."

"Okay, I won't give her any bug spray. Can you think of anything she'd like?"

"Sure," Scott said. "She likes long baths with those smelly things that melt."

"Smelly things that melt? What are those?"

"Bath-oil beads," Scott said. "If you can get her those, she might listen to you."

It was worth a try. He'd hit a drugstore next trip to Fairbanks. He walked into the office and held the door open for Scott to follow. Everyone had left for the day, which suited Sawyer fine.

He sat down at his desk; Scott sat in the opposite chair. Leaning back, Sawyer propped his feet on the corner and linked his hands behind his head. Scott imitated his actions, knobby elbows sticking out like miniature moose antlers from the sides of his head.

There was a knock at the door, and Susan poked her head inside. Her smile widened. "Hi, Sawyer," she said. "I saw your bike outside," she told her brother. "Mom wants you."

"What for?" he asked.

"She needs you to help her carry some stuff home from the library."

"Okay," Scott said. He released a long-suffering sigh.

"Want me to come with you?" Sawyer offered. He didn't think Abbey would appreciate it, but then he hadn't seen her all day. Maybe, just maybe, she'd missed him as much as he'd missed her, and they could put this unpleasantness behind them.

"It's okay," Scott assured him. "I can do it." He started toward the door.

"I appreciate the advice, Scott. Next run I make into Fairbanks, I'll buy plenty of those smelly bath things for your mom."

"Uh, Sawyer." Scott's face broke into a grin. "There's something else you could do."

"What's that?"

Scott and Susan exchanged looks.

"You could always marry my mom," the boy said. "Of all the guys who've proposed so far, we like you the best."

Chapter
8

So Pete Livengood wasn't the only one who'd popped the question, Sawyer mused darkly. Scott and Susan had said as much, and they were in a position to know. It infuriated him that the men in this community would make such asses of themselves over the first woman to arrive. These were the very men who'd insisted all they wanted was a little female companionship. Yet the minute Abbey set foot in town, they were stumbling all over themselves to see which of them could marry her first.

What bothered him even more were his own confused feelings for Abbey. He didn't want any of the other men in town approaching her—offering her gifts, dinner dates, marriage proposals. No, if anyone was going to do those things, he wanted it to be him. He just wasn't sure about the marriage part; he *was* sure about wanting to see Abbey. On an exclusive basis.

There, he'd owned up to it. But from the looks she'd given him lately, she'd rather go out with a rattlesnake than with him.

He sulked for a few minutes before leaving the office. He wondered if Mitch Harris had taken a liking to Abbey, too. Mitch hardly knew Abbey, but then, that hadn't stopped Pete from proposing. Mitch, a widower, was a good guy. Chrissie Harris and Susan had been hanging around together; he hoped that wouldn't give Mitch an unfair advantage.

There were a number of other unmarried men in town. Ben Hamilton, for one. The owner of the Hard Luck Café was around the same age as Pete Livengood, and Sawyer considered him a good friend. But that didn't mean Ben didn't have eyes in his head. Abbey was a beautiful woman, and Sawyer could understand why any man would be attracted to her.

There was no telling how many had lined up to offer Abbey their hearts and their homes. Not that he had any right to complain. It was more than he'd done. And a whole lot more than he intended to do.

Marriage was a lifetime commitment. Make that a life sentence. In his experience, marriage meant the death of love. It had killed whatever love his parents had started out with. Well, he wouldn't let that happen to him. No, sirree. He was frustrated and annoyed that the men of Hard Luck were so careless about their freedom.

As he continued his unsatisfying reflections, Sawyer strolled over to Ben's. It was too early for the dinner crowd, such as it was, and too late for lunch. The café was empty.

Sawyer slid onto a stool and uprighted a mug.

Almost immediately, Ben appeared from the kitchen and reached for the coffeepot. "What's bugging you?"

Sawyer smiled to himself, amused and rather impressed that the cook could read him so easily. "How'd you know something's bothering me?"

"You came in for coffee, right?"

"Right."

"You got a pot at your office, same as I do here. I know I'm a good-lookin' cuss, but I don't think you'd be willing to pay a buck-fifty for a cup of coffee unless you needed to talk. What's up?"

"It's that obvious?"

"Yeah." Ben picked up the empty sugar canister and refilled it.

Sawyer didn't know where to begin. He didn't want to let on that what he'd really come here to learn was whether Ben had proposed to Abbey, along with everyone else in town.

"Let me help you out," Ben said when he'd finished with the sugar canister. "A man doesn't wear that damned-if-you-do damned-if-you-don't look smeared across his face unless a woman's involved. Is it Abbey?"

"Yeah." Sawyer couldn't see any reason to deny it. "Pete Livengood proposed to her." He raised the coffee mug and studied Ben's reaction through the rising steam. The cook gave nothing away.

"So I heard."

"Apparently a few other men in town had the same idea."

Ben chuckled and brushed the sugar from his palms. "Someone else being interested in Abbey upsets you?"

That was putting it mildly. "Well, you could say I'm concerned," Sawyer admitted grudgingly.

Ben leaned against the counter, obviously waiting for him to proceed.

"I know what you're going to say," Sawyer said before Ben could prod him. "You want to know what's holding me back. If I'm so worried Abbey'll marry someone else, why don't I propose myself? For a number of very good reasons, if you must know," he said, raising his voice. "First and foremost, I refuse to be forced into this. A man doesn't offer marriage lightly, or at least he shouldn't." He was thinking of Pete and the others. "Another thing. I won't have any woman dictating to me what I should and shouldn't do with my life."

Ben's face creased with a smug look. "Why are you yelling at me?"

Sawyer shut his eyes for a moment and shook his head helplessly. "Darned if I know." Once again, he found himself thinking about his own parents and how miserable they'd been together. Abbey had already been married once. Badly burned, too, as far as he could tell.

The cocky smile vanished from Ben's face. "Maybe what you need to figure out is if you love her."

That debate had been going on inside him all day. "I don't *know* what I feel," he blurted out.

"What about her kids?"

Some of the tension left him. "I'm crazy about those two."

Ben studied him as if seeing Sawyer in a whole new light. "You didn't think you'd ever really fall for a woman, did you? The fact is, before Abbey and her children got here, you thought you were happy."

"I am happy," Sawyer insisted.

"Sure you are," Ben muttered. Chuckling to himself, he returned to the kitchen.

"I'm damn happy," Sawyer shouted after him.

"Right," Ben called back. The old coot seemed highly amused. "You're so happy you're crying in your coffee, afraid Abbey Sutherland's going to marry someone else. Careful, Sawyer, she just might, and then what'll you do?"

Sawyer slapped a handful of coins down on the counter and stomped out.

Abbey inserted a card into the catalog and reached for the next one. This low-tech approach to librarianship was a far cry from the computerized system she was used to, but for the moment, it was manageable. She glanced up as the door opened and Pearl Inman stepped in. "Are you coming down to the airfield?" she asked. "John Henderson's due back any time with Allison Reynolds."

"Give me a minute."

"I don't know about you, but I'm looking forward to meeting this young woman," Pearl said. "Ben baked a cake to welcome her. I just hope the men don't make fools of themselves the way they did when you got here."

Abbey's heart fluttered with a mixture of dread and excitement as she pulled on her sweater and headed out the door. She was eager to meet Allison, eager to have another woman move to Hard Luck. If she remembered correctly, Allison was the woman Christian had mentioned the night he'd phoned—his dinner date.

It was inevitable that she'd run into Sawyer at the airfield;

avoiding him in a town the size of Hard Luck was impossible. Nor did she wish to. She'd been angry and upset the last time they spoke. She wasn't accustomed to a lot of attention from men—it flustered and alarmed her. Then, without intending to, Sawyer had made everything worse. What upset her most was the way he'd insinuated she was hoping to trap him into marriage.

Despite what Sawyer might have thought, she *wasn't* planning to remarry. When she'd applied for the job, she'd done so because that was what she needed—a job. Going to Alaska had sounded adventurous, and small-town life had appealed to her. She *hadn't* come to "be friendly" to a bunch of love-starved men.

Unfortunately, once her children learned that Pete Livengood had proposed to her, they'd jumped on the bandwagon. Not that they wanted her to marry Pete. Oh, no, they were campaigning for Sawyer. Both Scott and Susan made sure they casually dropped his name at every opportunity. It was Sawyer this and Sawyer that, until she was sick of hearing about him. Abbey didn't have the heart to tell them he was the last man she'd marry—even if he asked her. Not with that attitude of his. He'd always believe she'd tricked him into marriage.

The day was overcast and cool, a contrast to the warm sunshine the area had enjoyed all week. Shivering a little, she walked to the airfield with Pearl.

Half the town was there waiting for the plane's arrival. Scott pulled up next to her on Sawyer's old bicycle, shading his eyes as he gazed up into the sky.

"What's the big deal?" he asked.

"Sawyer's new secretary's coming."

"Does she have any kids?"

The question amused Abbey. She wondered what Sawyer would do if another woman showed up on his doorstep with a family in tow.

"Probably not," she said.

"Are the men gonna want to marry her, too?"

"Maybe."

"What about Sawyer?"

"I wouldn't know," she answered, more emphatically this time.

"We want *you* to marry Sawyer," her son persisted. "Susan and me like him a whole lot, and he likes us."

"Scott, please!"

"But if he might marry this new lady, don't you think you should do something about it?"

"No," she said in her sternest voice, praying no one was listening in on their conversation.

"I hear the plane," Pearl shouted.

Abbey squinted into the hazy skies. She heard the buzz of an approaching aircraft, but couldn't see anything just yet. She recalled the excitement she'd felt when she'd flown into Hard Luck and looked down to find such a large welcoming committee.

The plane appeared over the horizon and slowly descended toward the dirt runway. Once it had taxied to a stop, Duke Porter hurried over and lowered the steps.

A minute later, a woman dressed in a hot-pink silk jumpsuit moved slowly down the steps. Like royalty, Abbey thought.

Allison Reynolds was beautiful, she saw with a small pang of jealousy. Knock-your-eyes-out gorgeous. Long legs that seemed to reach all the way to her earlobes, a more-than-ample bosom and a body that would stop New York City traffic. Allison gave a beauty-queen wave and the smile she bestowed on the crowd of welcomers was bright enough to create a glare.

Abbey suspected every man present was wiping drool off his chin. Until that moment, she'd avoided looking for Sawyer, but now she scanned the crowd, seeking him out. She found him, his intense blue eyes glued to the latest arrival with undeniable interest. Just like the others.

Her heart chilled as she admitted to herself that he really wasn't any different. Disillusioned—and determined to ignore it—she squared her shoulders and looked away.

Lonely men, indeed. Well, they were getting what they wanted with Allison Reynolds. Thank heaven.

Just as they had the day Abbey and the kids came, everyone assembled at the Hard Luck Café for introductions. Allison Reynolds was ushered inside and seated while the town put forth its best effort to impress her.

Abbey stood back and waited for a chance to welcome her. From her position by the wall, she had a clear view of the newcomer. Abbey sincerely hoped she and Allison would be friends. At the moment she could do with a friend.

"I'd like to talk to you."

Abbey started, then turned to discover Sawyer standing next to her. "Do you always sneak up behind people?" she asked in an angry whisper.

"Only when I'm desperate." He leaned one shoulder against the wall and crossed his arms. "It's Mitch Harris, isn't it?"

"What is?"

"The other man who proposed."

"That's none of your business."

"I'm making it my business. Was it Mitch?" he growled in a low whisper. Then not giving her time to answer, he asked again. "What about Ben Hamilton? I wouldn't put it past the old goat. He probably did it just to rile me." He sighed, shaking his head. "It worked, too."

"As I said earlier, none of this concerns you." If there'd been anywhere to move, Abbey would have moved, but the café was packed. Why on earth would Sawyer choose this precise minute to talk to her?

"You aren't marrying any of them."

"I beg your pardon?"

"I'm serious, Abbey. Call me a male chauvinist or whatever else you want, but if you're so intent on finding a husband, I'll marry you myself." His voice was harsh.

"You'll marry me yourself?" she asked, incredulous. "How generous of you. How benevolent!"

"I mean it," he said.

"Tell me, Sawyer, why would you do anything so…so drastic?" Mingled with her anger was a pain that cut deep, despite her disenchantment. This was exactly the type of behavior she'd come to expect from Sawyer—yet she was disappointed.

Her question appeared to hit its mark. His face tensed and the muscle in his jaw leapt. Unable to listen to any more, Abbey walked out of the café. She'd introduce herself to Allison later.

She'd gone only a few feet when she heard the screen door slam behind her. Quickening her steps, she hurried away.

"Abbey, wait!"

Half a minute later, he'd caught up with her. "For heaven's sake, will you stop long enough to listen to me?"

Her throat was so clogged with tears, it was impossible to answer him. He steered her onto the airfield and into a nearby hangar, then turned to face her. His outstretched arms touched her shoulder.

Abbey kept her face averted, praying he'd say whatever he intended to say so she could leave.

"Why do I want to marry you?" He sounded as confused as she did.

"You don't want me," she accused. "All you care about is making sure I don't accept anyone else's proposal. Your ridiculous male pride couldn't take that! Well, if you thought you were appeasing me with this insulting offer of marriage, you're dead wrong."

"I do want you," he argued, pulling her into his arms.

Her heart stopped, then jerked back to life as he directed her mouth to his. The kiss was long and thorough. Groaning softly, he kissed her again, hungrily this time. Her lips parted, and she slid her arms tightly around his hard waist.

They engaged in a series of warm, moist kisses that became more and more intense. He drew her closer until the full lengths of their bodies were pressed together. She felt the rise and fall of his chest and knew her own breathing was as labored.

Suddenly, looking stunned, he dragged his mouth from hers. He dropped his hands, releasing her, and stepped back.

Abbey studied him for a moment. "Don't look so worried, Sawyer," she said with wounded dignity. "I'm not going to accept your proposal." She spun on her heel and walked away, grateful he chose not to follow her.

As it happened, Abbey got a chance to talk to Allison Reynolds later that same afternoon. They met in the road outside the library. After a few minutes' conversation, it was apparent— at least to Abbey—that the other woman had no intention of staying in Hard Luck and probably never had.

"You're Abbey," Allison said, smiling. "Christian told me he'd hired you." She crossed her arms and swatted at a mosquito. "Can we talk?" Allison asked, doing a poor imitation of Joan Rivers. "I'm dying to find out how things have gone for you since you arrived." Allison glanced both ways, then lowered her voice conspiratorially. "Are you going to stay?"

"I plan to. So far, I love Alaska."

"But it's summer," Allison said as if this was something Abbey hadn't yet figured out. "I don't think anyone was serious about us staying all winter, do you? I mean, this is the *Arctic*. I don't go anywhere in the winter where there isn't a hot tub."

"I've never lived through an Arctic winter before, so I can't say, but I do know I'm going to try."

"You are?" The new secretary for Midnight Sons spoke as though Abbey was making a serious mistake. "Anyway, I can't talk long. I'm supposed to meet Ralph and Pearl, and they're going to drive me out to the cabin. I've never had a home of my own. Christian said it's a quaint little place. I can hardly wait to see it. But I do hope someone finds a way to get the rest of my luggage up here soon. They seemed to think I could pack everything in three suitcases."

Before Abbey could describe her own experience, Allison was gone. Actually Abbey was just as glad not to be around when Allison viewed her "quaint" new home.

The rest of the afternoon passed slowly, the main attraction being the vivacious and beautiful Allison Reynolds and not the newly opened Hard Luck Lending Library.

Pearl Inman was watering her cabbage plants when Abbey walked past on her way home.

"What a sorry disappointment Allison Reynolds is," Pearl Inman muttered. "That Christian's got mush for brains. I can't imagine what he was thinking when he hired her."

Abbey grinned. "Himself most likely."

"That girl got a free trip to Alaska—which was all she wanted," Pearl said with a disgruntled look. "Makes me down-right angry to think of the way everyone's been so excited about meeting her."

"She might change her mind and stay."

"It'd be a mistake if she did. Allison Reynolds is the type who causes more problems than she solves. My guess is she'll be out of here before the week's up."

Personally Abbey agreed with Pearl.

"I saw you and Sawyer talking. I'm glad to hear you decided to put that boy out of his misery."

Abbey wasn't aware that her troubles with Sawyer were common knowledge. "If Sawyer O'Halloran's miserable, he has no one to blame but himself."

"Isn't that the way it is with most folks?"

Abbey had no argument there.

"As for what happened to you this week, with the men and all, well—" Pearl sighed "—I have to say I blame Sawyer for that."

"So do I," Abbey said. And if he assumed he could make everything better by tossing her a marriage proposal, he was mistaken.

"The men wouldn't have come at you like a herd of buffalo if Sawyer hadn't tried to keep you for himself," Pearl was saying. "Way I hear it, some of them were up in arms because of all the rules and restrictions he put on them."

"Rules?"

"He didn't want anyone pestering you. However, he didn't include himself in that. But this is the only time I've ever seen Sawyer take advantage of a situation. You know," the older woman said thoughtfully, "I don't think he realized he was doing it. His intentions were to help you and the children get settled. I know for a fact that he never expected to fall in love with you."

Abbey looked away to hide her sudden tears. Sawyer *didn't* love her. His proposal told her that much. He was afraid she'd accept someone else, so he'd put his offer on the table. Only a day earlier, he'd vehemently insisted he wasn't marrying anyone.

"I'll see you later, Pearl," Abbey murmured.

Her friend cast her a look of concern. "You okay, sweetie?"

Abbey nodded, but she wasn't. What truly frightened her was that she'd fallen in love with Sawyer. Fallen fast and fallen hard. Once before, she'd proved what a poor judge of character she was when it came to men. She'd left the marriage broken, her confidence destroyed. She blinked back the tears that stung her eyes, feeling a strange new desolation.

Abbey was nearly home when she noticed a truck driving toward her. She knew almost everyone in town by now and stared at the unfamiliar—yet somewhat familiar—face as the truck slowed to a stop.

"Hello," the driver said.

"Hello," she responded, sniffling a bit.

"I'm Charles O'Halloran."

"Abbey Sutherland," she whispered.

Charles frowned. "Do you mind telling me what's going on around here?"

Sawyer sat in his office, rolling a pen between his palms. Every time he talked to Abbey he made matters worse. It started when he saw her standing on the airfield waiting for Allison Reynolds. His heart had actually hurt at the sight of her. Even now he didn't know what he'd done that was so terrible, and Abbey wouldn't tell him.

A man had his pride, but he'd been willing to swallow it one more time, so he'd followed her into Ben's place. Then, before he could stop himself, he was drilling her about other men, acting like a lunatic. He'd never been jealous in his life, and he didn't know how to handle it. John, Pete, Duke, Ralph, Mitch and the other guys were his friends. Or had been.

The office door opened and without a word of warning, in stepped his oldest brother. "Charles!" Sawyer bolted to his feet. "Hey, it's good to see you! When'd you get in?"

"About an hour ago." Charlie slipped the backpack from his shoulders and set it aside.

Charles looked tanned and healthy. He was a leaner, taller version of Sawyer, people often said.

Walking over to the coffeepot, Charles poured himself a mug.

Sawyer knew his brother well enough to recognize that he was upset. "You got a problem?"

His brother sighed and sipped his coffee. "Can you explain how you and Christian managed to let your brains go all soggy in the space of a few weeks?"

Sawyer laughed. "So you heard about the women."

"That's exactly what I'm talking about."

"We flew them here. And there's more coming."

"To live?"

Sawyer nodded, the humor leaving him. Just as he'd expected, Charles didn't think much of their scheme. "We came up with the idea of offering them those old cabins Dad built, plus twenty acres of land. In exchange, they have to live and work in Hard Luck for a year." As he spoke, Sawyer realized how ludicrous the idea must sound to their levelheaded older brother. It had to him at first, too, but his arguments had grown less convincing after Abbey's arrival.

"The women are supposed to *live* in those old cabins?" Charles asked incredulously.

"We cleaned them out, Charlie. They're actually quite...clean."

With unexpected violence, Charles slammed down his mug. "Have you two lost your minds?"

"No. We did what we thought was necessary to help the community grow." Sawyer was aware that he came across as stiff and pompous.

"It wasn't Hard Luck you were thinking about when you advertised for women," Charles countered. "You were thinking of yourselves."

"We were losing pilots left and right," Sawyer snapped. "Phil's gone, and we were about to lose Ralph and John as well. The men were willing to stay if we could bring in a few women."

"How many do you have coming?"

"I don't know," Sawyer confessed, trying to suppress his own anger. "Christian took care of that end of it."

"Was it Christian who sent up the beauty queen, or are you the one responsible for that?"

"Beauty queen? Oh, you mean Allison. No, she was Christian's idea. Okay, she probably won't work out. We're bound to have a few failures, but that's the law of averages. Some women are going to adjust and become part of our community. Others won't."

"Allison Reynolds wants out of the deal. Claims she was sold a false bill of goods. I talked to her myself—ran into her at Ben's."

"Fine. I told you, I didn't expect her to last. I'll arrange for her flight back to Seattle. All I have to do is tell Christian, and he can send up another secretary. From what I understand, there are plenty of applicants."

"Which brings up something else neither of you seemed to trouble yourself with. The media."

Sawyer had gotten a number of inquiries, but he'd steadfastly refused to give interviews. Way up here, he felt relatively safe from the press.

"You aren't so naive as to think the press doesn't know, are you?" Charles asked.

"Of course they know," Sawyer answered. "But they didn't hear about it from me. Before long, it'll be old news and everyone'll leave us alone."

"For your information," Charles said tersely, "I read about your scheme in the Anchorage newspaper while I was in Valdez."

"Okay, so the news is out," Sawyer muttered, unconcerned. He had more important things to worry about than some unwanted publicity.

"How do you think the media are going to react when they learn you've already got a failure on your hands? These women don't know anything about Alaska. They left everything they had and flew up here, thinking God knows what and expecting something far different than they were promised."

"Okay, Allison's a failure, and frankly that's Christian's fault. But Abbey Sutherland's one of the best things that's ever happened to Hard Luck. She's already got the library organized and in operation."

"Abbey Sutherland's the one living in Christian's house, right?"

"Yes." He didn't think now was the time to admit the mistake they'd made with the application form. Nor did he want Charles to know he'd contacted Catherine Fletcher's daughter about the use of Catherine's home for Abbey and her children.

"It seems you've misjudged the situation with her."

Sawyer's head snapped up. "Just what do you mean by that?"

"She isn't staying."

Sawyer's eyes narrowed. "Who told you that?"

"Abbey herself."

Sawyer felt as if he'd had the wind knocked out of him. It took a long moment before he could think clearly. "You met Abbey?"

Charles nodded.

"She's staying," Sawyer said, not waiting to hear his brother's argument.

"Sawyer, damn it, will you listen to reason?" Charles shouted.

"I couldn't care less what Allison Reynolds decides," he told his brother. "But Abbey and her kids are staying."

Charles groaned. "She has children?"

Sawyer rushed toward the door.

"Where are you going?" his brother demanded.

"To see Abbey."

He made the trek between the office and Christian's place in record time. He arrived, breathless with anger and exertion, at her front door, his shoulders heaving. Instead of knocking, he hammered his fist against the door.

Abbey answered it and stared at him through the screen.

"You aren't leaving." His voice was a harsh whisper.

"Sawyer," Charles shouted from behind him. "What do you think you're doing?" He leapt up the porch steps. "We've already talked about you going back to Seattle, remember?" he said to Abbey, lowering his voice.

Abbey stood on the other side of the screen door, her hand over her mouth.

It was all Sawyer could do not to rip the door off its hinges and haul her into his arms. "Abbey, listen, I—"

"Sawyer, leave the poor woman alone," Charles broke in.

Sawyer whirled around. "Stay out of this, Charles. This has

nothing to do with you and everything to do with me." The two men glared at each other.

"Abbey," Charles said, looking past his brother. "Like I said, you don't have to live in Hard Luck if you don't want to. I'll personally pay for your tickets back to Seattle."

"I said I'd marry you," Sawyer reminded her, his voice raised. "Isn't that what you want?" His brother's words felt like a knife between his shoulder blades.

"No. It isn't what I want." With that, she started to close the door.

"Abbey," he cried, frantic to talk some sense into her.

The door closed. He fought back the temptation to open it and follow her inside.

The realization hit him that he was going to lose her, and there wasn't anything he could do about it. The last time he'd experienced such a feeling of hopelessness was the afternoon his father died.

Chapter
9

"What's for dinner?" Scott asked on his way through the kitchen. He didn't give Abbey time to answer. "Can we have macaroni and cheese? Not from a box, but the kind you bake in the oven?"

"Sure." Abbey kept her back to her son, trying to disguise how upset she was. Her hands were shaking and her eyes were brimming with tears.

All the contradictory emotions that had buffeted her for the past few days had reduced her to a helpless inertia. For the first time since her divorce, Abbey had allowed herself to fall in love—with a man who didn't know how to love, who didn't *want* to love.

Allison Reynolds was going to leave. She was the smart one, Abbey thought bitterly. The one who owned up to a mistake and took measures to correct it. That was what Abbey should've done—only earlier, much earlier, before her heart became so completely involved.

She'd made one devastating mistake by marrying Dick. She'd known it almost immediately, but instead of admitting her error, she'd tried to make the best of a bad situation. She'd had to struggle for years afterward to get her life back in shape.

Then, a few weeks ago, she'd begun to dream again, to hope, to believe it was possible to find happiness with a man. Her illusions had been painfully shattered, one by one. It'd all started when she realized her position as Hard Luck's librarian had been a ruse—she'd been brought to Alaska to provide "female companionship" to a bunch of love-starved bush pilots.

Sawyer didn't want her to leave; she wasn't sure why and knew he wasn't, either. He was resisting whatever feelings he had for her, resenting them. He'd offered to marry her, but from the way he'd proposed, he seemed to consider marriage to Abbey some kind of punishment.

"Can Eagle Catcher come inside while we eat?" Scott asked, breaking into her thoughts.

Despite her misery, Abbey smiled. "You know the answer to that."

"But, Mom," Scott said in a singsong voice, "I was hoping you'd change your mind. Eagle Catcher may be a dog on the outside, but on the inside he's a regular guy."

Her son lingered in the kitchen. He poked through cupboards, then opened the refrigerator and took out a pitcher of juice to pour himself a glass. "I saw you talking to some strange man earlier. In a truck." Scott waited as if he expected her to fill him in on the details. When she didn't, he added, "I thought it was Sawyer at first, but he doesn't have a beard."

She sighed. "That was Charles O'Halloran, Sawyer's brother."

"Oh." Scott pulled out a chair and sat down at the table. He didn't say anything for a long moment. Finally he asked, "Are you all right, Mom?"

"Sure," she said with forced enthusiasm. "Where's Susan?"

"She's playing with Chrissie Harris, like always. Do you want me to get her?"

"In a bit."

Scott finished off his juice, then headed for the back door. "Don't be late for dinner," she called after him.

"I won't, especially if we're having macaroni and cheese."

Her mind preoccupied with her own problems, Abbey thought it was quite an accomplishment that she didn't burn dinner. In spite of her earlier resolve to stay, in spite of the fact that she'd invested everything she had in moving here, Abbey came to a decision. By the time her children trooped in, the table was set and she was ready to address the unpleasant task of telling them they'd be leaving Hard Luck. Abbey knew Scott and Susan weren't going to like it.

They sat down at the dinner table together, and Abbey waited until they were halfway through the meal before broaching the subject. "I hear Allison Reynolds has decided she doesn't want to stay," she said casually. "She's flying out first thing in the morning."

"The new lady looked like a ditz to me," Scott commented between mouthfuls of macaroni and cheese.

"She's real pretty," Susan said.

"She's dumb."

"Scott!" Abbey interjected.

"Well, she is. Anyone who didn't like this place after we threw a party for her is more than dumb, she's *rude*."

"Allison looked nice, though," Susan said. She stopped eating and studied Abbey.

Scott seemed far more concerned with shoveling in as much macaroni and cheese as possible, as quickly as possible. If Abbey had been a betting woman, she'd have said Eagle Catcher was on the front porch waiting for him.

"You know," Abbey said carefully. "I'm not so sure it's the right place for us, either."

"You gotta be kidding!" Scott cried. "I like it here. I was kinda worried if I'd find new friends when we got here. But it's neat being the new kid on the block. Everyone wants to be my friend, and now that Sawyer let me have his old bike, it's like being back home."

"There's no ice-cream man," Susan said, gesturing with her fork. She continued to study Abbey.

"There's no place for us to live, either. When Mr. O'Halloran offered me the job, I didn't tell him I had a family."

"Why can't we stay right here?" Susan wanted to know. "This is a nice house."

"Because it belongs to Sawyer's brother Christian," Scott answered for her. "Sawyer told me he was going to phone some old lady who used to live in town. He thinks we should be able to rent her house. We don't have a problem, Mom. Sawyer's taking care of everything."

"It's not just the living arrangements," Abbey went on. "The trucking company can only take our furniture as far as Fairbanks. There's no way to get it to Hard Luck until winter."

"I can wait," Scott volunteered.

"Me, too," Susan agreed.

"What about our supplies for winter?" she asked.

Both children stared at her as if she were speaking another language. "What does everyone else do?" Scott asked.

"They buy enough supplies to last them a year. Best as I can figure, that'd be nearly five thousand dollars for the three of us. I can't afford that."

"Can't you get a loan?" Scott suggested.

"No. I didn't know any of this, and now, well, it just makes sense for us to go back home."

"But Sawyer—"

"Please," she said, cutting Scott off. The last person she wanted to hear about was Sawyer. But she could see it was going to take more than excuses to convince her family they had to leave Hard Luck.

"I'm beginning to think we made a mistake in coming here," she whispered, barely able to look across the table at her children.

"A mistake? No way!"

"We *like* it here!" Susan protested.

"It's been a wonderful experience," Abbey said, "but it's time to stand back and assess the situation. We have some important decisions to make."

"You already made the decision," Scott insisted. "Don't you remember what you told us? You said that no matter what, we'd give it a year, and then we'd decide what we wanted to do. It isn't even a full month yet and you're already talking about quitting."

"There are things you don't understand," Abbey said. No one had told her that when she agreed to move to Alaska, she'd be putting her heart at risk. She would never have taken the gamble had she known the stakes were so high.

Over the past few weeks, she'd learned she could live without indoor plumbing. She could manage without electricity. She could do without the luxury of a shopping mall close at hand. But she could not tolerate another man crushing her heart.

And Sawyer would.

He didn't know about love, didn't trust it. His parents' difficult marriage had left him wary and cautious; she wasn't much better.

She'd taken all the pain she could bear from one man. She wasn't giving Sawyer the opportunity to take over where Dick had left off. As cowardly as it was, she'd made up her mind to leave.

She didn't expect her children to understand or appreciate that, which made everything so much more difficult.

"You aren't serious about moving, are you, Mom?"

Abbey swallowed past the tightness in her throat and nodded.

"I thought you liked it here," Susan wailed.

Everyone stopped eating. Scott and Susan stared at her, their eyes huge and forlorn.

"It just isn't working out the way I hoped," she told them brokenly.

"Is it because of Sawyer?" Scott asked.

Preferring not to lie, Abbey didn't answer him. "Since you both enjoy Alaska so much...I was thinking we could find a place in Fairbanks. Since that's where the truck's delivering our furniture, I thought we could rent a house and...and settle in before school starts again."

"I don't want to live in Fairbanks," Susan said emphatically. "I want to live here."

"I'm not leaving Eagle Catcher," Scott told her in a deceptively calm voice. From past experience, Abbey knew it wouldn't be easy to change her son's mind.

"There'll be lots of dogs in Fairbanks."

Susan began to sob. "Why do we have to leave?" she asked.

"Because...because we have to. Hard Luck is a wonderful town with friendly people, but...but it hasn't worked out for us."

"Why not?" Scott pressed. "I thought you liked it, too. Sawyer even named a lake after you, remember?"

There wasn't much she *didn't* remember about her times with Sawyer. The emotion that had hovered so close to the surface all day broke through, and hot, blistering tears filled her eyes.

"I'm so sorry..." Angry with herself for succumbing to her emotions, Abbey swiped at her face and drew in a deep breath, hoping it would relieve some of her tension.

"Why are you crying, Mommy?" Susan asked, sniffling herself.

Abbey patted her daughter's shoulder and stood up to reach for a couple of tissues.

"Is this because of Sawyer?" Scott demanded for the second time. "Is *he* the one who made you cry?"

"No. No!"

"You were mad at him before."

Abbey didn't need to be reminded of Sawyer's role in this drama. But ultimately she didn't blame him. If anyone was at fault, she was—for believing, for lowering her guard and falling in love again. For making herself vulnerable.

"Everyone says you should marry Sawyer," Susan put in. "If you did, would we still have to leave Hard Luck?"

"If you don't want to marry Sawyer," Scott said, "what about Pete? He's not as good-looking as Sawyer and he's kinda old, but he's real nice, even if he does have his hair in a ponytail. We could live with him, and he's got enough supplies to last us all year."

"I'm not marrying anyone," Abbey said, laughing and crying simultaneously.

"But if you did want to marry someone, it'd be Sawyer, right?" Scott persisted, his eyes serious. "You really like him. I know you do, because Susan and me saw you kissing, and it looked like you both thought it was fun."

"We're friends," Abbey told her children. "But Sawyer doesn't love me and... Oh, I know you're disappointed. I am, too, but we have to move."

Neither of the children said anything.

Abbey sniffed. She wiped her nose with her tissue, then rested her hands on the back of the dining-room chair. The sooner they were gone, she decided, the easier it would be. "Pack everything in your suitcases tonight. We're leaving first thing in the morning with Allison Reynolds."

Sawyer sat alone at the dinner table, his meal untouched. When Charles returned to Hard Luck from one of his jaunts, the two brothers usually sat up and talked most of the night.

Not this time.

In fact, if he saw his older brother just then, Sawyer wouldn't be held accountable for what he said or did.

His own brother had betrayed him by offering to fly Abbey out of Hard Luck. Sawyer had hoped she'd have the sense to realize she belonged right here with him. But apparently not.

Thanks to Charles's interference, his encouraging Abbey to leave, the two brothers had become involved in a heated argument. They'd parted, furious with each other.

Even now Sawyer couldn't understand how the brother he would've trusted with his life could do this to him. It was obvious that Charles didn't know a thing about falling in love. And even less about women...

Sawyer prayed that his older brother would experience—and soon—the intense frustration of loving a woman and being barricaded at every turn. And he *did* love her, damn it.

It was particularly disconcerting when one of those barricades came in the form of his own flesh and blood.

Not for the first time since meeting Abbey, Sawyer appreciated the dilemma his father had been in when his mother had said she wanted a separation. Soon afterward, Ellen had packed her bags and returned to England with Christian.

Sawyer still didn't fully grasp the dynamics of his parents' relationship. He'd known for years that his mother was deeply unhappy. As a child, he'd realized she wasn't like the other women in Hard Luck. She spoke with an accent and tended to keep to herself. As far as Sawyer knew, Pearl Inman had been her only friend. The other women had club meetings and volunteered at the school, but Ellen was never included.

In some ways she'd been an embarrassment to her son. He'd

wanted her to be like his friends' mothers. All she ever seemed to care about were her books—and yet, ironically, it was those books that had brought Abbey to Hard Luck.

Like his father before him, Sawyer was going to walk down to the airfield come morning and watch the woman he loved disappear into the horizon.

Then, like his father, Sawyer strongly suspected he was going to get royally soused, if not falling-down drunk.

Pushing away his untouched dinner plate, Sawyer stood. He walked into the living room and gazed longingly out the window. Abbey was directly across the street, but she might as well be on the other side of the world.

The urge to breach the distance and tell her everything that was in his heart was like a gnawing hunger that refused to go away. If there was the slightest chance she'd listen to him, he would've done it.

From the corner of his eye, Sawyer saw Scott wheel his old bike toward his house. The boy threw the bike down, then kicked it hard enough to make Sawyer wince.

First the mother and now the boy. Exhaling a deep breath, Sawyer went resolutely to the front door and opened it. He stepped onto the porch. "Is something wrong, son?"

"I'm not your son!" Scott shouted.

"What's wrong?"

Scott kicked the bicycle again. "You can have your dumb old bike. I don't want it. It's stupid and I never liked it."

"Thank you for returning it," Sawyer said without emotion. Scott's display of pain and anger was unlike him. Wondering what—if anything—he should say, Sawyer walked down the steps. "Would you like to help me put it back in the storage shed?"

"No."

Sawyer stooped to pick up the bicycle. The moment he bent to retrieve it, he was attacked with fists and feet. The blows didn't hurt as much as surprise him.

"You made my mother cry!" Scott screamed. "Now we have to leave!"

Sawyer easily deflected the impact of the small fists and wild punches. Scott kicked him for all he was worth, his shoe connecting with Sawyer's shin a number of times.

In an effort to protect himself and Scott, Sawyer dropped the old bike and wrapped his arms around the boy's shoulders. He knelt down on the grass in front of him. By now Scott was crying openly and his breath came in ragged gasps.

Sawyer held him tight, absorbing the boy's pain and feeling as though his own heart was about to break. Losing Abbey was bad enough. It seemed unfair that he'd lose the children, too.

In the short time they'd lived in Hard Luck, Scott and Susan had captured his heart. A day didn't seem right without Scott there to greet him and ask if he could get Eagle Catcher out of his pen. And Susan... With her wide grins and charming enthusiasm, she could always wrap him around her little finger.

"I'm sorry I made your mother cry," Sawyer whispered over and over, although he was sure the boy didn't hear him.

Sobbing, Scott buried his face in Sawyer's shoulder. Soon his thin arms were wrapped around Sawyer's neck and he clung to him as if he'd never let go. "Your bike isn't really stupid," he mumbled.

"I know."

"We have to put everything back in our suitcases," Scott said. "Mom told us at dinner that we're leaving in the morning."

"I know." He didn't bother to hide his regret.

Scott's head jerked back and he stared at Sawyer through swollen eyes. "You do?"

Sawyer nodded.

"And you were just gonna let us leave, without even saying goodbye?"

"I was going to walk down to the field in the morning and see you off," Sawyer explained. *And then silently stand by and watch you fly away.* He had no choice. What else could he do?

"Susan and I don't want to leave."

Sawyer's heart lightened a little. Perhaps Abbey's children could succeed where he'd failed. "Did you tell your mother that?"

Scott's eyes glistened with his recently shed tears. "That made her cry even more. I thought you cared about Mom and Susan and me."

"I do, Scott, more than you'll ever know."

Scott yanked himself free. "Then why does Mom want to move away so bad?"

"Because…" Sawyer struggled for words. "Sometimes it isn't easy to understand, especially when you're just nine and—"

"I wouldn't understand it if I live to be as old as…as forty."

Sawyer smiled, despite himself. "I wish I understood it myself so I could explain it to you." He stroked the boy's hair. "Do you want to talk about it some more?"

"No," Scott said, and shook his head. Rubbing his eyes with

the heel of his hand, he turned and ran in the opposite direction as fast as his legs would carry him.

Sawyer's heart contracted at the boy's distress. He wanted to follow Scott and swear that he'd do anything to convince Abbey to stay in Hard Luck. Anything. Instead, he remained on the front lawn, staring after her son. He hardly noticed that Mitch Harris was walking in his direction.

At Mitch's greeting, he raised a hand and smiled wanly. Presumably the public safety officer wasn't there on official business. In his calm, quiet way, Mitch was the most effective cop they'd ever had, but right now, Sawyer didn't need a cop.

"You certainly look glum," Mitch said, continuing toward him.

Sawyer kept his gaze on the house across the street. "Abbey's leaving," he said flatly.

"You're kidding, I hope. Her daughter and my Chrissie hit it off like gangbusters."

Sawyer nodded.

"It's been great for Chrissie to have a friend her age," Mitch said, his eyes narrowed in concern. "Those two have been inseparable for the past month. What happened?"

"I can't figure it out." Sawyer massaged his forehead.

"I thought—or rather, I'd heard—that you and Abbey had become...good friends."

"I thought we were friends, too. I guess I was wrong. She wants out of Hard Luck."

"Are you going to let her go?"

For pride's sake, Sawyer shrugged as if her coming or going was of little consequence to him. "It seems that bringing women to town was nothing more than an expensive mistake."

"I'm sorry to hear about Abbey and her kids leaving, though," Mitch said. "Chrissie's going to miss Susan, and I suspect Hard Luck's going to miss having a librarian. Abbey would've done a good job if she'd decided to stay. It's a shame."

Sawyer couldn't agree more.

"That's not our only problem," Sawyer said. He went back into the house and brought back a letter addressed to the school board. It was from Margaret Simpson, the high school teacher. "I received this in today's mail," he said and handed it to Mitch.

Mitch quickly scanned the letter. "Margaret's decided not to teach next year, after all."

"That's what she says." She'd addressed the letter to Sawyer as president of the school board. He drew a deep breath. "Looks like we'll need another teacher before the end of the summer. I'll be calling a board meeting later in the week."

"Fine." Mitch paused, then said, "It seems like a lot of bad news all at once, doesn't it?"

Sawyer was staring at the house across the street. "That it does," he murmured.

The two men shook hands, and Mitch left, walking across the street to Abbey's house. Sawyer had never been the nosy type, but he was decidedly curious to learn what Mitch had to say.

Abbey answered the door. Although Sawyer couldn't hear the conversation, he guessed that Mitch was bidding her farewell. But whatever Mitch's business with Abbey, it didn't last long. Hoping he wasn't too obvious, Sawyer tried to sneak a look at her. It didn't work; she was back inside the house faster than a turtle retreating into its shell.

* * *

Neither of the children had been particularly cooperative about going to bed. Since the sun still shone brightly at ten o'clock, it was difficult for them to get to sleep. As usual, Abbey propped a board against the curtains to darken the room a little.

She was grateful when the talking quieted down. Sitting at the kitchen table with her feet on the opposite chair, she sipped from a glass of iced tea and considered her options.

Her suitcases were packed. So were the children's. They'd worked silently, not hiding their disappointment. It was such a contrast, Abbey thought, to their cheerful, excited chatter the night they'd packed to come here.

Before he went to bed, Scott had told her he'd returned Sawyer's bike. Abbey had hugged her son and kissed the top of his head.

Fairbanks wouldn't be so bad, she'd tried to convince herself and the children. It was Alaska's second-largest city, and it would have all the comforts they'd left behind in Seattle.

No reaction.

She'd assured them they'd be settled in and ready long before school started. Even the reminder that Fairbanks was the world's mushing capital didn't seem to raise Scott's spirits. He was going to miss Sawyer's husky.

"Will I ever see Eagle Catcher again?" he'd asked.

"I...I don't know," Abbey told him sadly.

Although she knew she wouldn't sleep, she trudged down the hall to her bedroom. Out of habit, she stopped to check on Scott and Susan. Knowing they hadn't been asleep for long, she opened the door a crack and glanced inside.

Both had the covers pulled up over their heads. Quietly she closed the door and slipped down the hall.

She got as far as the second bedroom when she stopped. Something wasn't right. She hesitated, unable to identify exactly what it was. Retracing her steps, she returned to the bedroom, opening the door a bit wider.

Standing where she was, her silhouette against the opposite wall, Abbey could see nothing wrong. Tiptoeing farther into the room, she sat on the edge of Scott's bed.

It was then that she realized it wasn't her son in the bed at all, but a rolled-up blanket and a football helmet.

Abbey gasped, surged to her feet and yanked back the covers. Scott was missing.

She rushed over to the second bed and discovered that Susan was gone, too.

Abbey turned on the light and saw an envelope leaning against the lamp on the nightstand. She reached for it, her fingers trembling, and tore it open.

Dear Mom,
We don't want to leave Hard Luck. You can go without Susan and me.
Don't worry about us.

Love,
Scott and Susan

Abbey read through it four times before the realization began to sink in. Her children had run away.

She raced to the phone and instinctively dialed Sawyer's number. She felt so shaky she had to punch in the numbers twice.

"Hello."

At least he wasn't asleep. "It's Abbey. Is Eagle Catcher there?"

"You want to talk to my dog?"

"Don't be ridiculous. I want you to check his pen and tell me if he's inside. Please, Sawyer, this is important."

"I can tell you right now that he is," Sawyer grumbled. "I locked him in no more than an hour ago."

"Please check."

He sighed. "Okay."

She heard the click as he set the phone down. Abbey closed her eyes and impatiently counted backward, starting at a hundred, while he left the house to check his backyard. She'd reached sixty-three by the time he got back.

"He's gone," Sawyer said breathlessly. "Abbey, what's going on? Are you okay?"

"No, I'm not okay." Her heart felt like it was about to explode inside her chest. "Scott and Susan are gone."

Without a second's hesitation, Sawyer said, "I'll be right over."

"Please hurry," she whispered, but he'd already severed the connection.

Chapter
10

"Where would they go?" Abbey asked even before Sawyer had entered the house. She handed him Scott's letter, which he read in a few seconds.

"I have no idea."

Abbey sank onto the sofa. Her legs were incapable of supporting her any longer. "This is all my fault."

"Blaming yourself isn't going to help find those kids. Think, Abbey! You know Scott and Susan. Where would they hide?"

Abbey buried her face in her hands as she tried to reason, but her mind refused to function. Every time she closed her eyes, all she could see was her two children in the wilderness alone. Sawyer had repeatedly warned them about the dangers lurking out on the tundra. He'd told them about his aunt, who had disappeared without a trace at the age of five....

No one had ever explicitly described the danger brown bears presented, but it was very real. The day after her arrival she'd learned how to operate a can of pepper spray to ward them off. Now her children, the life and breath of her soul, were alone and defenseless, possibly wandering around in the wild. Eagle Catcher could only do so much to protect them.

"I'll find them, Abbey," Sawyer promised. He knelt in front of her and gripped her hands in both of his. "I swear to you I won't stop searching until they're home and safe."

Abbey reached for him. Despite their differences, despite the fact that she was walking out of his life in a few hours, she trusted Sawyer as she did no one else. He'd find her children or die in the attempt. She knew that.

His arms went around her, and they clung to each other.

"Abbey, don't forget—they've obviously got the dog with them. That's a good thing. Stay here," he instructed her. "I'll alert Mitch and we'll get a search team assembled."

She nodded, well aware that she wouldn't be of any help to them. But she didn't want to be here alone with her fears. Sawyer seemed to realize that, too.

"I'll ask Pearl Inman to come stay with you."

Her heart in her throat, Abbey walked Sawyer to the front door. He raised his hand and gently touched her cheek. Then he was gone.

Abbey moved onto the porch and sat in the swing, nearly choking on her fears. Mosquitoes buzzed nearby, but she paid them no heed. Again and again, her mind went back to the conversation she'd had with the children earlier that evening.

They loved Hard Luck. And Eagle Catcher and Sawyer.

Without a bit of trouble, they'd adjusted to their new lives in Alaska. Abbey had assumed it was too soon for any real attachments, but she'd been wrong.

Her son had bonded with Eagle Catcher. He'd become friends with Ronny Gold. Susan had struck up a friendship with Chrissie Harris. And she…well, she'd gone and done something really dangerous.

She'd fallen in love with Sawyer O'Halloran. She saw her actions with fresh clarity. Knowing she loved him frightened her so badly she'd decided to run. The fear of making another mistake had caused her to panic.

Pearl appeared on the top porch step. Caught up in her thoughts, Abbey hadn't noticed her right away.

"Abbey?"

"Oh, Pearl," she said in a broken whisper. "I'm so afraid."

The older woman sat next to her and squeezed her shoulders. "Sawyer will find those kids, don't you worry."

"But they could be anywhere."

"Mark my words, they'll be found in short order. At least they were smart enough to take Eagle Catcher. He's a good dog, and he isn't going to let anything happen to them."

Abbey tried to relax, but despite Pearl's assurances, she simply couldn't. The tension wouldn't ease until she knew her children were safe.

"Come on," Pearl said, "let's make a pot of coffee and some sandwiches. The men are going to need them."

Abbey agreed, although she knew Pearl was just trying to get her mind off the children. She moved into the kitchen and began the preparations by rote.

"Are you sure you want to use that much coffee?" Pearl asked, looking up from the bread she was efficiently buttering.

Abbey saw that she'd filled the basket to overflowing. "No," she said, laughing nervously. "Perhaps you'd better make the coffee."

"Sure thing. Just let me finish this."

They sat at the kitchen table and listened to the hot water dripping through the filter. The pot's gurgling seemed strangely loud in the unnatural quiet of the house.

An hour passed, the longest of her life. Mitch stopped by the house and asked Abbey some questions about the kids.

When he left, Pearl poured her a cup of coffee.

"The kids were upset about leaving," Abbey confessed to her.

"You're leaving?" Pearl sounded shocked. "Whatever for?"

"Because...oh, I don't know, because nothing seems right anymore. I'm afraid, Pearl... I don't want to be in love. It scares me. And Sawyer... I wouldn't have thought it possible to insult a woman with a marriage proposal, but he managed it. He seems to believe that every woman wants to trap him!"

Pearl patted her hand gently. "If that's the case, he must feel very strongly about you, otherwise he'd never have asked."

Despite everything, Abbey smiled. "I think Sawyer's as confused as I am."

When the phone rang, it startled Abbey so much she didn't know what to do. She sat paralyzed, unable to move or even breathe.

Pearl picked up the receiver. "Yes, yes..." she said, nodding.

Abbey studied the older woman's face for any sign of news.

A moment later, Pearl held her hand over the mouthpiece. "It's Sawyer. He called to let you know they have two four-man teams searching the area. The first one just reported back. They didn't see any trace of the children. He wants to talk to you."

Abbey snatched the receiver. "Sawyer, what's happening?"

"Nothing yet." How calm and confident he sounded. "Don't worry, we'll find them. Are you all right?"

"No!" she cried. "I want my children!"

"We'll find them, Abbey," he said again. "Don't worry."

She took a deep breath and tried to remain calm. "Is there any sign of Eagle Catcher?" she asked. If they found the dog, then surely the children would be nearby.

"Not yet."

"Call me soon, please. Even if you haven't found them yet. I need to know what's happening."

"I will," he promised.

Pearl poured Abbey another coffee and brought it to her. She stared into it, trying to think.

Another hour dragged slowly by, and Abbey started to pace. This time when the phone rang, she leapt for it.

"Did you find them?" she blurted into the mouthpiece.

"Mom?"

"Scott, is that you?" Abbey asked, then burst into tears. The release of tension washed over her like...like the clear, clean waters of Abbey Lake.

"Don't cry, Mom. We're okay. I bet we're in a lot of trouble.... Here, you better talk to Sawyer."

Abbey tried to control her emotions, but the relief was too

great to do anything but give in to it. A moment later Sawyer was on the line.

"Abbey, it's me."

"Where were they?"

"We found them in the old lodge. They'd managed to make their way upstairs, where they were hiding. I found the three of them cuddled up together. Eagle Catcher was in the middle and they each had an arm around him."

"You mean to say they were that close to town all this time?"

Sawyer chuckled. "Yup. Eagle Catcher heard me calling him, but he wouldn't leave Scott and Susan."

"Remind me to kiss that dog." She laughed softly.

"I'd rather you kissed the dog's owner."

Abbey's laughter faded, and the tension returned.

"Never mind," Sawyer said, defeated. "It was only a suggestion. The important thing is, the kids are safe and sound. I'll be bringing them home."

"Thank you, Sawyer. Thank you!" She glanced over at Pearl as she replaced the receiver. "They're fine," she said, wiping the tears from her face. "Sawyer found them hiding in the lodge."

"Thank God," Pearl whispered.

"I do," Abbey responded.

"I don't imagine you'll be needing me here anymore." The older woman moved toward the door, then turned toward her. "I know it's none of my affair and I'm sticking my nose where it doesn't belong, but I'd hoped you'd stay on in Hard Luck. You don't need me to tell you how stubborn men can be—and Sawyer's more stubborn than most. But his heart's in the right place."

Uncomfortable with the conversation, Abbey averted her gaze.

"We're gonna miss you and those young'uns," Pearl said sadly, "but you're the one making the decisions."

Abbey walked her to the door, then stood and waited on the porch for Sawyer to deliver her family. He arrived in his truck, along with his brother. When he opened the door, Scott and Susan came charging out of the cab, running straight into Abbey's outstretched arms.

Both children were talking at once, telling their version of what had happened and why. After she'd hugged and kissed them both, she glanced up to see Sawyer standing beside the truck, watching them. Charles was inside the cab.

"It seems to me you've caused a lot of trouble," she told the children. "You'll both be writing letters of apology to each and every person who searched for you."

Scott hung his head and nodded. Susan did, too.

"I'm sorry, Mom," Scott said, "but we don't want to move to Fairbanks. We like it here."

"We'll discuss this in the morning. We'll also discuss your punishment, and it's going to be more than just writing the letters. Understand?"

They nodded again.

"Now go and take a bath, both of you—you're absolutely filthy. Then get back into bed. We have a busy day ahead of us."

"But, Mom—"

"Good night, Scott. Good night, Susan," she said pointedly.

Their heads hanging, the two youngsters went inside the house.

Abbey looked at Sawyer. Swallowing hard, she approached him. "Sawyer, I don't have the words to thank you properly," she said, wrapping her arms around her waist. She smiled hesitantly at him. Even now, the temptation to walk into his arms tempted her almost beyond endurance. It struck her as deeply significant that when she'd discovered her children were missing, he was the person she'd turned to.

"I'm glad they're safe," Sawyer said. "That's what matters."

They stared at each other, neither of them saying a word or moving a step closer.

An eternity seemed to pass before Charles stuck his head out the cab window and cleared his throat. "We'll be seeing you in the morning, right?"

Abbey glanced from Sawyer to Charles. "In the morning," she said, then turned and walked away.

"You look like you could use a good, stiff drink," Charles said when Sawyer climbed back into the truck.

Sawyer's eyes were fixed on the front door of the house. It'd take a lot more than whiskey to cure what ailed him.

"I'll drive you back to your place," he said impassively. His hands tightened around the steering wheel until the knuckles showed white.

"You're in love with her." Charles's voice was matter-of-fact.

"Is that so hard to believe?"

"You barely know the woman!"

Hot anger surged through Sawyer. "I know what I feel. I know that when Abbey and those two kids board the plane you're piloting tomorrow, they're taking a part of me with them."

"You're serious?"

"Yes, I'm serious!" Sawyer snapped.

Charles didn't say anything until his brother pulled up in front of his house, which was at the other end of town near the lodge. "I was wrong to get involved."

It was of absolutely no comfort to hear Charles admit it now.

"I sure don't think this scheme of yours and Christian's was one of your brighter moves, but you obviously care for Abbey and those children."

His brother wouldn't understand how much he did care until he'd fallen in love himself. "That's putting it mildly."

"So, are you going to let her leave?"

"What choice do I have?" Sawyer asked, frustration ringing in his voice. How many people were going to ask him this? "I can't hold her hostage. I've tried talking to her, and that doesn't do any good. Mainly because every time I open my mouth to tell her how I feel, I end up insulting her. I get all tongue-tied and stupid."

Charles seemed to find Sawyer's confession amusing. He smiled.

"I've never...felt this way before," Sawyer said in his own defense, "and I'm telling you right now, watch out, because it's like getting hit with the worse case of flu you've ever had. Your turn's coming, so get that smug smile off your face."

"No way," Charles insisted. "I don't want any part of it. Look what it's done to you."

"You think I wanted this? It just *happened*. Abbey arrived—and there I was with my tongue hanging out."

Charles laughed outright. "How is it, little brother, that we've lived to the ripe old ages of thirty-three and thirty-five without falling in love?"

"And we were proud of it, weren't we, big brother?" Now it was Sawyer's turn to be amused. "Not anymore. When I met Abbey, I felt like I'd been sucker-punched. So I did everything I could to get rid of her."

"What made her finally decide to leave?"

"You mean other than my marriage proposal?"

Charles laughed. "So you scared her into it."

"I was serious," he said with a sigh. "All right, maybe I didn't use fancy words and tell her the angels smiled on her the day she was born and drivel like that, but I meant what I said." He paused as the regret sank in. "Maybe I could've been a bit more romantic, though."

"What'd you say to her?"

"Well—" Sawyer thought back to their conversation "—I don't exactly remember. We were at Ben's and there were a lot of people around, so I sort of stood next to her and said I didn't think it was a good idea for her to marry Pete or any of the other men who'd proposed."

"You mean to say she had more than one offer?"

"Yes." Sawyer's fingers threatened to dent the steering wheel. "Besides Pete, I think Ralph might've asked her, too."

"So you stood next to her at Ben's..."

"Right. We were welcoming Allison Reynolds, and basically I told Abbey that if she was so keen to get married she should've spoken up earlier because I was willing to marry her."

Charles was quiet for a long time. "That's it?" he eventually said.

Sawyer nodded.

"You didn't ask for my advice, but I'll give it to you, anyway. If I were you I'd propose again, and this time I'd use a few of those fancy words you frown on."

"I don't know if I can," Sawyer said sadly.

"Can you live with the alternative?" Charles asked.

"I don't know," he said. "I just don't know."

After dropping his brother off, Sawyer returned to his own place. He checked on Eagle Catcher, talking to the dog for a few minutes, then walked into the house. It felt empty and silent. He fixed a drink and took it into his bedroom, where he spent some time studying the photographs of his parents that stood on the dresser.

Tugging his shirttail free, he undressed and readied for bed. It was going to be a long night. Lying on his back, hands behind his head, he stared at the ceiling and tried to work out his options.

What he'd told his brother was true. When Abbey left Hard Luck she'd be taking part of him with her. He had to prove that to her. He just didn't know how.

He wasn't a man of words. He'd demonstrated that repeatedly; he'd made a mess of things whenever he opened his mouth. But there *had* to be a way to show Abbey he loved her.

He hardly slept at all.

By six he was up and dressed again. He sat at the kitchen table, nursing his coffee, devising a plan.

He waited until eight, then gathered together what he needed. He walked purposefully across the street to Abbey's.

He hadn't even reached the front door when she opened it. She wore a pretty pink sweater and jeans, and she'd never looked more beautiful.

"Good morning," she said. He noticed how pale she was. Pale and miserable. As miserable as he felt.

"Morning."

"I know you're busy getting ready to leave, so I won't take any more of your time than necessary. I brought something over for Scott and Susan," he said. "And you."

"The children are still sleeping."

"It doesn't matter. I'll give everything to you, and you can see that they get it later."

"Sawyer, I've been thinking and really there isn't any need—"

"Would it be all right if we sat down?" He motioned toward the swing.

Abbey sighed and perched on the swing's edge. Sawyer had the impression she'd rather avoid this last encounter. He didn't blame her.

They sat on opposite sides, as if they were uncomfortable strangers. He handed her an envelope. "These are Eagle Catcher's registration papers. I'm giving him to Scott—it'll make the transition easier. Once you're settled, let me know and I'll have him delivered."

"But he's *your* dog."

Sawyer's smile was sad. He wouldn't tell her that relinquishing the husky was more difficult than she'd ever know. "Those two belong together."

"But Sawyer—"

"Please, Abbey, let me do this one thing."

She looked as though she wanted to argue, then bit her lower lip and nodded.

"Susan is a wonderful little girl," Sawyer said. "I thought long and hard about what I could give her." He reached inside his shirt pocket and withdrew a gold, heart-shaped pendant. "This is a locket that belonged to my grandmother." He opened the tiny clasp with difficulty. "The picture inside is of Emily, the daughter she lost. She gave it to me shortly before she died. I'd like you to keep it until Susan's old enough to wear it."

Tears welled in Abbey's eyes as he placed the locket and its delicate chain in the palm of her hand. "Sawyer, I...I don't know what to say."

Sawyer's heart was heavy. "I have no other way of showing you how much I love you and Scott and Susan." He stood and took out an envelope from his pants pocket. It contained two marbles, a bobby pin and several folded sheets of paper. He sat down, then retrieved a second envelope from his shirt pocket.

"The last things I have are for you." He gave her the bobby pin first. "This saved my life when I was sixteen. It's a long, complicated story that I won't go into, but I was flying alone in the dead of winter and I had engine trouble. Had to make an emergency landing. This bobby pin was on the floor of the plane, and it helped me fix the problem so I could get back in the air and home. Otherwise I would've frozen to death. I saved the pin." He set it carefully aside.

Abbey smiled.

"The marbles were my two favorites as a kid. I was better than anyone, and these were the prize of my collection. Mom ordered them for me from a Sears catalog."

Abbey held the two marbles in her free hand.

He passed her the folded sheets of paper. "These are old and a bit yellowed, but you should still be able to read them. The first is an essay I wrote when I was in junior high. I won a writing contest with it and got a letter of commendation from the governor. His letter's with the story."

Abbey used the back of her hand to wipe the tears from her face.

Sawyer withdrew a plain gold band from the second envelope. "This is my father's wedding ring." Sawyer held it up between two fingers. His heart seized with pride and pain at the sight of it. "Since I was the one with Dad when he died, Charles and Christian thought I should have it. It's probably not worth much, but I treasure it." He leaned forward to place the ring in Abbey's hand and closed her fingers over it. Afraid he might have said more than he should, he stood up and awkwardly shoved his hands in his pockets. "Goodbye, Abbey."

As he turned to leave, she called to him. "Sawyer."

He faced her.

"Why are you giving me these things?"

"The bobby pin and marbles and the essay and Dad's ring—they represent what I am. I can't go with you and I can't make you stay, so I'm giving you part of me to take when you leave."

He was halfway down the steps when he heard her whisper. "You might have said you loved me earlier."

He kept his back to her and answered. "I want to marry you. A man doesn't propose to a woman unless he loves her."

"He does if he's afraid some other man might beat him to the punch. He does if he's confused about what he really wants."

"I know what I want," Sawyer said, turning, and his eyes met hers.

"Do you, Sawyer?"

"I want to spend the rest of my life with you, right here in Hard Luck. I want to raise Scott and Susan as my own children, and if you and God are willing, I'd like another child or two."

They stood staring at each other, the depth of their emotion visible. Abbey's beautiful brown eyes glistened with tears. It demanded every bit of self-control Sawyer possessed not to bridge the distance between them and take her in his arms.

"But I can't have that," he said, "so I'm giving you the most valuable things I own to do with as you please." Having said that, he hurried down the remaining steps.

"If you walk away from me now, Sawyer O'Halloran, I swear I'll never forgive you."

He turned around again to find her standing on the top step, her arms open. The sweetest smile he'd ever seen lit her eyes, curved her mouth.

His heart came to a sudden standstill. Then he rushed back, throwing his arms around her waist, pulling her tight against him. He trembled with the shock of it. He kissed her gently at first, for fear of frightening her with the power of his need.

Abbey slipped her arms around his neck and moaned. A stronger, more disciplined man might have been able to resist her, but not Sawyer. Not when he feared he'd never hold her and kiss her again. Not when he'd laid his heart and his life at her feet.

They kissed once more, too hungry for each other to attempt restraint. It was as if all the barriers had disappeared.

When he could, Sawyer pulled his mouth from hers, inhaled deeply and buried his face in her neck. He prayed for the strength to stop; otherwise, he was afraid he'd end up making love to her right then and there. But Abbey drew his face to hers, and the kissing began all over again.

"I think you should marry me," he breathed between kisses.

"A woman prefers to be asked, Sawyer O'Halloran."

"Please, Abbey, if you have any feelings for me whatsoever, put me out of this misery and marry me."

"Are you asking me or telling me?"

"Begging."

He felt the rush of air from Abbey's laugh before she kissed him. A kiss that was deep, passionate, thorough.

"Is that your answer?" he panted when she'd finished.

"Yes. But first you need to understand something. I'm not very good at this wife thing. I've got one failure behind me, and... Oh, Sawyer, I'm scared."

"Of what? Making another mistake?"

"No, not that. Not with you. I'm afraid...of so many things. Dick had several affairs, and when we divorced, he said...he said I'd never make a man happy."

"You make me happy. Did I ever tell you how much I love it when you smile?"

Abbey blushed. "I don't mean it like that. I don't know if I'll...satisfy you."

Sawyer threw back his head and laughed. "Oh, Abbey, just holding you gives me so much pleasure I can't even begin to imagine what it's going to be like in bed."

Sawyer could see that she was about to argue with him, so he guided her mouth to his and kissed her with all the love in his heart. He tasted her hesitation and her anxiety, then felt her yield to his kiss.

For the first time Sawyer understood the root of Abbey's fears. "You satisfy me," he whispered. "And tantalize me and torment me."

"Mom?"

Sawyer looked past Abbey to see Scott and Susan in the doorway. They were both still in their pajamas, their faces eager and wide-awake.

"Good morning," Sawyer said. "I've got some great news for you."

"You do?" Susan asked.

"Your mother's agreed to marry me."

Scott seemed mildly puzzled. "Already? Mom, I thought you said it would take a while to work everything out. The problems between you and Sawyer, I mean."

"Work out our problems?" Sawyer was the one wearing the perplexed frown this time.

"The children and I talked after you found them last night," Abbey explained. "We decided it would be a mistake to leave Hard Luck. Furthermore, we decided we're in love with you."

"You mean you weren't going to leave this morning?"

Abbey's arms tightened around him. "Don't sound so disappointed."

"I'm not. It's just that…" He stiffened. "You might have told me."

"I tried, but you wouldn't let me. Are you sorry about…what you said? The things you gave me?"

"No," he said fervently. "Not in the least."

"Are you really going to marry us?" Susan wanted to know.

"Yup."

"When?" This was from Scott, who continued to look unsure.

Sawyer and Abbey exchanged a glance. "Two weeks," Sawyer said, making the decision for them.

"Two weeks!" Abbey cried.

"I've been waiting thirty-three years for you, Abbey Sutherland, and I refuse to wait a minute longer than I have to. We'll do this as plain or as fancy as you want. Ben can cater the wedding, and we'll open up the school gym for the reception."

A truck pulled up in front of the house and the driver honked. "Looks like you two have everything settled," Charles called, leaning his elbow out the window.

"Sure do."

"Guess you won't be needing me, then."

"Sawyer's going to marry Mom and us," Susan informed him with her wide, delightful grin.

"In two weeks," Scott added.

"So you're not letting any grass grow under your feet," Charles commented.

"Nope," Sawyer said.

"Is this a secret or can I spread the word?" Charles asked.

Abbey and Sawyer looked at each other and smiled. "Feel free," Sawyer told him.

Charles pounded the horn and stuck his head out the window as he drove down the street, shouting, "There's going to be a wedding in Hard Luck!"

"You can't change your mind now, Sawyer."

"No chance of that," he whispered. "No chance at all."

* * * * *

THE MARRIAGE RISK

Chapter
1

July 1995

So this was Hard Luck.

Lanni Caldwell slung her backpack over her shoulders, picked up her suitcase and crossed the gravel road that ran past the mobile office for Midnight Sons. The small airline—which served the Alaskan interior—had been mentioned in the news several times during the past month. Her curiosity piqued, Lanni had read the Anchorage paper eagerly and watched the television reporters tell their tale. And what a tale it was. Midnight Sons had apparently spearheaded a campaign to attract women to Hard Luck with offers of jobs and housing.

Leave it to a bunch of lonely bush pilots to come up with such a crazy scheme! A number of single women had already arrived, and more would soon be joining them. TV reporters from down south were calling them "mail-order brides"—they weren't—and referring to Hard Luck as "the frozen north." It wasn't, at least not in July.

The sun shone bright and golden in a clear blue sky. The weather was in the comfortable seventies, with wildflowers blooming in a lively array of colors that stretched from one end of the tundra to the other.

Lanni, who'd grown up in Anchorage, had only been north of the Arctic Circle once before on a childhood visit to Hard Luck. But this all seemed familiar because her grandmother, Catherine Fletcher, had often spoken of the town and her life here. Lanni could remember sitting on Grammy's knee as a child and listening to wondrous descriptions and exciting adventures, but those times with her grandmother had been few. Catherine's visits had come less and less often as the years went on.

With Catherine's failing health, this might well be Lanni's last chance to learn about her grandmother's early life. It was the reason she'd agreed to spend her summer in Hard Luck. Beginning in September, she would become an intern at the Anchorage daily paper. After four years in college, her dream of working as a journalist was about to be realized. Lanni knew how fortunate she was to be chosen for the coveted position, and she was thrilled with the opportunity.

Her visit to Hard Luck had been prompted by a call from Sawyer O'Halloran to her mother, Kate, the month before. Kate had been surprised to hear from one of the O'Hallorans, and even a bit annoyed. Lanni only vaguely understood why. She was aware of bad blood between her grandmother and the

O'Hallorans, but she'd never really heard the reasons. It was something the family simply didn't talk about.

Sawyer O'Halloran had politely explained that with so many women moving into town, Hard Luck was in desperate need of housing. Catherine's home sat vacant, and Sawyer had asked if Kate would talk to her about renting it out.

Lanni wasn't sure her mother had discussed the situation with Grammy. But Catherine Fletcher's health had worsened since her move to the nursing home in Anchorage, so perhaps it was best that she hadn't been consulted.

"Hi." A young, freckle-faced boy smiled at her from his bicycle. A large, blue-eyed husky trotted along at his side. They both came to a halt and the dog's gaze quickly assessed Lanni as a friend. He sat on his haunches, panting.

"Are you here for the wedding?" the boy asked.

"The wedding?" Lanni echoed.

"Yeah, my mom's marrying Sawyer O'Halloran. Lots of people are coming to Hard Luck for the wedding. Ben's making his special sweet-and-sour meatballs and everything. He said he'd let me and Susan roll some, too."

"Ben?"

"Yeah, he owns the Hard Luck Café. You're not a reporter or anything, are you?"

"No."

"It's a good thing, 'cause Sawyer said he wanted to kick their butts."

Lanni laughed. This obviously wasn't the time to announce that she was a journalism graduate. "I'm Lanni Caldwell."

"Scott Sutherland," he said, and grinned broadly, revealing

front teeth too big for his mouth. "I bet you're the woman Sawyer's waiting for. He's been kind of frazzled lately."

No one had told Lanni she needed to check in with the O'Hallorans, but it couldn't hurt to introduce herself. After all, they were responsible for her being in town. She had reason to thank them, too. This summer was her one chance to explore some of the questions left unanswered by her family's official version of the past. There was so much she didn't know about Grammy, so many secrets, so many memories too painful to share. In many ways Lanni felt cheated out of part of her heritage, and it was because of this grandmother she barely knew.

"You want me to take you to meet Sawyer?" Scott asked.

"Sure." Lanni shifted her backpack and followed the boy to the mobile structure with *Midnight Sons* scrawled in bold red paint across the side.

"Sawyer," Scott called as he threw open the door. The dog followed him inside. "Lanni Caldwell's here."

The man behind the desk looked up with a sigh of relief. "Thank heaven. Christian didn't think you'd get here until after the wedding. You couldn't have picked a better time to show up."

It was clear to Lanni, if to no one else, that Sawyer O'Halloran had her confused with another person. Maybe he hadn't heard her surname.

"Listen," he went on, "I have to get to a school-board meeting. I know it's a bit of a rush asking you to take over like this, but I can't very well sit here answering the phones when I'm supposed to chair a meeting at the school."

"Uh..." Lanni hedged, wondering what she should do. Sawyer seemed to think she was a secretary.

"If you have any questions, just write them down. I'll be back in an hour or two."

She opened her mouth to explain the mix-up when Sawyer bolted out the door. "I really appreciate this," he said as he flew past her.

"See what I mean?" Scott commented, flopping down in the chair Sawyer had vacated. "You'd think he was gonna have a baby or something. Mom says she's never seen anything like it."

Lanni slipped the backpack from her shoulders and put it next to her suitcase. "Unfortunately he didn't give me a chance to tell him I'm not a secretary."

"You're not?"

Lanni shook her head.

"You sure you don't have anything to do with those newspapers that've been bugging him?"

"I'm sure."

Scott relaxed visibly. "Why are you here then? Did Christian send you?"

"No. I'm here to clean out my grandmother's home so one or two of the women will have someplace to live."

"Christian didn't hire you?" This information obviously surprised the boy and he sat up straight. "I bet Charles didn't, either. He doesn't seem to think much of Sawyer and Christian's idea. He even offered to pay for my mom, my sister and me to fly back to Seattle. We almost did it, too, but Susan and I didn't want to go. Now," he said, and his face brightened, "Mom and Sawyer are getting married."

"You sound pleased about that."

"You bet. Sawyer's neat. I never said anything to Mom, but I sorta missed having a dad. Sawyer's going to adopt me and Susan, and we're gonna be a real family."

"That's wonderful."

The phone rang then. Lanni stared at it.

"Just answer 'Midnight Sons,'" Scott told her, "and take a message."

Lanni reached for the receiver and did as Scott suggested.

"Sawyer won't be gone long," Scott said confidently when she'd finished writing down the caller's information. "He'll probably end the meeting early." Scott clasped his hands behind his head, his thin elbows jutting out awkwardly. "He's real nervous about the wedding. Maybe he'll faint right in front of the whole town before he can say *I do*." The image appeared to amuse Scott.

Lanni sat down at the desk across from the boy. "How many women have come to Hard Luck so far?" she asked.

"Not sure. A bunch, I guess. My mom was the first, though. Then there was this real pretty lady, but she didn't stay long. Everyone said she wouldn't, and they were right. Christian was really sad when he found out she left. That was when he went through all the applications again and hired another secretary. We thought you were her."

"That's an easy mistake."

"Dotty got here last week. She's living with Mrs. Inman right now and learning all about running the health clinic. She's not young and pretty like my mom and you, but everyone's happy she moved here. Mrs. Inman wants to go live with her daughter.

She couldn't before because the town needed her to run the clinic."

"Well, I'm glad she can go to her daughter's now."

"If you want, I'll show you around later," Scott volunteered.

"Thanks." It would help to have someone escort her about town. Lanni had been too young to remember that visit to Hard Luck more than twenty years ago. It was much easier for Grammy to fly into Anchorage than for everyone else to make the long trek to Hard Luck. Besides, Kate Caldwell had never been close to her mother, and the years had only served to widen that gap.

"Oh, this is Eagle Catcher," Scott said, petting the husky's neck. "He was Sawyer's dog, but then Sawyer gave him to me. I've got the papers and everything."

"He's a beautiful dog."

"He likes you, too, and he doesn't like just anyone."

"I'm honored." Lanni ran her hand along the dog's thick coat. Before she could say anything further, the phone rang again. From that point on, her conversation with Scott was intermittent as she dealt with a variety of calls.

True to his word, Sawyer returned to the office an hour later. "I'm sorry to leave you like that," he muttered, reading through his messages.

"Oh, it wasn't any problem," Lanni said breezily.

"Lanni isn't the new secretary," Scott announced, leaping out of Sawyer's chair.

Sawyer's expression went blank. "You're not?"

Lanni grinned, extending her hand. "I'm Lanni Caldwell. Catherine Fletcher's my grandmother." It might have been her imagination, but it seemed to Lanni that Sawyer's eyes hardened for an instant.

"I see."

"I've come to clean out the house."

"You mean Catherine's actually agreed to let us rent the place?"

"To be honest, I don't think my mother discussed it with her. My grandmother's in very poor health."

"I'm...sorry to hear it."

Lanni wondered if that was true. The bad feelings between the two families clearly existed on both sides. Lanni wished she understood what had happened, and why. "I'd be willing to help out until your new secretary arrives," she offered, surprising herself. Someone needed to build a bridge of friendship, and she supposed it might as well be her.

"You'd do that?" Sawyer eyed her speculatively, as if he wasn't sure he should trust her.

"I'd be happy to help out in any way I can," Lanni said with certainty. She had the impression that she'd learn more about her grandmother working with the O'Halloran brothers than she ever would sorting through Grammy's things.

"It'd only be now and then," Sawyer said hesitantly. "Until things settle down."

"Mom and Sawyer will be married in ten days," Scott piped in. "Not that I'm counting or anything."

"Then it's a deal." People said Lanni could charm a snake when she smiled, and she'd always considered her mouth her most attractive feature. It was full and classically shaped and expressive. Her teeth were even and white.

"You're sure you won't mind?" Sawyer asked, raking his fingers through his hair. "With Christian away, I'm shorthanded, and then the wedding... To top everything off, the school board needs to hire a new teacher."

"I'm happy to lend a hand," Lanni assured him again. "Really."

"It won't be for long. Christian'll be back soon. He's still in Seattle, but he'll be heading for British Columbia to visit our mother."

"If he isn't back soon," Scott added, "Sawyer said he was gonna throttle his scrawny neck."

Lanni laughed.

"Do you want me to carry your suitcase?" the boy asked.

"It's pretty heavy," Lanni cautioned.

"I may be skinny," Scott said with mock defiance, "but I'm strong."

"Uh, Lanni, would it be possible for you to come in to-morrow?" Sawyer's voice was casual, but she heard the eagerness behind it.

"What time would you like me?" she asked as she slid her arms into the backpack straps.

"Is eight too early?"

"Not at all. See you then."

"Thanks," he said, and he still seemed astonished by her willingness to assist him. "I mean that."

Charles O'Halloran stepped into the Midnight Sons office and glared at his brother. Not that it did any good. Sawyer had been in a world of his own from the moment Abbey Sutherland agreed to marry him.

Sawyer getting married.

Charles still had difficulty believing that his levelheaded brother was leaping into the abyss.

Charles had long accepted that Christian would probably marry someday, but not Sawyer. *Definitely* not Sawyer. Charles and Sawyer had both seen what could happen to two decent people when a marriage soured. They knew firsthand how the heartache spilled over into the lives of every family member. Charles wanted no part of that. He'd assumed Sawyer felt the same way.

From the moment he was old enough to leave home, Charles had struck out on his own. Following his high school graduation, he'd enlisted in the marines. Afterward he'd gone on to college, obtaining a degree in geology. Now he was a surveyor for Alaska Oil—the perfect job for him. He was often gone for weeks at a time, searching for natural gas deposits in the Alaskan interior.

"I talked with two reporters this afternoon," Charles muttered, making no effort to conceal his disgust. Not that he expected Sawyer to pay him any heed. His brother's head was so high in the clouds these days Charles suspected he was suffering from oxygen deprivation. That must be what had affected his thinking lately.

Sawyer stared at him blankly.

"They wanted to know about the women."

"There're only a few here," Sawyer said flatly, "and one of them is in her fifties."

"Yes, but the first one's getting married—practically before she had time to unpack her suitcase." It wasn't that Charles begrudged Sawyer his happiness. What bothered him was, first, his distrust of the institution of marriage and, second, the fact that the town his grandparents had built was being turned into a national laughingstock.

"Did you tell them to take a flying leap into the nearest moose pile?"

Charles grinned despite his surly mood. "No, but I should've. What I did was give them the number of the hotel where Christian's staying."

Sawyer nodded approvingly.

"I don't want you to get the wrong idea," Charles said, claiming a chair. "But frankly I don't think it was so smart to bring women to Hard Luck. The tabloids are having a field day with this. I read a headline this morning that was downright insulting."

"I don't care. I don't have a single regret."

Given Sawyer's present state of mind, Charles would've been shocked had he admitted to anything else.

"You're going to fall in love yourself one day," Sawyer said, eyeing him closely, "and then you'll know what I mean."

"God save me." Charles had managed to reach the age of thirty-five without getting snagged, and he planned to continue the trend.

"Someday you're going to meet someone you'll really fall for," Sawyer said thoughtfully. "And I mean hard."

Charles laughed. "Not me."

Sawyer arched his brows. "Sounds like you're tempting fate."

"Listen, I'm happy for you, Sawyer. You're obviously in love with Abbey and her kids, and I think that's wonderful—for you."

"But…"

"But I still don't condone what you and Christian did. It's a mistake to bring women to Hard Luck."

"Really?"

"Look at all the commotion caused by the ones who've already arrived. Just wait'll the day of the wedding. I bet you anything there'll be six or seven reporters here."

"Let 'em come," Sawyer said, seemingly unconcerned. "Inquiring minds want to know, and I say let 'em."

"You've got to be joking." Charles couldn't believe what he was hearing.

"I've got more important things on my mind." Sawyer riffled through the papers on his desk and pulled out a packet of airline tickets. He kissed it, an expression of ecstasy on his face. "Two weeks in Hawaii—with my wife," he said, closing his eyes. "I can't imagine anything closer to heaven."

"What about the kids?"

Sawyer grinned. "Abbey's parents are taking them to Disneyland. Later Abbey and I will meet them there and we'll fly home together."

Charles couldn't really respond to his brother's enthusiasm for Hawaii. He'd seen all he wanted of the outside world. Nothing held the lure or the beauty he'd found in Alaska.

He'd let others do the traveling. There wasn't anything he wanted that he couldn't find right here in Hard Luck. Their father and grandfather had felt the same way. Even when it might've saved his marriage, David O'Halloran hadn't been willing to move. As far as Charles was concerned, his father had made the only decision he could.

He realized how cold and hard his feelings might seem. It wasn't that he didn't love his mother. He felt very protective of Ellen. He cared more than words could express for both of his parents. He missed David still, with a grief that hadn't diminished in the years since his death. But he'd understood his father far better than he ever would his delicate English mother.

"You look like you're deep in thought," Sawyer said, breaking into his musings.

"Not really," Charles muttered, not wanting to continue the discussion with his younger brother. He stood abruptly. "I just came by to tell you I've spent my day fending off the press."

"I appreciate it."

"But you should know that nothing's going to stop them from crashing your wedding."

Sawyer shrugged. "Then so be it."

If he lived to a hundred, Charles would never truly understand the changes he'd seen in his brother the past few weeks.

Stepping out of the trailer, Charles walked over to the Hard Luck Café, where Ben Hamilton served the freshest cup of coffee in town.

Charles slid onto a bar stool and turned the mug right side up.

Ben, who'd been a longtime friend and confidant, reached for the coffeepot. "Looks like you could use this."

"I could. Tell me something. Has everyone in town gone along with this crazy idea?"

"What are you talking about?"

"Bringing in women, what else? I'm in Valdez minding my

own business, having a pretty decent day. Then I open the paper, and lo and behold there's a picture of Sawyer—and another one of Christian. My brothers! There's this article about some idiotic scheme of theirs—enticing women to move to Hard Luck."

"I've heard there are women in Anchorage who're upset Christian didn't take applications there."

"You've got to be kidding!"

"Nope. That's what I heard," Ben said, leaning against the counter. "You want anything with that coffee?"

Charles shook his head, befuddled that the one person he'd expected to get a straight answer from was as caught up in this craziness as everyone else.

"Don't worry about it," Ben said. "It isn't as bad as it seems." The retired navy man—currently chief cook and bottle washer—returned to the kitchen, leaving Charles to his discontent.

"By the way, did you see her?" Ben called out unexpectedly.

"See who?"

"The new gal in town. Pretty as a bug's ear. She's got long blond hair and a real cute nose. Young, though. Couldn't be more than twenty-two, twenty-three. Duke flew her in earlier. Scott took her over to the office. Looks like she's the new secretary Christian hired. I wish we'd known she was coming. I would've baked a cake to welcome her. Seems all this town can talk about these days is Sawyer and Abbey's wedding." He paused, rubbing the side of his jaw. "Fact is, I can't remember the last time there was a wedding here. Can you?"

"No," Charles barked and slid off the stool. No matter where he went, he couldn't escape it. Even Ben had lost his grip on the real world. It was as if every male within a two-hundred-mile radius couldn't think about anything other than romance. They were all waiting for love to strike—but they didn't realize how undignified they'd look with Cupid's arrow sticking out of their rear ends!

"So you haven't met her?"

"No," Charles answered.

"Do you know where she's staying, then?"

"Haven't got a clue."

Ben frowned. "I hope someone showed her around. I'd hate for her to think we aren't hospitable."

In that case, Charles thought, he'd make a special point of staying away from this latest arrival.

Still grumbling, he left the café. He walked toward his house, intent on finding a moment's privacy, when he heard someone call his name.

"Charles, look!"

He turned to see nine-year-old Scott Sutherland pumping away on an old bicycle that had belonged to Sawyer. Behind him, standing with her suitcase in the dirt, was a blond woman. No doubt the one Ben had mentioned.

The wind whipped her long hair about her face. She wore a sleeveless, pale blue summer dress. The straw sun hat perched on her head, a bright yellow daisy attached to the front, suited her perfectly.

Eagle Catcher raced at Scott's side, barking.

Charles waved, fighting the urge to smile, and turned away.

"Wait up," Scott called. "You gotta meet Lanni."

Charles had no desire to be introduced to the latest instance of his brothers' folly. He buried his hands in his pockets and increased his pace.

"Uncle Charles!"

That got to him. He was about to become an uncle—and he hadn't even realized it. Scott would soon be his nephew. He liked Scott, so the thought appealed to him. He turned back.

"Hello," Lanni said, walking toward them.

"Hello." Ben was right. She *was* pretty. Her whole face seemed to sparkle. Her eyes were blue, their color enhanced by her dress. Her mouth was wide and expressive, curved in an expectant smile.

"Charles O'Halloran," he said, thrusting out his hand. The last thing he wanted was to be accused of staring.

She blinked once, then placed her hand in his. "Lanni Caldwell." She seemed to be waiting for him to say something more—yet she looked relieved when he didn't.

"It's nice to meet you, Charles."

"You, too." The full force of that smile was leveled on him. Charles frowned. He didn't like this sensation, whatever it was. Nor was he keen on making small talk with a stranger.

"Mom's having Lanni over for dinner tonight," Scott announced. "Do you wanna come?"

Did he? Charles couldn't believe he was actually considering the invitation. "Sorry, I've got other plans," he muttered, before he could find a reason to change his mind.

"Mrs. Inman and Dotty'll be there."

"Sorry," he said again. "I wish I could." Charles managed to look disappointed, or so he thought until he caught the twinkle in Lanni's eye. She knew. She could see straight through him.

"If you don't come, I think Mom'll invite Duke," Scott said, sounding disappointed. "She left a message on your answering machine and asked you to call her back. Where've you been all afternoon?"

"Busy." This didn't seem the moment to explain that he'd spent most of the day fighting off the news media. Aside from his instinctive urge to stay away from Lanni Caldwell, that had left him in no mood for a dinner party. "Another time," he said. "Uh, see you around, Lanni."

"Bye, Charles."

A couple of hours later, Charles regretted turning down the best invitation he'd had in weeks. What on earth was wrong with him?

Wanting to kick himself, he decided to eat at Ben's. He walked out of the house just in time to see Duke strolling toward Christian's house, where Abbey and the kids were temporarily living. The bush pilot's hair was slickly combed into place, and he wore a clean shirt. Even from this distance, Charles could smell the other man's aftershave. Duke must've doused himself from head to foot with spice- and rum-scented cologne.

Charles found himself glaring at Duke as they made their way down opposite sides of the street. He was angry with the pilot for no reason he could name.

Ben usually offered a decent meal, but Charles might've been eating sawdust for all the pleasure his spaghetti dinner gave him.

"You want another piece of garlic bread?" Ben asked.

"No, thanks."

"You don't seem to have much of an appetite this evening."

"I had a big lunch." It was a slight stretch of the truth.

"You interested in playing a little cribbage?" Ben asked.

Charles nodded. Wasting an hour or two with his old friend sounded a lot better than spending what remained of the evening alone, wondering what was going on at his brother's house.

Before long, the two men faced each other across one of the small tables. Neither said much. Conversation wasn't really necessary when they sat down to play. They'd done this often enough through the years.

"You thinking about opening the lodge?" Ben asked him out of the blue.

"The lodge? Why? What brings that up?" The lodge had once been the largest building in Hard Luck. It'd been filled with tourists eager to explore the Alaskan interior. His father had owned and operated the business, but that, like so much else, had died with him.

Later a fire had destroyed part of the building. Repairing it now would be a costly, time-consuming affair. He hadn't the heart for it. Apparently Sawyer and Christian didn't, either, because neither of them had said anything about getting the place fixed up.

"It'd be a good idea to open the lodge, wouldn't it?" Ben persisted, moving his peg forward after counting his cards. "All the women coming to town—they need a place to live. Those cabins might work in the summer, but you can't expect greenhorn women to last the winter there, can you?"

Charles wasn't even going to *think* about that. Where the

"imported" women lived wasn't his concern. "Why don't you ask Sawyer or Christian what they plan to do?"

Ben looked directly at him, his expression as serious as Charles had ever seen it. "I'm asking you."

"Then you're asking the wrong guy. It wasn't me who enticed those women to move north. According to Christian, these gals all knew what they were getting themselves into. Far be it from me to interfere with my brothers' schemes."

"If you say so," Ben muttered.

Charles lost the game on a fluke. He had good card sense, and it wasn't like him to make stupid mistakes. He left soon afterward.

He was walking home, staring down at the ground, and when he looked up, he saw Lanni Caldwell. He couldn't seem to take his eyes off her. She saw him, too, and her eyes rose to meet his. For an instant he was mesmerized by the warmth she exuded.

She smiled.

Without thinking, he smiled in return.

There was nothing coy in their exchange. Nothing flirtatious. She didn't blink or sweep her lashes downward or blush like a shy schoolgirl. He didn't bother to camouflage his interest.

Neither did she.

"Evening, Charles."

Duke Porter's voice caught him by surprise. For the first time he noticed that Lanni wasn't alone. Duke had been a few feet behind and had now drawn even with Lanni.

"Evening," Charles said gruffly, and moved on. He passed them and had taken two, possibly three, steps when he turned around.

At the same moment, Lanni cast a glance over her shoulder and turned, too.

Once more their eyes met.

Then, as if she felt the urgent need to escape, Lanni whirled around and hurried to catch up with Duke.

With his heart in his throat, Charles walked straight past his own house and continued until he reached Christian's. Sawyer stood on the front porch, wearing a cocky grin.

"All right," Charles said with ill grace. "Tell me about her."

Chapter
2

"Who am I supposed to tell you about?" Sawyer asked.

Charles hated the smug look on his brother's face. Sawyer was going to make him suffer before giving him the information he wanted.

"You know who I mean!" Charles snapped.

"You don't by any chance mean Lanni Caldwell, do you?"

"Yes," Charles said impatiently, "I do."

Striking a casual pose, Sawyer leaned against the porch railing and folded his arms. He was clearly enjoying this more than necessary. "What do you want to know?"

"First, what's she doing in Hard Luck?"

Sawyer seemed to consider the question. "For the moment she's working as my secretary."

Charles didn't question the "for the moment" part. "She's not staying in one of those dilapidated cabins, is she?"

"No. As a matter of fact, Catherine Fletcher has agreed to let us rent her house. Lanni's living there."

That was a relief. Those pitiful excuses for cabins hadn't been used in years. Charles knew that his brothers and their crew of bush pilots, as well as some of the townsfolk, had worked hard to clean them, but Charles didn't like the idea of Lanni— or anyone else—living in them. Furthermore, he didn't want Lanni sleeping outside town, away from everything and everyone, particularly on her first night. People seemed to conveniently forget there were dangers lurking about, especially to someone unfamiliar with life this far north.

"Are you saying you're...romantically interested in Lanni?" Sawyer asked in the smooth easy drawl he used when he knew he had the upper hand. "You don't realize..."

"Realize what?"

"Never mind." Sawyer had a smug look on his face—a look that meant he knew something his brother didn't. Charles refused to play his game.

"You're attracted to Lanni," Sawyer said now. "Remember what I told you about tempting the fates? I love it. I absolutely love it."

Charles gave a short, derisive laugh. "How could I be attracted to the woman? I don't even know her. I only want to make sure nothing happens to her. The one thing we don't need is more bad press."

"You weren't this concerned when you first met Abbey."

"Sure I was," Charles said defensively. "I offered her airfare home, didn't I? I was worried about her and the kids—the same way I'm worried about Lanni...whatever her name is."

Sawyer lowered his head in an unsuccessful attempt to hide a knowing grin. Charles hated to think his brother could read him that easily. Apparently his sudden interest in Lanni was as clear as glacial runoff.

"Lanni seems like a sweet kid," Charles added, trying to justify his concern. He feared, however, that he was only digging himself in deeper. "I don't want to see anything happen to her," he insisted. "That's all."

"She's not a kid, Charles. She's a woman."

Remembering the almost dizzying attraction he'd experienced moments earlier, Charles didn't need to be reminded of that.

"Do you think it's a good idea for Duke to be walking her home?" he asked a little anxiously.

Sawyer laughed outright. "She'll be fine."

Charles let his gaze follow the road to the point where he'd last seen Lanni. It wasn't *entirely* that he didn't trust Duke Porter. His main objection, he had to admit, was that Lanni was spending time with another man. And that wasn't even logical.

Something was wrong. Charles barely knew Lanni, and here he was, jealous because someone else had walked her home. He'd better leave before he made a complete fool of himself over a woman who was just a stranger. And too young for him, besides.

"See you in the morning," Charles told his brother abruptly. He stepped off the porch and made it all the way to the gate before Sawyer called him.

"There's more to Lanni Caldwell than meets the eye."

Charles said nothing, although he'd already decided the same thing for himself.

"She's intelligent and witty and has a wonderful heart."

"A wonderful heart" was an expression their grandmother had used. He'd almost forgotten it. Anna O'Halloran had a talent for seeing the good in others. She'd always described those who were generous and caring as having a wonderful heart. Perhaps that was what Charles had sensed when he'd met Lanni. Her wonderful heart.

"I wish you'd cancelled your plans and joined us for dinner," Sawyer added.

Sawyer wasn't the only one who regretted that decision. Charles nodded, which was all the admission he was willing to make. Once again he set out for his own place.

"Charles?"

Sighing, he turned back.

Sawyer was grinning again. "Are you going to offer Lanni Caldwell airfare home?"

Abbey Sutherland joined her husband-to-be on the front porch. He slipped his arm around her waist and bent down to kiss her. Even now, it didn't seem possible that she and Sawyer would be married in such a short time. They'd come so close to losing each other.

"Was that Charles I heard you talking to?" she asked.

Sawyer answered her with a distracted nod. "He met Lanni. He doesn't know she's related to Catherine. I should've told him, but I want my brother to see her for herself. I want him to judge her as the woman she is, rather than as a member of the family that brought so much pain to ours."

Abbey rested her cheek against his chest. "It's more than that, isn't it?"

He rubbed his hand down the length of Abbey's arm. "I like Lanni."

"Does that surprise you?"

"Yes," he said, "in a way it does."

"She's a lovely person."

"I know," Sawyer agreed quickly. "It's just that I find it hard to believe someone as *nice* as Lanni Caldwell could be related to Catherine Fletcher." Then, almost in afterthought, he said, "My diehard bachelor brother is attracted to her. He's having enough trouble admitting that. If he found out about Lanni's relationship to Catherine, his interest would shrivel up and die. I don't want that to happen. I have a feeling Lanni's the one for him. And she might just teach my arrogant brother a lesson or two."

Abbey grinned, raising her head to look into Sawyer's eyes. "Charles vulnerable to a woman—my, my. I can't imagine who *that* sounds like, can you?" she asked, her voice warm with teasing.

"As far as I'm concerned, falling in love could only do Charles good. But I wish..."

"You wish the woman was someone who isn't related to Catherine Fletcher."

"Exactly," Sawyer muttered.

Although it was past midnight, Lanni couldn't sleep. She would've blamed the light if she hadn't been born and raised in Anchorage. The midnight sun was nothing new to her.

Filled with nervous energy, she showered and changed into her favorite loose-fitting pajamas. After that, she brewed herself a small pot of tea. She moved into her grandmother's living room and sat on the couch with her legs folded beneath her, then took a tentative sip of the steaming tea. Across from her, on top of the ancient television, sat two framed photographs. High school graduation photos. One was of Matt, her older brother, and the other was of herself.

Seeing the photographs comforted Lanni. It made her feel less…guilty about moving into her grandmother's house. Less as if she were invading her privacy. Catherine had suffered a slight stroke several months earlier. She hadn't wanted to move into the Anchorage nursing facility and had always intended to return home to Hard Luck. Even now, she considered her stay in Anchorage temporary. Grammy didn't seem to realize she wasn't getting better. Perhaps that was a blessing.

Lanni glanced at the photograph again. Her grandmother loved her and Matt enough to display their pictures to anyone who came into her home. But that fact led to a hundred other questions. Why had Catherine never shown any real pride or interest in her grandchildren? Why had she hidden her feelings from them? Lanni found it incredibly sad that Catherine had such a difficult time showing affection. She knew her own mother had often felt cheated and hurt by the things Catherine had said and done. Yet Kate Caldwell had cared tenderly for her mother during the months after Catherine's stroke.

Not wanting to dwell on the problems confronting her mother and grandmother in Anchorage, Lanni studied her brother's youthful face. She was worried about him, especially since his divorce from Karen.

Lanni longed to shake some sense into both her brother and his ex-wife. She refused to believe that two people who loved each other so deeply would allow their marriage to fall apart.

But if she was going to blame anyone, it would be Matt. At thirty, he was five years older than Lanni—and about five years younger in attitude. Matt still hadn't made a decision about what he wanted to do with his life. Throughout his marriage, he'd drifted from one area of interest to another, uprooting Karen every time. He'd tried his hand at accounting, commercial fishing, and perhaps most interesting, he'd attended cooking school.

Six months into each venture, just when Karen had readjusted her life, Matt decided this new interest wasn't what he wanted, after all.

Lanni didn't think her brother was irresponsible or reckless, but his driving need for change and his general dissatisfaction with life had led to the breakup of his marriage.

Lanni forced her thoughts away from Matt. It was after midnight—she should be asleep. Her day had started in the wee hours of the previous morning, and she was exhausted.

Suddenly, the image of Charles O'Halloran's face entered her mind. Their meeting on the road that evening had been the oddest thing. Attraction—an attraction unlike any she'd ever experienced—had charged the air between them.

Somehow Lanni had known what Charles was feeling, because she'd felt the same bewildering sensations herself.

Had she not been with Duke, Lanni feared she would have closed the distance that separated them and walked straight into Charles's arms.

He would have welcomed her, too. Of that Lanni was certain.

Perhaps it was the lure of the forbidden. The grass-is-greener syndrome. Wanting what you know you can't have. Lanni wished she'd paid more attention in her psychology classes.

Charles was an O'Halloran. An enemy of the Fletchers—
except that Lanni didn't know the reasons for their enmity.
Perhaps she was doing something terribly disloyal by dining
with members of his family.

But Charles hadn't been there for dinner.

Technically Sawyer hadn't invited her, either. It was Abbey
who'd insisted she come. Over the meal and the conversation
that followed, no mention was made of the problems between
the O'Hallorans and the Fletchers.

She would phone her mother, Lanni decided, and this time
she'd insist on some answers. She had a right to know. A right
to make her own decisions and choices.

It didn't help that she was so strongly attracted to Charles
O'Halloran. She didn't understand why, but she felt what she
could only describe as a sense of destiny, of fate, when she was
near him—and that was something she wasn't even sure she
believed in!

Lanni stayed awake until her head felt heavy and her eyelids
stung. She slipped between the clean sheets and cradled the
thick feather pillow. Closing her eyes, she walked mentally
through each room of the house. It should take a couple of
weeks to pack everything and arrange to have it delivered to
Anchorage. She planned to start with Catherine's bedroom.
Perhaps she'd find something there that would help her figure
out why the O'Hallorans so adamantly disliked her family...and
why her family felt the same way.

Charles spent the first part of his morning on the phone trying
to keep busy. He didn't want to think about his brothers' new

secretary. Yet time and again his mind wandered down to the mobile office next to the runway. Lanni was bound to stir up interest among the pilots. His jaw tensed at the thought that John, Ralph, Duke and the rest would be falling all over each other in an effort to impress her.

He could picture them gathering around her desk, disturbing her while she worked. They'd be telling her stories and making her laugh, and generally acting like fools.

Well, Charles wasn't going to join them. *He* wasn't willing to play the fool over a woman, no matter who she was. At least that was what he repeatedly told himself.

By ten o'clock he'd had a change of heart. He left his house and headed briskly down the road.

"Morning," Pete Livengood, the proprietor of the grocery store, called out as he walked past.

"Morning," Charles returned, wondering if Pete had heard about Lanni's arrival. From Sawyer's stories, he knew that Pete had taken an instant liking to Abbey and proposed almost within the first five minutes of meeting her. He smiled at the memory of Sawyer's outrage over their friend's interest.

Then Charles thought of Lanni and wondered if the old coot had proposed marriage—or anything else—to her. Involuntarily his hands tightened into fists.

The green-eyed monster had struck again, Charles realized. And this time *he* was the victim.

As he stepped up to the mobile, he felt his heart kick into high gear. He didn't have much of an excuse for stopping by. Although he was a partner in the air service with Sawyer and Christian, his role wasn't an active one. They rarely consulted him on business decisions—and they sure hadn't consulted him before embarking on this latest scheme!

He went into the office to discover Lanni sitting behind a desk typing. Her long hair was pulled back from her face, fastened with a clip at the base of her neck. Her eyes widened when she saw him and her hands froze over the keyboard.

"Hello again," he said, attempting to look as though he had an important reason for being there. "Is Sawyer around?"

"He took a flight this morning. One of the pilots—John, I think he said his name is—came down with the flu. Sawyer said he'd be back around one."

Charles immediately wondered if John's flu had been a way to get Sawyer out of the office so he could spend time with Lanni. John Henderson had made a point of letting Charles know where he stood on the issue of bringing women to Hard Luck. Either women came to live here or he was moving on to another air service.

This was a familiar complaint among the pilots, especially in the bleak, dark months of winter. Charles didn't understand why Christian and Sawyer had given in to what amounted to blackmail, but then, he reminded himself, he wasn't making the decisions. Obviously.

"Is there anything you'd like me to tell Sawyer?" Lanni asked, picking up a pad and pen. For the life of him, Charles couldn't come up with a single thing to say to his brother.

"I'll talk to him later," he said on a decisive note. "Thanks, anyway."

"I'll leave a message for Sawyer that you stopped by."

Charles shoved his hands into his pockets. "Great."

He hesitated. His heart seemed to be leaping and dancing inside his chest. "I don't suppose you've ever gone panning for gold, have you?"

Her eyes revealed her interest. "No. No, I haven't."

"My grandfather's claim is still active, and I was thinking I'd take a trip up there this afternoon. I was wondering if you'd, uh, like to come along and see how it's done, that is, of course, if, uh—"

She nodded even before he'd finished. "I'd love to. What time are you leaving?"

Charles had to think fast. "Any time is fine. Whenever you can get away from here, just let me know."

"I'll ask Sawyer as soon as he's back."

"Good," he said, doing his best to hide his delight. "Give me a call when you're ready."

Charles thought her smile could melt ice. "Thank you for asking me, Charles."

Thank you for asking me. Charles hardly dared to believe she'd actually agreed. It was all he could do to keep from clicking his heels as he walked out of the office.

Whatever it was, he had it bad. *Real* bad.

Charles hurried to the house and gathered together his supplies. Within half an hour he'd loaded the back of his pickup. Now all he had to do was wait for Lanni's call.

"Where are you going?" Scott asked as he rode up on his bicycle.

"To the gold claim my grandfather used to mine," Charles explained. He placed a second shovel in the bed of his truck. There were probably any number of shovels at the site, but he wanted to be sure. He'd also packed things that had nothing to do with gold mining: a bottle of wine, a loaf of sourdough bread and a hunk of cheddar cheese.

"Can I come?"

"Another time, Scott," Charles replied absently, checking to see if he'd forgotten anything.

"Promise?"

"Promise," Charles said, smiling. "We'll bring your sister, too."

"No girls," Scott protested. "Why do women have to ruin everything?"

A day earlier, Charles would have agreed with him, but not now. In an hour or two, Lanni would be joining him, and frankly nothing could have pleased Charles more.

"Susan wants to ride my bike," Scott complained. "I don't want her to, 'cause if I let her and she learns how, she'll want it all the time." He glanced over his shoulder and groaned. "Here she comes now."

The little girl raced toward Scott. "You said I could ride your bike," she said in an accusing voice, as if daring her older brother to refuse her.

"You don't know how," Scott muttered.

"Everyone has to learn sometime. Mom said you had to let me, remember?"

"All right, all right," Scott muttered, climbing off with a decided lack of enthusiasm. He cast Charles a forlorn look as he handed over the bike.

"Besides, I know how to ride a bike," Susan said righteously. "A little, anyway."

"The seat's too high and you can't reach the pedals and—"

"I can too reach the pedals."

The argument sounded like one that had been repeated often. Charles grinned as he watched the brother and sister engage in verbal battle. It didn't seem all that many years ago that he and Sawyer had fought over whose turn it was to ride the bike. Their parents had settled the issue by buying Sawyer his own bike for Christmas. The very one Scott had reluctantly passed over to his sister.

The boy climbed onto the back of Charles's truck and sat on the tailgate. "I don't want to watch," he said. "She's probably going to wreck the best bike I ever had, and all because she's a girl."

"Be patient," Charles advised the boy. "The harder you resist, the more attractive the bike will be to her. Women always want what they can't have."

"What about men?"

"Well, we're the same—but not as bad." Then, in afterthought, he added, "Don't tell your mother I said that. She might not understand. Okay?" He didn't want a war with his soon-to-be sister-in-law.

"Okay," Scott whispered.

With Charles's help, Susan climbed onto the bicycle. Her toes barely reached the pedals, even after Charles had lowered the seat as far as it would go. She looked up and beamed him a radiant smile of triumph.

"Thanks, Uncle Charles."

Being called uncle would take some getting used to, but as Charles had realized the day before, he rather liked it.

"I'll walk beside you until you get going," Charles said.

Scott got to his feet. "Just make sure she doesn't crash!" he shouted.

Susan started peddling, and the bike wobbled precariously from side to side. Charles trotted along beside her until she found her balance, then he stopped and waited for Susan to ride away on her own.

"She's doing all right," Scott mumbled, "for a girl."

"She's doing great." Charles felt a surge of pride as if he alone was responsible for Susan's success. He continued to watch as the seven-year-old turned the bike around and rode back.

"She shouldn't get so close to the side of the road," Scott warned. "There's all kinds of rocks there."

Charles was about to call out a warning when Susan made the unpleasant discovery for herself. The bicycle wobbled, then crashed into the bushes. Almost immediately they heard her howl of pain.

Scott leapt out of the truck and darted down the road toward his sister, with Charles following. When they reached Susan, Charles carefully pulled the bike away and handed it to Scott, who inspected the wheel to make sure it wasn't bent.

"Are you okay?" Charles asked as he gently helped her stand up. Tears streaked her face, and her shoulders jerked as she struggled to hold in her sobs.

Susan sat by the side of the road and twisted her arm so she could look at her elbow. "Here," she said, showing him the scraped skin. "Here, too." She pushed up the leg of her pants to examine her knee.

"You'd better let me wash that off and put on some disinfectant."

"It's not the kind that stings, is it?" Scott asked, sounding concerned. He stood over Charles and studied his sister's injuries.

"No," Charles said. "It isn't the kind that stings."

He carried Susan back and sat her on the tailgate, then hurried into the house for the necessary first-aid supplies. Although she didn't really need them, he brought out a couple of Band-Aids.

The little girl grimaced as he cleaned the scrapes. She gritted her teeth when he sprayed on the disinfectant. Then she released a slow smile and announced, "It didn't hurt."

"I told you it wouldn't," Charles said with an answering smile. He carefully placed the two small adhesive strips on her knee and elbow, then helped her down.

Before Susan's feet touched the ground, she wrapped her arms around his neck and hugged him tight. "Thank you, Uncle Charles." With that, she was off like a shot, running toward the library. Scott hopped on his bike and rode after her, with a wave and a "See you later" for Charles.

Watching them go, Charles felt his heart constrict. Sawyer was a lucky man, he thought. Not only had he fallen in love with Abbey, but she was bringing the priceless gift of her children to their marriage.

Back in the house, the phone rang. It was Lanni. Sawyer had returned and she was free to leave the office. Charles picked her up at Catherine Fletcher's house, and before long, she was sitting beside him in the cab of his truck. Feeling more light-hearted than he had in years, he headed north on the maintenance road out of Hard Luck.

"You said your grandfather used to mine this claim?" she asked conversationally.

He was pleased to note that she'd changed clothes and was dressed appropriately in blue jeans, a long-sleeved shirt and ankle-high boots. He'd brought some bug spray to ward off the mosquitoes, but unfortunately that went only so far in keeping the pesky critters away.

"My grandfather, Adam, and his wife, Anna, settled Hard Luck in the early 1930s. Like thousands of men and women before them, they came in search of a dream." He didn't mean to sound poetic, but he'd heard the story so often he found himself repeating it just the way his grandmother used to tell it. "The gold dredges working near Fairbanks were digging up huge quantities of gold. I don't recall the precise amount," he said, "but in a four- or five-year span one dredge was responsible for more than ten million dollars' worth of gold, and that was when the price was thirty-five dollars an ounce."

"Did your grandfather work on a dredge originally?"

"Yeah. That's when he got hit with gold fever. But he was convinced the real motherlode lay north. He planned to strike it rich someday."

"Did he?"

Charles sighed. "Not in the way he wanted or expected. He discovered some gold but never the huge vein he sought. He found something else, something far more valuable, though. He built a town and settled a land. He created a community that's grown and thrived. Without meaning to, my grandfather shaped the lives of several generations." Charles paused, wondering how much more he should say. "I believe the gold's there—the major strike he was hoping to discover. But now it might be one of Adam's descendants who finds it."

The maintenance road ended, and Charles slowed as they crossed the rugged tundra. The ride was far less smooth now. The track, what there was of it, was barely recognizable, even to him. But then, he only visited the site two or three times a year.

Soon they could hear the sound of rushing water. Lanni glanced at Charles questioningly.

"That's the Koyukuk River," he explained.

"Koyukuk," Lanni repeated. "It sounds like you're trying to clear your throat."

Charles laughed. "It's an Athabascan word. Although you've probably never heard of it, the Koyukuk is the third longest river in Alaska. It stretches over 550 miles."

"Then the longest must be the Yukon?"

"Right, but it covers three times the territory."

"That *is* impressive."

Charles threw her a look. He had the feeling she already knew this. "An Indian friend of mine lives close by. I hope you don't mind if we drop in," he said. "Fred's a trapper, and I haven't seen him in some time."

"I'd like that," Lanni assured him.

Charles smiled at her. Being with Lanni felt completely natural. When he'd first spoken to her that morning, his mouth had been so dry he could barely talk. Not now.

Soon they approached Fred Susitna's cabin, a weathered log structure nestled among scrub trees. A tin-covered porch extended halfway across the front, and a row of lanterns hung from hooks along the roof edge.

Charles had no sooner turned off the engine than Fred appeared. His tanned, leathery face broke into a wide grin of welcome. Charles had been making impromptu visits to Fred's cabin for years, and his friend never seemed to age. Fred could be forty or sixty, Charles didn't know.

"Welcome!" Fred hugged him as though it had been ten years since his last visit, instead of ten months. He slapped Charles on the back, then turned to meet Lanni.

"Fred Susitna, this is Lanni Caldwell."

The trapper greeted her as he had Charles, with a hug of welcome. He ushered them into his home and went about heating oil to fry bread. In the Alaskan interior it was a custom to feed visitors.

Within minutes they were served hot coffee and deep-fried bread coated with sugar. Charles smiled as Lanni finished the warm bread and licked the sugar from her fingertips.

His friend murmured something in Athabascan. Although Charles didn't understand the words Fred spoke, their meaning was clear.

Charles could feel his face grow hot.

He managed to make small talk for a while, asking about the line Fred trapped each winter. Lanni was full of questions when Fred proudly brought out and showed her the furs.

It didn't take Charles long to realize it had been a mistake to bring Lanni. Not because of her questions, but because Fred saw through him far too easily. As soon as he could do so without rudeness, Charles made an excuse to leave.

"Good to see you again," he said, edging his way to the door.

"It is always a pleasure," Fred said, walking out to the truck with him. "Come again soon and bring your woman."

He waited for Lanni to deny that she belonged to him or any other man. "Lanni isn't my woman," Charles corrected when she didn't say anything.

"No?" Fred Susitna asked, dark eyes twinkling. "I've never seen you run from the truth before, my friend."

If Lanni heard his remark, she didn't comment, and Charles was grateful.

The old mining site was less than five miles down the river. Charles parked the truck and helped Lanni out. Gazing around her, she walked over to the shore of the Koyukuk River. The water rushed past like a roaring freight train, drowning out every other sound.

When Charles came to stand by her side, she turned and smiled up at him, a smile of excitement and pure rapture at the river's fierce power. He swore he didn't mean to kiss her. It just happened. One minute he was thinking how lovely she looked, how…kissable her mouth seemed, and the next she was in his arms.

What started out as something unexpected, a moment's gratification, quickly became much more. They kissed again and again, tenderly, then heatedly; gently, then with a restless hunger that left him breathless and confused.

He needed to read what was in her eyes. He had to know what she was thinking, but realized he was afraid to ask. He eased his mouth from hers and searched her beautiful deep blue eyes. What he found there gave him pause.

"Lanni," he whispered, shocked by the openheartedness he saw, the acceptance.

"Have we both gone crazy?" she asked him, whispering despite their solitude.

"We must have."

They kissed again, a lazy, sensuous kiss, and when they broke apart, Charles was trembling. Trembling. Charles O'Halloran, ever calm and unemotional. Ever sensible and prudent. The man who'd been so sure where he stood on the subject of love.

Only the day before, his brother had suggested he was tempting the fates. And now the fates had sent Lanni into his life to teach him a well-deserved lesson.

"I...I need to sit down," Lanni said.

Charles could barely hear her above the noise of the rushing water. Truth be known, his own legs weren't too steady, either. He slid an arm around Lanni, and together they leaned against a boulder; he caught his breath and let his heartbeat slow down.

Charles considered apologizing—except that he wasn't sorry. Instead, he tightened his arm, and she snuggled against him. He looked into those blue, blue eyes so filled with promise.

"Charles, there's something—"

Unable to resist her a moment longer, he brought his lips down to brush hers.

She moaned softly, the sound mingled with a tantalizing sigh of pleasure. "I should tell you—"

"Whatever it is, it doesn't matter. Only this does." He kissed her again, deciding that if this was craziness, it was the most wonderful feeling he'd ever experienced.

"We came for gold," she reminded him when she could speak again.

"I've already found it," Charles said, and kissed her once more.

Chapter
3

Lanni's hand shook as she dialed her family home. Her father answered on the second ring.

"Hi, Dad," she said cheerfully.

"Lanni, it's good to hear from you. How's everything in Hard Luck?"

"Just great."

"Your mother wishes she could've come up with you. But we've already been over that—she's needed here, and it made sense for you to be the one clearing out your grandmother's house."

"Speaking of Mom, is she there? I need to talk to her."

"I'm sorry, sweetheart, she's at the nursing home with your grandmother."

"Oh." It was difficult to keep the disappointment out of her voice.

"Is there anything I can help you with?"

Lanni bit her lip. "It has to do with the O'Hallorans." Before she could say anything else, her father interrupted.

"Are they bothering you? You might remind those trouble-makers that *we're* the ones doing *them* the favor. The least they could do is be cooperative."

"Daddy, they are! They've been fantastic. Sawyer and his fiancée had me over for dinner last night, and Charles—he's the oldest brother—took me out to his grandfather's gold stake this afternoon." She didn't say that they'd never gotten around to panning for gold; the afternoon had been spent touring the campsite and sipping wine over a camp stove and talking for hours on end. She'd told him about her studies at the University of Washington and her dreams of being a writer. Although she'd known it was deceptive, she didn't mention her grand-mother. She talked about her brother, though, and confessed how worried she was about him.

Her father hesitated. "Well, I'm glad to hear they've made you feel welcome."

"I need to know what that old feud is all about, Dad. All I can remember is the little bit Mom told me."

"It's not important anymore, sweetheart," her father insisted. "It all happened a long time ago and it's best forgotten."

"But I'm dealing with the O'Hallorans now! I *need* to know what happened."

Her father was silent for a moment. Finally he said, "I think this is something you should discuss with your mother. If you want, I'll have her phone you later."

"Please."

They chatted a while longer, then said their goodbyes. Disappointed that she was still in the dark, Lanni made herself a sandwich and wandered into her grandmother's bedroom.

The bulky headboard and matching dresser dated from the forties. The meticulously kept room told Lanni little about Catherine's life.

She started with the closet and emptied the contents onto the bed. A row of shoe boxes lined the top shelf. As she brought them down, Lanni saw that not all the boxes contained shoes. A peek inside one revealed several orderly stacks of black-and-white photographs.

Lanni carried the box into the kitchen and sat down at the table. The first pile of photos was of her mother as a child. Lanni smiled as she saw her mother's toddler face glaring into the camera from the top of a snowbank outside the house. Grammy and the grandfather who'd died before Lanni was born looked on.

From what Lanni knew of her family history, her grandparents had divorced shortly after those photos were taken. Their daughter, Kate, Lanni's mother, had been much closer to her father, Willie, than to Catherine. Willie Fletcher had moved to Anchorage, and Kate had lived there with him, occasionally visiting her mother for a few weeks at a time. Catherine Harmon Fletcher had steadfastly refused to leave Hard Luck, even though it meant giving up custody of her only child.

Most of the photographs were of people Lanni didn't recognize. She found a few of her grandmother's wedding to William Fletcher. Catherine wore a lovely pastel-colored suit and held a small bouquet of white rosebuds.

Lanni spread the photos across the table and carefully

examined each picture, searching for an answer. None revealed itself. When she'd finished, she placed the snapshots back inside the shoe box and returned it to the bedroom.

It was when she emptied the drawers that Lanni found the faded manila envelope. Sitting on the edge of the bed, she unfastened the metal tab and pulled out an eight-by-ten professionally taken photograph of her grandmother. Catherine couldn't have been more than twenty. Her eyes were bright with happiness, and a smile softened her face. Scrawled across the top of the picture were the words "Sent to My Darling David, May 1944." At the bottom was "From His Loving Bride-to-Be, Catherine."

David.

Lanni couldn't remember anyone ever mentioning a David. The second photo showed her grandmother in a long, flowing white wedding dress with a satin train that circled her feet. She turned over the picture to find the address of a Fairbanks photographer stamped on the back.

Her grandmother had married twice? Lanni had already examined the pictures of her grandparents' wedding, and Catherine had worn a pastel suit. There'd been no white wedding dress and traditional veil.

The phone rang just then, and Lanni leapt up to answer it. "Hello?"

"Sweetheart, your father said you called. Is everything all right?"

"Everything's fine." Only it wasn't, not really. Her heart pounded as if she'd stumbled upon something she was never meant to discover. "I called because I wanted to find out what I could about the feud with the O'Hallorans."

"That's what your father said. I don't think there'd be any

harm in telling you." Her mother hesitated, perhaps unsure where she should start. "More than fifty years ago, your grandmother was engaged to David O'Halloran."

"They were engaged," Lanni whispered, looking down at the photo in her hands.

"Unfortunately World War II got in the way of their wedding. My mother wanted to marry David before he was shipped to England, but with such an uncertain future, David preferred that they wait.

"Mom lived for David's letters. She wrote him each and every day. According to what she told me, they were very much in love. She even had her wedding dress made and her photograph taken, but I don't think she ever sent it to him."

That explained the picture.

"Then Charles—David's elder brother—was killed in France. The two were very close, and for three months afterward, Catherine didn't receive a single letter from David. She was frantic until she finally got word that David was coming home. But he didn't arrive alone. He came with an English bride—Ellen."

"Oh, no." Lanni closed her eyes, feeling her grandmother's pain and rejection as if it were her own.

"It seems that when David learned of his brother's death, he was inconsolable. He tried to explain his feelings to my mother, but Catherine wouldn't listen. She didn't want to hear that this beautiful young Englishwoman had helped him through his grief.

"Apparently Ellen's family had died in the war, and she and David were both lost, lonely people. I suppose it's understandable that they'd fall in love."

"Poor Grammy," Lanni murmured.

"You see, Lanni, your grandmother never loved another man. I'm not really sure why she married my father. She never loved him, never wanted him. It was always David O'Halloran. She pined for him all her life. When he died, it was as though she lost her reason for living."

"Oh, Mom, what a sad story." It clarified so many things. No wonder her mother and grandmother had never been close. Kate was the product of a marriage to a man her grandmother had never loved. And her mother had always known that.

"It would've been much better if it was David who'd died in the war, instead of Charles," Kate said in a low, harsh voice.

Lanni tensed at the words. If David had died, there would've been no sons. No Sawyer. No Christian. *No Charles.*

"Naturally I don't know everything that happened after David brought Ellen home with him," Kate went on, sounding almost normal again. "Knowing my mother, she didn't do anything to make Ellen feel welcome. I'm sure the town's sympathy went to Catherine, and I'm also sure she took full advantage of that. Knowing her, I'm fairly certain she made Ellen's life as miserable as her own."

"Why would she stay in Hard Luck?" Lanni asked. It must have been torture for Catherine to watch the man she loved with another woman.

"I can't answer that. I believe Mother lived with the hope that David and Ellen would eventually divorce. I understand there were problems with the marriage from the first. And my mother was there on the sidelines—patiently waiting for David to leave Ellen. Only he never did."

"She never stopped loving him," Lanni said.

"Or hating him," Kate added. "I believe there was a fine line between love and hate as far as my mother and David O'Halloran were concerned."

"I've met two of his sons. The oldest is Charles—they probably named him after the Charles who died in the war. Sawyer's the middle one. His wedding is at the end of next week—he's marrying one of the women who answered the newspaper ad. They seem very much in love."

"It certainly didn't take him long."

"Charles claims Sawyer barely gave Abbey time to unpack her suitcase. I didn't know two people could fall in love so fast. It was as if they knew from the moment they met that they were meant to be together."

"It goes like that sometimes."

"Abbey's got two children from a previous marriage. Seeing the four of them together, you'd never know Sawyer wasn't their father. Whatever they have is very special."

"I'm happy for him," her mother said, but she seemed distracted. "You won't stay there longer than necessary, will you?"

"No," Lanni replied, but she knew what her mother was thinking. She was worried that Lanni, too, would be swept off her feet. She opened her mouth to reassure Kate, then abruptly closed it.

She wasn't too sure it hadn't happened already.

At the Midnight Sons office late that afternoon, Charles propped his feet on the corner of Sawyer's desk and twisted the cap off a cold bottle of beer. Across from him, Sawyer leaned forward, resting his elbows on his knees.

"In a few days, I'll be a married man," his brother said meaningfully.

"Are you having second thoughts?" Charles asked, watching Sawyer closely. If Sawyer *had* had a change of heart, it wasn't too late, but Charles sincerely hoped that wasn't the case.

"Second thoughts? Are you nuts?" Sawyer burst out. "I want to marry Abbey more than I've ever wanted anything in my life. It's just that all at once I realize what a huge responsibility it is to become a husband and a father."

Charles lifted the beer bottle in a silent toast. "Better you than me, little brother."

"I didn't know it was possible to love anyone this much," he said, apparently speaking to himself. "It's almost...frightening."

Charles said nothing. Never having been in love, he couldn't entirely relate to his brother's feelings. Or could he? He thought of Lanni with her wistful, soul-deep eyes and the way her cheeks flushed when he kissed her. Lanni. She'd felt so soft in his arms. And he remembered how easy and companionable their conversation had been. Charles had always considered himself a somewhat solitary man, self-sufficient and happy with his own company. Now, after meeting Lanni, his life just seemed...lonely. He couldn't help wondering if this was what his brother had experienced when he met Abbey.

Charles didn't know and he wasn't about to ask. Not after the way he'd chided Sawyer for rushing into marriage.

The office door flew open, and John Henderson stepped inside. "Ralph needs to talk to you," he told Sawyer, nodding politely in Charles's direction.

"Problems?"

"Nothing you can't fix," John assured him.

"You go on," Charles said. "I'll finish my beer and get out of your way."

Sawyer disappeared and John was about to leave, as well.

"John," Charles said, stopping him. "I have a question for you."

"Sure." John looked at him expectantly.

"You've met Lanni Caldwell?"

"Sure thing. Duke has, too. He flew her in."

Charles rubbed the side of his jaw. Either the beer was more potent than he realized or he was about to stick his foot halfway down his throat. "Is there a reason you and the other pilots aren't…you know, interested in her?"

"We can't see the point," John replied without a pause. "She's already got her eye on you." Having said that, he walked away, leaving the screen door to slam behind him.

Boxes were stacked against the living room wall. Lanni groaned and pressed her hands to the small of her back. She'd worked all morning without a break.

A timid knock sounded on the front door. Grateful for the distraction, Lanni opened the door to find Scott and Susan standing on the porch. They both wore forlorn expressions.

"Hiya, kids," Lanni said with a smile.

"Hi," Scott said.

"Do you want to pick wildflowers with us?" Susan asked. Her eyes seemed incredibly large in her small face. "We wanted to get my mom and Sawyer some flowers for the wedding, but—"

"But Mom said," Scott picked up the conversation, "we can't go out on the tundra without an adult, and we can't—"

"We can't find an adult to go with us," Susan finished.

"So, you wanna come?" Both children looked up at her hopefully.

"The flowers are real pretty," Susan said.

"We even have a book," Scott told Lanni. He knelt down and removed his backpack. "Mom gave it to us. It's from the library. See?" He handed her the small book, full of color photos and numerous drawings.

"So will you come with us?" Susan asked softly, gazing up at her.

Lanni wasn't sure how anyone could refuse these two. "I haven't had lunch yet," she said, "but I suppose I could make a sandwich and take it with me."

Scott's and Susan's eyes lighted up as if they couldn't believe what they were hearing.

"I have to be back before five," Lanni said, glancing at her watch. Charles had phoned and asked her to dinner at his house at six. That would give her plenty of time to shower and change before meeting him.

"That's okay. We have to be home before that."

The kids followed her into the kitchen, chatting about Scott's dog, Eagle Catcher, while Lanni made herself a cheese-and-tomato sandwich. Since she had the fixings out, she made extras for Scott and Susan, then added cookies and a thermos of juice. Might as well make a regular picnic of it. Almost in afterthought, she packed a can of pepper spray in case they had any trouble with bears.

"I'll change my shoes and be ready in a minute," she said.

"I'll run and tell Mom you're going with us," Scott offered.

Lanni had just laced up her boots when the boy returned. "Mom told me to tell you she appreciates it."

"We'll have fun. We'll learn about wildflowers together, and we'll get a beautiful bouquet of flowers for the wedding." Refrigerated, they should last until then, she thought.

They walked, Lanni in the middle, until Hard Luck was out of sight. The snow-covered peaks of the Brooks Range were visible through the cloud layer to the north, and a cool breeze whistled across the tundra. The flowers bloomed all around them in colorful array.

They found several patches of alpine arnica along their route. The yellow, daisylike flower with its pointed leaves was one of Lanni's favorites.

"We can't get all the same kind," Scott insisted.

"What's the pink flower?" Lanni asked, leafing through the book, which was coded by color. She knelt down beside the plant. "It looks like it might be this one," she said, pointing to a picture.

"Parry's wallflower," Susan read slowly.

"It's a member of the mustard family."

"I don't think Mom and Sawyer want a mustard plant at their wedding!" Scott said scornfully.

"But it's pretty," Susan protested. "We don't have to tell them it's really some old mustard plant."

"All right, we'll cut some of those, too," Scott agreed, but he didn't sound happy about it.

They walked farther and gathered arctic daisies and calla as well as a handful of northern primroses.

"We aren't supposed to go near the berry bushes," Scott said. He seemed to consider it a silly warning. "I told Mom we wouldn't pick any berries for her wedding, anyway."

"She wasn't worried about that," Lanni explained, relieved that she'd remembered the can of pepper spray. "Brown bears love the berries, and they wouldn't take kindly to sharing with us."

"Bears?" Susan repeated. Her head jerked up and she looked frantically around.

"What's this?" Scott asked, kneeling down on the tundra to point out a deep impression made in the soft, spongy grass.

Lanni crouched down and examined the large footprint. "I think a bear recently crossed here," she said, making sure her voice was calm. "They're probably all over this section of land, especially with so many berries getting ready to ripen."

"A bear was here?" Susan asked.

"Yes, sweetheart, but you don't need to worry. He isn't here now."

"You're sure?"

"No," Lanni said. "But I don't see any bears, do you?"

Both children glanced around.

"Don't worry," Lanni said. "Their natural diet is about eighty percent vegetarian. Brown bears much prefer berries and roots to meat."

"So one might kill us, but he probably wouldn't eat us," Scott suggested.

"I think we have enough wildflowers," Susan said nervously, "don't you?"

Scott nodded. "I think so, too."

"We can go back to Hard Luck if you want," Lanni said, sorry now that she'd mentioned the eating habits of bears. "We can have our picnic on my porch."

"I want to," Susan declared, and Scott nodded again.

Lanni gathered the wildflowers in her arms, and the three of them turned back toward town. Scott and Susan stayed close to her side.

"What's that?" Scott asked suddenly, his voice cold with fear. He gestured across the tundra.

Lanni had to squint to make out the minuscule brown figure. Her heart thumped wildly. "It…looks like it might be a bear," she whispered.

Charles couldn't believe he'd actually invited Lanni to eat a meal he'd cooked himself. Who did he think he was—some gourmet chef? His expertise was limited to a small number of dishes, most of which went into a microwave. He was pretty handy with a camp stove, but he wasn't going to impress Lanni if he poured their dinner out of a pouch.

It was either prepare the meal himself or take her to dinner at the Hard Luck Café. Charles was well aware that he had no culinary skills whatsoever. But serving his own limited fare was better than taking her to Ben's. By morning, the entire population of Hard Luck would've heard about him and Lanni and would be speculating about their relationship.

He could see it now. If they went to the café, he wouldn't have a moment's peace with her tonight—or any other night. First Ben would be over to fill their water glasses. Then he'd hang around, sharing the latest gossip the way he always did.

When Ben left, one of the other patrons would pick up the conversation. Before Charles knew it, everyone in the diner would be asking them questions. And they'd all hurry home to spread the word....

More determined than ever to make dinner himself, Charles scanned his cupboards. He had a box of macaroni and cheese. He could whip that up and serve it with smoked salmon. For dessert there was always canned peaches. Or maybe dried fruit.

The freezer had several moose steaks left from last winter, but he didn't know how Lanni felt about eating game.

After several minutes Charles slumped down on a kitchen chair. No wonder he was a bachelor. Macaroni and cheese just didn't cut it—not for dinner with company.

He needed help. Tucking his pride in his back pocket, Charles hurried down to the Hard Luck Café. He found Ben writing out the day's menu on a blackboard.

"It's a little early for dinner, isn't it?" Ben asked when he saw Charles reading over the specials.

"Yeah," he agreed. "Uh, how's the Norwegian pot roast?"

"Excellent, if I do say so myself. I cook it in a Dutch oven with lots of garlic and bacon fat. Then I add a couple bay leaves and some ginger, and I make the gravy with plenty of sour cream." He pressed his fingertips to his lips and made a loud smacking noise. "You haven't tasted anything better this side of Fairbanks."

Charles grinned. "What do you serve with it?"

"Mashed potatoes, green beans and a jellied salad." Ben eyed him curiously. "Is there a reason for all these questions?"

"Yeah," Charles said uncomfortably. "I don't suppose you'd consider selling me a couple of those dinners as takeout."

"Takeout? What's the matter, have I got bad breath or something?"

Charles shook his head. "I'm having...a friend over for dinner."

"Who?" Ben raised his eyebrows.

"None of your business."

"I could make an intelligent guess. Obviously it's someone you don't want to bring here. Hmm, there's got to be a reason for that."

"Will you or will you not sell me two pot-roast dinners to go?" Charles demanded. Ben was as bad as Sawyer when it came to tramping all over his ego.

"I don't suppose it's Lanni Caldwell?" Ben asked.

"What if it is?"

"Then you got yourself two of the best Norwegian pot-roast dinners you're ever going to taste, and at a bargain price to boot."

Charles pulled out his wallet. "And you've got yourself a deal." He set the cash on the counter. "I'll be back in an hour to pick them up."

"You want a little candlelight and romance to go with that?" Ben teased as he walked out the door.

Charles ignored him.

He was halfway back to the house when he ran into Sawyer.

"Have you seen Scott and Susan?"

"No." Charles wondered at the urgency in his brother's voice.

"What about Lanni?"

"Not since yesterday. Why?"

Sawyer frowned, rubbing his jaw with one hand. "Abbey just

told me the three of them went for a walk on the tundra. They were going to collect wildflowers for the wedding bouquet. I'd feel better if the dog was with them."

"How long have they been gone?"

"Three hours. They were due back an hour ago. Something's wrong. I can feel it in my gut."

Charles stiffened, an unfamiliar fear gnawing at his composure. "Do you know which way they went?" he asked, trotting toward his truck.

"South, Abbey thinks."

Within minutes the two men were out of Hard Luck, bumping and jolting over the tundra in Charles's truck. Sawyer lifted a pair of binoculars to his eyes and scanned the rolling landscape.

Nothing.

The tundra had already claimed one life in his family. An aunt had disappeared at age five without a trace. Neither man spoke, but Charles knew what Sawyer was thinking, because the same thoughts were crashing through his own mind.

Lanni with those two kids. Talk about the blind leading the blind!

Charles wasn't a man who often prayed. But he did so now, seeking protection for three precious lives.

"There," Sawyer shouted, pointing southwest. "It looks like Lanni's carrying Susan piggyback."

Although Charles couldn't make out the figures yet, he steered in the direction Sawyer indicated. When he saw them, he murmured a silent prayer of thanksgiving.

Lanni and the kids stopped walking as soon as they saw the

truck. Susan slid off Lanni's back, and they stood there waiting. The second Charles pulled to a stop Sawyer jumped out, and the children ran toward him.

When he crouched down, they scrambled into his arms.

"A bear came after us!" Scott cried, his voice trembling.

"Lanni saved us," Susan sobbed, circling Sawyer's neck with her arms and squeezing tightly.

Lanni stood no more than two feet from Charles. For an unguarded moment he simply absorbed the sight of her. Her hair was disheveled, her face red with perspiration and streaked with dirt. Nevertheless he was convinced he'd never seen anyone more beautiful.

"Are you all right?" he asked when he found his voice.

She nodded slowly. "We crossed paths with a bear."

The hair rose on the back of Charles's neck. "Were you hurt?" he asked frantically.

Lanni raised a shaking hand to her mouth. "Oh, God, I was so scared."

Not caring that his brother was watching, Charles hauled her into his arms and hugged her as if he never intended to release her. She came without resistance, buried her face in his chest and wept.

"It's okay," he whispered, stroking her hair. "You're safe now. Nothing's going to happen."

"At first the bear was a long ways away," Scott was saying. "He was just a brown dot."

"We could hardly see him," Susan added.

"Then he started to run straight for us."

"We ran, too," Susan said, "as fast as we could."

"Boy, can those bears run fast," Scott said.

"Then I fell," Susan cried, squeezing Sawyer's neck even tighter.

"I thought she was gonna be dead meat, but Lanni stopped and helped her up. Then Lanni stood on top of a rock and waved her arms and told me and Susan to hide. Lanni shouted like crazy, and when the bear got close she sprayed him with pepper spray. At first it didn't look like it was gonna work. We were afraid the bear was going to get Lanni, but he went away...and then Lanni started to shake real bad."

"The pepper spray worked," Susan said. "But if it hadn't, Lanni'd be dead, and me and Scott next."

"Oh, Lanni," Charles groaned. Lanni would've sacrificed herself to save the children.

"The bear stood up, too, and he's bigger'n a building!" Scott said.

"He was real, real big," Susan put in.

Sawyer loaded Scott and Susan into the back of the pickup and climbed in after them. The three of them sat there while Charles assisted Lanni into the cab, then got in himself.

She leaned her head against his shoulder as if she no longer had the strength to hold it up. "Thank you for coming," she whispered.

Emotion clogged his throat, and it was all he could do to keep from kissing her. To keep from thanking her for being alive.

He brushed the hair from her cheek, and she placed her hand over his fingers. At her touch, he shuddered with emotion.

"Lanni."

She lifted her head from his shoulder. He didn't know what

to say—how to say what was in his heart. Raising her hand to his lips, he planted tender, desperate kisses there.

He struggled for words. "Dear God, Lanni, you could've been killed."

"I know...I know."

Pulling her to him, he searched blindly for her lips. With his kiss he told her what he couldn't communicate in any other way. They kissed with the urgency of two people who recognize how close they've come to losing each other, an urgency mingled with fear. They kissed until the tremors of apprehension were replaced with tremors of passion and need.

"I don't know why we aren't leaving," Sawyer said to the kids. They were still waiting for Charles to switch on the ignition.

Scott got to his feet and clumped across the bed of the truck to the small window in back of the cab.

"I do," the boy muttered. "Uncle Charles is kissing Lanni."

Chapter

4

"Has everyone around here gone crazy?" Charles asked as he walked into the Hard Luck Café two mornings later.

"I guess you're talking about the wedding," Ben commented, reaching automatically for the coffeepot. He filled a cup for Charles and one for himself.

"Is there anything else?" Charles grumbled under his breath, taking a seat at the counter. He'd never seen anything like it. The entire town was being spruced up for the event. Folks were mowing lawns and cleaning out flower beds. You'd think the president was stopping by for a visit.

The school gymnasium, which was generally used for town meetings and the get-together at Christmas, had never been more elaborately decorated. Even the basketball hoop was filled with silk flowers. He'd like to know what Larry Bird would say if he ever laid eyes on that!

Since Charles was standing up as best man for his brother,

he'd been informed that he'd need to rent a tuxedo. Tuxedos weren't the only wedding paraphernalia that couldn't be obtained in Hard Luck. Sawyer had kept his pilots busy for two days making runs to Fairbanks and beyond, collecting everything from tuxes to table napkins. The last he heard, Duke Porter had been sent on a wild-goose chase after a silver punch bowl. Charles wouldn't have believed it if he hadn't heard it with his own ears.

"Are you baking the wedding cake?" he asked Ben.

"Not me," the café-owner said, raising both hands as if he wouldn't touch that task with a ten-foot pole. "I've got enough on my mind worrying about the rehearsal dinner and the hors d'oeuvres for the reception."

"Tell me," Charles said, shaking his head, "just where does my brother intend to put everyone? Abbey's parents arrive tomorrow, which is fine. Sawyer's putting them up in his house, and he's moving in with me. But there's Abbey's best friend and her husband, plus other family."

Charles wasn't keen on the idea of sharing his home with his brother, even if it *was* only for one night. Sawyer was an emotional wreck. The closer the wedding, the worse Sawyer got. Charles feared his brother would disintegrate into a hopeless idiot before noon tomorrow. He wasn't far from it now.

"You think that's bad," Ben said, smiling ironically. "Abbey's got every woman in town rolling these tiny scrolls and tying them with satin ribbons. Darned if I know what she intends to do with them."

Charles merely nodded. "I have no idea," he muttered.

"Thank goodness *you're* levelheaded enough not to be gettin' married."

Charles's eyes avoided Ben's. He cleared his throat and glanced over his shoulder to be sure they were alone. "Actually that's something I wanted to talk to you about."

Ben straightened. "Don't tell me you're next? You've gone and fallen in love with Lanni, haven't you?"

"No!" Charles snapped. "Of course not." But then, what did he know? If Sawyer's state of mind was any indication, then Charles would have to compare love with a bad case of the flu.

"You're protesting just a bit too loud for me to believe you," Ben said. He walked around the counter and slid onto the stool next to Charles's.

Charles didn't argue. He wished he could find a way to explain away what was happening between him and Lanni. "Have you ever met a woman and known right from that precise moment that—I don't know how to describe it."

"Like someone kicked you in the gut?"

"Yes," Charles said, grasping at his friend's definition. It was the best way he'd come across to describe how he'd felt the night he'd passed Lanni walking with Duke Porter. It didn't matter that she was with another man. It didn't matter that he and Lanni hadn't said more than a handful of words to each other. It felt as if God had sent a fist straight through the bright cloudless sky. A fist that connected—hard—and practically knocked him off his feet.

"It happened to me once," Ben said hoarsely, cradling his mug with both hands. He stared into the distance, frowning.

"You know what I'm talking about, then?" Charles prodded.

"I think so," Ben muttered. "But it was a long time ago. Longer than I care to admit." He shrugged, then took a sip of his coffee. "I was a kid, still wet behind the ears. I'd had a little college and kicked around for a while. Then I enlisted and when I finished boot camp, I was in San Francisco waiting for my orders to go to Vietnam.

"I met Marilyn at Golden Gate Park. She had long blond hair and was so damned pretty I couldn't take my eyes off her. She was going into her sophomore year in college. We had six weeks together."

"You mean before you were shipped out?" Charles asked.

"Yeah. She didn't want me to go, like I had a choice about it. Marilyn was against the war. But what college kid wasn't? She seemed to believe that if I really loved her, I'd stay with her. We argued about it. I said some things I regretted later. I'd like to think she regretted what she said to me, too, but I have no way of knowing."

"What happened after you left?"

"Nothing. She was the one in the wrong, I figured. It made me mad she'd been so narrow-minded. What about honor and duty? Apparently they meant nothing to her. What kind of man did she think I was, asking me to turn my back on a commitment I made to my country? The way I saw it, we had nothing in common."

"So you broke it off?"

"Yeah," Ben answered, but he didn't sound happy about it. "She wrote me a couple times early on, but I never even opened the letters. Just sent them back."

"What about after the war? Did you see her?" If Ben still had strong feelings for her this many years later, surely he'd made some effort to patch things up.

"I was ready to swallow my pride the next year. When I was stateside again, I phoned her. That was when I learned she'd gotten married. According to her mother, she didn't let any grass grow under her feet, either. Four months after I left, she was engaged. I don't mind telling you, it was a shock. We might've had only six weeks together, but they were the best weeks of my life. I loved her then, and even now I've got a soft spot in my heart for her."

Charles didn't know what to say. It seemed to him that Marilyn must not have loved Ben the way he loved her, otherwise she wouldn't have married someone else.

"You know, I really loved her," Ben was saying. "Thinking about Marilyn was what got me through the craziness in 'Nam. I've got plenty of regrets in this life, but the biggest one is what happened between me and her. I was a fool."

Charles had a few regrets of his own.

"We were both too young, too idealistic in our different ways," Ben continued. "I've paid for that."

Once more Charles felt at a loss. He was surprised and saddened by Ben's story. Although he considered Ben a good friend, the older man rarely spoke of his past.

"Are you offering me any advice?" Charles asked.

Ben pondered a moment. "For one thing you gotta trust your feelings."

"My feelings?" He hardly knew what his feelings *were*. As for trusting them…

"Yeah. You've met Lanni, and you like her and she likes you. That's great. It doesn't mean you have to leap off the nearest bridge—or into marriage."

Charles thought about Sawyer. Less than a month after meeting Abbey, his brother was taking on a wife and two children. If that didn't constitute a major life change, Charles didn't know what did.

"Tell you the truth, I'm surprised at you," Ben said candidly.

"You mean because I made such a fuss about Sawyer and Christian bringing women to Hard Luck?"

"No." Ben's voice was thoughtful. "Until now, I'd always kind of figured the two of us were alike. Cast from the same mold, two peas in a pod, that sort of thing."

"How's that?"

"You're pretty stubborn."

"True." Charles couldn't deny it.

"And a bit of a loner."

Charles nodded.

"I guess what I'm trying to say is, I never expected a woman to affect you like this."

"I don't know what you mean," Charles insisted. All he was doing was trying to sort out his thoughts—and emotions.

Ben swallowed the rest of his coffee and slid off the stool. "You asked for my advice, so I'll give it to you. Quit analyzing your feelings to death. Like I said, you gotta trust 'em. No need to make any decisions right now. Nothing has to change this minute. Just enjoy being with her."

"I do," Charles mumbled. Too much. That was part of his problem. Soon he'd be back in the field, doing what he loved best. Surveying. He'd always thought of those months alone as necessary. It had always seemed to him that was when his soul caught up with his body. But for the first time, he wasn't looking forward to the solitude he normally craved. He wanted Lanni with him.

Worst of all, when he left for the field, Lanni would be here in Hard Luck with a bunch of love-starved bush pilots eager for her attention. Eager to have him out of the picture. And before long, Bill Landgrin and his pipeline crew would be making excuses to visit town.

Charles gritted his teeth. He didn't want Lanni with any other man. He wanted her with *him*.

"Abbey!" Sawyer burst into the library. "I forgot the mints." He announced this as if the world were about to end.

Abbey looked up from the stack of books she was replacing on the shelves and blinked. "The mints?"

"You asked me to have John pick them up this afternoon, but I forgot."

"Oh, the mints. Don't worry about it. You had more than enough on your mind. Just remember to have someone pick up my parents in Fairbanks tomorrow afternoon."

"Tomorrow," he repeated. "I have the time on my schedule at the office. Right?"

"Right." Abbey had given Sawyer the information a week earlier. "What about your mother and Robert?" Robert was Sawyer's stepfather.

"She's coming with Christian the morning of the wedding. Oh, I forgot to tell you. Robert won't be with her. With his broken leg, he's finding it too hard to travel. He phoned his regrets."

"I'll meet him later, I guess," Abbey said.

Sawyer slowly lowered himself into a chair. The panicked expression on his face said that keeping track of everyone's comings and goings had become more than he could manage. "I've never looked forward to getting something over with this much."

Abbey shrugged. "You're the one who insisted on putting together a wedding in two weeks' time!"

"Don't remind me. I have no one to blame but myself."

Abbey was about to put an encyclopedia back on the shelf when Sawyer reached out and grabbed her around the waist.

She let out a small cry of surprise as he pulled her onto his lap. His arms brought her close.

"Why didn't you just suggest we elope and be done with it?" he chided. "I've never gone through this before, and like a fool, I thought organizing a wedding was no big deal. In case you haven't noticed, I'm a wreck."

"I've noticed," she said seriously, resting her hands on his shoulders, "but I agreed with you that a formal wedding was a good idea." She paused. "For me, for my children and parents, it's a symbol of our love. Our marriage. It also marks the beginning of our new life. I happen to think symbols and ceremonies are important." She dropped a kiss on his forehead. "I love you all the more for insisting on it."

"I swear I'm going crazy."

"It'll all be over in two days," she told him.

"I wish it was over now."

"Patience, my love."

He stroked her cheek with his callused palm. "I had no idea waiting to make love to you would be this difficult," he said in a husky murmur.

The gentleness of his touch and the agony in his words pierced Abbey's heart. She closed her eyes and buried her face in his shoulder. It was at her request that they'd decided to wait until their wedding night. And it moved her deeply that Sawyer had agreed. Emotion filled her chest, making it difficult to breathe.

"I love you, Sawyer O'Halloran," she said after a moment.

"Good thing you do, because I'd hate to think I was putting on a cummerbund for nothing."

Abbey giggled and kissed him with a thoroughness that left them both dizzy.

"I have a feeling," Sawyer said, pausing to clear his throat, "that you're going to be worth the wait."

The new secretary still hadn't arrived, so Lanni volunteered to answer the phones for Sawyer when Abbey's parents got in early Friday afternoon. Sawyer introduced her to Wayne and Marie Murray, and Lanni liked the middle-aged couple immediately.

"Entertain your guests," she urged Sawyer, "and don't worry about anything here. I can take care of the phones."

"You're sure you don't mind?" He looked apprehensive, as if he might be imposing. "You've been helping out almost every day this week."

"I'm positive. In fact I appreciate the break. I spent the morning cleaning out my grandmother's place, and it's tedious work."

Sawyer hesitated, glancing over his shoulder to check that he wasn't keeping his future in-laws waiting. Scott and Susan were busy introducing them around.

"Speaking of your grandmother," he began, "I don't suppose you've mentioned her to Charles yet, have you?"

"No." The answer was clipped. She avoided his gaze.

"I just wondered…"

"I thought you might have told him."

"No, I figured you'd want to do it."

She hadn't told Charles because she was afraid of what would happen once he learned she was related to Catherine Fletcher. And the longer she avoided the issue, the more difficult it was to tell him. She almost wished Sawyer *had* said something.

"You'll tell him?" Sawyer asked.

She nodded.

"When?"

"Soon," she promised. After the wedding, when life in Hard Luck had returned to normal. She hadn't purposely deceived him. Not any more than Sawyer had, or anyone else who knew her reason for being in Hard Luck.

"Good," the groom-to-be said decisively, then disappeared out the door.

Sawyer's desk was in a state of chaos. She was doing her best to straighten his papers, schedules and messages when the office door opened and Charles stepped inside. He stopped abruptly the instant he saw her.

Lanni stood up, her heartbeat thundering in her ears.

Their eyes met.

"Hello again," she said breathlessly. She sensed that Charles was uncomfortable with the strength of their attraction. She also knew he was fighting this feeling. She recognized that because she was fighting it herself.

"Hi," he said a little awkwardly. "Uh, where's Sawyer?"

"He's out of the office for a while," she said. "Abbey's parents just arrived."

"That's right—I'd forgotten." But he still didn't leave. "I came to ask about the wedding rehearsal this evening."

Lanni turned to Sawyer's appointment calendar, which lay on the corner of his desk. "Says here it's supposed to start at seven."

"I know that much. I was just wondering how formally I'm supposed to dress for this."

"Nothing fancy. What you have on now is fine."

"Great." Charles moved farther into the office. "Were you planning on attending the wedding tomorrow?"

"Yes. I'm looking forward to it." Although she hadn't received a formal invitation, both Sawyer and Abbey had asked her to come. "And I'll be playing the piano at the rehearsal tonight, too."

"You will?"

"The man bringing the recorded music won't be available until the wedding itself. He's coming from Fairbanks."

"I see. Speaking of the wedding," Charles said, "I was wondering if you'd…consider attending it with me—" he paused as if the words had stuck in his throat "—as my date?"

Lanni smiled softly. You'd almost think he dreaded her response. "I'd like that very much."

"Great," he said, grinning broadly. "Shall we meet at the church? I'd offer to stop by the house and personally escort you, but unfortunately I'm going to have my hands full with Sawyer."

"He told me you're his best man."

"I just hope he lasts through the ceremony. I've never met a more nervous groom."

"He'll be fine."

"Yeah, I'm sure he will."

Lanni's fingers fumbled with the papers on Sawyer's desk.

"Will you be going over to Ben's for the dinner tonight?" Charles asked.

She nodded. From what she'd heard, at least half the town would be on hand for the after-rehearsal dinner.

"I'll look for you there." Charles seemed to brighten.

"I'll probably be a little late, though," Lanni said, regretting now that she'd volunteered to be part of the crew that would decorate the church. "I promised I'd help get the sanctuary ready for the wedding."

"I'll save a seat for you," Charles promised, "next to me."

Lanni liked the idea of that and smiled.

"I'll see you at seven, then," he said, backing out of the trailer.

She raised her hand in farewell. "Until seven."

Feeling oddly shaky after the short encounter, Lanni sat down again. It wasn't the first time she'd observed that being around Charles left her feeling distinctly weak in the knees.

Charles was having real difficulty paying attention. This was supposed to be a practice before the actual wedding. A rehearsal, so everyone would know when to sit and stand. So Charles would know when to steer his lovesick brother toward the altar, when to jab him in the ribs signaling it was time to repeat his vows.

He *should* be paying attention. Instead, his gaze repeatedly wandered over to Lanni, who sat behind the old upright piano.

Again and again his eyes were drawn to her lips. Why he

should choose that precise moment to remember how soft and sweet her mouth was, he'd never know.

Thank goodness no one could read his mind. He'd probably be arrested for harboring such sensual thoughts in a church. If the evening was starting out like this—with him so distracted he couldn't see straight—Charles hated to think about the dinner.

It was bad enough that—

"Charles," Reverend Wilson, the circuit minister, cut into his musings. "Were you listening?"

"Sorry," he muttered, pulling his eyes and thoughts away from Lanni.

"Pay attention," Sawyer grumbled. "I'm going to need you."

Charles had certainly figured that out. What he *hadn't* figured out, though, was where all these people had come from, and more importantly, where they were going to sleep. Thank goodness his mother and Christian weren't arriving until the morning, especially since Sawyer had given Christian's bed to Abbey's matron of honor and her husband.

Reverend Wilson stood in front of the group. "I think we'd better run through this one more time. I sense some…confusion here, and we want the actual ceremony to go as smoothly as possible."

Charles groaned inwardly.

"All right, let's start from the beginning."

It took most of an hour to go through the ceremony one last time. Charles did his best to pay attention, although it remained a struggle to keep his eyes off Lanni. She looked so beautiful in her white cotton dress that he wondered how anyone could *not* stare at her.

When Reverend Wilson finally dismissed them, Charles casually made his way over to the piano. Almost everyone else had vacated the church in a rush—as if fearful that the good pastor might find some excuse to call them back.

As Charles approached the piano, Lanni was straightening a stack of sheet music.

"You did a great job," he told her, but in fact he couldn't have identified a single piece she'd played.

"Thank you."

"If you want, I'll wait for you and we can walk over to Ben's together," he suggested.

Lanni looked at Pearl Inman, who stood at the back of the church holding a bag of huge white ribbons. "You'd better go on without me," she said with obvious reluctance. "It'll take ten or fifteen minutes to put up the pew bows, and everyone will wonder where you are if you don't show up right away."

"Okay," he agreed, although he would've preferred to stay. Unfortunately his duties as best man were interfering with his plans to spend time with Lanni.

When Charles got to the Hard Luck Café most of the others were already there. He barely recognized the place. Ben had set up six-foot-long tables and covered them with white linen cloths. Each table was adorned with a decorative paper wedding bell and a scattering of brightly colored confetti.

Charles went straight to the head table to greet Abbey and Sawyer and the other members of the wedding party. "We need an extra chair here," he said, edging past the adjoining table to grab one before anyone else could claim it.

"An extra chair?" Sawyer asked. "Who for?"

"Lanni," Charles answered, glaring at his brother, daring him to make an issue of it. He shoved the chair viciously into place beside his.

"Lanni. Of course," Sawyer said, sliding Charles another of his know-it-all looks. His brother leaned over and whispered something to Abbey, who glanced in Charles's direction and grinned.

Charles resisted the urge to remind his brother and Abbey that it was impolite to whisper.

Instead, he took his seat. Tantalizing smells wafted from the kitchen. Ben stepped into the crowded room, wearing a chef's hat and a fresh white apron.

"Dinner is served," he said with uncharacteristic formality. Then he instructed everyone to take their plates to the buffet table.

Rather than stand in line, Charles decided to wait until Lanni could join him. As she'd promised, it didn't take long. The side door opened and both she and Pearl walked in.

Because of the noise, he raised his hand to attract her attention, rather than call out. With any luck she'd see he was seated at the head table.

However, before she noticed Charles, Ted Richards, one of Sawyer's new pilots, waylaid her. It was clear that the man had asked Lanni to join him at his table.

Charles held his breath, wondering what she'd do. Even from this distance, he could see how persuasive the pilot was. With a sweeping gesture, Ted held out a chair for Lanni as if to say that her sitting next to him would be the greatest honor of his life.

Charles's hands tightened.

"It looks to me like Ted's about to steal your girl," someone whispered from behind him. So intent was Charles on what was happening between Lanni and the pilot, he didn't know who'd spoken.

"Excuse me," he said, stepping impatiently around several other people.

"Lanni," he said, interrupting Ted. "I've got a seat for you up front."

"I asked her to sit with me," Ted pointed out.

"I asked her first."

"Charles did ask me earlier this afternoon," Lanni explained in what Charles thought was a much too apologetic tone.

"What is it with those O'Halloran men?" Ted loudly asked a pilot sitting nearby. "Bringing women to Hard Luck was to keep us pilots happy. It was the main reason I took the job! We don't get so much as a chance with them, though, do we? The minute a decent woman arrives, one of the O'Hallorans takes her for himself."

Charles would have asked the hotheaded pilot to apologize if Lanni hadn't quickly announced, "I'm starved!"

"Ben outdid himself," Charles said, steering her toward the buffet line. "He ordered honey-baked ham from Anchorage and cooked up his own scalloped potatoes. It looks like there might be a salad or two up there, as well. And I heard a rumor about blueberry cobbler for dessert."

"It all sounds wonderful."

And it was. The meal proved as delicious as Charles had expected. Afterward, there were a few short humorous speeches. Charles made one himself, about his brother being a man who knew what he wanted and knew how to get it.

Together Abbey and Sawyer stood, their arms around each other's waists. They took turns thanking all those who had contributed to making their wedding day possible. Scott and Susan sat with their grandparents, beaming.

Hardly aware of what he was doing, Charles reached for Lanni's hand under the table. "I'll walk you home," he whispered in her ear.

"What about the bachelor party?" Lanni asked. "Doesn't that start now?"

"So I'll be a few minutes late. It's no big deal."

"You're sure?"

He nodded. He hoped Lanni was as eager to be alone with him as he was with her. No doubt their leaving together would be cause for speculation, but it didn't worry him. Not at all.

He made his farewells and promised to return soon.

They walked hand in hand toward Catherine Fletcher's old house. Charles tried not to think about Lanni living there. It bothered him, yet he knew his reaction should be gratitude that she had a decent place to stay. The only other alternative was one of those worthless cabins, and Charles certainly didn't want her there.

"You should've stuck around for the party," Lanni said, a smile in her voice. "You know what they're going to say, don't you?"

"No." He did of course, but he really didn't care.

Her smile was sassy and provocative as she turned, walking backward in front of him, hands clasped behind her. "Pearl Inman said there's going to be another wedding in Hard Luck soon," she murmured in a low, sultry voice. "If I were you, I'd be running for cover."

Charles swallowed. Another wedding. He and Lanni? He tensed, then remembered Ben's advice. *Nothing has to change this minute.* "Let folks talk if it makes them happy."

"Fortunately for you I don't think Pearl was referring to us."

Charles frowned. "Then who was she talking about?"

Lanni blinked. "You mean you don't know?"

"I haven't got any idea."

"Dotty Harlow and Pete Livengood."

"Dotty? You mean the nurse who's going to take over at the health clinic?" He watched as the breeze flirted with Lanni's long hair. Its magical fingers stirred up the softness, and once more his gaze was drawn to her enticing, kissable lips.

"Dotty and Pete have been quite an item of late," Lanni informed him.

"You're so beautiful." The words were out before he could censor them.

She lowered her eyes and blushed.

Embarrassed that he'd let the remark slip, Charles opened the small gate outside the house and walked her to the front porch. With all the men in town gathering for Sawyer's bachelor party, he didn't need to worry about Ted or John or any of the others showing up here, at her place.

"Thank you for walking me home," Lanni said, standing on the first step.

"Thank *you* for allowing me to do it." The proper little speech made him feel a bit old-fashioned—"gentlemanly" his mother would have said—but it felt...right.

Neither of them spoke, then at precisely the same moment, they moved together.

Lanni brought her arms around his neck as he slid his around her waist. Their kiss was sweet, then grew passionate. It was better than he'd imagined, better than he'd remembered.

All at once they broke apart, as if they were afraid to continue. As if they were afraid of where it would lead.

After a moment she suggested, "Maybe you should...join your friends."

Charles didn't want to leave. Not now. But he knew she was right. Still, the temptation to stay was almost more than he could resist.

"There's a dance after the wedding," he said.

"Yes, I know."

"I'm not very light on my feet."

She said nothing.

"Save the first dance for me, okay?"

Lanni broke into a smile and nodded.

Charles turned away and hurried back to Ben's. He winced as he realized he'd actually asked her to save him a dance. Well, he supposed a man didn't voluntarily make a fool of himself without a good reason. A sentimental fool, yet. True, he didn't want anyone else dancing with her, but it was more than that. He was looking for an excuse to hold her. An excuse to wrap his arms around her.

Intuitively Charles knew that whatever he felt for Lanni was an emotion he shouldn't label.

Chapter
5

Charles gazed up at the bright blue sky. The Baron twin-engine aircraft with its Midnight Sons logo descended toward the field at Hard Luck. The last time he'd seen his mother had been six months ago. He didn't consider himself a very good son. Since their father's death, Christian and Sawyer had made much more of an effort to keep in touch with her.

Ellen was content, and for that Charles was grateful. She deserved a bit of happiness after the hardship of the past forty years. First the war in Europe, which had wiped out her family, then the years spent in a miserable marriage to his father.

The plane touched down smoothly and taxied to a standstill. Charles opened the door. Christian descended first, then turned back to help his mother out. Duke Porter, the pilot, climbed out next, and with a respectful wave, left them alone.

Ellen surveyed the field, and the town just beyond. It took

her a moment to realize Charles was waiting for her. A smile touched her lips as she hurried down the steps.

She looked small and fragile in her pale blue suit. She was a beautiful woman, graceful and exquisitely boned, and as out of place in this harsh land as a hothouse orchid. Charles had never understood what had possessed his father to marry such a delicate woman, knowing where he'd be bringing her to live.

"Charles," Ellen cried, hugging him. "Don't you look handsome!"

Charles edged his index finger between his neck and the confining collar of his starched white dress shirt. He'd be lucky if it didn't strangle him before the end of the day.

"You in a tuxedo!" Christian exclaimed. "I don't believe it."

"Believe it," Charles said with a cocky grin. "Sawyer rented one for you, too. It's at the house waiting for you as we speak."

The laughter drained out of Christian's eyes. "You're joking."

"Do I *look* like I'm making this up?" Charles asked. "You'd better hurry. Sawyer's on pins and needles as it is. It's your turn to keep him occupied while I take Mother over to meet Abbey."

Christian muttered something Charles couldn't hear, but from his tone, that was probably just as well. "It's good to see you, too, big brother," he said in a louder voice.

Charles chuckled and offered Ellen his arm. "You're going to like Abbey," he told her.

"I'm crazy about her already," she said, and slipped her hand into the crook of his arm. "She's managed something I thought was impossible."

"What's that?"

Ellen's eyes filled with surprise, as if to say Charles should know very well what she was talking about. "She convinced one of my sons to get married. You have no idea how long I've been waiting for one of you to come to your senses. Not only that, she's made me an instant grandmother. I could kiss her feet."

Charles was astonished. "You *want* to be a grandmother?"

"What woman my age doesn't?" Ellen asked. "I waited long enough to have children, but I swear I've been far more impatient for grandchildren. I can't tell you how grateful I am that Robert's daughter had the good sense to marry young."

"Scott and Susan are going to love you."

"As well they should," Ellen said, and laughed softly. "I plan to spoil them rotten."

Charles was still reeling from his mother's revelation.

"Now let me take a good look at you," she said. She stepped back and studied Charles, then raised her hand to her lips. "Oh, Charles…" She smiled tremulously. "You make me proud."

Charles wasn't accustomed to dealing with praise, especially from his mother. "Uh, thank you."

Ellen moved resolutely into place beside him and squared her shoulders. "Now take me to meet my daughter-in-law before I make a fool of myself by breaking into tears." She snapped open her handbag and withdrew a lace-edged handkerchief, which she pressed to the corner of each eye.

"Aw, Mom," Charles said, guiding her toward the pickup. "Don't tell me you're going to cry at Sawyer's wedding."

"Of course I am," she said. "It's my right and I've earned it."

Not a single seat remained empty in the small community church. Lanni felt fortunate to find a place to sit. An air of festivity pervaded the room, as though each person present felt in some way responsible for Sawyer's marrying Abbey Sutherland.

A hush fell over the gathering when Charles and Sawyer appeared and walked toward the altar. They turned slightly to await the approach of Abbey and her attendants.

Because the church didn't have a pipe organ, the couple had chosen taped music and a rented sound system. The first notes of the wedding march soared through the small church. Everyone stood and faced the center aisle as Abbey entered on her father's arm.

She wore a pale peach, floor-length dress, her hair wreathed in a garland of white roses. She carried a bouquet of more white roses mingled with yellow and lavender wildflowers.

They were similar to the ones Lanni had picked with the children the fateful day they'd encountered the bear. Those flowers had gotten lost in the trauma that followed. But apparently Abbey had made sure that a few of the delicate tundra blossoms were added to her bouquet.

Lanni had seen many a bride and participated in more weddings than she cared to count. Every bride was beautiful. Every wedding was special. But the happiness shining in Abbey's face as she looked toward the front of the church where Sawyer stood waiting brought unexpected tears to Lanni's eyes. The love that flowed between them was visible to all.

Lanni wasn't the only one affected. Across the aisle from her stood Ben Hamilton. She nearly didn't recognize him without his apron. He reached into his back pocket and took out a crumpled handkerchief and loudly blew his nose. He glanced around self-consciously, then rubbed his fist across his eyes.

Ben weeping! She was astounded by that for some reason. But since her own vision was blurry with tears, Lanni couldn't very well blame anyone else for reacting the same way.

At that moment Abbey and Sawyer joined hands and stepped in front of Reverend Wilson. Susan and Scott stood beside them. Susan's dress was made from the same material as Abbey's, and her hair was adorned with a garland. Scott stood next to Sawyer in a miniature tuxedo and cummerbund.

When her eyes had cleared, Lanni turned her attention to Charles. She experienced a twinge of pride at what a distinguished-looking man he was. But watching Charles reminded her that time was fast running out.

Soon she would no longer have an excuse to stay in Hard Luck. Her family was already asking questions. But she could hardly admit that she strongly suspected she was falling in love with Charles O'Halloran!

Abbey handed her bridal bouquet to her matron of honor and joined hands with Sawyer. Reverend Wilson asked her to repeat her vows. Her voice didn't hesitate, didn't waver. She seemed to be saying she'd never been more confident of any action she'd ever taken.

"I solemnly swear to love..."

Love. Charles heard Abbey speak, and the word echoed in his mind. All this time he hadn't understood why Sawyer found it so necessary to rush Abbey to the altar. He didn't understand why his brother was in such an all-fired hurry to tie the knot. He'd already waited thirty-three years—what was another three or four months?

To Charles's way of thinking, the least Sawyer could've done was give Abbey time to get settled in Hard Luck. The move from Seattle was a major transition for her and the children. One life change was enough, without adding a marriage with all its adjustments to the equation.

But right now, at this moment, Charles recognized the depth of emotion that bound Sawyer and Abbey. They were very much in love. Waiting a month, three months, a year, would change nothing. Their commitment was as strong now as it would be in twenty years' time.

One look at the two of them standing before God, family and friends was all Charles needed to convince him of that truth. Funny he hadn't been aware of it sooner. Funny how blind he'd been to what was obvious to everyone else.

Love. He risked glancing in Lanni's direction. Breathless emotion grabbed at his chest as their eyes met. He could see the bright tears that sparkled in hers as she sent him a smile.

"...honor," Abbey continued.

Honor. Lanni tore her gaze away from Charles. Her heart pounded so fast she grew dizzy. Abbey, Sawyer, the children and Reverend Wilson slowly faded from view as she focused her attention solely on Charles. Although they'd been together only hours earlier, she felt almost desperate for the sight of him.

She loved this man. Loved him. Briefly she closed her eyes while her mind acknowledged the truth. She wasn't falling in love. She *was* in love.

It wasn't possible, the logical side of her argued. They hadn't known each other very long. He was older. A loner. *An O'Hal-*

loran. She couldn't love him. Not without creating all kinds of problems for both of them.

Lanni opened her eyes and raised her head. Once again her gaze slid deeply into his. What she saw there was enough to convince her that nothing was worth more than having this man in her life. If she lived another hundred years, she'd never find anyone she'd love as much.

Had they not been in a church, in the midst of a wedding ceremony, she would have pushed her way into the aisle and run to his side.

Abbey finished repeating her vows and Sawyer began his. *"Before God, I hereby solemnly vow to cherish…"*

Cherish. He'd talk to Lanni, Charles decided. Reason this out. Together, they'd make some sense of their feelings. Plan for the future. He wouldn't rush her, wouldn't pressure her. It had taken him thirty-five years to meet a woman like Lanni, but now that he had, he'd do whatever was necessary to keep her in his life.

"I do," Abbey said, her voice ringing clearly through the church.

"I do, too," Scott added.

"Me, too," Susan chimed in, not wanting to be left out.

The congregation laughed, and Lanni saw there was more than one wet eye in the crowd. Reverend Wilson made his final statement, and then Sawyer O'Halloran kissed his wife.

A spontaneous burst of applause broke out. Ben reached for his handkerchief a second time. He blew his nose, and the sound, which resembled the honk of a goose, echoed against the church walls.

Scott and Susan led the procession out of the church, and the people of Hard Luck spilled out after them.

Somehow in the crush Charles found Lanni. His hand reached for hers and he drew her aside. She knew he was needed at the reception; she was, too. Abbey had asked her to cut the cake.

Neither moved. Or spoke.

Did she dare hope he'd felt the same magic she had during the service? Did she dare believe Charles loved her? Her heart refused to beat. Her lungs forgot to breathe.

People stepped around them, laughing, talking, joking.

Slowly, because she desperately needed to touch him, she raised her hand. Her palm settled against his cheek. He was warm and solid and wonderful.

Wordlessly he drew her into his arms.

"Lanni—"

"I know. I know."

"You felt it, too?"

She nodded.

Charles struggled for words, then shrugged helplessly. "I can't talk now."

She nodded, understanding.

"Later. All right?" Releasing her, he moved away. Then—as if he couldn't bear to leave her—he turned back. Holding her face between his hands, he kissed her, a long kiss that told her everything he felt. He took a deep, calming breath before he hurried toward the school gymnasium, where the reception was being held.

It took Lanni a minute to compose herself. She wanted to

laugh and weep at the same time. How she'd ever explain this to her family she didn't know. Didn't *want* to know. They'd tell her she'd lost her mind. It was only natural, they'd say, to feel this kind of joy in the middle of a wedding service.

They wanted her to fall in love, but not with Charles O'Halloran.

She'd tell them soon, she decided. For the first time in her life she was truly in love. If no one else, Matt, her brother, would understand. Karen, her former sister-in-law, would, too. And if she was lucky, so would her parents. But before she told them anything, she needed to tell Charles that Catherine Fletcher was her grandmother.

He was possibly the worst best man Sawyer could have chosen, Charles thought later. He was part of the reception line, but he couldn't concentrate on greeting family and friends. He was sure he hadn't spoken a single sensible word from the moment he took his place beside his mother. Fortunately, despite his previous fears, only two reporters showed up, both from Seattle. So that was one less thing to worry about.

"Charles," Ellen whispered when the crowd began to thin. "What's wrong with you?"

"Wrong?"

"Who is it you keep craning your neck to see?"

Charles wasn't convinced she was ready for this. "I met someone very special, Mother. As soon as we're finished here, I'd like to introduce you."

Ellen's jaw went slack, and she laid a hand on his forearm.

"Charles, are you telling me— Are you saying you've fallen in love?"

This time he didn't hesitate. "Yes."

"Oh, my heavens!" Ellen placed her free hand over her heart. "When? Who is she? Why didn't you say something sooner?"

Charles grinned. "Actually Lanni and I haven't known each other long."

"That certainly didn't stop Sawyer."

He laughed outright. "So I noticed."

"I don't care what anyone might think, the minute I met Abbey I realized she was perfect for him."

Charles eyed his mother skeptically. "You'd say that if Sawyer announced he was marrying a gorilla. The fact that Abbey comes complete with grandchildren must elevate her to the level of sainthood."

"Don't you pooh-pooh me, young man," Ellen said, tapping his arm in reproach. "It's true I'm overjoyed that at least one of my sons is getting married. But I want it understood that I couldn't be happier with Sawyer's choice."

"Yes, Mother," Charles replied with mock timidity.

Ellen frowned at him. "Now stop. Tell me about your young lady."

"She isn't mine. Not yet," he said. "Lanni's another one of the women Christian hired. She's working for Midnight Sons as a secretary. She's from Seattle, at least I think she is. That's where she's been living for the past four years, anyway. She recently graduated from the University of Washington."

"Point her out to me," Ellen urged.

Charles directed her attention across the room to the table

where Lanni was busy cutting and serving slices of wedding cake. He couldn't look at her and not be stirred in some way. He observed with pleasure how friendly and open she was, taking time to chat with each person in line. He found it difficult to pull his gaze back to his mother.

"The blonde?" Ellen asked.

"Yes."

"Oh, Charles, she's lovely."

"She's the most beautiful person I ever met."

Ellen patted his hand. "What a sweet thing to say."

Charles still couldn't force his eyes away from Lanni. "She's too young for me."

"Nonsense. You're what—six, seven years older?"

"Ten."

"Does the age difference bother her?"

He had to think about that. "She's never said."

"Then I doubt she cares."

"I'm often gone weeks on end." He tried another argument. "I have to be—it's my job."

"Does she object?"

"I don't know. We've never discussed it."

"Ask her," Ellen advised with perfect logic.

He paused, marveling at her easy acceptance of Lanni—and of her son's feelings for a woman who was a virtual stranger. "I want you to get to know her, Mother."

"I'll enjoy that."

Abbey and Sawyer broke away from the reception line. The disc jockey who'd been hired for the dance had set up his equipment, and the first strains of a haunting melody filled the gymnasium.

Sawyer drew Abbey into his arms and danced with his bride. Studying his brother, Charles noticed that he moved with grace and a surprisingly relaxed air.

He heard Ellen's voice and turned back to her. "I want you to be happy," she was saying. "I mean that, Charles. I'd be delighted to see you find happiness with that lovely girl. I am really looking forward to a houseful of grandchildren."

The way he was feeling at the moment, Charles would have enjoyed getting started on that project just as soon as it could be arranged.

He settled his mother in a comfortable chair. Pearl Inman joined Ellen, and the two women hugged.

"If you'll excuse me," Charles said, eager to hurry over to Lanni.

"Of course." Ellen seemed just as eager to dismiss him.

He was halfway across the room when he turned back to see Ellen and Pearl with their heads close together, their mouths going a mile a minute. Charles considered the nurse his mother's only real friend in Hard Luck.

His mother had never adjusted to life in Alaska. Charles believed, perhaps unfairly, that she'd never tried hard enough. True, there'd been a brief period when she might have found happiness in Hard Luck and in her marriage—but Catherine Fletcher's bitterness had destroyed that, and in the process whatever joy his parents had achieved.

Charles didn't wish Catherine ill, but he was thankful she no longer lived in town. It would be just like her to try to ruin this day for his mother.

Lanni smiled when he approached her. "Are you ready for some cake?"

"Sure, but how about a dance first?"

Lanni glanced at Louise Gold, one of the townspeople and a particular friend of Abbey's. "Go on," Louise urged. "Most everyone's had cake."

Charles thanked her. He noticed that nine-year-old Ronny was attempting to help his mother—if help was the word—by scooping up any discarded frosting with the tip of his index finger and sneaking it inside his suit pocket. Little Chrissie Harris and her dad, Mitch, stood nearby, watching him with amusement and enjoying their generous slices of cake.

"I've been looking forward to dancing with you," Lanni told Charles, stretching out her hand.

"Just remember I'm not good at this," he said. They moved onto the makeshift dance floor. Charles was willing to agree to just about anything for an excuse to hold her. Even if it meant acting like a fool in front of the whole town.

Fortunately the disc jockey had chosen a slow number. Charles gathered Lanni in his embrace and nearly sighed aloud when she slipped her arms around him. He didn't do much more than shuffle back and forth, but at least he wasn't stepping on her feet.

Lanni rested her head against his shoulder, and he closed his eyes. His chest ached with what he felt for her. He wanted to ask her about what had happened between them in the church. But he couldn't bear to release her, so the question would have to wait.

The song ended, and Charles made a pretense of breaking away. But before the next song started, he already had her in his arms.

Unfortunately the disc jockey started playing one of the fast-paced songs from the seventies. High-pitched male voices chanted something about staying alive. Couples jerked their bodies in every direction. Charles figured if he and Lanni were going to survive the song, it wouldn't be on the dance floor.

He scanned the room, then reached for her hand and drew her away. There was absolutely no chance of finding a quiet corner in which to talk. So Charles led her out of the building and into the bright sunlight.

"You want us to dance out here?" Lanni teased.

"Not dance," he said, bringing her back into his arms. The distance between their mouths felt like the most urgent journey he'd ever made. Charles didn't stop to consider what he was doing. He realized in some vague way that anyone walking outside would stumble upon them. He didn't care.

Lanni moaned and responded with the same pent-up desperation that had driven him. He was greedy for her, needed to express everything he felt. She tasted good, so good. Her softness, the smoothness of her skin, the glitter of her satiny hair in the sunlight, made him want to hold her, touch her, forever.

"I couldn't wait a second longer," he said in a husky whisper.

"I couldn't, either."

He waited until he'd had a chance to catch his breath. Glancing quickly around, he steered her toward the playground, his arms still around her.

"Where are we going?" Lanni asked.

"To the swings."

She pressed her head to his shoulder. "I've always loved the swings. When I was a little girl I'd pump and pump and aim for the sky."

Charles set her in the U-shaped seat and stood in front of her. He grasped the heavy chains. "I think the Fates must have an excellent sense of humor," he said as he drew the swing forward.

"Why's that?"

He released the chains and stepped away as Lanni swayed gently back and forth.

"I gave Sawyer such a hard time about falling in love with Abbey. I was so sure something like that couldn't really happen, let alone practically overnight."

For a breathless moment, Lanni said nothing. "You believe differently now?"

"Yes. I *know* differently. Sawyer nearly lost Abbey because of me."

Her eyes widened with surprise.

"I was worried about what was going on with my levelheaded brother. Like I told you, I just didn't think it was possible to feel the way he did. So in my own stupid way I tried to fix things by offering Abbey and the kids their airfare home. I figured out of sight, out of mind."

"But Abbey didn't leave."

"No, thank heaven. She stayed. And now you're here, and I'd probably shoot any man who tried to convince you to go."

She looked away from him. "Charles, I need to—"

"No," he interrupted, "let me finish. I have to say this. The moment we met, I felt a connection with you. Later, when you were walking home with Duke Porter—" He shook his head. "I can't find the words to describe what happened."

"And in church this afternoon."

"Yes, again, only much stronger."

"I felt it, too, Charles." Her voice was faint.

"I know nothing about love, Lanni. All I know is what I feel for you. I'm not comfortable with it. The fact is, I'm not sure what to do about it."

"Are you trying to say you love me?" she asked.

"Yes," he answered starkly.

"Oh, Charles."

The one reaction he hadn't expected was this woebegone look that spread over her face.

"I realize I shouldn't be throwing this at you now," he said hurriedly, "but I had a feeling that I *had* to tell you or it was going to burn a hole straight through me."

"I...love you, too."

His shoulders relaxed. At least he wasn't in this predicament alone. "Well, where do we go from here?"

"Do we have to go anywhere?" she asked.

"I guess not." He was almost ashamed to hear the relief in his voice. But the idea of going where Sawyer had gone terrified Charles. He wasn't ready for marriage. His feelings were too new. He needed time to adjust to the fact that he was in love before complicating his life with an irrevocable commitment. Because if he ever *did* get married, it had to be forever.

He pulled the swing toward him and gave her a loving kiss. "We should get back to the reception."

"I know." She didn't sound eager to return.

"My mother's dying to meet you."

"I want to meet her, too."

Hand in hand, they entered the gymnasium. Several couples were dancing, but because of the shortage of women, Ben Hamilton and John Henderson were waltzing around the room alone, without partners. Duke Porter eyed Lanni—and Charles—as if to gauge how likely she'd be to accept a dance with him. Every other unattached man seemed to be gazing at her just as avidly.

The last person Charles expected to have to give her up to, though, was his own younger brother.

"Hello, beautiful," Christian said, planting himself in front of Lanni.

"Hello, yourself," Charles answered.

"I wasn't talking to you."

"Hello," Lanni responded.

"Can I have this dance and the next one and the one after that?" Christian asked.

Uncertain, Lanni looked at Charles. "Perhaps later," she said kindly. "I promised Charles I'd meet his mother."

"Great," Christian muttered. "I'll tag along, and if I'm lucky my big bad brother might find it in his heart to introduce you to me, as well."

Charles didn't know what kind of game Christian was playing. His brother knew darn well who Lanni was. He'd hired her!

He decided to ignore Christian, but his irritating brother would have none of it. Like a playful puppy, he followed them across the room to where Ellen sat.

"Mother," Charles said, placing his arm around Lanni's shoulders, "this is Lanni Caldwell. Lanni, my mother, Ellen Greenleaf."

"Hello, Lanni."

"Hello." They exchanged smiles and brief handshakes.

"Please sit down," Ellen said, patting the empty chair next to her. "Charles has told me very little about you."

Christian made a show of clearing his throat. "I know I'm stiff competition, but I still deserve an introduction," he insisted for the second time.

Charles frowned. "Don't tell me you don't recognize Lanni."

"I don't," Christian said blankly.

"She's Sawyer's secretary. You hired her, remember?"

Christian's look revealed his confusion. "I've never seen this woman before in my life."

"I think I can explain all this," Lanni said, her voice trembling slightly.

"The woman I hired is named Mariah Douglas," Christian continued. "She gets here next week. I finished making the arrangements a couple of days ago."

Charles's frown deepened. "Lanni?"

"He's right," she said. Charles watched as her whole body tensed. "I came to Hard Luck to clean out my grandmother's house. Sawyer called my mother and asked if Midnight Sons could rent it."

"Your grandmother's house," Charles repeated. "Who's your grandmother?"

"Catherine Harmon Fletcher," she said.

Chapter
6

"Charles?" Ellen turned to her son as if seeking an explanation. "Surely there's some mistake."

Charles ignored his mother, his eyes searing Lanni's. She squared her shoulders and met his gaze without flinching.

"There's no mistake, Mother," Charles said icily. "It seems I've been taken for a fool." With that he turned and walked away.

Lanni resisted the urge to run after him. "I apologize if I caused you any discomfort, Mrs. Greenleaf," she said calmly, trying to keep her voice void of emotion.

Ellen stared after Charles. "I'm sorry, Lanni." Her eyes filled with sadness. "You see, there's been so much hurt to both families it's difficult to overlook. I don't wish your grandmother any harm, but I don't want anything to do with her, either."

"I understand." In essence Ellen was asking Lanni to leave. "I'm...glad to have met you."

Ellen didn't return the sentiment. Instead, she simply nodded.

With her heart in her throat, Lanni left Ellen and Christian. The need to talk about this with Charles burned in her chest. He was hurt and angry, justifiably so. But she hadn't *meant* to deceive him. She'd tried to tell him—twice—but both times he'd stopped her. She'd been almost grateful, fearing exactly this.

Lanni walked to the other side of the gymnasium and slumped weakly into a chair.

"Lanni, is something wrong?"

She glanced up to find Abbey standing over her. "Charles rushed out of here so fast," she went on.

"It's nothing," Lanni insisted, not wanting to ruin Abbey's wedding day with her own troubles.

Abbey sat down in the seat next to her. "I don't believe that. Now tell me what happened."

Lanni took a deep breath. "Charles learned that Catherine Fletcher's my grandmother. I should've told him from the first, but I didn't really think it would matter. I thought that once he got to know me he'd realize neither one of us has anything to do with the history between our families."

Abbey squeezed Lanni's hand reassuringly. "Give him time," she murmured.

Lanni had already made that decision herself, although she thought she'd never forget the shock and anger in his eyes. The outrage seem to spit and boil inside him. He couldn't get away from her fast enough.

"Don't worry about Charles and me," Lanni said, forcing

herself to smile. "This is your day, and I don't want anything to spoil it."

"Nothing could," Abbey assured her. After a few more minutes of low-key conversation, she rejoined her husband.

Lanni's throat felt dry and scratchy so she walked over to the punch bowl. She hadn't taken more than a sip of her sweet, fruity drink when Sawyer walked up to her.

"Abbey told me what happened," he said grimly.

"Charles needs time to get used to the idea, that's all," she said, making light of his reaction.

Sawyer's eyes revealed his own remorse. "I should've told him."

"It wasn't your job."

"I purposely let him think you were the secretary Christian hired." A gathering frown darkened Sawyer's features. "Charles was so self-righteous when he learned what Christian and I had done to bring women to Hard Luck. When I saw how taken he was with you, I thought it was poetic justice. Frankly I felt it would do him good."

"I'm the one who's responsible here," she argued, "not you."

"If you want, I'll talk to him."

As tempting as the offer was, Lanni refused to involve anyone else. "Thank you, but no. Either Charles and I work this out ourselves or we don't. It's not up to anyone else."

It pained her that Charles found it so difficult to accept her background. As Ellen had said earlier, sins were committed by both families. Lanni was willing to forgive what his family had done to hers, but apparently the reverse wasn't true.

"He's stubborn," Sawyer told her. "Be patient."

Lanni didn't answer. She had other commitments and responsibilities waiting for her in Anchorage. She'd be starting
her internship with the newspaper less than two months from
now, and she had plenty to do before then. She wasn't willing
to delay her return home, hoping Charles would suddenly
come to his senses. He wasn't the only one who could be
stubborn.

Sawyer left and Lanni finished her punch. The drink felt cool
and soothing against the dryness of her throat. Then, just as she
was setting aside the empty crystal cup, she noticed Charles.

He'd come back to the reception. He stood at the other side,
as far away from her as he could get and still be in the same
room. His eyes followed her intently. She tried to smile, tried
to tell him without words how sorry she was.

The minute her eyes met his he turned and walked to his
mother's side. That action told Lanni everything she needed to
know. His loyalty was with his family. He wanted nothing more
to do with her.

"Hello, Lanni."

She looked up to see Duke Porter. "Hi, Duke."

"Would I get my head bitten off if I asked you to dance?"

"Of course not," she said.

"I didn't mean by you." Duke cast a look in Charles's direction. "You two seem to be an item. I don't want to cause
problems, but Charles is sitting over there and you're here all
alone—and you seem a little depressed."

Pride elevated Lanni's chin. She'd had no idea others could
see how miserable she was. "No one's going to object if we
dance," she said, "least of all Charles O'Halloran."

* * *

Anger poured through Charles like liquid fire. Lanni hadn't been the only person to mislead him. Sawyer and Abbey had been in on this deception, too, making him the brunt of their joke. Still, he didn't really blame Sawyer. His brother was so much in love he needed a compass to find his way to the john. Nor was Charles sure how much Abbey knew of the family history.

That left Lanni.

He might've been inclined to think she was unaware of the facts, if it wasn't for one small thing. She'd purposely led him to believe she was someone else. No wonder she hadn't talked much about herself. She knew. His stomach churned, and it was all he could do not to vent his rage.

He'd made a first-class idiot of himself over Lanni Caldwell. Granddaughter of the woman he hated. Earlier that afternoon he'd laid his heart at her feet. He cringed when he remembered his disjointed speech about falling in love with her. She must have been snickering over that one!

Charles clung to his anger. It was necessary, otherwise those pleading looks she sent his way would dissolve the wall of grievances he'd built against her.

Unlike Lanni, he'd been old enough to remember some of what had happened. He'd seen with his own eyes what Catherine Fletcher had done to his family. That woman was responsible for ruining his parents' marriage, and his father's life. Charles would never forgive or forget.

He turned away, unwilling to allow Lanni the satisfaction of knowing he was watching her. The determination to focus his attention elsewhere lasted all of two minutes. When he sought her again, he found she wasn't standing by the punch bowl anymore.

She was dancing with Duke Porter.

The anger brewing inside him intensified to glass-melting degrees. The gentle sway of her hips was nearly his undoing. The fact that Duke had his hand plastered against those hips demanded every ounce of restraint he possessed. He was a fraction of a heartbeat from shoving his way through his brother's wedding guests and plowing his fist halfway down Duke Porter's throat.

Even knowing what he did about Lanni couldn't keep Charles from wanting her. He'd never thought of himself as a weak man—but then, he hadn't known he was this much of a fool, either. What he needed, Charles decided, was a beer.

"Is everything all right?" Christian asked him a few minutes later.

Charles lifted the beer bottle to his lips. "Couldn't be better," he said gruffly, unable to tear his gaze from Lanni and Duke. It certainly hadn't taken *her* long to turn her attention to greener pastures.

"What's going on with you and Lanni?" Christian pressed.

"Not a thing." He wanted to tear off his brother's head for even asking.

"Peace, peace," Christian said, raising both hands. "All I did was ask a simple question."

"You got a simple answer."

Christian's gaze followed his. "She sure is pretty," he murmured. "It's a damn shame she's related to Catherine."

Having said that much, he wandered away. Charles was glad to be rid of him.

He wasn't in the mood for company, especially his own brother reminding him how pretty Lanni was. He downed another swig of beer, but it did little to douse the burning anger.

Lanni wrapped her arms loosely around Duke's shoulders. The pilot's no-doubt clammy hands slid from the gentle swell of her hips to her waist and down again. That did it. Charles smacked the beer bottle down on the table and headed for the dance floor.

Sawyer waylaid him. "Do you have a problem?" he asked.

Charles glared at his brother. "Not really. Duke does. In another two minutes he's going to need a set of dentures."

"It's time you went outside and cooled down." Christian joined forces against Charles, and together, one at each side, his brothers escorted him out of the building.

The sun was so bright it nearly blinded him. "It isn't Duke you're angry with," Sawyer said evenly. "It's me. Only, I'm your brother and this is my wedding day."

Charles ground his teeth, recognizing the truth of his brother's words. He was angriest with Lanni, but that didn't completely absolve Sawyer of complicity in the deception.

"I should have told you."

Charles stiffened. "You're damn right you should have."

"I'll admit, it was a stupid trick. But, Charles, does it matter who Lanni's related to? She didn't have anything to do with the past. She's her own woman. Judging her by Catherine's sins isn't fair, any more than it'd be fair if she blamed you for what Dad did."

"There are things you don't know!" Charles snapped. He wiped his face with a shaking hand in an effort to cool his temper. He knew far better than Sawyer or Christian the damage Catherine Fletcher had done to their family.

Every time he looked at Lanni he'd be reminded that she was a blood relative of Catherine's. He couldn't forget, and perhaps more importantly, he couldn't forgive.

"If that's the way he feels," Christian said to Sawyer, "nothing we say is going to change his mind."

"I'm wondering, though," Sawyer said with a thoughtful frown, "if he can live with the consequences."

Charles threw his brothers a look that told them exactly where they could go and that he'd be more than happy to see to their arrival there.

"I'm getting out of here," Charles announced.

Sawyer and Christian exchanged a look.

"And I don't want or need any company, understand?" He had all the companionship he needed in the form of a bottle. He'd never purposely gotten drunk in his life. But there was a first time for everything.

Lanni saw Charles disappear with his two brothers. Shortly afterward, Sawyer and Christian reappeared without him, and she didn't see him again. She tried to pretend it didn't matter, but couldn't hide the fact that it did.

Deciding to leave the reception herself, she found Abbey and Sawyer and hugged them both. "I hope you'll be very happy," she whispered, fearing her voice would break if she tried to speak normally. "My love goes with you."

"Everything will work out for the best," Abbey whispered in her ear.

Lanni managed a smile and nodded. "I'll remember that."

Sawyer's eyes were somber. "I'm sorry, Lanni."

"What for?" she asked with feigned cheerfulness. "You didn't do anything wrong." She was grateful he didn't offer her platitudes.

The reception broke up before Lanni could leave. Abbey and Sawyer were scheduled to fly into Fairbanks that evening, and then the next day take a flight to Hawaii for two glorious weeks. Abbey had mentioned earlier that Scott and Susan were flying out with their grandparents and that Charles would be looking after Eagle Catcher, Scott's husky. In the flurry of departures and teary goodbyes, Lanni quietly slipped out.

It seemed as though every ally she had in town was deserting her.

Her grandmother's house felt like a prison when she walked inside. Boxes lined one entire living room wall, ready to be mailed to Anchorage. That was something she'd learned soon after coming to Hard Luck—everything was sent via the United States Mail, even groceries. Transport by any other means was prohibitively expensive.

The phone rang, startling her. She stared at it until it rang again. With her heart hammering wildly, she grabbed the receiver.

"Hello," she said into the mouthpiece.

"Hiya, little sister."

"Matt." Just the sound of his voice was comforting. "It's so good to hear from you."

"Miss me, do you?"

He hadn't a clue how much. She'd always idolized Matt; he'd been her knight in shining armor. Even when they were children, at an age when most siblings fought, Lanni had considered Matt as near perfect as it was possible for any human to be. Not until his marriage failed had Lanni found fault with him.

"So," Matt said, breaking into her thoughts, "you're hobnobbing with the O'Halloran brothers."

"Not exactly," she said, wanting to minimize her contact with Charles and his family.

"That's not what I hear. Mom said you filled in for Sawyer's secretary and that you met Charles."

"Yes." She swallowed painfully. "We've met."

"According to Mom, you two hit it off."

Lanni's hand tightened around the receiver. The temptation to spill her heart out to her older brother and seek his advice was almost overwhelming. But she wouldn't do that.

"Come on, Lanni. Don't keep me in the dark."

She moistened her lips. "Charles is...a good man."

"Mom said you seemed quite enthralled with him."

"How's Karen?" Lanni asked in a desperate effort to change the subject. Then she sighed—Matt had struggled with the breakup of his marriage, and Lanni was still worried about him. "I'm sorry, Matt. I can't seem to remember that you two aren't together anymore."

"Karen moved."

"Moved? What do you mean, she moved?"

"As in packed up her bags and headed south."

"How far south?"

"California."

Any hope Lanni harbored of a reconciliation between her brother and his wife was dashed. With Karen living thousands of miles from Anchorage, the likelihood of those two settling their differences seemed practically nil.

"When did that happen?" Lanni generally stayed in close contact with Karen and hadn't heard a word about her leaving Alaska.

"Last week. Paragon, Inc. offered her a giant promotion. Unfortunately it entailed a transfer, and I gather she leapt at the chance. Naturally she didn't call to talk it over with me. I heard through the grapevine that she packed up and was out of here in two days flat."

Lanni closed her eyes. No wonder her brother didn't recognize her anguish; he was dealing with his own.

"I'm sorry to hear that."

"Mom said Karen tried to contact you before she left." *But not Matt.* "I want only the best for her." He said the words as if by rote. Lanni knew he didn't dare admit—least of all to himself—how much he loved and missed his ex-wife; admitting it would leave him too vulnerable, too ravaged. "Only the best," he said again.

"I know you do, Matt."

"Listen," he said, brightening, "I didn't call to get us both depressed."

"Good." Lanni could do with a bit of cheering up.

"I heard a rumor I want you to check out for me."

"Sure."

"Is it true there's some kind of lodge in Hard Luck?"

"Yes, sort of. There was a fire years back that burned part of it. No one ever bothered to repair it."

"That's great!"

"Great? If you want the truth, I wonder why Charles's family hasn't torn it down by now. The place is completely boarded up. My feeling is it needs to be either rebuilt or demolished."

"Do you think they'd be willing to sell it?"

"The lodge?"

"Of course the lodge."

"Why?" It made no sense to Lanni.

"Why?" her brother repeated.

It was beginning to sound as if the phone had developed an echo. "Because I'd like a chance to do something with it. Gate of the Arctic National Park's close by, isn't it? The lodge would be perfect tourist accommodation."

Tourist accommodation? Her brother must have lost every shred of reason he'd ever possessed. "But, Matt, what about the winters? What tourist in his right mind would visit the Arctic in December and January? You'd go broke."

"Dogs, Lanni. There are hundreds of adventure-seekers out there looking for a new thrill. I'll take them mushing. Just look at the popularity of the Iditarod and the other races."

"But you'd have to raise the dogs first." Surely this project would cost more than he could possibly afford.

"Not necessarily. I'll rent them and whatever else I need from the pros. This is the opportunity of a lifetime, Lanni, and I'm getting in on the ground floor."

Lanni wondered again if her brother had finally lost his mind.

He routinely came up with these crazy ideas, but this was the craziest yet. None of them held his attention for long. He'd get started on some fabulous plan, some wonderful new career that was bound to make him rich, and tire of it within six months. Lanni had seen the pattern countless times.

"Ask Charles for me, would you, Lanni?"

Lanni pressed her hand to her forehead. "No..." She'd never refused her brother anything. Until now.

"No?"

"If you're truly interested in buying that burned-out lodge from the O'Hallorans, then you can ask them yourself."

Her words were followed by a lengthy pause. "Lanni, is everything all right?"

"It's great," she lied. "Just wonderful. I'm nearly finished with Grammy's house. I might even be home in a couple of days."

"You don't sound so good," Matt said gently. "You'd better tell me what happened."

"Nothing happened."

"You're sure?"

"Positive. Just answer one question."

"Anything."

She took a shaky breath. "Are all men born bastards, or do they have to work hard to achieve it?"

Matt chuckled. "You've locked horns with the O'Hallorans, have you?"

"Something like that."

"Well, I don't know about the O'Hallorans, but I guess the answer depends on who you ask. Karen would agree I'm a bastard, and she'd tell you I worked hard to achieve it. But I gotta say I seem to have come by the talent naturally."

Luring women to Hard Luck wasn't working out the way Christian had expected. One of his brothers was married and the other wasn't speaking to him.

Since he'd been away from his desk for so long, Christian decided he'd walk down to the airfield to check out the office.

The morning was clear and sunny. Abbey and Sawyer and their entourage had gotten off safely the day before. The kids and their grandparents had left today. Christian glanced at his watch. By now the honeymoon couple would be on a plane headed for beautiful Waikiki.

Christian was about to enter the mobile office when he heard the buzz of an approaching aircraft. None of Midnight Sons' planes was in the air, which meant that another of the flying services was making a run into Hard Luck. He stood outside the trailer and watched the descent of the single-engine aircraft.

Frontier was a well-known flight-service contractor flying out of Fairbanks. The pilots made regular stops in Hard Luck. Only this wasn't one of their regular runs.

The Cessna landed, coasting to a stop.

The door lowered, and a young woman with long red hair descended cautiously. She paused when she stepped onto the runway, apparently surveying the town.

Christian was sure he recognized her, but he couldn't recall exactly when they'd met or where. In the past five weeks, he'd interviewed more women than he cared to count.

The plane's engine continued to purr in the early-morning

stillness. The pilot handed the redhead a piece of luggage, which she promptly dropped. Her expensive-looking suitcase hit the ground and snapped open.

At least half a dozen pairs of lacy panties spilled onto the dirt-and-gravel runway. The whirling blades of the Cessna created a strong breeze, which sent the panties flying. The woman gave a frustrated cry and chased after her underwear, leaving the suitcase open. The wind caught several other items, lifting them from the neatly folded stack.

A second suitcase appeared while the woman chased hither and yon.

Christian would have volunteered to help, but he suspected his assistance wouldn't be appreciated.

The woman snatched up a delicate black bra and several other skimpy items, then hurriedly stuffed them back into the suitcase, slamming it shut.

Christian resisted the urge to laugh.

The redhead managed to retrieve everything. She lifted the suitcase and carried it awkwardly under her arm. One bra strap and some lacy odds and ends dangled from the sides.

The Frontier pilot spoke to her for a few minutes, then they solemnly shook hands and he prepared to leave. She waved enthusiastically as the plane began its takeoff.

"Hello," she said, smiling brightly when she saw Christian.

"Hello," he answered, coming forward. "Would you like some help with your luggage?"

"No thanks, I've got everything under control." With some difficulty she looped her purse strap over her shoulder and picked up the second suitcase.

"Welcome to Hard Luck." Christian still hadn't figured out where he'd met this woman.

"I can't tell you how good it is to finally get here," she said, sighing. "I had no idea how far from civilization this place is."

Although she claimed she didn't want any help, she was obviously in need of it. He removed both suitcases from her hands.

"I hope it isn't a problem that I arrived a day early," she said.

"A day early?"

"Yes. I'm Mariah Douglas, the secretary you hired. Don't you remember?"

Lanni never spent a more miserable day in her life. She worked all morning and afternoon, sorting through Grammy's personal things. When she happened upon a thick manila envelope tucked in the back of the bookcase, she suspected it had something to do with David O'Halloran. She was right.

Inside she discovered the letters he'd mailed her from Europe during the war. Lanni fingered them, but hadn't the heart to read them. For more than fifty years, her grandmother had saved love letters from a man who'd betrayed her.

Lanni sighed as she thought about this again. She hadn't eaten all day and decided a walk would do her good. Maybe she could grab a sandwich or something at Ben's.

Burying her hands deep in her sweater pockets, she started toward the Hard Luck Café. As she turned off Main Street, she saw Charles walking toward her. Her first inclination was to ignore him, to pretend she hadn't seen him.

He'd obviously recognized her at the same moment she saw

him. His step faltered slightly, as if the mere sight of her was enough to throw him off balance.

They continued toward each other at the same slow pace, their eyes wary, until only a few feet separated them. Lanni spoke first. "Charles, please..."

"What?" he asked gruffly.

"If I misled you, I'm sorry."

"*If?*"

She had no response, and the silence stretched between them.

"I assume you're looking for an apology," she eventually said, trying one last time, "and I'll admit I was wrong. I should've told you the first day we met, but I was hoping that once you got to know me you'd be willing to put old grievances aside." She struggled to keep the hurt out of her voice.

He gave a smile that lacked any hint of pleasure.

Lanni could feel her anger take hold. She pointed a finger at Charles. "Something is very wrong here. *Your* father left *my* grandmother standing at the altar fifty years ago, and *I'm* the one apologizing to *you*."

Charles frowned, but he said nothing.

"You know what I found this morning?" Of course he didn't, but she was going to tell him. "Letters. My grandmother kept the letters your father wrote her while he was away at war. All these years she's treasured them. I found them with ribbons wrapped around them, hidden in the back of her bookcase."

Charles clenched his fists at his sides. "Your grandmother ruined my father's life."

"Oh, please. He did it to himself."

"There are things you don't know."

"I know enough. My grandmother was so much in love with him she went down to Fairbanks and had her photograph taken in her wedding dress—the one she intended to wear for him. Can you imagine how she must've felt when she learned he'd married someone else? Do you have any idea how difficult it is to stop loving someone?"

Fire leapt into his eyes; again he said nothing.

"What is this?" she shouted in frustration. "A family trait?"

"What are you talking about *now?*"

Lanni's nails bit into her palms. "You," she said, unable to conceal her emotion any longer. "Did you or did you not claim you loved me? Apparently the words mean nothing to an O'Halloran. Not to your father, and not to you."

She thought she saw a look of regret cross his face, but he didn't speak.

"I see," she said softly.

"You should've told me who you were," he mumbled at last.

"I did," she returned stiffly.

"No, you didn't."

She held her hand over her heart. "I'm Lanni Caldwell. What more would you need to know?"

He closed his eyes as if to block her out.

Swallowing her pride, Lanni tried one final time. "What happened, happened. It's true my grandmother was no saint, but then neither was your father. And, Charles, neither are you. Nor am I."

"I'm sorry, Lanni," he said, pushing back his dark hair with one hand.

"Sorry?" She didn't understand. "What are you saying?" It came to her then with a sickening sense of dread. "Charles," she whispered, her voice catching, *"what are you saying?"*

He sucked in a deep breath.

"You don't want anything to do with me?"

He nodded slowly.

Anger and frustration boiled inside her. "Then say it!" she shouted. "At least have the courage to say it to my face."

The pain in his eyes was almost more than she could bear. He stroked her face gently. "It was never meant to be, Lanni. Not for us."

Chapter
7

Lanni had told Charles she'd studied journalism. He sat nursing his coffee in the Hard Luck Café, mulling over the way things had gone between him and Lanni. Mitch Harris, who worked for the Department of the Interior, and his daughter, Chrissie, were at another table, having breakfast.

He remembered the day he'd taken her to his grandfather's original claim, when they'd sat by the camp stove and talked. He'd wondered at the time what she was doing working as a secretary if she had a journalism degree, but the truth was, he hadn't cared. He was so glad she was in Hard Luck he hadn't questioned the whys or wherefores.

Since his behavior at the wedding reception, recriminations had been coming at him from all sides. Even Ben seemed ready to take him to task.

"Ready for a refill?" Ben stopped at the table, coffeepot in hand.

Charles stared down at his cup, the coffee long since cooled. "No thanks."

Ben lingered. "Normally I don't butt into someone else's business unless I'm asked, but—"

"I'd advise you to do the same now," Charles said evenly. He'd been friends with Ben for a good many years. He didn't want that relationship ruined now, especially over Lanni.

"I'd keep my trap shut if it wasn't for one thing." Ben set the coffeepot on the table, and glancing over at Mitch, lowered his voice. "I told you about Marilyn. I haven't said her name aloud in ten, maybe fifteen years. Talking about her stirred up a lot of old feelings that should've stayed at rest. The way I figure it, you owe me."

"I owe you for the coffee, nothing else."

"Not this time, Charlie."

No one called him Charlie. Ben knew that.

"Lanni's leaving town," Ben said. "I heard her making the arrangements."

"I know." What did Ben think he'd been doing for the last thirty minutes? Charles had been sitting there, trying to figure out where he was going to find the strength to let her walk out of his life.

Ben's mouth thinned. "You know?"

Charles's hand tightened around his mug until his knuckles showed white. "It's inevitable, don't you think?"

The older man didn't answer. "You're going to *let* her?"

Charles expelled his breath forcefully and nodded.

Ben cocked his head as if he couldn't believe what he'd heard. Or, more to the point, as if he simply hadn't *liked* what he'd heard. "You mean to say you're actually going to let Lanni Caldwell walk out of your life even after what I told you?" Ben sounded incredulous. "If you do anything so damn stupid, I guarantee you're going to regret it for the rest of your life."

"Maybe."

"Okay, so you don't owe me anything, but what do you owe yourself? Lanni, too. She deserves better than this. Maybe you're just looking for an excuse to be rid of her. That's what it seems like to me."

"Stay out of this, Ben," Charles warned. "What happens between Lanni and me isn't any of your business."

"I don't understand it," Ben muttered. "I really don't understand it." He picked up the coffeepot and returned to the kitchen. "College-educated, smart as a tack when it comes to book learning, yet I've never met a stupider, more stubborn—"

"Bastard," Charles supplied for him.

Ben just shook his head.

It was useless for Charles to explain that there were certain elements of his relationship with Lanni that Ben couldn't possibly understand.

"One last word of advice," Ben called. "I'm telling you this because I know." He splayed his fingers across his chest. "I've lived with my mistakes for the past twenty-five years. I didn't know when I refused to read Marilyn's letters that we wouldn't see each other again. There was never anyone else for me, Charles. Think about that. Would you let Lanni go if you knew you'd never see her again?"

"Yes. I would." Charles stood up and slapped a fistful of change on the table, then walked out of the café.

* * *

Duke Porter would be arriving with the Midnight Sons' truck shortly after noon. Lanni was ready for him. She'd transferred the boxes from the living room onto the porch, then sat on the top step to wait. Her muscles ached, but she welcomed the physical pain.

A cloud of dust appeared down the road. Wiping the perspiration from her brow with the back of her wrist, she got to her feet, assuming it was Duke. She quickly realized she was wrong—it was Charles driving past. He kept his eyes trained ahead, avoiding even a glance in her direction. For all the notice he gave her, she might have been invisible.

Lanni sank back onto the step, struggling with her emotions. She covered her face with her hands and drew in one deep breath after another in an effort to distance the pain.

How often, she wondered, had her grandmother's heart raced at the sound of an approaching car? Had David come to her? Ever? All those years she'd waited for him. Hoped. Pined. Suffered. Now Grammy was dying, and Lanni knew why. The doctors said it was her heart. In a manner of speaking they were right. Her grandmother had been slowly dying for the past ten years because she had no reason to continue living. David, the man she'd loved from the time she was a teenager, was dead. The only hope she had of ever being with him again lay on the other side of life.

Lanni knew that, like his father before him, Charles wasn't free to love her. But it wasn't another woman who stood between them. Family loyalty had destroyed their love. Now Charles wanted nothing to do with her.

Unlike her grandmother, Lanni would leave voluntarily. But not without pain or regret. Head held high, unwilling to apologize for who she was, she would walk away.

Duke pulled up a few minutes later and loaded the truck himself. She signed the necessary papers, gave him her parents' address for the bill and returned to the house.

In the morning she'd leave Hard Luck.

That night, Lanni sat on the swing on her grandmother's front porch. A light breeze, scented with tundra wildflowers, stirred restlessly. Lanni closed her eyes and recalled the last time she'd sat on a swing. A child's swing, very different from this one. A night very different from this one, too...

Lanni basked in the silence. She listened to the crickets, the birds, the sounds of evening—an evening as bright as noontime—searching for solace she knew she wouldn't find.

She didn't understand how her grandmother could have remained in Hard Luck waiting for a man who'd never love her. Year after year, until she was old and bitter.

How unhappy she must have been.

Lanni closed her eyes. These final hours in town were agony for her. Yet Catherine had stayed on year after year, never giving up hope that one day David would be hers again.

The sound of footsteps alerted her to the fact that she was no longer alone.

Lanni opened her eyes to see Charles standing on the other side of the fence that framed her grandmother's yard. Her pulse quickened.

Was he real or some figment of her imagination? Had this happened to Grammy, too? Had she been so desperate for

David that she'd pictured him coming to her the way Lanni was seeing Charles?

"I shouldn't be here."

Yes, so he was real. One look told her he hadn't wanted to come. His eyes were filled with a pain that reflected her own. He turned to leave.

She rushed down the steps. "Don't go."

He hesitated.

"Come sit with me," she invited, gesturing toward the swing.

Charles moved closer. Watching him, she could almost see the battle being waged inside him. She realized he didn't understand what had driven him to her. She suspected he considered it a deficiency of character, a weakness. If that was the case, then she was weak, too.

Lanni turned to climb the steps and sat where she'd been sitting moments earlier, on the swing, leaving space beside her.

Charles opened the gate and came through. He climbed the steps, too, but paused at the top. His face revealed nothing; nevertheless Lanni could tell how tightly he'd reined in his emotions.

"I'm not as different from my father as I thought," he said hoarsely. "He couldn't stay away, either."

Lanni didn't know what he meant, but she wasn't sure it mattered. Not right now. Charles was here, with her, on her last night in Hard Luck.

She stared at him, feeling a jolt of pain when she saw the lines about his eyes and the rigid way he held himself. He was hurting, just as she was.

"Years ago," he continued in an emotionless voice, "my

mother returned to England. She took Christian with her. My father was devastated. At first he found comfort in the bottle, but that didn't last long. He was never much of a drinking man."

Charles rubbed his hand along the back of his neck. "Later it was Catherine who...comforted him."

If that was true, Lanni didn't understand why Charles hated her grandmother so much. She couldn't decide whether to be shocked—or pleased that Catherine had even a little time with the man she loved.

"Dad didn't think Sawyer or I knew where he went at night," he said. "But we did. We never talked about it. Catherine became an addiction to him."

"That was a long time ago."

"He couldn't stay away from Catherine, and I can't stay away from you." It sounded like a confession. "I don't have the strength to resist you, Lanni."

She stood, causing the swing to sway gently behind her. Wordlessly she walked over to him and touched his face. "I love you, Charles."

He pulled her toward him, urgently seeking her mouth. Again and again he kissed her, as though he couldn't get enough. She sensed that whatever she gave him now would need to last them both a lifetime.

Charles buried his fingers in her hair and groaned.

She slipped her arms around his neck, pressing herself against him. He drew in a swift breath and kissed her with an intensity that left her reeling.

Then he caught hold of her arms and pulled them down to her sides. "No more," he said roughly. "We can't do this...."

Lanni hugged him, molding her body to his. The quick surge of his heart, the hardening of his body, told her what she needed to know. After a moment she felt his hand move lightly on her hair.

She slipped out of his embrace and led him into the house, her heart beating heavily. He turned to close the door.

"Just hold me," she said in a whisper, nestling in his arms. "That's all I want."

They sat on the sofa, the same one her grandmother must have sat on with his father. Charles seemed to realize this at the precise moment she did.

"My father was with Catherine—here."

"I know. We can move," she said quickly.

"It's not important." When he brought her back into his embrace, his touch was tender. He kissed her face, her eyes and nose and chin. Lanni's heart fluttered with excitement, with passion. With hope.

He eased away from her, his breathing ragged. "We have to stop," he whispered in a voice she barely recognized as his.

She nodded.

Charles settled back on the sofa. He gathered Lanni to him, her back against his chest.

"Tell me what you meant earlier," she said when she found her voice. "About David not being able to stay away from Catherine. Did they...have an affair?"

"They did," Charles answered, breathing softly into her hair. "Maybe it wasn't such a big deal...."

"But you haven't forgotten. Neither has your mother." She leaned back far enough so she could look into his eyes.

He didn't answer her, not right away. His arms, still holding her, tightened. "Eventually we got word that Ellen was returning to Alaska. To Hard Luck. She didn't want a divorce. She wanted to come home."

Lanni closed her eyes, thinking of two teenage boys eager to have their mother back. At the same time, she understood how the news must have crushed her grandmother.

"My father had to tell Catherine. She'd come to our house— I was doing my homework in the kitchen at the time." He paused. "Catherine was hysterical. She yelled and screamed and hit my father. He didn't even try to defend himself, and he stopped me when I tried to intervene. I'd come running in when I heard the noise. I'm just glad Sawyer wasn't there. Over and over Catherine told him he couldn't do this to her. Not again. Not a second time."

Lanni's eyes flooded with tears.

"She started sobbing. She told Dad he'd be sorry, and then she ran out the door."

Charles's fingers bit into her arms. Lanni was sure he wasn't even aware of it.

"After she left—" he hesitated "—Dad broke down. It's the only time in my life I ever saw him weep. At first I thought she might have physically hurt him. Later, I realized what was wrong."

He stopped, as if telling her was too much.

"I need to know. Please, Charles, just tell me," Lanni pleaded.

"He wept because he loved Catherine. He'd always loved her."

"Then why..." Lanni was confused. If David had truly cared

for Catherine, why had he taken Ellen back? Why had he married her in the first place?

Charles understood her unfinished question. "I'd like to believe my father loved my mother, too," he said. "My brothers think so, but I don't know. I just don't know. They'd been married nearly twenty-five years by that time. Ellen had no one. Except her sons. Her family had been dead for years, wiped out in the war, and when she returned to England there was no one there for her. All the years she lived in Alaska she'd built up a fantasy of what her life would've been like in England. But when she went back, she discovered she wasn't happy there, either."

"How long was she away?"

"Eighteen months."

Poor Ellen. She belonged to two different worlds, but to neither one completely.

"Mother missed Sawyer and me, and wanted another chance to make her marriage work. To her credit she tried hard. For a while after her return she was involved in the community, volunteered at the school, that sort of thing."

"Until?"

Charles's hands caressed her forearms. "Until Catherine made good on her threat."

Lanni stiffened.

"Catherine made my mother the town laughingstock. The first thing she did was tell Ellen about her affair with my father. She supplied plenty of details, too. And she made sure everyone in Hard Luck heard the whole story. More important, she took delight in purposely destroying whatever chance my parents had of fixing their marriage."

"You hate my grandmother, don't you?"

"Yes." Charles didn't hesitate. "My mother made plenty of mistakes over the years, but she didn't deserve that.

"She'd done nothing wrong except fall in love with a man who loved someone else. I'll never understand why they got married at all. Although, I guess people often behave very differently in wartime than they otherwise would."

"Your father allowed Catherine to taunt Ellen?"

Charles didn't answer her question. "Catherine wasn't content with making Ellen miserable. She did whatever she could to hurt my father, as well. Remember the old saying 'Hell hath no fury like a woman scorned'? I swear Catherine Fletcher was the bitterest woman there ever was.

"My father betrayed my mother with his affair, and then Catherine humiliated her. I can't hurt her again. I can't get involved with someone who'll be a constant reminder of the woman who brought so much pain into her life."

Lanni jerked herself free of Charles's embrace. She moved off the sofa, backing away from him. "What about *my* grandmother? Don't you think *she* deserved better? Twice your father used her. Twice he cast her aside. Can you blame her? Can you honestly blame her? You claim he loved her. I doubt it. He did nothing but use her!"

Charles didn't answer, not that she expected him to. With trembling hands, Lanni brushed aside the hair that had fallen in her face.

"You say my grandmother ruined your father's marriage and his life. I wonder." She inhaled deeply. "I wonder if you've considered what he did to her. She married shortly after he returned from the war with Ellen—his bride—but that marriage didn't last more than two years.

"She gave up custody of her only child so she could stay close to David. Catherine is a stranger to my mother. A stranger to me. All because of your father."

Leaning forward, Charles braced his elbows on his knees and hung his head. "Now you know why there can never be anything between us," he whispered.

Lanni stood rigidly beside him. "I'm sorry, Charles, for the pain my family caused yours. And the pain yours has caused mine."

"I'm sorry, too. For all of it."

"But it doesn't change anything."

He shook his head. "Your leaving is for the best."

She fought to keep her voice even. "I'm not going to make the mistakes my grandmother did," she told him, her voice quavering despite her efforts. "I'm not going to spend the rest of my life pining away for you."

"I wouldn't want that."

"I'm going home to Anchorage and I'll do my absolute best to forget I ever met you." Using one hand, she swiped at the tears running down her face.

He gave a brief nod.

"I'm not coming back to Hard Luck." She swiped at her face again, hating the weakness that let the tears fall. Slowly she backed even farther away.

Charles stood up, raking his hand through his hair. "I thought you should know," he said.

She lowered her head. "It helps. Now that I've been properly informed, everything's evened out. I can hate your family, too."

He turned and, shoulders hunched, walked out of her life. This time, she knew, it was forever.

Sawyer sat up in bed with Abbey leaning against him as they listened to the surf. The lanai door was open and a tropical breeze rustled through the palm trees just outside.

"Eventually we're going to have to leave this room," Abbey murmured.

Sawyer stroked her hair. "Why?"

She moved her head to look into her husband's clear gray-blue eyes. "In case you haven't noticed, paradise is right outside."

"Paradise is being right here with you."

Not for the first time, Abbey marveled at her husband's romantic heart. This side of Sawyer had come as a pleasant surprise—along with what she'd learned about his sensual nature. Marriage to Sawyer was going to be a wonderful adventure.

The first night of their honeymoon, in Fairbanks, they'd made love again and again before falling asleep in each other's arms. The next morning, they were on a flight to Hawaii.

When they arrived, all Abbey wanted was a feather pillow and a bed. Sawyer was interested in a bed, too, but not for the purpose of sleep. This man she'd married, Abbey soon discovered, was inexhaustible. Their dinner had been delivered to the room, followed by a late breakfast some hours later. Still they lingered in bed.

"I'd like to play tourist for a while," she said. "Would you mind?"

Sawyer ran his hand down her bare back. He released a slow,

long-suffering sigh. "I suppose I could drag myself out of bed, but only if you promise one thing."

"What's that?"

"We'll play a different kind of game first..."

"Now?" What she really meant was, "Again?"

"No time like the present." He slanted his mouth over hers, and Abbey groaned, sliding toward him.

"Sawyer," she protested without any real fervor, "it's already ten-thirty and——" ·

"You're right," he said. "It's much too late to get started today. We'll have to wait until tomorrow to explore the island."

Abbey giggled. "That wasn't what I meant."

His tongue slid across her lips.

"Then again..." she said breathlessly, "you might be right."

"I thought you'd see the error of your ways."

Hours later they did leave the room. Abbey even managed to convince Sawyer to buy them matching shirts and straw hats in the hotel gift shop.

"I look like I'm wearing a pineapple," he complained, studying himself in the shop mirror.

Abbey laughed, feeling lighthearted and very much in love.

Sawyer rented a car and they drove to the north shore of Oahu, stopping at an outdoor café for lunch. They discovered a deserted beach and lay there soaking up the sunshine. Abbey asked him to spread suntan lotion on her back.

"Do you need any help with the front?" he asked.

"No." She squeezed the lotion onto her arms and rubbed it vigorously into her pale skin. She paused when she found Sawyer watching her every move.

"Will you quit that?" she said.

"Quit what?"

"Looking at me like that."

His expression was one of complete innocence. "Like what?"

Abbey rolled her eyes. "Like you're going to ravish me the first chance you get."

He lowered his sunglasses, his eyes dancing. "That's exactly what I intend."

Abbey smiled. Although she'd been married before, she'd never felt this loved or cherished. And she'd never felt this sexy. "It'd serve you right if I got pregnant during the honeymoon," she told him absently, snapping the lid on the bottle of suntan lotion.

Sawyer went still. "Is there a chance?"

She glanced at him, fearing his reaction. They hadn't talked about birth control. They should have, but… "Yes," she whispered. "There wasn't time to start on the pill, and we…we haven't stopped long enough for any precautions."

Sawyer let out a shout of sheer delight and sent his hat flying toward the cloudless blue sky. "Hot damn, woman, if I'd known that, we'd *never* have left the hotel room."

"You mean to say you wouldn't object?"

"Object? If you were to get pregnant on this trip it would be the second-best thing that ever happened to me."

"What's the first?"

He seemed surprised she didn't know. "Meeting you, Abbey. What else?"

She leapt up from the beach towel and stuffed it in her bag. Once that was done, she shoved in everything else she'd so carefully unpacked.

"Come on," she said to her husband.

He looked at her as if he wasn't sure what to make of her abrupt movements. "Where are we going?"

"Back to the hotel room of course!"

Lanni stopped at the Hard Luck Café on her way to the airfield early the next morning.

"Hi, Ben," she said, slipping the backpack off her shoulders and setting it aside.

"Morning." He eyed her bags. "Looks to me like you're getting ready to head out of here."

She smiled sadly. "I thought I'd come in for one last coffee and to tell you goodbye." She held out her hand to him.

He shook it, his hand firmly clasping hers.

"We're going to miss you around here," Ben said.

"I'm going to miss you, too."

"Miss me? My guess is I'm not the one you're gonna miss when you're back home."

She bent her head, refusing to react to his comment. "Well, I have to say it's been interesting."

"Yup, I suppose it has."

He poured her a cup of coffee and she reached for her purse. Ben shook his head. "On the house."

"Thanks." She sipped the coffee, needing it. She hadn't slept much and hoped the caffeine would revive her enough to see her through the morning.

"It's too bad about you and Charles."

She shrugged as if their relationship mattered little. "You win some, you lose some."

"You fit in this town a lot better than some of those women Christian hired. One of 'em didn't stay long enough to give it a chance. Another woman—a teacher—wouldn't even get off the plane."

"You're joking!"

"It's true," he said, leaning both hands on the counter. "Ask anyone."

"I believe you."

"Pity you have to go back."

She didn't contradict him.

"Who's flying you into Fairbanks?"

"Ralph," she answered. He wasn't one of the pilots she'd gotten to know. She checked her watch. "I'd better get on over to the office before they take off without me."

"We're gonna miss you, Lanni," Ben said again as she collected her bags.

Blinking fiercely to force back the tears, she raised her hand in farewell and hurried out the door.

Charles's truck, loaded with camping equipment, was parked in front of the mobile office. She waited there, reluctant to go in, until she recognized Ralph, who stood just inside the door. He looked up from his clipboard and smiled when he saw her.

"I'm almost ready," he called. "Go ahead and get on the plane."

The office door opened then and Charles walked out. He stopped abruptly when he saw her.

Lanni looked longingly at the plane. They'd said their farewells; there was nothing more to say.

"Bye, Charles," she said, holding out her hand in a business-like manner.

He stared at it for a moment, then his fingers closed convulsively over hers. "Goodbye, Lanni."

She offered him a proud smile and turned away. Climbing into the plane, she took her seat and snapped the belt into place.

With tears burning her eyes, she gazed out the small window to see Charles standing next to his truck, watching her. He didn't move.

Ralph put her luggage aboard and climbed in. He reviewed the safety instructions with her, although she wasn't really listening, then started the engine.

Lanni kept her eyes trained on Charles. Her face was pressed to the window as the engine roared to life.

The plane taxied down the runway.

Lanni craned her neck as far as possible in order to see Charles.

He stepped forward a few paces, then came to a halt. She stared out the window until he disappeared from view.

Chapter

8

August 1995

"Hello, Grammy, it's me. Lanni." Catherine Fletcher gave Lanni an odd look, as though she didn't recognize her.

Catherine was in her early seventies, but she appeared older. There were deeply etched lines of bitterness around her mouth and eyes. "I know who you are. Where's Kate?"

"Mom's coming."

"Your mother hasn't been to see me all week. If my daughter's going to shuffle me off to die, the least she can do is come and visit."

Lanni knew her mother had been to the nursing home practically every day. The burden of these daily visits had taken their toll on her. Yet Kate remained faithful, doing whatever she could to make Catherine as comfortable as possible.

"Well, don't just stand there," Catherine said sourly. "Bring me my robe. I want out of this bed."

For all her bluster, Lanni's grandmother was as fragile as a spider's web. She was thinner than Lanni remembered and terribly frail.

"Mother, you know you can't get out of bed without a nurse." Kate stood in the doorway, her voice filled with concern and frustration. "And there's no reason to snap at Lanni."

Lanni was greatly relieved her mother had chosen that moment to arrive.

Catherine looked away sheepishly.

"I thought we'd wash and dry your hair this afternoon," Kate said, her tone gentler. Catherine's hair was tied at the back, but the frizzy sides stuck out in every direction. "We've let it go for several days now."

Catherine pinched her lips in disapproval.

"I wish you'd let someone cut it," Kate went on.

"No," came Catherine's sharp retort. "No one's touching my hair but me."

"Whatever you say, Mother."

Lanni marveled at her mother's patience.

An hour later she accompanied Kate out of the nursing home. "How do you do it?" she asked, impressed by her mother's tender care for a woman who seemed so mean-spirited.

"She's my mother," Kate explained simply. "She wasn't the best mother in the world, but I suppose she wasn't the worst, either. Adjusting to life in the nursing home is difficult for her. We need to remember how independent Catherine was for all those years."

"But she's so..."

"Ungrateful?" Kate supplied.

"Yes."

"She doesn't mean to be," Kate said. "Mother's miserable. I don't think she's had much happiness in her life. Her health is failing, and I'm afraid we won't have her much longer. I don't want any regrets when the time comes to bury her."

Lanni understood what her mother meant about regrets. She felt trapped in a mire of her own might-have-beens. Not a minute passed that she didn't think about Charles. Since her return to Anchorage, Lanni was constantly on the verge of tears.

"Are you ready for lunch?" Kate asked, linking her arm through Lanni's.

Lanni nodded, managing a smile.

"Good."

Kate took Lanni to her favorite seafood place. Generally Lanni was treated to this particular restaurant only on special occasions like her birthday.

They were seated in a comfortable upholstered booth; it was situated in front of a window overlooking Turnagain Arm, an elongated waterway that extended from Cook Inlet. If Lanni remembered her history correctly, Turnagain Arm had been discovered by Captain James Cook on his third and final voyage in 1778 while he was searching for the Northwest Passage. The name came from the fact that Cook and his crew had had to turn back yet again.

"Are we celebrating something?" Lanni asked, surprised by her mother's choice of restaurant.

"You're home."

"I've been back almost a month." Twenty-seven days to be exact. Every minute of those days had felt like a year to Lanni. It astonished her that she could have known Charles so briefly and yet loved him so intently. Every day without him was a struggle; her appetite was nonexistent, and she wasn't sleeping well.

"Something happened while you were in Hard Luck," her mother said quietly, studying Lanni over the top of her menu. "You haven't said anything, but it's obvious to your father and me that you're unhappy."

"It's nothing, Mom. I'm fine."

"You've lost weight, and Lanni... Oh, sweetheart, I want you to know there isn't *anything* you can't tell me. I'm your mother, and if I can't help you, I'll find someone who can. Please tell me what's troubling you."

Lanni had always been close to her mother, but never more than at that moment. She'd watched her deal effectively with her own mother's bitterness and was aware of what a good daughter she was. Now Kate was proving once again that she was an equally good mother.

"It's almost embarrassing to say," Lanni began, crumpling her napkin in one fist. "I fell in love. Unfortunately the man I fell in love with is...Charles O'Halloran."

Her mother's eyes closed. "David O'Halloran's son?"

"Yes," Lanni whispered. "You told me some of what went on between David and Grammy, and Charles filled in the rest."

"Perhaps one day you can tell me what you learned. There's a lot I've never heard. But not now. What I want to know now is what happened with you and Charles. What hurt you so much?"

"He didn't know I was related to Catherine. I…purposely hid it from him. Once he found out he wanted nothing more to do with me."

Kate frowned. "Then the man's a fool."

Lanni grinned; it was a relief to smile again. "If I ever see him, which is doubtful, I'll tell him you said so."

Kate's features relaxed. "Do you want to talk about him?"

Surprisingly Lanni discovered she did. She told her mother about the instant attraction she'd felt toward him, the bond they seemed to share. She described what had happened at the wedding ceremony—and afterward, when Charles had learned the painful truth about her family.

The wetness on her face shocked Lanni. She hadn't realized she was crying. Her mother's hand gripped hers tightly. "I'm so sorry, sweetheart. I'd give anything to have spared you this."

"But you know, Mom, the funny part is I don't regret loving Charles. Someday I'll look back and I'll see how knowing him, loving him, changed my life. At the moment, it's still too raw, too painful, to see what good could possibly come of all this." Her voice shook but she continued despite that. "It's difficult, but I'm trusting that we were never meant to be together— just the way his father and Grammy were never meant to marry."

Kate wiped a tear from her own eye. "You astonish me," her mother said softly. "When did you grow up to be so wise?"

Lanni laughed and dabbed at her eyes with the napkin. "I don't feel wise at all—the only thing I feel is empty."

"That will change," Kate assured her.

Lanni knew that a time of peace and acceptance would come, but it would still take a while.

All at once her mother's face grew thoughtful. "Speaking of Charles O'Halloran, I seem to remember Matt saying something about him recently."

"Matt wants the O'Hallorans to sell him the lodge in Hard Luck," Lanni explained. She'd had several other conversations with him regarding the purchase of the lodge.

"Your brother's on another of his kicks, isn't he?" Kate gave an exaggerated sigh.

Lanni couldn't help laughing. "This time might be different," she said with a shrug. "I think he could do a great job with it."

"Remember when he went to cooking school?"

"How could I forget?" Lanni asked. Matt had hoped to make his fortune with the most absurd assortment of recipes—all of which he insisted his family sample. Somehow his concoctions, teriyaki moose being his favorite, just hadn't been the success he'd expected.

"He was a fisherman for a while, too," her mother reminded her.

"Was that before or after he studied to be an accountant? You know, Mom, maybe—just maybe—he'll pull this off. He *is* serious about wanting the lodge."

"I only wish he'd done something earlier, before…"

Kate left the rest unsaid, but Lanni knew what her mother was thinking. If Matt had thought of buying the lodge sooner, he might have been able to save his marriage.

"I'm meeting him for dinner tomorrow evening," Lanni said.

"I'll try to find out how his plans are going." The real trick, she mused, would be to find out what she could about Charles without being obvious.

No, she decided abruptly, she wouldn't ask. Charles was part of her past. He was someone she'd always love, but she wouldn't look back.

Charles stood outside Matt Caldwell's apartment building. He wasn't quite sure why this meeting was necessary. Matt had phoned and said there were papers they needed to review; since Charles was already in Anchorage, he couldn't think of a reason to refuse.

It didn't surprise him to discover he liked Matt. Under different circumstances he would've been happy to call Lanni's older brother his friend. But selling the lodge to a member of Catherine's family was more than a gesture of goodwill. It was his own way of telling Lanni he'd always love her.

Convincing Sawyer and Christian to go along with him hadn't been nearly as difficult as he'd assumed. Both his brothers were relieved that someone was going to do something about the lodge their father had built. They weren't any more interested than Charles was, but it seemed a shame to tear it down. The three of them had set a reasonable price, with excellent terms.

He checked the slip of paper for the apartment number and walked into the low-rise building. After locating the apartment, he rang the doorbell and waited.

Lanni answered.

Charles felt as if the wind had been knocked out of him.

Speechless, they stared at each other.

Shock widened her eyes, and he noticed the way her fingers tightened around the doorknob. "Charles."

"Lanni." He'd forgotten how soft her voice was, soft and melodic. Stupidly, he glanced down at the slip of paper, frowning at the apartment number.

She stepped aside, obviously realizing she was blocking the door. "Come in, please."

It was all he could do to look away from her. She was thinner and a bit pale, but he'd never seen a more beautiful woman in his life.

"Is Matt here?" he asked.

"Matt?" Once again her eyes betrayed her surprise.

"He gave me this address. Apparently there are some papers regarding the sale of the lodge that he wanted me to read over."

"I see." She closed her eyes.

"What is it?"

"It seems we've both been tricked." She sank onto the couch. "This is my place. Matt was supposed to pick me up for dinner."

"Perhaps he intended to meet us both."

"Perhaps," she agreed uncertainly. "If you'll wait here, I'll give him a call." She stepped out of the room and returned a moment later, paler than before.

"I apologize, Charles. My brother left a message for me on his answering machine. He purposely arranged for the two of us to meet this evening," she said, her voice trembling. "He sent you here on a wild-goose chase and then made sure I'd be home when you arrived."

Charles nodded. He wasn't sorry, but he didn't tell her that.

Lanni had haunted him from the morning she'd flown out of Hard Luck. He couldn't sleep or eat or think for want of her. No other woman had ever affected him this way.

"How are you?" he asked, his voice uncharacteristically gruff.

"Fine," she said quietly, "and you?"

He sat on the chair across from her. "Fine. Sawyer and Abbey are back from their honeymoon, and Pearl Inman's getting ready to move in with her daughter."

She lowered her gaze to her hands. "I understand Matt's negotiations with you are going well."

Charles raised a shoulder in acknowledgment. "The fact that he's taking over the lodge helps us all." He couldn't very well admit that Lanni was the real reason he'd agreed to go ahead with the sale.

"How's Ben?" she asked.

"Cantankerous as ever."

Lanni smiled, and the knots inside him grew even tighter.

"How's the new secretary doing?"

"Mariah Douglas?" Charles's smile was involuntary. "I don't think she's had much office experience. Last I heard, Christian had to show her how to change the paper in the photocopier."

"But she's stayed."

Charles nodded. "She seems determined to make a go of it. She insists on living in one of the old cabins, without electricity, because she wants those twenty acres my brothers promised her."

"Good for Mariah."

Several minutes of silence came next, but for some reason, it didn't bother him.

"Do you like Anchorage?" she asked.

Charles hoped she was looking for ways to continue the conversation, because he didn't want to leave, but he had no excuse to stay. "Anchorage? As far as I'm concerned it's about half an hour away from Alaska."

Lanni smiled and stared down at her hands, which were clenched in her lap.

Charles had never met another woman he felt as comfortable with as Lanni. Their conversation had been a little awkward at first, but once they'd both relaxed, it flowed smoothly. Had it been like this with his father and Catherine? Had David found his soul mate in one woman while married to another?

Lanni was *his* soul mate; Charles had realized that with complete certainty after she left Hard Luck. The loneliness had closed in around him. Until he'd met her, Charles had preferred his own company; in the past few weeks it felt as if a part of him was missing.

Countless times he reviewed their situation. But he'd seen the pain in Ellen's eyes when she discovered Lanni was related to Catherine. Charles couldn't bear to inflict that pain on Ellen again. Not when she was happy for perhaps the first time in her life.

Charles told himself to leave, but he couldn't seem to stand up and walk away.

"I have coffee on," she said. "Would you like a cup?" Her dark, luminous eyes were pleading.

He shouldn't stay. Every minute he lingered made it more difficult to go. "All right," he said, agreeing quickly before he could change his mind.

He followed her into the kitchen. She opened the cupboard to reach for a mug, but his hand on her forearm stopped her.

"It isn't coffee I want," he told her. His eyes boldly met hers.

Her lips parted, and warm color blossomed in her cheeks. "I...I don't think this is a good idea—not for us. I—"

He cut off her words by lowering his head and kissing her. As she responded, he wondered how he'd managed to last this long without her. When he ended the kiss, they were both breathing heavily. He ran his lips down the curve of her cheek to her ear.

Then he slid his mouth back to hers, and his kiss was filled with urgency. He couldn't seem to get enough of her. This was dangerous—to him *and* her. Dragging his mouth away, he struggled for control.

Lanni hid her face in his shoulder.

"Charles..." she gasped.

"I know. I know." He was equally shaken. "It scares me how much I want you." He was desperate for a solution, but every time he closed his eyes, all he could see was the pain on his mother's face.

"Let me make love to you," he whispered.

Her body tensed and she shook her head.

The rejection tore at his heart. He might not know a lot about a woman's wants and needs, but he'd have staked his life on the fact that she wanted him too.

He caught her hand and flattened it against his heart. "You want me, don't you?"

"Yes, but..." At least she was honest enough not to deny it.

"I've been half-crazy these last few weeks without you." Charles nuzzled her throat, then drew her into another lengthy kiss. When he finished, she buried her face in his shoulder once more. Her body shuddered.

He kissed her again. Gently. Lips meeting lips. The mere act of touching her made him feel as though he were on fire. Lanni filled him with a tenderness he didn't recognize.

He wove his fingers through her long blond hair and held her protectively close.

She hung her head. "We can't go on like this."

He didn't answer, but his heart pounded wildly.

"Will our being together change anything?" she asked, her voice low and trembling. "Will I stop being Catherine Fletcher's granddaughter? Will you stop being David and Ellen's son?"

He had no argument to give her, no answer to make things right.

All he knew was how badly he needed her. Emotionally. Physically. And in every possible way you could need someone. Taking a deep breath, he began, "Lanni, please…"

She moved away and brushed the tumble of hair from her face in the habitual gesture he loved.

He closed his eyes.

"Tell me, Charles. Would you have sought me out if Matt hadn't tricked us into this meeting?"

It would've been easy to lie, but he wouldn't do that. Not to Lanni. "No."

She flinched. "I didn't plan on seeing you again, either."

"But we *have* met," he argued, "and it's obvious we still feel the same way about each other."

"I'll always love you, Charles, but I refuse to live like this, sneaking around—"

"If we're in love, then—"

"I can't. I'm afraid that history will repeat itself. My grandmother loved your father—and she was never more than his mistress—a small part of his life. It's not enough for me."

"I'd never ask that of you. *I'm* not married to someone else!"

"But you'll always feel torn," she said. "You love me, but you love your family, too, and so you should. But your mother could never accept me."

He didn't reply.

"I apologize for what Matt did. I'll make sure it doesn't happen again," she whispered brokenly, moving into the living room and gesturing at the door. "Perhaps it'd be best if you left now."

Charles reached the door and stopped, his back to her. "I can't go," he said. "I can't just leave you." He wasn't sure what his staying would accomplish; it might do more harm than good. One thing was certain—he couldn't right the sins of generations past.

He blindly made his way back into the kitchen. He might not have wanted coffee earlier, but he felt a desperate need for something now.

By the time he found the mugs, Lanni had joined him.

"Do you want some?" he asked.

"Please."

He poured them each a cup and carried them to the small table. Lanni gave him a weak smile as they sat facing each other.

Knowing he was the one responsible for the shadows under her eyes broke his heart.

"I…I want to thank you," she said.

"Thank me?" He'd done nothing but bring pain into her life, just as his father had brought pain to her grandmother's.

"For what you're doing to help my brother."

The time for pretense was gone. "I sold the lodge for a number of reasons, not all of them noble."

"I don't understand."

"I'm not sure I do, either." The coffee tasted slightly burned and bitter. That seemed fitting somehow. "I suppose I thought that if your brother managed the lodge, I'd have a way of learning about you. Not that I intended to pry into your private life."

"I see."

"I figured your brother would let me know when you got married…" His heart seized at the thought of Lanni with another man. "I'm sorry for what happened this evening. I didn't mean to hurt you." His words were jagged. He took a hurried drink of coffee to cover how difficult it had been to say them.

Tears glistened in her eyes. "Some things were never meant to be. Isn't that what you said earlier?"

He stood up to carry the mug to the sink. He looked back at her and resisted the urge to tell her goodbye.

They'd already done that.

"So," Matt said when he phoned Lanni the following morning. "I don't suppose you had any company dropping by last night, did you?"

"Yes." Her brother didn't have any idea how much his actions had hurt her.

"Well, don't keep me in suspense. Tell me what happened."

"Why would you *do* such a thing?" Lanni asked, her throat aching as she struggled to control her voice. She knew her brother hadn't intentionally hurt her. Yet he might as well have driven a knife into her heart as invite Charles into her home.

"Why would I arrange for Charles and you to meet?" Matt repeated. "Because it was clear to me from the moment I met O'Halloran that he's in love with you."

Lanni said nothing.

"It was also clear to me that you're in love with him!"

Again she didn't bother to contradict him.

"I don't know what nonsense is keeping you apart, but I thought it was time someone did something."

"Of all people," she blurted, "I would think you'd know enough to respect another person's privacy." Lanni was close to tears. "You love Karen and—"

"What's she got to do with this?" he interjected.

"—she loves you!"

"Right. She couldn't get to that attorney fast enough to file for the divorce. In case you didn't realize it, that's not the act of a woman in love."

"I won't take sides, Matt. I didn't all through the divorce, and I won't now. All I know is that you love her, and I'm sure she still loves you. How would *you* feel if I tricked you into meeting her?"

Matt's voice hardened. "Don't even try it."

"That's what I thought."

Suddenly he chuckled as if something amused him. "Karen and I would probably end up killing each other. Now that she's moved, I can see the wisdom of having her gone."

"Wisdom?"

"I don't have to worry about seeing her with another man, do I?"

"No."

They both hesitated.

"I apologize if I did the wrong thing," Matt said brusquely. "It sounds like I made the situation worse instead of better."

"It doesn't matter."

"I'm not much of a matchmaker, am I?"

"Put it this way—the next time I want to meet a man, you're the last person I'll ask for help."

"Why's that?"

"I don't think I could go through another evening like last night."

When Matt spoke again, he seemed uncertain. "I did read you right, didn't I? You are in love with him?"

"Yes," she said hoarsely. "But it's over—the same as you and Karen. There's nothing left to resurrect. If you have any feelings for me as your sister, you won't pull this kind of stunt again."

"I won't," Matt promised.

Lanni believed him.

At noon she went to check her mailbox. There was one

letter—with a Canadian postmark. But she was positive she didn't know anyone living in Vancouver, British Columbia.

She waited until she was back in the apartment before opening the envelope. She pulled out a sheet of personalized stationery. The embossed letterhead said Ellen Greenleaf.

With shaky knees, Lanni pulled out a kitchen chair and sat down to read.

Dear Lanni,

I imagine this letter comes as a surprise. Sawyer was kind enough to obtain your address for me. I've debated for several weeks now on how to get in touch with you, and decided the best way was by letter.

First, I want to apologize for my behavior at Sawyer and Abbey's wedding. Discovering you're a relative of Catherine Fletcher's was a shock. I fear I was far less gracious than I should have been. I beg your forgiveness for anything I might have said or done to hurt you.

I'm not sure what you do or don't know about my relationship with Catherine—or more importantly, my late husband's relation-ship with her. As far as I'm concerned, all of that was laid to rest with David. I harbor Catherine no ill will. Nor you.

Before Charles learned about your connection with Catherine, he confided in me his feelings for you. I realize you have since returned to Anchorage. I tried to ask Charles about the two of you, but he re-fuses to discuss the matter.

However, I know my son. I've attempted to convince him, without success, that you shouldn't be blamed for the sins of another.

It breaks my heart to think that another generation is about to suffer because of me. I plan to be in Anchorage next week. Would it be possible for us to have lunch? I'll be staying at the Alaska Inn. If you could give me a call on Tuesday morning, perhaps we could arrange something.

It's time we buried the past.

Most Sincerely,

Ellen Greenleaf

Chapter
9

Sawyer was poring over a cookbook when Abbey walked in the front door. She stopped a minute, amused at what an incongruous sight her husband made with a lace-fringed apron around his waist.

"I'm home," she called, slipping off her shoes.

"Thank goodness." Sawyer stripped off the apron and tossed it aside. "I can't even begin to figure out these instructions."

"What did you want to cook?"

"Chicken cordon bleu."

"Cordon bleu? When you said you'd fix dinner, I assumed you'd pick something easy."

"This looked easy enough," he said, peering down at the photograph accompanying the recipe. "We've got the chicken, the cheese and just about everything else I need—except the patience."

Abbey slid her arms around him and smiled into his face. "You want me to come to the rescue, don't you?"

He kissed her. "Please."

"It's going to cost you," she teased.

"I'll pay—price is no object."

Abbey reached for the cookbook while Sawyer tied the apron around her.

"Well?" he asked when she'd finished reading the recipe.

"I'll do what I can," she said, feigning uncertainty. "But I'm not promising anything."

Sawyer poured a cup of coffee and sat down to watch her. Abbey efficiently assembled ingredients from the cupboard and the refrigerator. After a few minutes, he said, "Charles is back."

"Oh," Abbey said absently. "Has his mood improved?"

"No. If anything it's worse. I don't think I've ever seen him more miserable."

Abbey looked up, concerned. "Have you tried talking to him?"

"Twice, and both times he nearly bit my head off. You can take my word for it, he isn't feeling very communicative."

"It's Lanni, isn't it?"

Sawyer frowned. "That's my guess."

"Maybe *I* should try talking to him."

"I wouldn't advise it," Sawyer murmured. "Charles will work this out in his own time and his own way. He's struggling with the fact that he loves Lanni. My brother never expected to fall in love."

"You didn't, either," Abbey reminded him.

"That's true," Sawyer said with a wide grin. "As you recall, I

had some trouble getting used to the idea myself." More seriously he said, "It's even harder for Charles, because he didn't
fall in love with just anyone. Nope, that would've been too
easy. He had to go and fall for Catherine Fletcher's granddaughter. So he's making all kinds of excuses why a relationship
between them won't work."

"How do you mean?"

"Lanni's nearly ten years younger, so Charles announces she's
too young to know what she wants. Then he said something
about Lanni working for some newspaper." He shook his head.
"I haven't got a clue what he was talking about there."

"Lanni shouldn't be blamed for what her grandmother did."

"I don't think Charles blames her. I think he feels he's being
disloyal to our mother. You have to understand, Catherine did
everything in her power to destroy my family."

Abbey sat down across the table from her husband. "It seems
such a pity the way everything's turned out for Charles and
Lanni. They really care about each other."

"Being in love doesn't automatically make everything right,"
Sawyer said.

"No, it doesn't," Abbey agreed, "but it's a step in that direction."

Sawyer took her hand. "I sure hope so."

Scott burst into the kitchen just then, Eagle Catcher at his
heels. The boy's face was red and sweaty with exertion; her son
always went at full speed, Abbey thought with a smile.

"What's for dinner?" Scott asked. "I'm starved."

He looked at Sawyer, who'd made a grandiose announcement
that morning about cooking a special meal. Flustered, Sawyer
raised both shoulders in a shrug.

"Chicken with cheese and rice," Abbey answered.

Scott beamed with approval. "Sounds good."

"It's an old family recipe," Sawyer assured him. "Handed down from generation to generation."

"I bet I'll like it, then."

"I bet you will, too," Sawyer said and winked at his wife.

Lanni walked into the formal dining room of the Alaska Inn and glanced around. She was meeting Charles's mother here. The room's opulent decor was reminiscent of the Roaring Twenties, Alaska style, with red velvet wallpaper, a rich-looking red carpet and red velvet cushions on the chairs.

Lanni saw Ellen Greenleaf almost right away. Dignified and elegant, she sat at a table next to the window, apparently deep in thought, since she didn't seem to notice Lanni's approach.

"Mrs. Greenleaf," Lanni said quietly, not wanting to startle the woman.

"Lanni," Ellen said, smiling in welcome. "Please, sit down."

Lanni pulled out the chair across from Ellen and sat down. She took a nervous moment to tuck her purse between her feet and place her napkin on her lap.

"It's good of you to meet me," Ellen began.

"Oh, no, it's my pleasure," Lanni said. "I appreciated your letter more than I can say. And please, don't worry about what happened at Sawyer's wedding."

The waiter appeared and they both ordered quickly, getting that out of the way. Lanni's mind wasn't on food; she felt much too anxious to think about eating.

"How are you?" Charles's mother asked first.

Lanni didn't know if there was some hidden meaning in her question. "Uh, fine, thanks. And you?"

Ellen nodded. "I don't mean to hedge with small talk. It's just that I find what I'm about to tell you very…difficult. You see, it happened so many years ago, and I wonder if exhuming the past will do either of us any good."

Lanni sipped from her ice water, concentrating on the coldness of the glass. She'd noticed how drawn and pale Ellen looked. "I don't want you to say or do anything that makes you uncomfortable."

Ellen seemed not to have heard. "I remember your mother so well. Kate was a delightful little girl, with bright eyes and long braids. I used to see her when she visited her mother during the summer. I desperately longed for a child myself, and Catherine never lost an opportunity to taunt me."

Lanni lowered her gaze. "I'm sorry."

"No, I apologize," Ellen said, and sighed. "I didn't ask you to lunch to discuss your grandmother's faults. Actually I've come to confess my own."

Lanni grew more troubled. It was obvious that Ellen felt unsure about this conversation. She'd instigated their meeting, yet seemed to question the value of it.

"From what I've heard, there are grievances on both sides," Lanni said.

Ellen's nod was almost imperceptible. "That's true enough. Truer than you'll ever know."

"My grandmother isn't well these days."

"I'm sorry to hear it," Ellen murmured. "I'm sincere about that, whether you choose to believe me or not."

"I do believe you."

Ellen lifted the water glass to her lips; when she set it back on the table, she appeared to be readying herself for some sort of ordeal. She straightened, and Lanni noticed how she clenched and unclenched her hands.

"It's somewhat…ironic that you're the one I'm telling this to. My sons know nothing of what I'm about to explain. I've kept this secret for nearly fifty years."

Lanni was surprised herself. She was almost a stranger to Ellen Greenleaf; more than that, she was the granddaughter of Ellen's oldest enemy. Yet Ellen had chosen to confide in her.

"Mrs. Greenleaf—"

"Please, call me Ellen."

"Ellen, I'd rather you didn't—"

It was as if Ellen hadn't heard her. "In all fairness," she began, "I've decided Charles should be told the facts, as well. Whether or not to tell Sawyer and Christian is something I'll leave up to Charles."

Lanni didn't know what to say. She didn't want to mislead Ellen into thinking she had a relationship with Charles when she didn't. "I don't—it isn't likely I'll see Charles again."

"I hope that isn't the case." Ellen sighed again and gazed into the distance. "My son will live his own life, make his own decisions and live by them. What he does with this information is entirely up to him. The same way it'll be up to you."

"Ellen, I'm not sure you should tell me…whatever this is."

The older woman shook her head. "I feel differently, and I'll explain later."

Lanni might have argued further, but their food arrived.

Neither seemed to have any interest in eating. Lanni reached for her fork and ate a couple of shrimp, then contented herself with pushing the lettuce leaves around her plate.

Ellen moved her salad aside and picked up her water glass again. Then she began to speak. "It all started in the last days of World War II. I lost my parents in one of the London bombings. My older brother was a bombardier. His plane went down over Germany in June of 1943. Other than one older cousin, Elizabeth, I had no family left."

Lanni's heart constricted; she was close to her own family and losing them seemed unimaginable. "How alone you must have felt."

"I did. I was lost and lonely and desperately afraid. That was when I met a young American soldier."

David must have been lonely, too, Lanni realized. So far from home, enduring the shock and horror of war, devastated by the death of his brother.

"We fell in love. I've never loved as deeply or as completely in my life. We clung to each other, and the love we shared was the only thing that kept me sane in those last terrible months of the war." Ellen paused, her eyes shining with tears. It took her several minutes to compose herself.

"Perhaps we should continue later," Lanni suggested.

"No. That won't make it any easier. And I've come this far...."

Lanni leaned across the table and clasped Ellen's hand.

"I was raised in a God-fearing home," Ellen said in a low voice. "I'm not offering any excuses for what happened, but you have to understand how desperate the times were. I was in love, and I didn't know from one day to the next what the future held. My family was gone. He was so far from home. It seemed inevitable that we give in to our natural inclinations and make love."

"I would never judge you, Ellen."

Charles's mother smiled softly, sadly. "We lived for those few tender moments together. With each other, we found a confirmation of life, a solace that had escaped us."

She hesitated, and Lanni remained silent, not wanting to interrupt Ellen's painfully remembered—and painfully told—story.

"The inevitable happened. We were careless, and I soon discovered I was pregnant."

"Pregnant?" Lanni blinked in surprise.

Ellen nodded. "I was so afraid to tell him. So embarrassed that I'd been this foolish. I avoided him, but he confronted me. I was sure he wouldn't want me anymore, but when I told him about the baby, he was ecstatic." Her eyes grew warm with the memory. "He lifted me off the ground and kissed me until I was senseless. Because he was happy, I was, too." A smile brightened her pale face. "We planned to marry as quickly as possible. He…he was making the arrangements when…when he was sent on a mission." She paused and seemed to gather herself together.

"You see, he…he never returned. I didn't learn until two agonizing weeks later that he'd been killed."

Lanni frowned. "David killed?"

"No. The father of my child was Charles O'Halloran. David's brother."

Lanni was left speechless. She started to ask the most obvious questions but found that her throat had closed up.

"I think…I *know* I would've died had it not been for David and the baby. Losing my parents and my brother broke my heart. Losing Charles crushed my spirit. I had no will to go on."

"Did you ever find out what happened to Charles?"

Ellen shook her head. "No one will ever really know. The only thing I'm confident of is that he loved me and he wanted our child."

"So David came to see you?"

"Yes. Charles and his brother were very close. As I look back on that time, I think Charles might have known on some level that he wouldn't make it. David told me his brother had asked him to take care of me if anything happened. David gave Charles his word of honor that he would."

Lanni closed her eyes.

"At first all he intended to do was arrange for me to join his family in Alaska."

"And he couldn't," Lanni guessed.

"The only way it turned out to be possible was if he married me himself. I should never have agreed. Over the years I regretted it thousands of times. In my own defense, though, I was in a haze of pain and grief. The pregnancy wasn't going well, and the thought of being alone terrified me."

"You did eventually come to love him."

"Oh, yes." Ellen's eyes took on that faraway look again. "When I married him, I didn't know about Catherine. David never mentioned her, and if Charles had ever told me about his brother's fiancée, I'd forgotten."

"What about the baby?"

"Two months after the wedding—when I was six months pregnant—I gave birth to a daughter. She lived two days… We buried her in London. I named her Emily after the sister my Charles lost. I thought he'd approve."

"I'm sure he would have." Lanni felt the tears gathering, and her heart went out to Charles's mother. She'd lost her family, the father of her child and then her child.

"David was so gentle with me. We wept together, and he stood by my side when we buried Emily. I wanted to release him from the wedding vows, but he refused. Soon afterward, he was given his orders to return home. We went together."

"That was when you found out about Catherine?"

"Yes," Ellen answered softly. "In the beginning I was upset that David hadn't told me. But he insisted he'd made the decision to marry me and he wanted me as his wife. By that time we'd become lovers, although I don't believe we were in love. Not then. I'm ashamed to admit that in the beginning when David made love to me I pretended he was Charles. I prayed he never knew, but I suspect he did."

"You waited almost fifteen years to start a family."

Ellen shook her head. "It wasn't our choice. There never seemed to be any medical reason I couldn't conceive. I had easily enough before. Both David and I went through numerous tests and the doctors always came up blank." She sighed. "In retrospect I probably needed those years to heal emotionally. It wasn't until I was in my midthirties that I became pregnant with Charles."

Named after the brother who'd died. The lover who'd never returned.

"In many ways the two Charleses are alike," Ellen said on a wistful note. "I've marveled over the years at the similarities between them. Sawyer, on the other hand, is a lot like his father in looks and temperament."

"Christian must take after your side of the family, then," Lanni commented. "In appearance, anyway." The youngest O'Halloran brother's hair color was much lighter than that of his siblings.

Ellen answered with a nod. "I'd hoped for a daughter, but it was never to be."

"You and David were separated for a while, weren't you?"

"Yes. We'd been married close to thirty years by then. Charles was fifteen at the time, Sawyer a couple of years younger." Ellen hesitated as if she wasn't sure she should say any more. "I'd been back to England only once in all those years. I'd never done well in Alaska. I realize now that part of this was my own fault, but part of it was due to…other factors."

Lanni had a feeling some of those factors had to do with Catherine.

"I missed England. I'd always missed England. My cousin, Elizabeth, wrote and urged me to visit. David and I argued, which was something we frequently did in those days. He didn't want me to leave.

"In all the years we'd lived together, not once had he ever said he regretted marrying me. He did that day, in anger. That was when I knew how much my weakness had hurt him.

"I'm not proud of what happened next. In my outrage I told him I'd never loved him. It was a lie. A woman can't live with a man, bear his children and feel nothing. I'd grown to love David, but I was afraid to tell him that.

"The next morning I packed my bags and left for England with Christian."

"David didn't come after you?"

"No. His pride wouldn't allow that."

"How sad for you both."

"It was a very painful time," Ellen acknowledged simply. "I returned to England, the home I'd yearned for all those years, and discovered I no longer belonged. Christian was miserable, too. My own pride carried me through the first year, but the months that followed were…difficult."

"You were in touch with David?"

"Oh, yes. I had to keep in touch because of the boys. I missed them terribly and they missed me. I'd thought that with Charles and Sawyer in their teen years, my presence wouldn't be that important or necessary to them. I was wrong."

"What brought you home?"

Ellen smiled. "I admitted to David that I'd lied. I did love him, and had for many years. I asked him to forgive me for being so foolish. He said he was sorry, too. I told him I wanted to come home."

"And you were happy afterward?"

"Yes," she said, but her eyes revealed how short-lived that happiness was. "In the beginning we were. It was as if we'd both been given a fresh start. I tried in every way I could to show David how important he was to me.

"He'd sacrificed a great deal to fulfill a promise to his brother. For the first time since we were married he wanted me, and not because of any obligation. Or so I believed."

"That was when my grandmother destroyed your marriage, wasn't it?"

"No," Ellen surprised her by saying. "David and I did that on our own. Certainly she contributed to the problem, but I can't blame her for David's or my stubbornness. When I learned about their affair, I was deeply hurt. David had had the perfect opportunity to suggest a divorce. Instead, he'd invited me home. I came back because I thought he wanted me...."

"Why *did* he ask you to come back?"

"I don't think I'll ever fully understand his reasons. I'd like to believe he was sincere about wanting our marriage to work. For the boys' sake, yes, but for us, as well. England wasn't the homeland I'd left—almost against my will Alaska had become my home.

"When I found out about the affair, I moved out of David's bedroom and asked for a divorce. David wouldn't hear of it. That was when he built the lodge.

"I always hated that place, while David became more and more obsessed with it. Soon we were like strangers. We rarely spoke to each other. I fully expected him to leave me for Catherine, and I never understood why he didn't. To the best of my knowledge, he never slept with her again after I returned from England, but I can't be sure."

"She waited for him," Lanni said. "She waited for the marriage to end so she'd be free to take him for herself."

"I lived with that knowledge every day of our married life."

"My grandmother is a bitter, unhappy woman."

"I'm afraid she has been from the day I stepped off that plane with David and he introduced me as his wife."

Ellen didn't blame Catherine for ruining her marriage; by the same token, Catherine had to take responsibility for what she'd made of her own life.

"I'm still not sure why you've told me all this," Lanni said. Her salad remained virtually untouched, as did Ellen's.

"My son loves you."

"I love him."

"Then go to him, Lanni. Fight for him. Don't let the mistakes I made, the sins your grandmother and I committed, influence your life. Marry Charles, with my blessing. Make him happy and, if you're both willing, make me a grandmother."

Lanni's eyes held Ellen's. "I'll do what I can," she said decisively, "but Charles is a stubborn man."

"Be more stubborn, then," she advised. "I lost my Charles, not by choice, but by fate. Don't lose yours."

Lanni's eyes gleamed with determination. "I won't. Not now."

Ellen laughed. "You know, I almost feel sorry for the boy."

Before she was through with him, Lanni thought, Charles might well be in need of his mother's sympathy.

"I suppose you heard," Ben said when Charles walked into the Hard Luck Café.

"Heard what?"

"About Pete and Dotty. They've announced their engagement."

Charles slid onto a stool without comment. Feeling the way he had lately, he found it difficult to dredge up enthusiasm for much of anything. If Pete Livengood was marrying the nurse Christian had hired, then great. Wonderful.

"Aren't you going to say something?" Ben asked, pouring him a cup of coffee.

"Yeah, more power to them."

"The wedding's in two months."

The last thing Charles wanted to discuss was weddings.

Ben lingered at the counter. "Rumor has it you're selling the lodge."

"Yeah," he answered without elaborating.

"When did all this happen?"

"Last week."

"Well, who bought it? Anyone I know?" Ben was beginning to sound decidedly short-tempered.

"I doubt it."

"Listen, Charles, if talking with a friend is too much trouble for you, just say the word and I'll shut my trap."

Charles scowled. "I came in for coffee, not conversation."

"Fine." Ben set down the pot so hard coffee splashed on the counter. Then he marched back into the kitchen, where he slammed dishes and pans around with far more noise than Charles suspected was necessary.

Listening to the racket, he regretted his own outburst. Ben was a good friend and deserved better.

"Matt Caldwell bought the lodge," he said when Ben reappeared.

The older man ignored him.

"Matt is Lanni's brother."

Still Ben went about his business as if he was alone in the café.

The door opened and Mitch Harris stepped inside. He slipped onto a stool two down from Charles. The two men acknowledged each other with a brief nod. Mitch hadn't been in Hard Luck all that long, but Charles liked him. Liked his understated authority, his kindness—and the fact that Mitch, too, was a man of few words.

Ben took Mitch's order and continued to ignore Charles.

"All right," Charles muttered when his friend paraded past yet again. "If you're looking for an apology, you've got one."

To his amazement Ben whirled about, grinning broadly. "You know what your problem is, don't you?"

As a matter of fact, Charles did. His problem, as Ben referred to it, was about five six with long blond hair and eyes that could look straight through his soul.

Ben didn't give him a chance to respond. "In case no one's bothered to tell you, you've got a chip on your shoulder the size of this great state of ours."

"Thank you, I appreciate hearing that," Charles said sarcastically.

"Now if you want to make a mess of your life, that's your business. I told you what I thought. Most of the others share my opinion, but they don't have the guts to tell you. You seem to—"

"I saw Lanni while I was in Anchorage," Charles broke in, his voice low. He paused; he wasn't sure why he felt it was necessary for Ben to know that.

However, his comment had piqued Ben's interest. "You did?"

Charles stared into his coffee mug. "Her brother tricked us into a meeting. We both realize a relationship between us isn't meant to be. She feels as strongly about it as I do." Even now, Charles didn't understand why he'd stayed in her apartment once he knew what Matt had done. Any man with a lick of sense would've known better. The only thing he'd managed to prove was how much he loved her.

Instinctively he recognized that true satisfaction would

escape him with any other woman. He would find what he needed with Lanni and with no one else.

The door opened, and Christian entered the café, frowning. "Got anything stronger than coffee?" he asked Ben.

"You know I only sell beer on Friday and Saturday nights."

"I was hoping you'd make an exception this afternoon."

"What's up?" Charles asked.

Christian regarded him wanly. "Have you rejoined the living, or are you still a brooding, bad-tempered zombie?"

"I'm still brooding and bad-tempered, but that doesn't mean you don't need to answer the question."

"Mariah Douglas."

"Who?"

"The new secretary," Ben supplied.

"The woman's incompetent," Christian snapped.

"Then fire her," Charles said.

"I've tried. Three times to be exact, and then she bursts into tears and tells me how sorry she is, and before I know it she's talked me into giving her another chance."

"Is Sawyer having the same problems with her?" Charles wanted to know. It seemed to him that his brother wouldn't have any qualms about laying off an inept employee.

"That's what's so bizarre. I swear if Sawyer asks Mariah to type anything, she goes at it about a hundred miles an hour and produces a flawless copy."

"But not for you?"

"For me she spills coffee on the keyboard. For me she topples a hundred-pound filing cabinet onto my foot. For me she cuts off a phone call to an important client."

"I'd say you have a negative effect on the woman."

Christian rested his elbows on the counter and dropped his head into his hands. "I don't know what to do anymore."

"Is she still living in the cabin?" Ben asked.

"Oh, yes. I don't know what possessed me to actually think a woman from the big city, accustomed to modern conveniences, could live out there. But Mariah refuses to listen to reason. For the life of me, I can't convince her to move."

Charles found himself enjoying the fact that his youngest brother was experiencing troubles of the female variety. He obviously hadn't managed to conceal his reaction from Christian.

Christian raised his head and looked at Charles through narrowed eyes. "If I were you I wouldn't look so smug."

"Why's that?" Charles had to admit it felt good to smile.

"You know Matt Caldwell's in town?"

"Already?" Ben said. "The man isn't going to let any grass grow under his feet, is he?"

The two brothers ignored him. Charles said, "I understand he's bringing in supplies. What he said to me in Anchorage is that he wants to get as much done as possible before the weather changes."

"Supplies aren't the only thing he brought with him," Christian said.

Charles frowned. "What do you mean?"

"Nothing." His brother slid off the stool. He set a dollar bill and some change down on the counter, then gave a jaunty wave. "Thanks for the coffee, Ben. I'll be back Friday night when you can serve me something more to my liking."

Charles knew that Matt had come in on the morning flight.

One of the air services out of Fairbanks had brought him, along with enough building supplies to keep him busy the entire winter.

He'd need at least that much time. While part of the structure hadn't been seriously damaged by the flames, much of it was in bad shape. Matt would have to work fast if he intended to live in the lodge this year. Winter arrived early in Hard Luck; it wasn't uncommon for the rivers to freeze over in September.

Wondering about his brother's cryptic remark, Charles got up from the counter and strolled outside. He didn't intend to become close friends with Matt Caldwell, but the least he could do was stop by to say hello and see if there was anything he needed.

Knowing his new sister-in-law, he figured Abbey had probably invited Matt to dinner. She and Sawyer would provide a hearty welcome to their community. He smiled when he thought of the changes in Sawyer since he'd met Abbey.

When Charles got to the lodge, he heard a volley of hammering. The sound of voices followed. Charles hadn't realized Matt had brought anyone with him; actually he'd been smart to do so. With everything that needed to be done before the weather became prohibitive, getting the lodge in shape would take more than one pair of hands.

It felt strange to knock at the front door of a place he'd once considered his own. A moment later Matt was there, greeting him warmly. "Charles! Come in. Uh, I take it you heard."

"Heard what?"

"It's Charles," he shouted over his shoulder. "And I don't

think it's me he's come to see." Matt's deep brown eyes sparkled with mischief.

"Is something going on here that I don't know about?"

"Hello, Charles." Lanni stepped out from one of the back rooms. She wore jeans and carried a hammer, which she swung idly at her side. "I wondered how long it would take you to discover I'd moved to Hard Luck."

Chapter
10

"What do you mean you've moved to Hard Luck?" Charles demanded. He scowled, but his lack of enthusiasm didn't appear to discourage her.

The hammer continued to swing at her side, and she wore a sassy grin. "What do you think I mean?"

That she planned to make his life a living hell, Charles decided. "What about your job with the paper?"

She shrugged, as if that was of no importance. Charles knew otherwise. Matt had bragged to him about Lanni's talents. Being accepted as an intern at the Anchorage daily paper was no small feat. If he remembered correctly, Lanni was supposed to begin work at the beginning of September. It was the chance of a lifetime, and he refused to let her abandon the opportunity because of him. Or because of some misguided belief that they could work things out.

"Damn it, Lanni, you were supposed to be working for the paper in another two weeks."

Her saucy look began to waver. "I guess I won't be, after all."

"Why not?"

"Lanni," Matt called out. He stuck his head around the corner and saw the two of them talking. A smile spread across his face. "Never mind," he said, looking pleased with himself.

"Answer my question!" Charles glared at her.

"If you must know," she said stiffly, "I've turned down the internship."

"You can't do that!"

"I tried to talk sense into her," Matt insisted, peeking around the corner again, "but she refused to listen."

"Go away, Matt," Lanni said. "This conversation doesn't include you."

"Sorry." Matt stepped onto the porch and stood, feet braced apart, gunslinger-style, thumbs tucked into his toolbelt. A hammer hung from one side like a six-shooter. "I don't think she should turn it down, either. Maybe *you* can talk sense into her."

"What happens with my career is entirely up to me," Lanni said calmly.

"Take the job!" Charles barked. It was simple: he didn't want her in Hard Luck. Not where she could torment him day and night. He had enough trouble resisting her when she was half a state away; he'd be in serious trouble if she moved virtually next door.

"He's right, sis."

"Matt," Lanni said in a low, angry whisper. "Let me repeat— this conversation is between Charles and me."

"All right, all right," Matt said. He held up both hands in sur-render. "I'll leave." He strode sheepishly past them and out the front door, stopping to whisper something to Lanni that Charles couldn't hear.

The door closed with an ominous slam.

"Perhaps we should sit down and talk about this," Lanni said.

Charles shook his head, unwilling to be drawn into an argument. He felt himself weakening just being close to Lanni. Her smile cut straight through his pride and sliced away his resolve. "There's nothing to discuss."

"That's not true." Her voice remained calm and controlled.

"You'll be wasting your time."

"I don't see it that way."

"I'm leaving town this afternoon," he said sharply. That much was true—for some unknown reason his mother wanted to see him. She'd arranged to meet in Fairbanks. Initially he'd agreed with reluctance, but was grateful now for the excuse.

"I'll be here waiting for you when you get back," Lanni promised—or was that a threat?

His hands knotted into tight fists. "Lanni, no."

The tender look she gave him told Charles it would take an act of God to get her to return to Anchorage. He could disappear into the tundra for weeks on end, often did, and it wouldn't matter. Not to her. She'd still be here, waiting.

He ran his fingers through his hair. "Why are you doing this?" he asked in exasperation.

"Because I love you. We belong together. I didn't understand that until...recently. Your mother helped me see—"

"My mother?" He was unable to hide his surprise. "What's she got to do with this?"

Lanni's eyes widened. "You mean to say she hasn't talked to you yet?"

He didn't answer. Frankly he didn't like the idea of his mother meddling in his life.

"I've never been one to believe in fate," Lanni continued, "but now I'm not so sure. It's as if the two of us are destined for each other. I feel I was sent into your life and you into mine. And one of the reasons for that is to right a wrong done half a century ago. We didn't fall in love by accident," she said, her expression intent. "You, Charles O'Halloran, are my destiny. Love me or not, I'm yours."

Charles could see that no amount of logic would help. So the only option she'd left him was cruelty. "I suggest you leave Hard Luck now. If you don't, you'll become just like your grandmother, wasting your life over a man she can't have."

Lanni blanched, and he saw how she took a step back as if he'd physically threatened her. The temptation to rush to her and beg her forgiveness was nearly overpowering.

"There's something you're forgetting in all this," she said in a shaky voice. "David loved Catherine. You told me so yourself. Just like you love me. Insulting me and my family isn't going to make any difference."

It *had* to. Insults were the only tool he still had in his fast-depleting arsenal.

"I refuse to believe you don't love me, Charles. You can try of course, but I don't know how you'll manage to keep up the facade when we live in the same town."

"Fine, then. We'll be lovers if that's what you want." He tried again, desperate to get her to see reason. "It was all my father was willing to offer your grandmother. And it's all I'm offering you."

She hesitated, her eyes revealing her pain. The confidence she'd exuded earlier had vanished. Once again Charles had to restrain himself from reaching for her, comforting her. He didn't know what madness had possessed her to return. There was no hope for their relationship. As far as he was concerned, the matter was settled.

She said nothing.

"So what do you intend to do?" he demanded. His patience hung by a fraying thread.

"Exactly what I planned from the first. I'll help Matt for as long as I can."

"Then what?" he pressed.

A slow, satisfied smile curved her lips. "I came back for you, Charles O'Halloran, and I'll be waiting for you."

"You've been quiet all evening," Abbey said to her husband.

Sawyer sat in his favorite chair, feet propped on the matching ottoman. The Fairbanks newspaper lay unread in his lap as he stared blankly into the distance. "Something's not right," he murmured.

Abbey sat on the arm of the chair and rested her cheek on his shoulder. "Not right with what?"

"My brother."

Abbey kissed the top of Sawyer's head. "You know, Charles has to figure things out for himself."

"I suppose," he said absently. He slid his arm around her waist. "I got word that Bethany Ross, one of the new schoolteachers, is flying into town the first of next week."

Abbey was relieved. The kids were just about ready for school if Susan's recent chatter was anything to go by. That morning she'd found her playing school with Chrissie Harris. The two girls had become almost inseparable over the summer months, and Abbey was grateful her children had adjusted so readily to life in the Alaskan interior. They'd need to adjust to school here, too, but they wouldn't be the only ones. The teachers—one for elementary school to the sixth grade, the other for seventh grade through high school—were also new this year.

It still seemed odd to Abbey that there were fewer students in Hard Luck than there were teachers in the Seattle school her kids had attended. Considering the size of the community, Abbey reflected, her children had made friends very quickly here. Scott and Ronny Gold had discovered each other the very day they arrived. It was almost the same story with Susan and Chrissie, who spent her days with Ronny's mother, Louise.

"Charles flew into Fairbanks this afternoon. He didn't say why he was going," Sawyer said, breaking into Abbey's thoughts.

"He doesn't need to check in with you, does he?"

"No. It's just that…"

"Just what?"

"He wasn't the same when he returned."

"Don't you think that might have something to do with Lanni moving back to town?"

"Possibly," Sawyer agreed, "but he knew she was living at the lodge before he left. Fact is, he was telling me what a damn fool she was."

Abbey hid a smile. "A fool, you say. She must be in love with an O'Halloran."

Sawyer chuckled and pulled Abbey into his lap. "I could take offense at that."

Abbey's eyes met his and the laughter drained away. "I was only teasing. You know how much I love you."

"I know." He touched his forehead to hers. "I'm worried. About Charles."

"Don't be," Abbey told him gently. "From my admittedly limited experience, I've learned that things usually have a way of righting themselves."

"My wife, the eternal optimist." Sawyer kissed the tip of her nose.

"Don't you feel Charles and Lanni should be together?" Abbey asked. It was something she'd sensed almost from the first. Fate. Providence. Whatever you wanted to call it.

"I don't know." Sawyer shook his head. "In the beginning I felt the same as you do."

"And now?"

"Now I don't know what to think. Charles is obviously miserable, not that he'll admit it. At first I blamed myself—I should've told him who Lanni's related to, and I'm still not sure why I didn't. I guess I liked seeing him flustered over a woman."

"Flustered?"

"The way you flustered me from the moment we met," Sawyer said, touching his lips to hers. "Later I realized what a dirty trick I'd pulled on him, and I regretted it."

"I don't believe it would have mattered," Abbey said thought-fully. "Lanni's being related to Catherine, I mean. He fell for her hook, line and sinker."

"The poor man's doomed."

"Doomed?" Abbey raised her eyebrows. "You might've come up with a more flattering term. I believe they were meant to be together," she said again. "Maybe this is too poetic, but what if the two of them are supposed to make up for the wrongs of the past?"

Sawyer grinned. "In other words, my poor brother really is doomed."

Abbey tickled her husband in retaliation, and then Sawyer found an even more effective revenge. It was a very long time before either of them worried about Charles or Lanni again.

Lanni sat on the top step of the porch while her brother worked inside the lodge. Matt was reviewing his finances, trying to calculate how soon he could advertise for paying customers. She knew money was going to be tight, but somehow he'd manage. He always had in the past.

As August dwindled to a close, Lanni could feel a new chill in the air. She drew her sweater about her. Mentally she reviewed her confrontation with Charles. It had gone much worse than she'd expected. She'd been completely confident she was doing the right thing when she returned to Hard Luck.

Now she wasn't so sure.

When her brother realized she had no intention of going home to Anchorage, he'd been furious. He'd made his feelings on the subject extremely clear. He told her she was throwing away an opportunity that might not come again.

It was true; she might not get another internship at the newspaper. It was also true that if she didn't take this last chance to salvage their love, she'd regret it for the rest of her life.

But Charles didn't want her in Hard Luck, and now it looked as if her brother would find a way to send her packing.

Lanni hugged her legs and pressed her forehead against her knees.

Despite everything, she couldn't forget the gleam in Ellen's eyes when she'd advised her to fight for Charles. What Ellen hadn't told her was how hard Charles would fight back.

Although she'd tried to hide her reaction, his cruel words had hit their mark. By staying in Hard Luck, she was taking a risk—a risk that she might end up like her grandmother, loving a man she could never have.

She heaved a deep sigh, then raised her head.

A shadow appeared, stretched across the still-bright ground. Lanni's heart quickened, not with fear, but with a breathless emotion.

It was Charles.

He didn't speak. She straightened her back, and her heart banged unmercifully against her ribs. For one wild moment Lanni wondered if her imagination had conjured him up. It didn't seem possible, after their confrontation earlier, that he was here.

Slowly she rose to her feet. She reached for the railing, needing its support. With a complete lack of haste, almost as if he was being drawn against his will, Charles approached her. One step at a time. One heartbeat at a time. One breath at a time.

When he stood before her, she could read the wildness in

his eyes. She recognized his uncertainty, his pain. It hurt her to see him like this.

When she'd worked up the courage, she lifted one hand and brought it to his face.

Charles covered her hand with his and closed his eyes.

After a moment he opened them again. His gaze searched hers, and she felt the tension leave him.

"I'm tired of fighting a battle I can't win," he whispered. Then he pulled her, almost roughly, into his arms.

Lanni went willingly and buried her face in his neck. "It's about time!" she cried, throwing her arms around him.

Not satisfied simply to hold her, Charles kissed her with an urgency that told her how difficult his struggle had been.

He inched his mouth from hers with a reluctance that thrilled her. "I met with my mother this afternoon," he said, his voice low and ragged with emotion.

"Then you know about your uncle and…and the baby?" she asked.

Charles nodded. "Mother said she met with you earlier in the week."

"Yes…"

"She's happy, you know. Perhaps for the first time in her life."

They sat on the porch steps, Charles on the top step, Lanni on the one below. He leaned down to clasp her hands with both of his.

"She told me how much I remind her of my uncle Charles." He frowned as if he found it impossible to assimilate everything she'd said.

"It took a lot of courage for her to talk about him after all these years." Lanni hoped Charles could appreciate what it had cost his mother to share her secret.

"My father always loved Catherine."

"But he loved his brother more," Lanni whispered. "And he did love your mother."

"What you said about being my destiny," he murmured, his hands cradling her face. "It makes sense now. I want us to get married, Lanni."

It took one millisecond for her head and her heart to grasp what he was saying.

"Married?"

"Don't tell me you've changed your mind."

"I haven't changed my mind." She laughed through her glistening tears. "Are you *nuts?*"

"I hope you don't want a long engagement."

"No. The shorter the better." Happiness filled her.

"I'm too old for you."

"Would you stop making excuses?"

Charles grinned. His smile was lopsided and irresistible. Lanni moved up to sit beside him and brought her mouth to his.

They kissed again and again until finally he tore his mouth from hers, his breathing fast. His lips trailed the length of her neck, spreading kisses.

"Oh, Lanni, you tempt me."

"You do the same to me," she whispered.

He wrapped his arms about her. He didn't speak for several minutes and seemed to be collecting his thoughts. "It sounds strange, but I think my father's found a way to be with Catherine through me."

"I know what you mean," Lanni said. "It's almost as if he's...reached out from the other side and given us to each other."

Charles kissed the top of her head. "I don't know what we're going to do about your internship," he said in a brisk, practical tone, as if he'd had enough of fate and fanciful notions and wanted to return to the reality of *their* lives.

"We'll figure something out later." A career in journalism didn't seem to matter all that much just then.

"But I thought journalism was important to you."

Lanni leaned against him and settled into his arms. "It is, but I'd like to stay in Hard Luck. Perhaps publish a newspaper here."

"You'll need training and experience before you take that on. You'd have it, too, if you worked at the Anchorage paper."

"But, Charles, my commitment would be for nine months. We'd have to delay the wedding. I don't think that's what either of us wants."

"I'm not going to change my mind about us getting married," he assured her. "I'm going to love you for the rest of my life. I knew that the day Sawyer married Abbey. I know it now."

"I'd love to produce a newspaper for Hard Luck. But be warned, life might get a bit hectic, especially after we start a family."

"A family?"

"Children, Charles. You do want children, don't you?" She twisted around to look at him, her eyes suddenly worried.

He struggled for words, then nodded. "Yes, Lanni, I very much want children. With you."

"Oh, Charles." She shifted so that she faced him completely and took his face between her hands. "We're going to be so happy."

"Lanni—" he kissed her softly "—I already am."

* * * * *

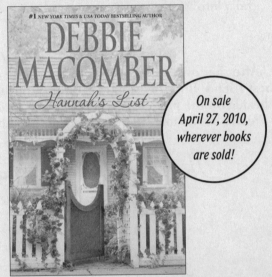
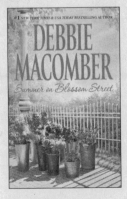

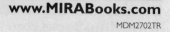

#1 *New York Times*
bestselling author

DEBBIE MACOMBER

Dear Reader,

I'm not much of a letter writer. As the sheriff here, I'm used to writing incident reports, not chatty letters. But my daughter, Megan—who'll be making me a grandfather soon—told me I had to do this. So here goes.

I'll tell you straight out that I'd hoped to marry Faith Beckwith (my onetime high school girlfriend) but she ended the relationship last month, even though we're both widowed and available.

However, I've got plenty to keep me occupied, like the unidentified remains found in a cave outside town. And the fact that my friend Judge Olivia Griffin is fighting cancer. And the break-ins at 204 Rosewood Lane—the house Faith happens to be renting from Grace Harding...

If you want to hear more, come on over to my place or to the sheriff's office (if you can stand the stale coffee!).

Troy Davis

92 Pacific Boulevard

#1 *NEW YORK TIMES* BESTSELLING AUTHOR

DEBBIE MACOMBER

Denim and Diamonds

Rancher Chase Brown has always loved Letty Ellison, but
nine years ago she left their small Wyoming town, heading
for Hollywood. Now she's returned, dreams in tatters, five-
year-old child in tow, and she's ready to trade the glitz to be
a rancher's wife. Chase's wife. But is it too late?

The Wyoming Kid

Rancher Lonny Ellison is an ex-rodeo cowboy who's used
to the adulation of women—something Joy Fuller doesn't
dole out. Can Lonny convince Joy that marriage to the
Wyoming Kid will be as exciting as a bull ride and as
sweet as the cookies she bakes?

Wyoming Brides

Available now wherever books are sold!

#1 *NEW YORK TIMES*
BESTSELLING AUTHOR
DEBBIE MACOMBER

What do you want most in the world?

Anne Marie Roche wants to find happiness again. At 38,
she's childless, a recent widow and alone. On Valentine's
Day, Anne Marie and several other widows get together to
celebrate…what? Hope, possibility, the future. They each
begin a list of twenty wishes.

Anne Marie's list includes learning to knit, doing good for
someone else and falling in love again. She begins to act on
her wishes, and when she volunteers at a school, little Ellen
enters her life. It's a relationship that becomes far more
important than she ever imagined, one in which they both
learn that wishes can come true.

Twenty Wishes

"These involving stories…continue the Blossom Street
themes of friendship and personal growth that readers
find so moving."—*Booklist* on *Back on Blossom Street*

Available wherever books are sold!

MIRA®